THE NEW FOLGER LIBRARY SHAKESPEARE

Designed to make Shakespeare's great plays available to all readers, the new Folger Library edition of Shakespeare's plays provides accurate texts in modern spelling and punctuation, as well as scene-by-scene action summaries, full explanatory notes, many pictures clarifying Shakespeare's language, and notes recording all significant departures from the early printed versions. Each play is prefaced by a brief introduction, by a guide to reading Shakespeare's language, and by accounts of his life and theater. Each play is followed by an annotated list of further readings and by a "Modern Perspective" written by an expert on that particular play.

Barbara A. Mowat is Director of Academic Programs at the Folger Shakespeare Library, Editor of *Shakespeare Quarterly*, Chair of the Folger Institute, and author of *The Dramaturgy of Shakespeare's Romances* and of essays on Shakespeare's plays and on the editing of the plays.

Paul Werstine is Professor of English at King's College and the Graduate School of the University of Western Ontario, Canada. He is author of many papers and articles on the printing and editing of Shakespeare's plays and was Associate Editor of the annual *Medieval and Renaissance Drama in England* from 1980 to 1989.

The Folger Shakespeare Library

The Folger Shakespeare Library in Washington, D.C., a privately funded research library dedicated to Shakespeare and the civilization of early modern Europe, was founded in 1932 by Henry Clay and Emily Jordan Folger. In addition to its role as the world's preeminent Shakespeare collection and its emergence as a leading center for Renaissance studies, the Folger Library offers a wide array of cultural and educational programs and services for the general public.

EDITORS

BARBARA A. MOWAT
Director of Academic Programs
Folger Shakespeare Library

PAUL WERSTINE
Professor of English
King's College and the University of Western Ontario

.THE NEW.
FOLGER LIBRARY
SHAKESPEARE

The Tragedy of

HAMLET,

Prince of Denmark

BY

WILLIAM SHAKESPEARE

WASHINGTON SQUARE PRESS
PUBLISHED BY POCKET BOOKS
New York   London   Toronto   Sydney   Tokyo   Singapore

A WASHINGTON SQUARE PRESS *Original* Publication

WSP

A Washington Square Press Publication of
POCKET BOOKS, a division of Simon & Schuster Inc.
1230 Avenue of the Americas, New York, NY 10020

ISBN: 0-671-72262-X

Washington Square Press New Folger Edition August 1992

10

WASHINGTON SQUARE PRESS and colophon are
registered trademarks of Simon & Schuster Inc.

Cover design by David Stevenson
Cover illustration by Kinuko Y. Craft

Printed in the U.S.A.

From the Director of the Library

For over thirty-five years, the Folger Library General Reader's Shakespeare has provided accurate and accessible texts of the plays and poems to students, teachers, and hundreds of thousands of other interested readers. Today, in an age often impatient with the past, the passion for Shakespeare continues to grow. No author speaks more powerfully to the human condition, in all its variety, than this actor/playwright from a minor sixteenth-century English village.

Over three decades, much has changed in the way Shakespeare's works are edited, performed, studied, and taught. It is time to replace the earlier Folger Shakespeare with an entirely new version, one that incorporates the best and most current thinking concerning both the texts and their interpretation. Professors Barbara Mowat and Paul Werstine are uniquely qualified to produce this New Folger Shakespeare for a new generation of readers. The Library is grateful for the learning, clarity, and imagination they have brought to this ambitious project.

Werner Gundersheimer, Director
The Folger Shakespeare Library

From the Director of the Library

For over thirty-five years, the Folger Library General Readers' Shakespeare has provided accurate and accessible texts of the plays and poems to students and general readers. Today, in an age often impatient with the past, the passion for Shakespeare's continuing vitality speaks more profoundly to the human condition in all its variety than did the earlier portrayals from a major sixteenth-century English culture.

Over three decades, though, an advance in the way Shakespeare's works are edited, annotated, studied, and taught, it is time to replace the earlier Folger Shakespeare with an entirely new version, one that incorporates the best and most current thinking concerning both the texts and their presentations. These new Folger editions, and their accompanying materials, are designed to carry this vision forward for a new generation of readers. The Folger is proud of the learning, clarity, and imagination they have brought to this ambitious project.

Werner Gundersheimer, Director
The Folger Shakespeare Library

Contents

Contents

Editors' Preface

In recent years, ways of dealing with Shakespeare's texts and with the interpretation of his plays have been undergoing significant change. This edition, while retaining many of the features that have always made the Folger Shakespeare so attractive to the general reader, at the same time reflects these current ways of thinking about Shakespeare. For example, modern readers, actors, and teachers have become interested in the differences between, on the one hand, the early forms in which Shakespeare's plays were first published and, on the other hand, the forms in which editors through the centuries have presented them. In response to this interest, we have based our edition on what we consider the best early printed version of a particular play (explaining our rationale in a section called "An Introduction to This Text") and have marked our changes in the text—unobtrusively, we hope, but in such a way that the curious reader can be aware that a change has been made and can consult the "Textual Notes" to discover what appeared in the early printed version.

Current ways of looking at the plays are reflected in our brief introductions, in many of the commentary notes, in the annotated lists of "Further Reading," and especially in each play's "Modern Perspective," an essay written by an outstanding scholar who brings to the reader his or her fresh assessment of the play in the light of today's interests and concerns.

As in the Folger Library General Reader's Shakespeare, which this edition replaces, we include explanatory notes designed to help make Shakespeare's language clearer to a modern reader, and we place the notes on the page facing the text that they explain. We also follow the earlier edition in including illustrations —of objects, of clothing, of mythological figures—from books and manuscripts in the Folger Library collection. We provide fresh accounts of the life of Shakespeare, of the publishing of his plays, and of the theaters in which his plays were performed, as well as an introduction to the text itself. We also include a section called "Reading Shakespeare's Language," in which we try to help readers learn to "break the code" of Elizabethan poetic language.

For each section of each volume, we are indebted to a host of generous experts and fellow scholars. The "Reading Shakespeare's Language" sections, for example, could not have been written had not Arthur King, of Brigham Young University, and Randal Robinson, author of *Unlocking Shakespeare's Language*, led the way in untangling Shakespearean language puzzles and shared their insights and methodologies generously with us. "Shakespeare's Life" profited by the careful reading given it by S. Schoenbaum, "Shakespeare's Theater" was read and strengthened by Andrew Gurr and John Astington, and "The Publication of Shakespeare's Plays" is indebted to the comments of Peter W. M. Blayney. We, as editors, take sole responsibility for any errors in our editions.

We are grateful to the authors of the "Modern Perspectives," to Leeds Barroll and David Bevington for their generous encouragement, to the Huntington and Newberry Libraries for fellowship support, to King's College for the grants it has provided to Paul Werstine, to the Social Sciences and Humanities Research Council of Canada, which provided him with a Research Time Stipend for 1990–91, and to the Folger Institute's Center for Shakespeare Studies for its fortuitous sponsorship of a workshop on "Shakespeare's Texts for Students and

Teachers" (funded by the National Endowment for the Humanities and led by Richard Knowles of the University of Wisconsin), a workshop from which we learned an enormous amount about what is wanted by college and high-school teachers of Shakespeare today.

Our biggest debt is to the Folger Shakespeare Library: to Werner Gundersheimer, Director of the Library, who has made possible our edition; to Jean Miller, the Library's Art Curator, who combed the Library holdings for illustrations, and to Julie Ainsworth, Head of the Photography Department, who carefully photographed them; to Peggy O'Brien, Director of Education, who gave us expert advice about the needs being expressed by Shakespeare teachers and students (and to Martha Christian and other "master teachers" who used our texts in manuscript in their classrooms); to the staff of the Academic Programs Division, especially Paul Menzer (who drafted "Further Reading" material), Mary Tonkinson, Lena Cowen Orlin, Molly Haws, and Jessica Hymowitz; and, finally, to the staff of the Library Reading Room, whose patience and support have been invaluable.

Barbara A. Mowat and Paul Werstine

Shakespeare's *Hamlet*

Hamlet is the most popular of Shakespeare's plays for readers and theater audiences, and it is also one of the most puzzling. Many questions about the play continue to fascinate readers and playgoers, making *Hamlet* not only a revenge tragedy but also very much a mystery. What is this Ghost that appears to Hamlet? Is it Hamlet's murdered father returned from the everlasting fire to demand justice upon his murderer? Is it a "goblin damned"—that is, a demon bent on claiming Hamlet's soul by tempting him to assassinate his king? Or is the Ghost "a spirit of health," an angelic messenger revealing to Hamlet that the young man's mission in life is to cleanse the kingdom of Denmark of its corrupt king?

And what happens to Hamlet after the Ghost commands that the throne of Denmark be cleansed? Does Hamlet actually go mad, becoming unhinged by the accusation that his uncle murdered his father or by the ugly picture the Ghost paints of Hamlet's lustful mother? Or does Hamlet merely pretend to be mad, pretend so well that he makes us wonder if we can tell the difference between sanity and madness? Why is he so hostile to women, both to his mother and to the woman whom he once courted and whom he claims to have loved dearly? Why does he wait so long to confirm the guilt of the king after the Ghost has accused the king of murder? And once he is convinced that the king is a murderer, why does Hamlet not act immediately?

And what about Gertrude? Was she unfaithful to her husband during his lifetime? Was she complicit in his murder? What does she come to believe about Hamlet's madness? And about her new husband?

Beyond such questions about the play and its characters lie deeper issues about the rightness of revenge, about how to achieve an ethical life, and about how to live in a world where tears of sorrow, loving smiles, and friendly words are all suspect because all are "actions that a man might *play*." Hamlet's world is bleak and cold because almost no one and nothing can be trusted. But his world, and Hamlet himself, continue to draw us to them, speaking to every generation of its own problems and its own yearnings. It is a play that seems particularly pertinent today—just as it has seemed particularly pertinent to any number of generations before us.

For "A Modern Perspective" on *Hamlet*, we invite you, after you have read the play, to read the essay by Professor Michael Neill of the University of Auckland, printed at the back of this book.

Reading Shakespeare's Language

For many people today, reading Shakespeare's language can be a problem—but it is a problem that can be solved. Those who have studied Latin (or even French or German or Spanish) and those who are used to reading poetry will have little difficulty understanding the language of Shakespeare's poetic drama. Others, however, need to develop the skills of untangling unusual sentence structures and of recognizing and understanding poetic compressions, omissions, and wordplay. And even those skilled in reading unusual sentence structures may have occasional trouble with Shakespeare's words. Four hundred years of "static"—caused by changes in language and life—intervene between his speaking and our hearing. Most of his immense vocabulary is still in use, but a few of his words are not, and, worse, some of his words now have meanings quite different from those they had in the sixteenth and seventeenth centuries. In the theater, most of these difficulties are solved for us by actors who study the language and articulate it for us so that the essential meaning is heard—or, when combined with stage action, is at least *felt*. When reading on one's own, one must do what each actor does: go over the lines (often with a dictionary close at hand) until the puzzles are solved and the lines yield up their poetry and the characters speak in words and phrases that are, suddenly, rewarding and wonderfully memorable.

Shakespeare's Words

As you begin to read the opening scenes of a play by Shakespeare, you may notice occasional unfamiliar words. Some are unfamiliar simply because we no longer use them. In the opening scenes of *Hamlet*, for example, we find such words as *parle* (i.e., discussion, meeting), *soft* (an exclamation meaning "hold" or "enough" or "wait a minute"), and *marry* (an oath "by the Virgin Mary," which had by Shakespeare's time become a mere interjection, like "indeed"). Words of this kind are explained in notes to the text and will become familiar the more of Shakespeare's plays you read.

Some words are strange not because of the "static" introduced by changes in language over the past centuries but because these are words that Shakespeare is using to build a dramatic world that has its own geography and history and story. *Hamlet*, for example, builds, in its opening scenes, a location, a past history, and a background mythology through references to "the

Dane," to "buried Denmark," to Elsinore, to partisans and jointresses, to Hyperion and Niobe and Hercules. These "local" words and references (each of which is explained in notes to this text) build the world of Denmark that Hamlet, Gertrude, and Claudius inhabit and that will become increasingly familiar to you as you get further into the play.

In *Hamlet*, as in all of Shakespeare's writing, the most problematic words are those that we still use but that we use with a different meaning. In the first scene of *Hamlet* (1.1.14), the word *rivals* is used where we would use "companions." At 1.1.44 we find the word *his* where we would use "its" and at 1.1.134 the word *still* used (as it most often is in Shakespeare) to mean "always." At 1.1.67, *sensible* means "confirmed by the senses"; at 1.1.169, *extravagant* means "wandering"; and at 1.2.66, *cousin* is used (as it is generally in Shakespeare) to mean simply "kinsman." And at 1.2.278, where Hamlet says, "I doubt some foul play," we would say, "I suspect some treacherous action." Again, such words are explained in the notes to the text, but they, too, will become familiar as you continue to read Shakespeare's language.

Shakespeare's Sentences

In an English sentence, meaning is quite dependent on the place given each word. "The dog bit the boy" and "The boy bit the dog" mean very different things, even though the individual words are the same. Because English places such importance on the positions of words in sentences, on the way words are arranged, unusual arrangements can puzzle a reader. Shakespeare frequently shifts his sentences away from "normal" English arrangements—often to create the rhythm he seeks, sometimes to use a line's poetic rhythm to emphasize a particular word, sometimes to give a character his or her own speech patterns or to allow the character to speak in a special way. Again, when we attend a good performance of the play, the actors will have worked out the sentence structures and will articulate the sentences so that the meaning is clear. In reading for yourself, do as the actor does. That is, when you are puzzled by a character's speech, check to see if the words are being presented in an unusual sequence.

Look first for the placement of subject and verb. Shakespeare often places the verb before the subject (e.g., instead of "He goes," we find "Goes he"). In the opening scene of *Hamlet*, when, at line 73, Horatio says "So frowned he once," he is using such a construction, as he is at line 91, when he says "That can I." Such inversions rarely cause much confusion. More problematic is Shakespeare's frequent placing of the object before the subject and verb (e.g., instead of "I hit him," we might find "Him I hit"). When Horatio says, at 1.1.78, "In what particular thought to work I know not," he is using such an inverted construction (the normal order would be "I know not in what particular thought to work"). Horatio uses another such inversion later in the same scene when he says (at lines 170–71), "of the truth herein / This present object made probation."

In some plays Shakespeare makes systematic use of inversions (*Julius Caesar* is one such play). In *Hamlet*, he more often uses sentence structures that depend instead on the separation of words that would normally appear together. (Again, this is often done to create a particular rhythm or to stress a particular word.) Claudius's "which have freely gone / With this affair along" (1.2.15–16) interrupts the phrase "gone along"; Horatio's "When he the ambitious Norway combated" (1.1.72) separates the subject and verb ("he combated"), interjecting between them the object of the verb ("the ambitious Norway"). To create for yourself sentences that seem more like the English of everyday speech, you may wish to rearrange the words, putting together the word clusters and placing the remaining words in their more familiar order. You will usually find that the sentences will gain in clarity but will lose their rhythm or shift their emphases. You can then see for yourself why Shakespeare chose his unusual arrangement.

Locating and, if necessary, rearranging words that "belong together" is especially necessary in passages that separate subjects from verbs and verbs from objects by long delaying or expanding interruptions—a structure that is used frequently in *Hamlet*. For example, when Horatio, at 1.1.92–110, tells the story of how King Hamlet won the Norwegian lands and how the prince of Norway seeks to regain them, he uses a series of such interrupted constructions:

>   *our last king,*
> Whose image even but now appeared to us,
> *Was,* as you know, by Fortinbras of Norway,
> Thereto pricked on by a most emulate pride,
> *Dared to the combat; in which* our valiant *Hamlet*
> (For so this side of our known world esteemed him)
> *Did slay this Fortinbras, who* by a sealed compact,
> *Did forfeit,* with his life, *all those his lands* . . .
>   Now, sir, young *Fortinbras,*
> Of unimprovèd mettle hot and full,
> *Hath* in the skirts of Norway here and there
> *Sharked up a list of lawless resolutes.* . . .

Here the interruptions provide details that catch the audience up in Horatio's story. The separation of the basic sentence elements ("our last king was dared to the combat") forces the audience to attend to supporting details while waiting for the basic sentence elements to come together. In the second scene of *Hamlet* (at 1.2.8–14), Claudius uses the same kind of interrupted construction in his opening speech:

Therefore *our sometime sister*, now our queen,
Th' imperial jointress to this warlike state,
Have we (as 'twere with a defeated joy,
With an auspicious and a dropping eye,
With mirth in funeral and with dirge in marriage,
In equal scale weighing delight and dole)
Taken to wife . . .

where the basic elements of the sentence are simply "we [i.e., I] have taken to wife our sometime sister [i.e., my former sister-in-law]." Claudius's speech, like Horatio's, is a narrative of past events, but the interrupted sentence structure here seems designed to add formality to the speech and, perhaps, to cover over the bald statement carried in the stripped-down sentence.

Occasionally, rather than separating basic sentence elements, Shakespeare simply holds them back, delaying them until much subordinate material has already been given. Marcellus uses this kind of delaying structure when he says, at 1.1.76–77, "Thus twice before, and jump [i.e., exactly] at this dead hour, / With martial stalk hath he gone by our watch" (where a "normally" constructed English sentence would have begun with the basic sentence elements: "He hath gone by our watch"); Barnardo's sentence that precedes the entrance of the Ghost at line 46 uses this same delayed construction, though the Ghost's entrance breaks off Barnardo's words before the subject of the sentence ("Marcellus and myself") finds a verb. Hamlet, in his first soliloquy (1.2.133–64), uses a delayed construction when he says (lines 158–61) "Within a month, / Ere yet

the salt of most unrighteous tears / Had left the flushing
in her gallèd eyes, / She married."

Shakespeare's sentences are sometimes complicated
not because of unusual structures or interruptions or
delays but because he omits words and parts of words
that English sentences normally require. (In conversation, we, too, often omit words. We say "Heard from
him yet?" and our hearer supplies the missing "Have
you." Frequent reading of Shakespeare—and of other
poets—trains us to supply such missing words.) In plays
written five or ten years after *Hamlet*, Shakespeare uses
omissions both of verbs and of nouns to great dramatic
effect. In *Hamlet* omissions are less interesting and seem
to be used primarily for compressed expression. At
1.1.31–32, for instance, Marcellus says "Therefore I
have entreated him along / With us," omitting the words
"to come" or "to go" before "along"; a few lines later,
Barnardo omits the word "with" in the construction
"let us once again assail your ears [with] . . . what we
have . . . seen" (lines 37–39).

Shakespearean Wordplay

Shakespeare plays with language so often and so variously that books are written on the topic. Here we will
mention only two kinds of wordplay, puns and metaphors. A pun is a play on words that sound the same but
have different meanings. When, in the second scene of
Hamlet, Claudius calls Hamlet his "son" and asks him
why his mood is so cloudy, Hamlet replies that he is,
rather, "too much in the sun" (punning on son/sun). In
the exchange between Gertrude and Hamlet:

QUEEN
   Thou know'st 'tis common; all that lives must die,
   Passing through nature to eternity.

HAMLET
  Ay, madam, it is common.
QUEEN   If it be,
  Why seems it so particular with thee?
HAMLET
  "Seems," madam? Nay, it is. I know not "seems."
                              (1.2.74–79)

Hamlet's reply is a pun on "seems"; for Gertrude, the question was "Why are you acting as if this death were something particularly awful," but Hamlet responds as if she had asked "Why are you putting on this show of grief." In Polonius's conversation with Ophelia in the third scene of the play, much of his dialogue is based on puns: the word *tenders*, for example, introduced by Ophelia to mean "offers," is picked up by Polonius and used, first, to mean "coins" ("legal tender"), then shifted to its verb form "to tender" and used to mean "to regard," and then, in the phrase "tender me a fool," to mean, simultaneously, "present me," "make me look like," and "show yourself to me." In many of Shakespeare's plays, one may not be aware that a character is punning, and the dialogue can seem simply silly or unintelligible; one must thus stay alert to the sounds of words and to the possibility of double meanings. In *Hamlet*, puns carry a heavier burden (Hamlet packs much of his feeling about Claudius into his single-line "aside": "A little more than kin and less than kind," where "kind" has the double meaning of "kindred" and "kindhearted"; and many of Polonius's speeches are unintelligible until one untangles the puns and related plays on words).

A metaphor is a play on words in which one object or idea is expressed as if it were something else, something with which it shares common features. For instance, when Horatio refers to the appearance of the Ghost as "a mote . . . that troubles the mind's eye," he is using metaphoric language: the mind is irritated by a question as the eye is irritated by a speck of dust. Hamlet's description of the world as "an unweeded garden that grows to seed" uses metaphor to paint for us his bleak vision; behind his description of Gertrude and Claudius's hasty marriage ("O, most wicked speed, to post / With such dexterity to incestuous sheets") is the metaphor of post-horses running skillfully and swiftly. Metaphors are often used when the idea being conveyed is hard to express or, for Hamlet, simply beyond normal expression; through metaphor, the speaker is given language that helps to carry the idea or the feeling to his or her onstage listener—and to the audience.

Implied Stage Action

Finally, in reading Shakespeare's plays you should always remember that what you are reading is a performance script. The dialogue is written to be spoken by actors who, at the same time, are moving, gesturing, picking up objects, weeping, shaking their fists. Some stage action is described in what are called "stage directions"; some is suggested within the dialogue itself. Learn to be alert to such signals as you stage the play in your imagination. When, in the first scene of *Hamlet*, Barnardo says "Last night of all, / When yond same star that's westward from the pole / Had made his course t' illume that part of heaven / Where now it burns," it is clear that, on the word "yond," he points toward the imagined star. When Barnardo says of the Ghost "See, it stalks away!" the stage action is obvious. It is less obvious, later in the scene, exactly what is to take place when Horatio says "I'll cross it though it blast me" (line 139). The director and the actor (and the reader, in imagination) must decide whether Horatio makes a cross of his body by spreading his arms, or whether he simply means he will stand in the Ghost's path; again, as the Ghost once again exits, the lines "Shall I strike it with my partisan?" "Do, if it will not stand," clearly involve some violent action. Marcellus describes their gestures as a "show of violence" and mentions their "vain blows," but the question of who strikes at the Ghost and with how much vigor will be answered variously from production to production. Learning to read the language of stage action repays one many times over when one reaches a crucial scene like that of the play within the play (3.2) or that of the final duel (5.2), in both of which scenes implied stage action vitally affects our response to the play.

It is immensely rewarding to work carefully with Shakespeare's language so that the words, the sentences, the wordplay, and the implied stage action all become clear—as readers for the past four centuries have discovered. It may be more pleasurable to attend a good performance of a play—though not everyone has thought so. But the joy of being able to stage one of Shakespeare's plays in one's imagination, to return to passages that continue to yield further meanings (or further questions) the more one reads them—these are pleasures that, for many, rival (or at least augment) those of the performed text, and certainly make it worth considerable effort to "break the code" of Elizabethan poetic drama and let free the remarkable language that makes up a Shakespeare text.

Shakespeare's Life

Surviving documents that give us glimpses into the life of William Shakespeare show us a playwright, poet, and actor who grew up in the market town of Stratford-upon-Avon, spent his professional life in London, and returned to Stratford a wealthy landowner. He was born in April 1564, died in April 1616, and is buried inside the chancel of Holy Trinity Church in Stratford.

We wish we could know more about the life of the world's greatest dramatist. His plays and poems are testaments to his wide reading—especially to his knowledge of Virgil, Ovid, Plutarch, Holinshed's *Chronicles*, and the Bible—and to his mastery of the English language, but we can only speculate about his education. We know that the King's New School in Stratford-upon-Avon was considered excellent. The school was one of the English "grammar schools" established to educate young men, primarily in Latin grammar and literature. As in other schools of the time, students began their studies at the age of four or five in the attached "petty school," and there learned to read and write in English, studying primarily the catechism from the Book of Common Prayer. After two years in the petty school, students entered the lower form (grade) of the grammar school, where they began the serious study of Latin grammar and Latin texts that would occupy most of the remainder of their school days. (Several Latin texts that Shakespeare used repeatedly in writing his plays and poems were texts that schoolboys memorized and recited.) Latin comedies were introduced early in the lower form; in the upper form, which the boys entered at age ten or eleven, students wrote their own Latin orations and declamations, studied Latin historians and rhetoricians, and began the study of Greek using the Greek New Testament.

Since the records of the Stratford "grammar school" do not survive, we cannot prove that William Shakespeare attended the school; however, every indication (his father's position as an alderman and bailiff of Stratford, the playwright's own knowledge of the Latin classics, scenes in the plays that recall grammar-school experiences—for example, *The Merry Wives of Windsor*, 4.1) suggests that he did. We also lack generally accepted documentation about Shakespeare's life after his schooling ended and his professional life in London began. His marriage in 1582 (at age eighteen) to Anne Hathaway and the subsequent births of his daughter Susanna (1583) and the twins Judith and Hamnet (1585) are recorded, but how he supported himself and where he lived are not known. Nor do we know when and why he left Stratford for the London theatrical world, nor how he rose to be the important figure in that world that he had become by the early 1590s.

We do know that by 1592 he had achieved some prominence in London as both an actor and a playwright. In that year was published a book by the playwright Robert Greene attacking an actor who had the audacity to write blank-verse drama and who was "in his own conceit [i.e., opinion] the only Shake-scene in a country." Since Greene's attack includes a parody of a line from one of Shakespeare's early plays, there is little doubt that it is Shakespeare to whom he refers, a "Shake-scene" who had aroused Greene's fury by successfully competing with university-educated dramatists like Greene himself. It was also in 1592 that Shakespeare became a published poet. In that year he published his long narrative poem *Venus and Adonis;* in 1593, he followed it with *The Rape of Lucrece.* Both poems were dedicated to the young earl of Southampton

(Henry Wriothesley), who may have become Shakespeare's patron.

It seems no coincidence that Shakespeare wrote these narrative poems in years in which the theaters were closed because of the plague, a contagious epidemic disease that devastated the population of London. When the theaters reopened late in 1594, Shakespeare apparently resumed his double career of actor and playwright and began his long (and seemingly profitable) service as an acting-company shareholder. Records from the fall of 1594 show him to be a leading member of the Lord Chamberlain's Men. It was this company of actors, later named the King's Men, for whom he would be a principal actor, dramatist, and shareholder for the rest of his career.

So far as we can tell, that career spanned about twenty years. In the 1590s, he wrote his plays on English history as well as several comedies and at least two tragedies (*Titus Andronicus* and *Romeo and Juliet*). These histories, comedies, and tragedies are the plays credited to him in 1598 in a work, *Palladis Tamia*, that in one chapter compares English writers with "Greek, Latin, and Italian Poets." There the author, Francis Meres, claims that Shakespeare is comparable to the Latin dramatists Seneca for tragedy and Plautus for comedy, and calls him "the most excellent in both kinds for the stage." He also names him "mellifluous and honey-tongued Shakespeare": "I say," writes Meres, "that the Muses would speak with Shakespeare's fine filed phrase, if they would speak English." Since Meres also mentions Shakespeare's "sugared sonnets among his private friends," it is assumed that many of Shakespeare's sonnets (not published until 1609) were also written in the 1590s.

In 1599, Shakespeare's company built a theater for themselves across the river from London, naming it the Globe. The plays that are considered by many to be Shakespeare's major tragedies (*Hamlet*, *Othello*, *King Lear*, and *Macbeth*) were written while the company was resident in this theater, as were such comedies as *Twelfth Night* and *Measure for Measure*. Many of Shakespeare's plays were performed at court (both for Queen Elizabeth I and, after her death in 1603, for King James I), some were presented at the Inns of Court (the residences of London's legal societies), and some were doubtless performed in other towns, at the universities, and at great houses when the King's Men went on tour; otherwise, his plays from 1599 to 1608 were, so far as we know, performed only at the Globe. Between 1608 and 1612, Shakespeare wrote several plays —among them *The Winter's Tale* and *The Tempest*— presumably for the company's new indoor Blackfriars theater, though the plays seem to have been performed also at the Globe and at court. Surviving documents describe a performance of *The Winter's Tale* in 1611 at the Globe, for example, and performances of *The Tempest* in 1611 and 1613 at the royal palace of Whitehall.

Shakespeare wrote very little after 1612, the year in which he probably wrote *King Henry VIII*. (It was at a performance of *Henry VIII* in 1613 that the Globe caught fire and burned to the ground.) Sometime between 1610 and 1613 he seems to have returned to live in Stratford-upon-Avon, where he owned a large house and considerable property, and where his wife and his two daughters and their husbands lived. (His son Hamnet had died in 1596.) During his professional years in London, Shakespeare had presumably derived income from the acting company's profits as well as from his own career as an

actor, from the sale of his play manuscripts to the acting
company, and, after 1599, from his shares as an owner
of the Globe. It was presumably that income, carefully
invested in land and other property, that made him the
wealthy man that surviving documents show him to
have become. It is also assumed that William Shakespeare's growing wealth and reputation played some
part in inclining the crown, in 1597, to grant John
Shakespeare, William's father, the coat of arms that he
had so long sought. William Shakespeare died in Stratford on April 23, 1616 (according to the epitaph carved
under his bust in Holy Trinity Church) and was buried
on April 25. Seven years after his death, his collected
plays were published as *Mr. William Shakespeares Comedies, Histories, & Tragedies* (the work now known as the
First Folio).

The years in which Shakespeare wrote were among
the most exciting in English history. Intellectually,
the discovery, translation, and printing of Greek and
Roman classics were making available a set of
works and worldviews that interacted complexly
with Christian texts and beliefs. The result was a questioning, a vital intellectual ferment, that provided
energy for the period's amazing dramatic and literary
output and that fed directly into Shakespeare's plays.
The Ghost in *Hamlet*, for example, is wonderfully complicated in part because he is a figure from Roman
tragedy—the spirit of the dead returning to seek revenge—who at the same time inhabits a Christian hell
(or purgatory); Hamlet's description of humankind
reflects at one moment the Neoplatonic wonder-
ment at mankind ("What a piece of work is a man!")
and, at the next, the Christian disparagement of human sinners ("And yet what to me is this quintessence
of dust?").

As intellectual horizons expanded, so also did geographical and cosmological horizons. New worlds—both North and South America—were explored, and in them were found human beings who lived and worshiped in ways radically different from those of Renaissance Europeans and Englishmen. The universe during these years also seemed to shift and expand. Copernicus had earlier theorized that the earth was not the center of the cosmos but revolved as a planet around the sun. Galileo's telescope, created in 1609, allowed scientists to see that Copernicus had been correct: the universe was not organized with the earth at the center, nor was it so nicely circumscribed as people had, until that time, thought. In terms of expanding horizons, the impact of these discoveries on people's beliefs—religious, scientific, and philosophical—cannot be overstated.

London, too, rapidly expanded and changed during the years (from the early 1590s to around 1610) that Shakespeare lived there. London—the center of England's government, its economy, its royal court, its overseas trade—was, during these years, becoming an exciting metropolis, drawing to it thousands of new citizens every year. Troubled by overcrowding, by poverty, by recurring epidemics of the plague, London was also a mecca for the wealthy and the aristocratic, and for those who sought advancement at court, or power in government or finance or trade. One hears in Shakespeare's plays the voices of London—the struggles for power, the fear of venereal disease, the language of buying and selling. One hears as well the voices of Stratford-upon-Avon—references to the nearby Forest of Arden, to sheep herding, to small-town gossip, to village fairs and markets. Part of the richness of Shakespeare's work

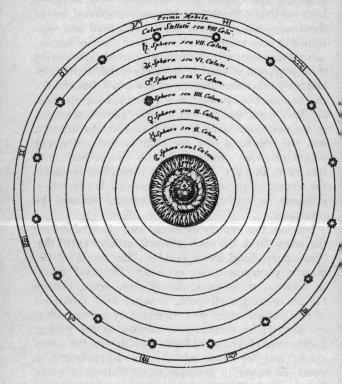

Ptolemaic universe.
From Marcus Manilius, *The sphere of . . .* (1675).

is the influence felt there of the various worlds in which he lived: the world of metropolitan London, the world of small-town and rural England, the world of the theater, and the worlds of craftsmen and shepherds.

That Shakespeare inhabited such worlds we know from surviving London and Stratford documents, as well as from the evidence of the plays and poems themselves. From such records we can sketch the dramatist's life. We know from his works that he was a voracious reader. We know from legal and business documents that he was a multifaceted theater man who became a wealthy landowner. We know a bit about his family life and a fair amount about his legal and financial dealings. Most scholars today depend upon such evidence as they draw their picture of the world's greatest playwright. Such, however, has not always been the case. Until the late eighteenth century, the William Shakespeare who lived in most biographies was the creation of legend and tradition. This was the Shakespeare who was supposedly caught poaching deer at Charlecote, the estate of Sir Thomas Lucy close by Stratford; this was the Shakespeare who fled from Sir Thomas's vengeance and made his way in London by taking care of horses outside a playhouse; this was the Shakespeare who reportedly could barely read, but whose natural gifts were extraordinary, whose father was a butcher who allowed his gifted son sometimes to help in the butcher shop, where William supposedly killed calves "in a high style," making a speech for the occasion. It was this legendary William Shakespeare whose Falstaff (in *1* and *2 Henry IV*) so pleased Queen Elizabeth that she demanded a play about Falstaff in love, and demanded that it be written in fourteen days (hence the existence of *The Merry Wives of Windsor*). It was this legendary Shakespeare who reached the top of his acting career in the roles of the Ghost in *Hamlet* and old Adam in *As You Like It*—and who died of·a fever contracted by drinking too hard at "a merry meeting" with the poets Michael Drayton and Ben Jonson. This legendary Shakespeare is a rambunctious, undisciplined man, as attractively "wild" as his plays were seen by earlier generations to be. Unfortunately, there is no trace of evidence to support these wonderful stories.

Perhaps in response to the disreputable Shakespeare of legend—or perhaps in response to the fragmentary and, for some, all-too-ordinary Shakespeare documented by surviving records—some people since the mid-nineteenth century have argued that William Shakespeare could not have written the plays that bear his name. These persons have put forward some dozen names as more likely authors, among them Queen Elizabeth, Sir Francis Bacon, Edward de Vere (earl of Oxford), and Christopher Marlowe. Such attempts to find what for these people is a more believable author of the plays is a tribute to the regard in which the plays are held. Unfortunately for their claims, the documents that exist that provide evidence for the facts of Shakespeare's life tie him inextricably to the body of plays and poems that bear his name. Unlikely as it seems to those who want the works to have been written by an aristocrat, a university graduate, or an "important" person, the plays and poems seem clearly to have been produced by a man from Stratford-upon-Avon with a very good "grammar school" education and a life of experience in London and in the world of the London theater. How this particular man produced the works that dominate the cultures of much of the world almost four hundred years after his death is one of life's mysteries—and one that will continue to tease our imaginations as we continue to delight in his plays and poems.

Shakespeare's Theater

The actors of Shakespeare's time are known to have performed plays in a great variety of locations. They played at court (that is, in the great halls of such royal residences as Whitehall, Hampton Court, and Greenwich); they played in halls at the universities of Oxford and Cambridge, and at the Inns of Court (the residences in London of the legal societies); and they also played in the private houses of great lords and civic officials. Sometimes acting companies went on tour from London into the provinces, often (but not only) when outbreaks of bubonic plague in the capital forced the closing of theaters to reduce the possibility of contagion in crowded audiences. In the provinces the actors usually staged their plays in churches (until around 1600) or in guildhalls. While surviving records show only a handful of occasions when actors played at inns while on tour, London inns were important playing places up until the 1590s.

The building of theaters in London had begun only shortly before Shakespeare wrote his first plays in the 1590s. These theaters were of two kinds: outdoor or public playhouses that could accommodate large numbers of playgoers, and indoor or private theaters for much smaller audiences. What is usually regarded as the first London outdoor public playhouse was called simply the Theatre. James Burbage—the father of Richard Burbage, who was perhaps the most famous actor in Shakespeare's company—built it in 1576 in an area north of the city of London called Shoreditch. Among the more famous of the other public playhouses that capitalized on the new fashion were the Curtain and the Fortune (both also built north of the city), the Rose, the Swan, the Globe, and the Hope (all located on the Bankside, a region just across the Thames south of the city of London). All these playhouses had to be built outside the jurisdiction of the city of London because many civic officials were hostile to the performance of drama and repeatedly petitioned the royal council to abolish it.

The theaters erected on the Bankside (a region under the authority of the Church of England, whose head was the monarch) shared the neighborhood with houses of prostitution and with the Paris Garden, where the blood sports of bearbaiting and bullbaiting were carried on. There may have been no clear distinction between playhouses and buildings for such sports, for we know that the Hope was used for both plays and baiting and that Philip Henslowe, owner of the Rose and, later, partner in the ownership of the Fortune, was also a partner in a monopoly on baiting. All these forms of entertainment were easily accessible to Londoners by boat across the Thames or over London Bridge.

Evidently Shakespeare's company prospered on the Bankside. They moved there in 1599. Threatened by difficulties in renewing the lease on the land where their first theater (the Theatre) had been built, Shakespeare's company took advantage of the Christmas holiday in 1598 to dismantle the Theatre and transport its timbers across the Thames to the Bankside, where, in 1599, these timbers were used in the building of the Globe. The weather in late December 1598 is recorded as having been especially harsh. It was so cold that the Thames was "nigh [nearly] frozen," and there was heavy snow. Perhaps the weather aided Shakespeare's company in eluding their landlord, the snow hiding their activity and the freezing of the Thames allowing them to slide the timbers across to the Bankside without paying tolls for repeated trips over London Bridge. Attractive as this narrative is, it remains just as likely that the heavy snow hampered transport of the timbers in wagons through the London streets to the river. It also must be remembered that the Thames was, according to report, only "nigh frozen" and therefore as impassable as it ever was. Whatever the precise circumstances of this fascinating event in English theater history, Shakespeare's company was able to begin playing at their new Globe theater on the Bankside in 1599. After the first Globe burned down in 1613 during the staging of Shakespeare's *Henry VIII* (its thatch roof was set alight by cannon fire called for by the performance), Shakespeare's company immediately rebuilt on the same location. The second Globe seems to have been a grander structure than its predecessor. It remained in use until the beginning of the English Civil War in 1642, when Parliament officially closed the theaters. Soon thereafter it was pulled down.

The public theaters of Shakespeare's time were very different buildings from our theaters today. First of all, they were open-air playhouses. As recent excavations of the Rose and the Globe confirm, some were polygonal or roughly circular in shape; the Fortune, however, was square. The most recent estimates of their size put the diameter of these buildings at 72 feet (the Rose) to 100 feet (the Globe), but we know that they held vast audiences of two or three thousand, who must have been squeezed together quite tightly. Some of these spectators paid extra to sit or stand in the two or three levels of roofed galleries that extended, on the upper levels, all the way around the theater and surrounded an open space. In this space were the stage and, perhaps, the tiring house (what we would call dressing rooms), as well as the so-called yard. In the yard stood the spectators who chose to pay less, the ones whom Hamlet contemptuously called "groundlings." For a roof they had only the sky, and so they were exposed to all kinds of weather. They stood on a floor that was sometimes made of mortar and sometimes of ash mixed with the shells of hazelnuts. The latter provided a porous and therefore dry footing for the crowd, and the shells may have been more comfortable to stand on because they were not as hard as mortar. Availability of shells may not have been a problem if hazelnuts were a favorite food for Shakespeare's audiences to munch on as they watched his plays. Archaeologists who are today unearthing the remains of theaters from this period have discovered quantities of these nutshells on theater sites.

Unlike the yard, the stage itself was covered by a roof. Its ceiling, called "the heavens," is thought to have been elaborately painted to depict the sun, moon, stars, and planets. Just how big the stage was remains hard to determine. We have a single sketch of part of the interior of the Swan. A Dutchman named Johannes de Witt visited this theater around 1596 and sent a sketch of it back to his friend, Arend van Buchel. Because van Buchel found de Witt's letter and sketch of interest, he copied both into a book. It is van Buchel's copy, adapted, it seems, to the shape and size of the page in his book, that survives. In this sketch, the stage appears to be a large rectangular platform that thrusts far out into the yard, perhaps even as far as the center of the circle formed by the surrounding galleries. This drawing, combined with the specifications for the size of the stage in the building contract for the Fortune, has led scholars to conjecture that the stage on which Shakespeare's plays were performed must have measured approximately 43 feet in width and 27 feet in depth, a vast acting area. But the digging up of a large part of the Rose by archaeologists has provided evidence of a quite different stage design. The Rose stage was a platform tapered at the corners and much shallower than what seems to be depicted in the van Buchel sketch. Indeed, its measurements seem to be about 37.5 feet across at its widest point and only 15.5 feet deep. Because the surviving indications of stage size and design differ from each other so much, it is possible that the stages in other theaters, like the Theatre, the Curtain, and the Globe (the outdoor playhouses where we know that Shakespeare's plays were performed), were different from those at both the Swan and the Rose.

After about 1608 Shakespeare's plays were staged not only at the Globe but also at an indoor or private playhouse in Blackfriars. This theater had been constructed in 1596 by James Burbage in an upper hall of a former Dominican priory or monastic house. Although Henry VIII had dissolved all English monasteries in the 1530s (shortly after he had founded the Church of England), the area remained under church, rather than hostile civic, control. The hall that Burbage had purchased and renovated was a large one in which Parliament had once met. In the private theater that he constructed, the stage, lit by candles, was built across the narrow end of the hall, with boxes flanking it.

The rest of the hall offered seating room only. Because there was no provision for standing room, the largest audience it could hold was less than a thousand, or about a quarter of what the Globe could accommodate. Admission to Blackfriars was correspondingly more expensive. Instead of a penny to stand in the yard at the Globe, it cost a minimum of sixpence to get into Blackfriars. The best seats at the Globe (in the Lords' Room in the gallery above and behind the stage) cost sixpence; but the boxes flanking the stage at Blackfriars were half a crown, or five times sixpence. Some spectators who were particularly interested in displaying themselves paid even more to sit on stools on the Blackfriars stage.

Whether in the outdoor or indoor playhouses, the stages of Shakespeare's time were different from ours. They were not separated from the audience by the dropping of a curtain between acts and scenes. Therefore the playwrights of the time had to find other ways of signaling to the audience that one scene (to be imagined as occurring in one location at a given time) had ended and the next (to be imagined at perhaps a different location at a later time) had begun. The customary way used by Shakespeare and many of his contemporaries was to have everyone onstage exit at the end of one scene and have one or more different characters enter to begin the next. In a few cases, where characters remain onstage from one scene to another, the dialogue or stage action makes the change of location clear, and the characters are generally to be imagined as having moved from one place to another. For example, in *Romeo and Juliet*, Romeo and his friends remain onstage in Act 1 from scene 4 to scene 5, but they are represented as having moved between scenes from the street that leads to Capulet's house into Capulet's house itself. The new location is signaled in part by the appearance onstage of Capulet's servingmen carrying napkins, something they would not take into the streets. Playwrights had to be quite resourceful in the use of hand properties, like the napkin, or in the use of dialogue to specify where the action was taking place in their plays because, in contrast to most of today's theaters, the playhouses of Shakespeare's time did not use movable scenery to dress the stage and make the setting precise. As another consequence of this difference, however, the playwrights of Shakespeare's time did not have to specify exactly where the action of their plays was set when they did not choose to do so, and much of the action of their plays is tied to no specific place.

Usually Shakespeare's stage is referred to as a "bare stage," to distinguish it from the stages of the last two or three centuries with their elaborate sets. But the stage in Shakespeare's time was not completely bare. Philip Henslowe, owner of the Rose, lists in his inventory of stage properties a rock, three tombs, and two mossy banks. Stage directions in plays of the time also call for such things as thrones (or "states"), banquets (presumably tables with plaster replicas of food on them), and beds and tombs to be pushed onto the stage. Thus the stage often held more than the actors.

The actors did not limit their performing to the stage alone. Occasionally they went beneath the stage, as the Ghost appears to do in the first act of *Hamlet*. From there they could emerge onto the stage through a trapdoor. They could retire behind the hangings across the back of the stage (or the front of the tiring house), as, for example, the actor playing Polonius does when he hides behind the arras. Sometimes the hangings could be drawn back during a performance to "discover" one or more actors behind them. When performance required that an actor appear "above," as when Juliet is imagined to stand at the window of her chamber in the famous and misnamed "balcony scene," then the actor probably climbed the stairs to the gallery over the back of the stage and temporarily shared it with some of the spectators. The stage was also provided with ropes and winches so that actors could descend from, and reascend to, the "heavens."

Perhaps the greatest difference between dramatic performances in Shakespeare's time and ours was that in Shakespeare's England the roles of women were played by boys. (Some of these boys grew up to take male roles in their maturity.) There were no women in the acting companies, only in the audience. It had not always been so in the history of the English stage. There are records of women on English stages in the thirteenth and fourteenth centuries, two hundred years before Shakespeare's plays were performed. After the accession of James I in 1603, the queen of England and her ladies took part in entertainments at court called masques, and with the reopening of the theaters in 1660 at the restoration of Charles II, women again took their place on the public stage.

The chief competitors for the companies of adult actors such as the one to which Shakespeare belonged and for which he wrote were companies of exclusively boy actors. The competition was most intense in the early 1600s. There were then two principal children's companies: the Children of Paul's (the choirboys from St. Paul's Cathedral, whose private playhouse was near the cathedral); and the Children of the Chapel Royal (the choirboys from the monarch's private chapel, who performed at the Blackfriars theater built by Burbage in 1596, which Shakespeare's company had been stopped from using by local residents who objected to crowds).

In *Hamlet* Shakespeare writes of "an aerie [nest] of children, little eyases [hawks], that cry out on the top of question and are most tyrannically clapped for 't. These are now the fashion and . . . berattle the common stages [attack the public theaters]." In the long run, the adult actors prevailed. The Children of Paul's dissolved around 1606. By about 1608 the Children of the Chapel Royal had been forced to stop playing at the Blackfriars theater, which was then taken over by the King's Men, Shakespeare's own troupe.

Acting companies and theaters of Shakespeare's time were organized in different ways. For example, Philip Henslowe owned the Rose and leased it to companies of actors, who paid him from their takings. Henslowe would act as manager of these companies, initially paying playwrights for their plays and buying properties, recovering his outlay from the actors. Shakespeare's company, however, managed itself, with the principal actors, Shakespeare among them, having the status of "sharers" and the right to a share in the takings, as well as the responsibility for a part of the expenses. Five of the sharers themselves, Shakespeare among them, owned the Globe. As actor, as sharer in an acting company and in ownership of theaters, and as playwright, Shakespeare was about as involved in the theatrical industry as one could imagine. Although Shakespeare and his fellows prospered, their status under the law was conditional upon the protection of powerful patrons. "Common players"—those who did not have patrons or masters—were classed in the language of the law with "vagabonds and sturdy beggars." So the actors had to secure for themselves the official rank of servants of patrons. Among the patrons under whose protection Shakespeare's company worked were the lord chamberlain and, after the accession of King James in 1603, the king himself.

We are now perhaps on the verge of learning a great deal more about the theaters in which Shakespeare and his contemporaries performed—or at least of opening up new questions about them. Already about 70 percent of the Rose has been excavated, as has about 10 percent of the second Globe, the one built in 1614. It is to be hoped that soon more will be available for study. These are exciting times for students of Shakespeare's stage.

The Publication of Shakespeare's Plays

Eighteen of Shakespeare's plays found their way into print during the playwright's lifetime, but there is nothing to suggest that he took any interest in their publication. These eighteen appeared separately in editions called quartos. Their pages were not much larger than the one you are now reading, and these little books were sold unbound for a few pence. The earliest of the quartos that still survive were printed in 1594, the year that both _Titus Andronicus_ and a version of the play now called _2 King Henry VI_ became available. While almost every one of these early quartos displays on its title page the name of the acting company that performed the play, only about half provide the name of the playwright, Shakespeare. The first quarto edition to bear the name Shakespeare on its title page is _Love's Labor's Lost_ of 1598. A few of these quartos were popular with the book-buying public of Shakespeare's lifetime; for example, quarto _Richard II_ went through five editions between 1597 and 1615. But most of the quartos were far from best-sellers; *Love's Labor's Lost* (1598), for instance, was not reprinted in quarto until 1631. After Shakespeare's death, two more of his plays appeared in quarto format: *Othello* in 1622 and *The Two Noble Kinsmen*, coauthored with John Fletcher, in 1634.

In 1623, seven years after Shakespeare's death, *Mr. William Shakespeares Comedies, Histories, & Tragedies* was published. This printing offered readers in a single book thirty-six of the thirty-eight plays now thought to have been written by Shakespeare, including eighteen that had never been printed before. And it offered them in a style that was then reserved for serious literature and scholarship. The plays were arranged in double columns on pages nearly a foot high. This large page size is called "folio," as opposed to the smaller "quarto," and the 1623 volume is usually called the Shakespeare First Folio. It is reputed to have sold for the lordly price of a pound. (One copy at the Folger Library is marked fifteen shillings—that is, three-quarters of a pound.)

In a preface to the First Folio entitled "To the great Variety of Readers," two of Shakespeare's former fellow actors in the King's Men, John Heminge and Henry Condell, wrote that they themselves had collected their dead companion's plays. They suggested that they had seen his own papers: "we have scarce received from him a blot in his papers." The title page of the Folio declared that the plays within it had been printed "according to the True Original Copies." Comparing the Folio to the quartos, Heminge and Condell disparaged the quartos, advising their readers that "before you were abused with divers stolen and surreptitious copies, maimed, and deformed by the frauds and stealths of injurious impostors." Many Shakespeareans of the eighteenth and nineteenth centuries believed Heminge and Condell and regarded the Folio plays as superior to anything in the quartos.

Once we begin to examine the Folio plays in detail, it becomes less easy to take at face value the word of Heminge and Condell about the superiority of the Folio texts. For example, of the first nine plays in the Folio (one quarter of the entire collection), four were essentially reprinted from earlier quarto printings that Heminge and Condell had disparaged; and four have now been identified as printed from copies written in the hand of a professional scribe of the 1620s named Ralph Crane; the ninth, *The Comedy of Errors*, was apparently also printed from a manuscript, but one whose origin cannot be readily identified. Evidently then, eight of the first nine plays in the First Folio were not printed, in spite of what the Folio title page announces, "according to the True Original Copies," or Shakespeare's own papers, and the source of the ninth is unknown. Since today's editors have been forced to treat Heminge and Condell's pronouncements with skepticism, they must choose whether to base their own editions upon quartos or the Folio on grounds other than Heminge and Condell's story of where the quarto and Folio versions originated.

Editors have often fashioned their own narratives to explain what lies behind the quartos and Folio. They have said that Heminge and Condell meant to criticize only a few of the early quartos, the ones that offer much shorter and sometimes quite different, often garbled, versions of plays. Among the examples of these are the 1600 quarto of *Henry V* (the Folio offers a much fuller version) or the 1603 *Hamlet* quarto (in 1604 a different, much longer form of the play got into print as a quarto).

Early in this century editors speculated that these questionable texts were produced when someone in the audience took notes from the plays' dialogue during performances and then employed "hack poets" to fill out the notes. The poor results were then sold to a publisher and presented in print as Shakespeare's plays. More recently this story has given way to another in which the shorter versions are said to be recreations from memory of Shakespeare's plays by actors who wanted to stage them in the provinces but lacked manuscript copies. Most of the quartos offer much better texts than these so-called bad quartos. Indeed, in most of the quartos we find texts that are at least equal to or better than what is printed in the Folio. Many of this century's Shakespeare enthusiasts have persuaded themselves that most of the quartos were set into type directly from Shakespeare's own papers, although there is nothing on which to base this conclusion except the desire for it to be true. Thus speculation continues about how the Shakespeare plays got to be printed. All that we have are the printed texts.

The book collector who was most successful in bringing together copies of the quartos and the First Folio was Henry Clay Folger, founder of the Folger Shakespeare Library in Washington, D.C. While it is estimated that there survive around the world only about 230 copies of the First Folio, Mr. Folger was able to acquire more than seventy-five copies, as well as a large number of fragments, for the library that bears his name. He also amassed a substantial number of quartos. For example, only fourteen copies of the First Quarto of *Love's Labor's Lost* are known to exist, and three are at the Folger Shakespeare Library. As a consequence of Mr. Folger's labors, twentieth-century scholars visiting the Folger Library have been able to learn a great deal about

THE
Tragicall Historie of
H A M L E T,
Prince of Denmarke.

By William Shakespeare.

Newly imprinted and enlarged to almost as much
againe as it was, according to the true and perfect
Coppie.

AT LONDON,
Printed by I. R. for N. L. and are to be sold at his
shoppe vnder Saint Dunstons Church in
1604.

Title page of *Hamlet* Second Quarto, 1604.

sixteenth- and seventeenth-century printing and, particularly, about the printing of Shakespeare's plays. And Mr. Folger did not stop at the First Folio, but collected many copies of later editions of Shakespeare, beginning with the Second Folio (1632), the Third (1663–64), and the Fourth (1685). Each of these later folios was based on its immediate predecessor and was edited anonymously. The first editor of Shakespeare whose name we know was Nicholas Rowe, whose first edition came out in 1709. Mr. Folger collected this edition and many, many more by Rowe's successors.

An Introduction to This Text

The play we call *Hamlet* was printed in three different versions in the first quarter of the seventeenth century.

In 1603 appeared *The Tragicall Historie of Hamlet Prince of Denmark by William Shake-speare*, a quarto or pocket-size book that provides a version of the play markedly different from the two subsequent printings and from the play most readers know. This version is little more than half as long as the others. Some of the characters have different names; for example, Polonius is called Corambis and his servant Reynaldo appears as Montano. The action of the play also varies considerably. Most scholars have found many passages in this version extremely difficult to read and have concluded that it is so full of errors that it is generally unreliable as a witness to what was written for the stage. This First Quarto has therefore been dubbed a "bad quarto."

The Second Quarto, often called the "good quarto," is dated in some copies 1604, in others 1605. Although it has exactly the same title as the First Quarto, the Second

Quarto's title page goes on to represent it as "Newly imprinted and enlarged to almost as much againe as it was, according to the true and perfect Coppie."

The third version to see print is found in the First Folio of Shakespeare's plays, published in 1623. Entitled *The Tragedie of Hamlet, Prince of Denmarke*, the Folio play has some eighty-five or so lines not found in the Second Quarto; but the Folio lacks about two hundred of the Second Quarto's lines. These two versions also differ from each other in their readings of hundreds of words.

Most modern editions offer various combinations of the Second Quarto and Folio versions. It is impossible in any edition to combine the whole of these two forms of the play because they often provide alternative readings that are mutually exclusive; for example, when the Second Quarto has Hamlet wish that his "too too sallied flesh would melt," the Folio prints "solid" for "sallied." In such cases (and there are a great many such cases) editors must choose whether to be guided by the Second Quarto, by the Folio, or perhaps even by the First Quarto in selecting what to print.

Twentieth-century editors have made the decision about which version to prefer according to their theories about the origins of the three early printed texts. Most recent editors have preferred the Second Quarto's readings in the belief that it was printed either directly from Shakespeare's own manuscript or from a scribe's copy of it. A few have, instead, adopted Folio readings in the belief that the Folio was set into type from a theater manuscript, and they wanted to give their readers the play as it was performed on Shakespeare's stage. Still fewer editors have granted the First Quarto much influence over their choices, since many believe that the First Quarto prints a manuscript put together from memory by a small-part actor who had a role in the play as it was performed outside of London. Editors who have been convinced of this story about the First Quarto sometimes have depended on it as a record of what was acted. In recent years, some editors have come to believe that the Second Quarto and Folio are distinct, independent Shakespearean versions of the play that ought never to be combined with each other in an edition. Nevertheless, as today's scholars reexamine the narratives about the origins of the printed texts, we discover that the evidence upon which they are based is questionable, and we become more skeptical about ever identifying with any certainty how the play assumed the forms in which it was printed.

The present edition is based upon a fresh examination of the early printed texts rather than upon any modern edition. It is designed both for those who prefer the traditional text of *Hamlet*, which is the combination of Second Quarto and First Folio, and for those who prefer to regard the Second Quarto and First Folio as distinct versions of the play. The present edition resembles most other modern editions in offering its readers a text of the Second Quarto combined with as much of the First Folio as it has been possible to include. It also resembles most other editions in its efforts to correct what are believed to be errors or deficiencies in the Second Quarto by substituting or introducing alternatives either from the First Folio or from the editorial tradition. Yet the present edition is unique in marking all passages that are found only in the Second Quarto and all words and passages found only in the Folio. Thus it becomes possible for a reader to use this book to discover the major and even many of the minor differences between the Second Quarto and First Folio versions of *Hamlet*. This edition ignores the First Quarto version because the First Quarto is so widely different from the Second Quarto and the Folio.

In order to enable its readers to tell the difference between the Folio and Second Quarto versions, the present edition uses a variety of signals:

(1) All the words in this edition that are printed only in the Folio version but not in the Second Quarto appear in pointed parentheses (⟨⟩).

(2) All lines that are found only in the Second Quarto and not in the Folio are printed in square brackets ([]).

(3) Sometimes neither the Second Quarto nor the Folio seems to offer a satisfactory reading, and it is necessary to print a word different from what is offered by either. Such words (called "emendations" by editors) are printed within superior half-brackets (⌈⌉).

Whenever we change the wording of the Second Quarto or add anything to its stage directions, we mark the change because we want our readers to be immediately aware that we have intervened. (Only when we correct an obvious typographical error in the Second Quarto or the First Folio does the change not get marked.) Whenever we change the Second Quarto's or First Folio's wording or change their punctuation so that meaning changes, we list the change in the textual notes at the back of the book, even if all we have done is fix an obvious error. Those who wish to find the Folio's alternatives to the Second Quarto's readings will be able to find these in the textual notes.

For the convenience of the reader, we have modernized the punctuation and the spelling of both the Second Quarto and the Folio. Thus, for example, our text supplies the modern standard spelling "sullied" for the Second Quarto's variant spelling "sallied." Sometimes we go so far as to modernize certain old forms of words; for example, when *a* means "he," we change it to *he;* we change *mo* to *more,* *ye* to *you,* and *God buy to you* to *good-bye to you.* But it is not our practice in editing any of the plays to modernize words that sound distinctly different from modern forms. For example, when the early printed texts read *sith* or *apricocks* or *porpentine*, we have not modernized to *since, apricots, porcupine.* When the forms *an, and,* or *and if* appear instead of the modern form *if,* we have reduced *and* to *an* but have not changed any of these forms to their modern equivalent, *if.* We also modernize and, where necessary, correct passages in foreign languages, unless an error in the early printed text can be reasonably explained as a joke.

We correct or regularize a number of the proper names, as is the usual practice in editions of the play. For example, the Second Quarto's "Gertrard" or "Gertrad" is changed to Folio's "Gertrude" because "Gertrude" has become the familiar form of the name; and there are a number of other comparable adjustments in the names.

This edition differs from many earlier ones in its efforts to aid the reader in imagining the play as a performance rather than as a series of historical events. Thus stage directions are written with reference to the stage. For example, the present edition reproduces the Second Quarto direction: "Ghost cries under the stage" (1.5.168). Whenever it is reasonably certain, in our view, that a speech is accompanied by a particular action, we provide a stage direction describing the action. (Occasional exceptions to this rule occur when the action is so obvious that to add a stage direction would insult the reader.) Stage directions for the entrance of characters in mid-scene are, with rare exceptions, placed so that they immediately precede the characters' participation in the scene, even though these entrances may appear somewhat earlier in the early printed texts. Whenever we move a stage direction, we record this change in the textual notes. Latin stage directions (e.g., *Exeunt*) are translated into English (e.g., *They exit*).

We expand the often severely abbreviated forms of

names used as speech headings in early printed texts into the full names of the characters. We also regularize the speakers' names in speech headings, using only a single designation for each character, even though the early printed texts sometimes use a variety of designations. Variations in the speech headings of the early printed texts are recorded in the textual notes.

In the present edition, as well, we mark with a dash any change of address within a speech, unless a stage direction intervenes. When the *-ed* ending of a word is to be pronounced, we mark it with an accent. Like editors for the last two centuries, we print metrically linked lines in the following way:

> MARCELLUS
>   It is offended.
> BARNARDO   See, it stalks away.

However, when there are a number of short verse-lines that can be linked in more than one way, we do not, with rare exceptions, indent any of them.

The Explanatory Notes

The notes that appear on the pages facing the text are designed to provide readers with the help that they may need to enjoy the play. Whenever the meaning of a word in the text is not readily accessible in a good contemporary dictionary, we offer the meaning in a note. Sometimes we provide a note even when the relevant meaning is to be found in the dictionary but when the word has acquired since Shakespeare's time other potentially confusing meanings. In our notes, we try to offer modern synonyms for Shakespeare's words. We also try to indicate to the reader the connection between the word in the play and the modern synonym. For example, Shakespeare sometimes uses the word *head* to mean "source," but, for modern readers, there may be no connection evident between these two words. We provide the connection by explaining Shakespeare's usage as follows: "**head:** fountainhead, source." On some occasions, a whole phrase or clause needs explanation. Then we rephrase in our own words the difficult passage, and add at the end synonyms for individual words in the passage. When scholars have been unable to determine the meaning of a word or phrase, we acknowledge the uncertainty.

world in the play and the modern audience. For example, Shakespeare sometimes uses the word "used" to mean "correct," but for modern readers there may be no connection between these two words. We provide the connection by explaining Shakespeare's usage as follows: "head romanticized, source." Of word locutions a whole phrase or clause needs explanation. Then we replace in our own words the difficult passage, and and at the end synonyms for individual words in the passage. When scholars have been unable to determine the meaning of a word or phrase, we acknowledge the uncertainty.

The Tragedy of

HAMLET,

Prince of Denmark

Characters in the Play

THE GHOST
HAMLET, Prince of Denmark, son of the late King Hamlet
   and Queen Gertrude
QUEEN GERTRUDE, widow of King Hamlet, now married
   to Claudius
KING CLAUDIUS, brother to the late King Hamlet

OPHELIA
LAERTES, her brother
POLONIUS, father of Ophelia and Laertes, councillor to
   King Claudius
REYNALDO, servant to Polonius

HORATIO, Hamlet's friend and confidant

VOLTEMAND
CORNELIUS
ROSENCRANTZ
GUILDENSTERN *courtiers at the Danish court*
OSRIC
Gentlemen
A Lord

FRANCISCO
BARNARDO *Danish soldiers*
MARCELLUS

FORTINBRAS, Prince of Norway
A Captain in Fortinbras's army

Ambassadors to Denmark from England

Players who take the roles of Prologue, Player King,
   Player Queen, and Lucianus in *The Murder of Gonzago*

3

Two Messengers
Sailors
Gravedigger
Gravedigger's companion
Doctor of Divinity

Attendants, Lords, Guards, Musicians, Laertes's Followers, Soldiers, Officers

The Tragedy of

HAMLET,
Prince of Denmark

ACT 1

1.1 On the guards' platform at Elsinore, Horatio waits with Barnardo and Marcellus to question a ghost that has twice before appeared. The Ghost, in the form of the late King Hamlet of Denmark, appears but will not speak. Horatio decides to tell his fellow student, Prince Hamlet, about the Ghost's appearance.

---

2. **unfold yourself:** disclose your identity
14. **The rivals of my watch:** my fellow sentries

⟨Scene 1⟩

Enter Barnardo and Francisco, two sentinels.

BARNARDO Who's there?

FRANCISCO
  Nay, answer me. Stand and unfold yourself.

BARNARDO Long live the King!

FRANCISCO Barnardo.

BARNARDO He.   5

FRANCISCO
  You come most carefully upon your hour.

BARNARDO
  'Tis now struck twelve. Get thee to bed, Francisco.

FRANCISCO
  For this relief much thanks. 'Tis bitter cold,
  And I am sick at heart.

BARNARDO Have you had quiet guard?   10

FRANCISCO Not a mouse stirring.

BARNARDO Well, good night.
  If you do meet Horatio and Marcellus,
  The rivals of my watch, bid them make haste.

Enter Horatio and Marcellus.

FRANCISCO
  I think I hear them.—Stand ho! Who is there?   15

HORATIO Friends to this ground.

17. **the Dane:** the Danish king
30. **of us:** by us
34. **approve our eyes:** confirm our observation
43. **pole:** Polaris, the North Star
44. **his:** its

Sledded warriors: "sledded Polacks on the ice." (1.1.74)
From Cesare Vecellio, *Habiti antichi et moderni* (1598).

MARCELLUS   And liegemen to the Dane.
FRANCISCO   Give you good night.
MARCELLUS
  O farewell, honest (soldier.) Who hath relieved
    you?   20
FRANCISCO
  Barnardo hath my place. Give you good night.
                                        Francisco exits.
MARCELLUS   Holla, Barnardo.
BARNARDO   Say, what, is Horatio there?
HORATIO   A piece of him.
BARNARDO
  Welcome, Horatio.—Welcome, good Marcellus.   25
HORATIO
  What, has this thing appeared again tonight?
BARNARDO   I have seen nothing.
MARCELLUS
  Horatio says 'tis but our fantasy
  And will not let belief take hold of him
  Touching this dreaded sight twice seen of us.   30
  Therefore I have entreated him along
  With us to watch the minutes of this night,
  That, if again this apparition come,
  He may approve our eyes and speak to it.
HORATIO
  Tush, tush, 'twill not appear.   35
BARNARDO   Sit down awhile,
  And let us once again assail your ears,
  That are so fortified against our story,
  What we have two nights seen.
HORATIO   Well, sit we down,   40
  And let us hear Barnardo speak of this.
BARNARDO   Last night of all,
  When yond same star that's westward from the pole
  Had made his course t' illume that part of heaven
  Where now it burns, Marcellus and myself,   45
  The bell then beating one—

51. harrows: torments (A harrow is a farm implement used to break up the ground.)

57. sometimes: formerly

67. sensible: attested by the senses; **avouch:** guarantee, testimony

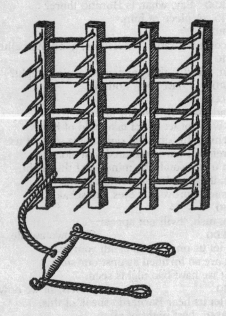

The harrow. (1.1.51)
From Gervase Markham, *The English husbandman* (1613).

Enter Ghost.

MARCELLUS
  Peace, break thee off! Look where it comes again.
BARNARDO
  In the same figure like the King that's dead.
MARCELLUS, ⌜*to Horatio*⌝
  Thou art a scholar. Speak to it, Horatio.
BARNARDO
  Looks he not like the King? Mark it, Horatio.   50
HORATIO
  Most like. It (harrows) me with fear and wonder.
BARNARDO
  It would be spoke to.
MARCELLUS   Speak to it, Horatio.
HORATIO
  What art thou that usurp'st this time of night,
  Together with that fair and warlike form   55
  In which the majesty of buried Denmark
  Did sometimes march? By heaven, I charge thee,
    speak.
MARCELLUS
  It is offended.
BARNARDO   See, it stalks away.   60
HORATIO
  Stay! speak! speak! I charge thee, speak!
                             Ghost exits.
MARCELLUS 'Tis gone and will not answer.
BARNARDO
  How now, Horatio, you tremble and look pale.
  Is not this something more than fantasy?
  What think you on 't?   65
HORATIO
  Before my God, I might not this believe
  Without the sensible and true avouch
  Of mine own eyes.

72. **Norway:** i.e., the king of Norway (the elder Fortinbras)

73. **parle:** parley, meeting

74. **smote:** attacked or, perhaps, defeated; **sledded Polacks:** Polish military riding in sleds

76. **jump:** exactly

78–79. **In what . . . opinion:** i.e., I cannot be precise, but in my general opinion

81. **tell . . . knows:** i.e., let him who knows tell me

83. **toils:** causes to labor; wearies; **subject of the land:** i.e., subjects of the realm

85. **foreign mart:** international trade

86. **impress:** enforced service

88. **toward:** approaching, about to happen

95. **Thereto . . . pride:** stirred to do this (i.e., to dare King Hamlet to combat) by a proud desire to rival the Danish king

99. **heraldry:** the law of arms, regulating tournaments and battles

101. **stood seized of:** legally possessed

MARCELLUS   Is it not like the King?
HORATIO   As thou art to thyself.   70
   Such was the very armor he had on
   When he the ambitious Norway combated.
   So frowned he once when, in an angry parle,
   He smote the sledded ⌈Polacks⌉ on the ice.
   'Tis strange.   75
MARCELLUS
   Thus twice before, and jump at this dead hour,
   With martial stalk hath he gone by our watch.
HORATIO
   In what particular thought to work I know not,
   But in the gross and scope of mine opinion
   This bodes some strange eruption to our state.   80
MARCELLUS
   Good now, sit down, and tell me, he that knows,
   Why this same strict and most observant watch
   So nightly toils the subject of the land,
   And ⟨why⟩ such daily ⟨cast⟩ of brazen cannon
   And foreign mart for implements of war,   85
   Why such impress of shipwrights, whose sore task
   Does not divide the Sunday from the week.
   What might be toward that this sweaty haste
   Doth make the night joint laborer with the day?
   Who is 't that can inform me?   90
HORATIO   That can I.
   At least the whisper goes so: our last king,
   Whose image even but now appeared to us,
   Was, as you know, by Fortinbras of Norway,
   Thereto pricked on by a most emulate pride,   95
   Dared to the combat; in which our valiant Hamlet
   (For so this side of our known world esteemed him)
   Did slay this Fortinbras, who by a sealed compact,
   Well ratified by law and heraldry,
   Did forfeit, with his life, all ⟨those⟩ his lands   100
   Which he stood seized of, to the conqueror.

102. **a moiety competent:** an appropriate portion
103. **gagèd:** engaged, i.e., pledged
105. **comart:** bargain
106. **carriage of the article designed:** i.e., meaning carried by the agreement drawn up
108. **unimprovèd:** uncontrolled
110. **Sharked up:** i.e., gathered indiscriminately
112. **stomach:** spirit of adventure
118. **head:** fountainhead, source
119. **rummage:** bustle, commotion
121. **Well may it sort:** i.e., it would thus be fitting
125. **palmy:** triumphant, worthy to "bear the palm"
127. **sheeted:** wrapped in their shrouds
129–30. **As stars . . . sun:** These lines are awkward; probably some text has been lost.
130. **Disasters:** threatening signs; **moist star:** the moon, which governs the tides
131. **Upon . . . stands:** i.e., by whose influence the sea is controlled   **Neptune:** Roman god of the sea
133. **precurse:** foreshadowing
134. **harbingers:** those that announce someone's or something's approach; **still:** always
135. **omen:** i.e., ominous event

Against the which a moiety competent
Was gagèd by our king, which had (returned)
To the inheritance of Fortinbras
Had he been vanquisher, as, by the same comart   105
And carriage of the article ⌜designed,⌝
His fell to Hamlet. Now, sir, young Fortinbras,
Of unimprovèd mettle hot and full,
Hath in the skirts of Norway here and there
Sharked up a list of lawless resolutes   110
For food and diet to some enterprise
That hath a stomach in 't; which is no other
(As it doth well appear unto our state)
But to recover of us, by strong hand
And terms compulsatory, those foresaid lands   115
So by his father lost. And this, I take it,
Is the main motive of our preparations,
The source of this our watch, and the chief head
Of this posthaste and rummage in the land.

⌜BARNARDO
I think it be no other but e'en so.   120
Well may it sort that this portentous figure
Comes armèd through our watch so like the king
That was and is the question of these wars.

HORATIO
A mote it is to trouble the mind's eye.
In the most high and palmy state of Rome,   125
A little ere the mightiest Julius fell,
The graves stood tenantless, and the sheeted dead
Did squeak and gibber in the Roman streets;
As stars with trains of fire and dews of blood,
Disasters in the sun; and the moist star,   130
Upon whose influence Neptune's empire stands,
Was sick almost to doomsday with eclipse.
And even the like precurse of ⌜feared⌝ events,
As harbingers preceding still the fates
And prologue to the omen coming on,   135

137. **climatures:** geographic regions
138. **soft:** "wait a minute"
146. **happily:** perhaps; or, fortunately

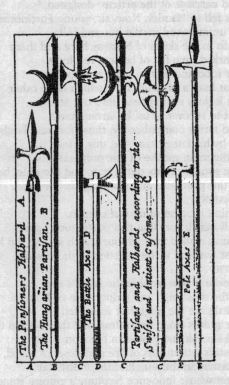

A — The Pensioners Halbard
B — The Hungarian Partisan.
D — The Battle Axe
C — Partisans and Halbards according to the Swisse and Antient Custome
E — Pole Axes

A   B   C   D   C   C   E   E

Partisans and other weapons. (1.1.153)
From Louis de Gaya, *A treatise of the arms . . .* (1678).

16

Have heaven and earth together demonstrated
Unto our climatures and countrymen.]

Enter Ghost.

But soft, behold! Lo, where it comes again!
I'll cross it though it blast me.—Stay, illusion!
                              It spreads his arms.
If thou hast any sound or use of voice,   140
Speak to me.
If there be any good thing to be done
That may to thee do ease and grace to me,
Speak to me.
If thou art privy to thy country's fate,   145
Which happily foreknowing may avoid,
O, speak!
Or if thou hast uphoarded in thy life
Extorted treasure in the womb of earth,
For which, they say, (you) spirits oft walk in death,   150
Speak of it.   *The cock crows.*
          Stay and speak!—Stop it, Marcellus.
MARCELLUS
  Shall I strike it with my partisan?
HORATIO   Do, if it will not stand.
BARNARDO   'Tis here.   155
HORATIO   'Tis here.
                              (Ghost exits.)
MARCELLUS   'Tis gone.
  We do it wrong, being so majestical,
  To offer it the show of violence,
  For it is as the air, invulnerable,   160
  And our vain blows malicious mockery.
BARNARDO
  It was about to speak when the cock crew.
HORATIO
  And then it started like a guilty thing
  Upon a fearful summons. I have heard

169. **extravagant:** out of bounds; **erring:** wandering

171. **made probation:** demonstrated

173. **'gainst:** just before

177. **strike:** destroy through malign influence

178. **takes:** puts under a magic spell

The cock, that is the trumpet to the morn,   165
Doth with his lofty and shrill-sounding throat
Awake the god of day, and at his warning,
Whether in sea or fire, in earth or air,
Th' extravagant and erring spirit hies
To his confine, and of the truth herein   170
This present object made probation.

MARCELLUS
It faded on the crowing of the cock.
Some say that ever 'gainst that season comes
Wherein our Savior's birth is celebrated,
This bird of dawning singeth all night long;   175
And then, they say, no spirit dare stir abroad,
The nights are wholesome; then no planets strike,
No fairy takes, nor witch hath power to charm,
So hallowed and so gracious is that time.

HORATIO
So have I heard and do in part believe it.   180
But look, the morn in russet mantle clad
Walks o'er the dew of yon high eastward hill.
Break we our watch up, and by my advice
Let us impart what we have seen tonight
Unto young Hamlet; for, upon my life,   185
This spirit, dumb to us, will speak to him.
Do you consent we shall acquaint him with it
As needful in our loves, fitting our duty?

MARCELLUS
Let's do 't, I pray, and I this morning know
Where we shall find him most convenient.   190

                                        They exit.

1.2 In an audience chamber in Elsinore, Claudius, the new king of Denmark, holds court. After thanking his subjects for their recent support, he dispatches ambassadors to Norway to halt a threatened attack from Fortinbras. He gives Laertes permission to return to France but denies Hamlet's request to return to the university in Wittenberg. Hamlet, mourning for his father's death, is left alone to vent his despair at what he regards as his mother's all too hasty marriage to his uncle, Claudius. The audience learns that the marriage took place "within a month" of the former king's death.

Horatio, Barnardo, and Marcellus arrive and tell Hamlet about the Ghost. Hamlet, aroused by the news, agrees to join them that night.

---

8. **our sometime sister:** my former sister-in-law (Claudius uses the royal "we" throughout, when he is speaking as king.)

9. **jointress:** a woman who owns property jointly with her husband

11. **With . . . eye:** as if smiling with one eye and crying with the other

18. **a weak . . . worth:** i.e., a low opinion of my ability

21. **Colleaguèd:** i.e., in league with; **advantage:** i.e., superior position

29. **impotent:** helpless

⟨Scene 2⟩

Flourish. Enter Claudius, King of Denmark, Gertrude the
Queen, ⌜*the*⌝ *Council, as Polonius, and his son Laertes,*
Hamlet, with others, ⌜*among them Voltemand and*
Cornelius.⌝

KING

Though yet of Hamlet our dear brother's death
The memory be green, and that it us befitted
To bear our hearts in grief, and our whole kingdom
To be contracted in one brow of woe,
Yet so far hath discretion fought with nature   5
That we with wisest sorrow think on him
Together with remembrance of ourselves.
Therefore our sometime sister, now our queen,
Th' imperial jointress to this warlike state,
Have we (as 'twere with a defeated joy,   10
With an auspicious and a dropping eye,
With mirth in funeral and with dirge in marriage,
In equal scale weighing delight and dole)
Taken to wife. Nor have we herein barred
Your better wisdoms, which have freely gone   15
With this affair along. For all, our thanks.
Now follows that you know. Young Fortinbras,
Holding a weak supposal of our worth
Or thinking by our late dear brother's death
Our state to be disjoint and out of frame,   20
Colleaguèd with this dream of his advantage,
He hath not failed to pester us with message
Importing the surrender of those lands
Lost by his father, with all bonds of law,
To our most valiant brother—so much for him.   25
Now for ourself and for this time of meeting.
Thus much the business is: we have here writ
To Norway, uncle of young Fortinbras,
Who, impotent and bedrid, scarcely hears

31. **gait:** course

31–33. **in that . . . subject:** i.e., since the troops and supplies are drawn from Norway's own subjects

37. **To business:** to negotiate

38. **these . . . articles:** this detailed written account

39. **let . . . duty:** i.e., let your speedy departure take the place of ceremonious leave-taking

45. **lose your voice:** i.e., waste your words

48. **native:** naturally connected

Of this his nephew's purpose, to suppress   30
His further gait herein, in that the levies,
The lists, and full proportions are all made
Out of his subject; and we here dispatch
You, good Cornelius, and you, Voltemand,
For bearers of this greeting to old Norway,   35
Giving to you no further personal power
To business with the King more than the scope
Of these dilated articles allow.
                              ⌜*Giving them a paper.*⌝
Farewell, and let your haste commend your duty.
CORNELIUS / VOLTEMAND
    In that and all things will we show our duty.   40
KING
    We doubt it nothing. Heartily farewell.
                        (*Voltemand and Cornelius exit.*)
And now, Laertes, what's the news with you?
You told us of some suit. What is 't, Laertes?
You cannot speak of reason to the Dane
And lose your voice. What wouldst thou beg,   45
    Laertes,
That shall not be my offer, not thy asking?
The head is not more native to the heart,
The hand more instrumental to the mouth,
Than is the throne of Denmark to thy father.   50
What wouldst thou have, Laertes?
LAERTES   My dread lord,
Your leave and favor to return to France,
From whence though willingly I came to Denmark
To show my duty in your coronation,   55
Yet now I must confess, that duty done,
My thoughts and wishes bend again toward France
And bow them to your gracious leave and pardon.
KING
Have you your father's leave? What says Polonius?

60–61. **wrung . . . petition:** i.e., finally persuaded me to allow him

62. **Upon . . . consent:** i.e., I reluctantly agreed to his wishes

64–65. **Take . . . will:** a courteous formula giving Laertes permission to return to France

66. **cousin:** kinsman

67. **more than kin:** i.e., twice related: uncle/nephew and "father"/"son"; **less than kind:** i.e., in a less-than-natural relationship

69. **in the sun:** a pun on sun/son

70. **nighted color:** i.e., black (mourning) clothing

72. **vailèd lids:** i.e., lowered eyes

74. **common:** belonging to all human beings

78. **particular:** special, personal

80–86. **'Tis . . . truly:** i.e., it is not only my black clothes, my sighs and tears, my downcast face, and other outward signs of grief that indicate my real feelings

POLONIUS
  Hath, my lord, [wrung from me my slow leave   60
  By laborsome petition, and at last
  Upon his will I sealed my hard consent.]
  I do beseech you give him leave to go.
KING
  Take thy fair hour, Laertes. Time be thine,
  And thy best graces spend it at thy will.—   65
  But now, my cousin Hamlet and my son—
HAMLET, ⌜*aside*⌝
  A little more than kin and less than kind.
KING
  How is it that the clouds still hang on you?
HAMLET
  Not so, my lord; I am too much in the sun.
QUEEN
  Good Hamlet, cast thy nighted color off,   70
  And let thine eye look like a friend on Denmark.
  Do not forever with thy vailèd lids
  Seek for thy noble father in the dust.
  Thou know'st 'tis common; all that lives must die,
  Passing through nature to eternity.   75
HAMLET
  Ay, madam, it is common.
QUEEN   If it be,
  Why seems it so particular with thee?
HAMLET
  "Seems," madam? Nay, it is. I know not "seems."
  'Tis not alone my inky cloak, (good) mother,   80
  Nor customary suits of solemn black,
  Nor windy suspiration of forced breath,
  No, nor the fruitful river in the eye,
  Nor the dejected havior of the visage,
  Together with all forms, moods, ⌜shapes⌝ of grief,   85
  That can (denote) me truly. These indeed "seem,"
  For they are actions that a man might play;

96. obsequious: dutiful (Claudius seems to be playing on the related word "obsequy," funeral service.)

97. obstinate condolement: sorrow that refuses comfort

99. incorrect to heaven: uncorrected by the divine will

103. most . . . sense: most familiar object of perception

108. still: always, habitually

109. corse: corpse

111. unprevailing: futile, useless

113. most immediate: next in line of succession

116. impart toward: give to

118. retrograde: opposite, contrary

But I have that within which passes show,
These but the trappings and the suits of woe.

KING

'Tis sweet and commendable in your nature, Hamlet,　　　90
To give these mourning duties to your father.
But you must know your father lost a father,
That father lost, lost his, and the survivor bound
In filial obligation for some term　　　95
To do obsequious sorrow. But to persever
In obstinate condolement is a course
Of impious stubbornness. 'Tis unmanly grief.
It shows a will most incorrect to heaven,
A heart unfortified, ⟨a⟩ mind impatient,　　　100
An understanding simple and unschooled.
For what we know must be and is as common
As any the most vulgar thing to sense,
Why should we in our peevish opposition
Take it to heart? Fie, 'tis a fault to heaven,　　　105
A fault against the dead, a fault to nature,
To reason most absurd, whose common theme
Is death of fathers, and who still hath cried,
From the first corse till he that died today,
"This must be so." We pray you, throw to earth　　　110
This unprevailing woe and think of us
As of a father; for let the world take note,
You are the most immediate to our throne,
And with no less nobility of love
Than that which dearest father bears his son　　　115
Do I impart toward you. For your intent
In going back to school in Wittenberg,
It is most retrograde to our desire,
And we beseech you, bend you to remain
Here in the cheer and comfort of our eye,　　　120
Our chiefest courtier, cousin, and our son.

129. **jocund health:** merry toast

130. **tell:** count out

131. **rouse:** deep drink; **bruit:** report

133. **sullied:** stained, defiled (The Second Quarto [Q2] reads "sallied," an alternate spelling for "sullied"; the Folio [F] reads "solid.")

136. **canon:** law

143. **that was to this:** i.e., that was, in comparison to *this* king (Claudius)

144. **Hyperion to a satyr:** i.e., like the sun god as compared to a goatlike satyr

145. **might not beteem:** would not allow

151. **or ere:** before

Niobe. (1.2.153)
From Giovanni Battista Cavalleriis,
Antiquarum statuarum (1585–94).

28

QUEEN
Let not thy mother lose her prayers, Hamlet.
I pray thee, stay with us. Go not to Wittenberg.

HAMLET
I shall in all my best obey you, madam.

KING
Why, 'tis a loving and a fair reply.   125
Be as ourself in Denmark.—Madam, come.
This gentle and unforced accord of Hamlet
Sits smiling to my heart, in grace whereof
No jocund health that Denmark drinks today
But the great cannon to the clouds shall tell,   130
And the King's rouse the heaven shall bruit again,
Respeaking earthly thunder. Come away.
Flourish. All but Hamlet exit.

HAMLET
O, that this too, too sullied flesh would melt,
Thaw, and resolve itself into a dew,
Or that the Everlasting had not fixed   135
His canon 'gainst (self-slaughter!) O God, God,
How (weary,) stale, flat, and unprofitable
Seem to me all the uses of this world!
Fie on 't, ah fie! 'Tis an unweeded garden
That grows to seed. Things rank and gross in nature   140
Possess it merely. That it should come (to this:)
But two months dead—nay, not so much, not two.
So excellent a king, that was to this
Hyperion to a satyr; so loving to my mother
That he might not beteem the winds of heaven   145
Visit her face too roughly. Heaven and earth,
Must I remember? Why, she (would) hang on him
As if increase of appetite had grown
By what it fed on. And yet, within a month
(Let me not think on 't; frailty, thy name is woman!),   150
A little month, or ere those shoes were old
With which she followed my poor father's body,

153. **Niobe:** In Greek mythology, Niobe, so grief-stricken at the loss of her children that she could not cease crying, was transformed into a stone from which water continually flowed.

154. **wants . . . reason:** lacks the ability to reason

158. **Hercules:** in Greek mythology, a hero of extraordinary strength and courage

160. **Had . . . eyes:** i.e., had stopped turning her eyes red

161. **post:** rush (as in riding a post-horse)

162. **incestuous:** Hamlet calls the marriage of his mother and his uncle "incestuous"—i.e., a violation of the laws against intercourse between close kin. The Ghost will also make this charge (1.5.49). Other members of the Danish court seem to see the marriage of Gertrude and Claudius as legal and legitimate. Debates about the incestuousness of a marriage between a widow and her dead husband's brother were heated in the 16th century (especially during the divorce trial of Henry VIII and Catherine of Aragon). The Bible gives conflicting commands about such marriages. How one is to view the marriage of Gertrude and Claudius is an ongoing focus of interest for students of *Hamlet*.

169. **I'll . . . you:** i.e., instead of your calling yourself my "servant," we'll call each other "friend"

170. **what . . . from:** what are you doing away from

Like Niobe, all tears—why she, ⟨even she⟩
(O God, a beast that wants discourse of reason
Would have mourned longer!), married with my   155
  uncle,
My father's brother, but no more like my father
Than I to Hercules. Within a month,
Ere yet the salt of most unrighteous tears
Had left the flushing in her gallèd eyes,   160
She married. O, most wicked speed, to post
With such dexterity to incestuous sheets!
It is not, nor it cannot come to good.
But break, my heart, for I must hold my tongue.

Enter Horatio, Marcellus, and Barnardo.

HORATIO   Hail to your lordship.   165
HAMLET   I am glad to see you well.
  Horatio—or I do forget myself!
HORATIO
  The same, my lord, and your poor servant ever.
HAMLET
  Sir, my good friend. I'll change that name with you.
  And what make you from Wittenberg, Horatio?—   170
  Marcellus?
MARCELLUS   My good lord.
HAMLET
  I am very glad to see you. ⌈*To Barnardo.*⌉ Good
    even, sir.—
  But what, in faith, make you from Wittenberg?   175
HORATIO
  A truant disposition, good my lord.
HAMLET
  I would not hear your enemy say so,
  Nor shall you do my ear that violence
  To make it truster of your own report
  Against yourself. I know you are no truant.   ⁶⁹
  But what is your affair in Elsinore?
  We'll teach you to drink ⟨deep⟩ ere you depart.

186. **hard upon:** soon after
188. **coldly:** served cold (as leftovers)
189. **dearest:** most grievous; bitterest
194. **goodly:** admirable, excellent
201. **Season your admiration:** i.e., control your astonishment
202. **attent:** attentive

HORATIO
  My lord, I came to see your father's funeral.
HAMLET
  I prithee, do not mock me, fellow student.
  I think it was to ⟨see⟩ my mother's wedding. 185
HORATIO
  Indeed, my lord, it followed hard upon.
HAMLET
  Thrift, thrift, Horatio. The funeral baked meats
  Did coldly furnish forth the marriage tables.
  Would I had met my dearest foe in heaven
  Or ever I had seen that day, Horatio! 190
  My father—methinks I see my father.
HORATIO
  Where, my lord?
HAMLET   In my mind's eye, Horatio.
HORATIO
  I saw him once. He was a goodly king.
HAMLET
  He was a man. Take him for all in all, 195
  I shall not look upon his like again.
HORATIO
  My lord, I think I saw him yesternight.
HAMLET   Saw who?
HORATIO
  My lord, the King your father.
HAMLET   The King my father? 200
HORATIO
  Season your admiration for a while
  With an attent ear, till I may deliver
  Upon the witness of these gentlemen
  This marvel to you.
HAMLET   For God's love, let me hear! 205
HORATIO
  Two nights together had these gentlemen,
  Marcellus and Barnardo, on their watch,

210. at point exactly; cap-à-pie: at every point, from head to foot

213. oppressed and fear-surprisèd: terrified

214. truncheon: short staff (here carried as a symbol of authority)

215. the act of fear: the action of fear upon them

"Armèd at point exactly, cap-à-pie." (1.2.210)
From Henry Peacham, *Minerua Britanna* (1612).

In the dead waste and middle of the night,
Been thus encountered: a figure like your father,
Armèd at point exactly, cap-à-pie,   210
Appears before them and with solemn march
Goes slow and stately by them. Thrice he walked
By their oppressed and fear-surprisèd eyes
Within his truncheon's length, whilst they, distilled
Almost to jelly with the act of fear,   215
Stand dumb and speak not to him. This to me
In dreadful secrecy impart they did,
And I with them the third night kept the watch,
⌜Where, as⌝ they had delivered, both in time,
Form of the thing (each word made true and good),   220
The apparition comes. I knew your father;
These hands are not more like.

HAMLET   But where was this?

MARCELLUS
My lord, upon the platform where we watch.

HAMLET
Did you not speak to it?   225

HORATIO   My lord, I did,
But answer made it none. Yet once methought
It lifted up its head and did address
Itself to motion, like as it would speak;
But even then the morning cock crew loud,   230
And at the sound it shrunk in haste away
And vanished from our sight.

HAMLET   'Tis very strange.

HORATIO
As I do live, my honored lord, 'tis true.
And we did think it writ down in our duty   235
To let you know of it.

HAMLET   Indeed, sirs, but this troubles me.
Hold you the watch tonight?

ALL   We do, my lord.

HAMLET
Armed, say you?   240

245. **beaver:** front piece of a helmet
259. **grizzled:** gray

Helmet with beaver down. (1.2.245)
From Henry Peacham, *Minerua Britanna* (1612).

ALL   Armed, my lord.
HAMLET   From top to toe?
ALL My lord, from head to foot.
HAMLET Then saw you not his face?
HORATIO
O, yes, my lord, he wore his beaver up.   245
HAMLET What, looked he frowningly?
HORATIO
A countenance more in sorrow than in anger.
HAMLET Pale or red?
HORATIO
Nay, very pale.
HAMLET   And fixed his eyes upon you?   250
HORATIO
Most constantly.
HAMLET   I would I had been there.
HORATIO It would have much amazed you.
HAMLET Very like. Stayed it long?
HORATIO
While one with moderate haste might tell a   255
hundred.
BARNARDO/MARCELLUS Longer, longer.
HORATIO
Not when I saw 't.
HAMLET   His beard was grizzled, no?
HORATIO
It was as I have seen it in his life,   260
A sable silvered.
HAMLET   I will watch ⌜tonight.⌝
Perchance 'twill walk again.
HORATIO   I warrant it will.
HAMLET
If it assume my noble father's person,   265
I'll speak to it, though hell itself should gape
And bid me hold my peace. I pray you all,
If you have hitherto concealed this sight,

269. **tenable:** withheld, kept secret

278. **doubt . . . play:** suspect some treacherous action

1.3 In Polonius's chambers, Laertes says good-bye to his sister, Ophelia, and tells her not to trust Hamlet's promises of love. Polonius joins them, sends Laertes off, then echoes Laertes's warnings to Ophelia, finally ordering her not to see Hamlet again.

———————

3. **convey is assistant:** ships are available

7. **fashion:** a temporary enthusiasm; **toy in blood:** amorous flirtation

8. **in . . . nature:** in the early days of its prime

9. **Forward:** ardent, eager

10. **perfume . . . minute:** that which makes the moment sweet and fills it with pleasure

Let it be tenable in your silence still;
And whatsomever else shall hap tonight,   270
Give it an understanding but no tongue.
I will requite your loves. So fare you well.
Upon the platform, 'twixt eleven and twelve,
I'll visit you.

ALL   Our duty to your Honor.   275

HAMLET
Your loves, as mine to you. Farewell.

⌜*All but Hamlet* ⌝ *exit.*

My father's spirit—in arms! All is not well.
I doubt some foul play. Would the night were come!
Till then, sit still, my soul. (Foul) deeds will rise,
Though all the earth o'erwhelm them, to men's   280
  eyes.

He exits.

(Scene 3)
Enter Laertes and Ophelia, his sister.

LAERTES
My necessaries are embarked. Farewell.
And, sister, as the winds give benefit
And convey ⟨is⟩ assistant, do not sleep,
But let me hear from you.

OPHELIA   Do you doubt that?   5

LAERTES
For Hamlet, and the trifling of his favor,
Hold it a fashion and a toy in blood,
A violet in the youth of primy nature,
Forward, not permanent, sweet, not lasting,
The perfume and suppliance of a minute,   10
No more.

OPHELIA   No more but so?

LAERTES   Think it no more.

14–15. nature ... bulk: i.e., a growing human does not increase only in strength and size

15. this temple: the body; **waxes:** grows larger

17. withal: at the same time

18. cautel: deceit

20. greatness: high rank

23. Carve: i.e., choose

26. that body: i.e., the Danish state

31. give his saying deed: put his words into action

34. credent: gullible; **list:** listen to

35–36. your chaste ... importunity: i.e., surrender your chastity to his uncontrolled pleading

38. keep ... affection: i.e., hold yourself back from actions your feelings would lead you into (The metaphor is from warfare, and is continued in the next line.)

40. chariest: most careful

43. The canker ... spring: the cankerworm destroys the early spring blossoms

44. buttons: buds

46. blastments: withering blights

48. Youth ... else near: i.e., youth loses self-control even without a tempter

For nature, crescent, does not grow alone
In thews and ⟨bulk,⟩ but, as this temple waxes,   15
The inward service of the mind and soul
Grows wide withal. Perhaps he loves you now,
And now no soil nor cautel doth besmirch
The virtue of his will; but you must fear,
His greatness weighed, his will is not his own,   20
⟨For he himself is subject to his birth.⟩
He may not, as unvalued persons do,
Carve for himself, for on his choice depends
The safety and ⌜the⌝ health of this whole state.
And therefore must his choice be circumscribed   25
Unto the voice and yielding of that body
Whereof he is the head. Then, if he says he loves
     you,
It fits your wisdom so far to believe it
As he in his particular act and place   30
May give his saying deed, which is no further
Than the main voice of Denmark goes withal.
Then weigh what loss your honor may sustain
If with too credent ear you list his songs
Or lose your heart or your chaste treasure open   35
To his unmastered importunity.
Fear it, Ophelia; fear it, my dear sister,
And keep you in the rear of your affection,
Out of the shot and danger of desire.
The chariest maid is prodigal enough   40
If she unmask her beauty to the moon.
Virtue itself 'scapes not calumnious strokes.
The canker galls the infants of the spring
Too oft before their buttons be disclosed,
And, in the morn and liquid dew of youth,   45
Contagious blastments are most imminent.
Be wary, then; best safety lies in fear.
Youth to itself rebels, though none else near.

OPHELIA
  I shall the effect of this good lesson keep

51. **ungracious:** ungodly

52–54. **Show me . . . treads:** i.e., show me how to live a strict and virtuous life while you yourself follow a life of self-indulgence (See Matthew 7.13–14.)

55. **recks not his own rede:** does not heed his own advice

58. **A double . . . grace:** i.e., to receive one's father's blessing twice is a double favor from heaven

59. **Occasion smiles upon:** i.e., opportunity (personified as "Occasion") kindly grants me

65. **Look thou character:** see that you inscribe

67. **familiar:** friendly; **vulgar:** i.e., indiscriminate

71. **unfledged courage:** spirited youngster

75. **censure:** synonymous with **judgment**

76. **habit:** clothing

80. **Are . . . in that:** This puzzling line reads, in Q2, "Or of a most select and generous, chiefe in that"; in F it reads, "Are of a most . . . cheff in that." The line seems to mean, generally: the French show their refinement chiefly in the way they choose their apparel.

As watchman to my heart. But, good my brother,   50
Do not, as some ungracious pastors do,
Show me the steep and thorny way to heaven,
Whiles, (like) a puffed and reckless libertine,
Himself the primrose path of dalliance treads
And recks not his own rede.   55

LAERTES   O, fear me not.

Enter Polonius.

I stay too long. But here my father comes.
A double blessing is a double grace.
Occasion smiles upon a second leave.

POLONIUS
Yet here, Laertes? Aboard, aboard, for shame!   60
The wind sits in the shoulder of your sail,
And you are stayed for. There, my blessing with
   thee.
And these few precepts in thy memory
Look thou character. Give thy thoughts no tongue,   65
Nor any unproportioned thought his act.
Be thou familiar, but by no means vulgar.
Those friends thou hast, and their adoption tried,
Grapple them unto thy soul with hoops of steel,
But do not dull thy palm with entertainment   70
Of each new-hatched, unfledged courage. Beware
Of entrance to a quarrel, but, being in,
Bear 't that th' opposèd may beware of thee.
Give every man thy ear, but few thy voice.
Take each man's censure, but reserve thy judgment.   75
Costly thy habit as thy purse can buy,
But not expressed in fancy (rich, not gaudy),
For the apparel oft proclaims the man,
And they in France of the best rank and station
(Are) of a most select and generous chief in that.   80
Neither a borrower nor a lender (be,)
For (loan) oft loses both itself and friend,

83. **husbandry:** management of one's money

89. **invests:** i.e., presses upon (Many editors prefer the Folio's "invites.")

98. **Marry:** indeed (formerly, a mild oath derived from "By the Virgin Mary")

103. **so 'tis put on me:** so I have been told

108–9. **tenders . . . to me:** offers to me of his affection

111. **Unsifted in:** i.e., naive about

And borrowing (dulls the) edge of husbandry.
This above all: to thine own self be true,
And it must follow, as the night the day,   85
Thou canst not then be false to any man.
Farewell. My blessing season this in thee.

LAERTES
Most humbly do I take my leave, my lord.

POLONIUS
The time invests you. Go, your servants tend.

LAERTES
Farewell, Ophelia, and remember well   90
What I have said to you.

OPHELIA 'Tis in my memory locked,
And you yourself shall keep the key of it.

LAERTES Farewell.   *Laertes exits.*

POLONIUS
What is 't, Ophelia, he hath said to you?   95

OPHELIA
So please you, something touching the Lord
   Hamlet.

POLONIUS Marry, well bethought.
'Tis told me he hath very oft of late
Given private time to you, and you yourself   100
Have of your audience been most free and
   bounteous.
If it be so (as so 'tis put on me,
And that in way of caution), I must tell you
You do not understand yourself so clearly   105
As it behooves my daughter and your honor.
What is between you? Give me up the truth.

OPHELIA
He hath, my lord, of late made many tenders
Of his affection to me.

POLONIUS
Affection, puh! You speak like a green girl   110
Unsifted in such perilous circumstance.
Do you believe his "tenders," as you call them?

115. tenders: coins that should be "legal tender" but are not because they are not **sterling**

116. Tender yourself more dearly: regard yourself at a higher rate

117–18. not to . . . thus: not to run the phrase, as if it were a horse, so hard that it becomes winded

118. tender me a fool: (1) show yourself to me as a fool; (2) make me look like a fool; (3) present me with a grandchild (The word "fool" was used as a term of endearment for a child.)

124. springes: snares; **woodcocks:** birds thought to be stupid and easily captured

127–28. extinct . . . a-making: i.e., both the light and the heat of such **blazes** die out almost as soon as they appear

131–32. Set . . . parle: Polonius here uses images from finance (**Set . . . at a higher rate**), diplomacy (**entreatments:** negotiations), and the military (**a command to parle:** an order to meet in conference) in order to tell Ophelia to spend less time talking to Hamlet.

136–40. brokers . . . beguile: i.e., they are panders (**brokers, bawds:** go-betweens in sexual intrigues) who are not as holy as their dress (**investments**) would indicate; instead, they are merely urgers (**implorators**) of sinful actions (**unholy suits**) speaking (**breathing**) as if they were holy, in order to entice (**beguile**) (Bawds was suggested by Lewis Theobald; Q2 and F read "bonds.")

142. slander: disgrace by misusing

OPHELIA
  I do not know, my lord, what I should think.
POLONIUS
  Marry, I will teach you. Think yourself a baby
  That you have ta'en these tenders for true pay,   115
  Which are not sterling. Tender yourself more dearly,
  Or (not to crack the wind of the poor phrase,
  ⌈Running⌉ it thus) you'll tender me a fool.
OPHELIA
  My lord, he hath importuned me with love
  In honorable fashion—   120
POLONIUS
  Ay, "fashion" you may call it. Go to, go to!
OPHELIA
  And hath given countenance to his speech, my lord,
  With almost all the holy vows of heaven.
POLONIUS
  Ay, ⟨springes⟩ to catch woodcocks. I do know,
  When the blood burns, how prodigal the soul   125
  Lends the tongue vows. These blazes, daughter,
  Giving more light than heat, extinct in both
  Even in their promise as it is a-making,
  You must not take for fire. From this time
  Be something scanter of your maiden presence.   130
  Set your entreatments at a higher rate
  Than a command to parle. For Lord Hamlet,
  Believe so much in him that he is young,
  And with a larger ⟨tether⟩ may he walk
  Than may be given you. In few, Ophelia,   135
  Do not believe his vows, for they are brokers,
  Not of that dye which their investments show,
  But mere ⟨implorators⟩ of unholy suits,
  Breathing like sanctified and pious ⌈bawds⌉
  The better to ⟨beguile.⟩ This is for all: 140
  I would not, in plain terms, from this time forth
  Have you so slander any moment leisure

1.4 While Claudius drinks away the night, Hamlet, Horatio, and Marcellus are visited by the Ghost. It signals to Hamlet. Hamlet's friends try to stop him from following the Ghost, but Hamlet will not be held back.

————————

1. **shrewdly:** keenly, intensely
2. **eager:** sharp (from the French *aigre*)
7. **held his wont:** has been accustomed
9. **doth . . . rouse:** stays awake tonight drinking
10. **Keeps wassail:** carouses; **upspring:** a German dance, particularly associated with heavy drinking
11. **Rhenish:** Rhine wine
13. **triumph of his pledge:** his feat of emptying the cup in one draft
17. **to the manner born:** destined through birth to accept this custom
20. **taxed of:** censured by
21. **clepe:** call
22. **addition:** titles of honor

As to give words or talk with the Lord Hamlet.
Look to 't, I charge you. Come your ways.
OPHELIA   I shall obey, my lord.   145

                                          They exit.

⌜Scene 4⌝
Enter Hamlet, Horatio, and Marcellus.

HAMLET
  The air bites shrewdly; it is very cold.
HORATIO
  It is ⟨a⟩ nipping and an eager air.
HAMLET   What hour now?
HORATIO   I think it lacks of twelve.
MARCELLUS   No, it is struck.   5
HORATIO
  Indeed, I heard it not. It then draws near the season
  Wherein the spirit held his wont to walk.
            A flourish of trumpets and two pieces goes off.
  What does this mean, my lord?
HAMLET
  The King doth wake tonight and takes his rouse,
  Keeps wassail, and the swagg'ring upspring reels;   10
  And, as he drains his draughts of Rhenish down,
  The kettledrum and trumpet thus bray out
  The triumph of his pledge.
HORATIO   Is it a custom?
HAMLET   Ay, marry, is 't,   15
  But, to my mind, though I am native here
  And to the manner born, it is a custom
  More honored in the breach than the observance.
  [This heavy-headed ⌜revel⌝ east and west
  Makes us traduced and taxed of other nations.   20
  They clepe us drunkards and with swinish phrase
  Soil our addition. And, indeed, it takes

25. pith and marrow: essence; **attribute:** reputation

26. So: in the same way; **oft it chances in:** it often happens with

27. mole of nature: natural fault

30. o'ergrowth . . . complexion: i.e., the increase of one of the four "humors," which were thought to control man's physical and emotional being

31. pales and forts: palings and ramparts

32. o'erleavens: radically changes

33. plausive: pleasing

35. nature's livery: i.e., something by which one is marked by nature (**as in their birth, or the o'er-growth of some complexion**); **fortune's star:** something determined by luck (as in the accidental forming of **some habit**)

36. His virtues else: the other virtues of these men

39–41. The dram . . . scandal: These difficult lines have never been satisfactorily repaired, but the general sense may be that a small amount of evil makes even something admirable seem disreputable.

48. questionable: problematic

52. canonized: i.e., buried in accord with the canons of the church (accent on second syllable)

From our achievements, though performed at
   height,
The pith and marrow of our attribute.   25
So oft it chances in particular men
That for some vicious mole of nature in them,
As in their birth (wherein they are not guilty,
Since nature cannot choose his origin),
By ⌜the⌝ o'ergrowth of some complexion   30
(Oft breaking down the pales and forts of reason),
Or by some habit that too much o'erleavens
The form of plausive manners—that these men,
Carrying, I say, the stamp of one defect,
Being nature's livery or fortune's star,   35
His virtues else, be they as pure as grace,
As infinite as man may undergo,
Shall in the general censure take corruption
From that particular fault. The dram of ⌜evil⌝
Doth all the noble substance of a doubt   40
To his own scandal.]

Enter Ghost.

HORATIO   Look, my lord, it comes.
HAMLET
Angels and ministers of grace, defend us!
Be thou a spirit of health or goblin damned,
Bring with thee airs from heaven or blasts from   45
   hell,
Be thy intents wicked or charitable,
Thou com'st in such a questionable shape
That I will speak to thee. I'll call thee "Hamlet,"
"King," "Father," "Royal Dane." O, answer me!   50
Let me not burst in ignorance, but tell
Why thy canonized bones, hearsèd in death,
Have burst their cerements; why the sepulcher,
Wherein we saw thee quietly interred,
Hath oped his ponderous and marble jaws   55

59–61. **and we ... our souls:** and causing us weak humans to agitate our minds with thoughts that go beyond what even our souls can reach to

64. **some ... desire:** did desire to impart something

73. **a pin's fee:** the cost of a pin

81. **deprive your sovereignty of reason:** depose reason as ruler of your mind

83. **toys of desperation:** desperate impulses

To cast thee up again. What may this mean
That thou, dead corse, again in complete steel,
Revisits thus the glimpses of the moon,
Making night hideous, and we fools of nature
So horridly to shake our disposition   60
With thoughts beyond the reaches of our souls?
Say, why is this? Wherefore? What should we do?
                              (Ghost) beckons.

HORATIO
It beckons you to go away with it
As if it some impartment did desire
To you alone.   65
MARCELLUS   Look with what courteous action
It waves you to a more removèd ground.
But do not go with it.
HORATIO   No, by no means.
HAMLET
It will not speak. Then I will follow it.   70
HORATIO
Do not, my lord.
HAMLET   Why, what should be the fear?
I do not set my life at a pin's fee.
And for my soul, what can it do to that,
Being a thing immortal as itself?   75
It waves me forth again. I'll follow it.
HORATIO
What if it tempt you toward the flood, my lord?
Or to the dreadful summit of the cliff
That beetles o'er his base into the sea,
And there assume some other horrible form   80
Which might deprive your sovereignty of reason
And draw you into madness? Think of it.
[The very place puts toys of desperation,
Without more motive, into every brain
That looks so many fathoms to the sea   85
And hears it roar beneath.]

92. **arture:** artery (Arteries were believed to be the veins that carried the body's invisible "vital spirits.")

93. **the Nemean lion's nerve:** the sinews of the lion killed by Hercules as one of his twelve "labors"

95. **lets me:** holds me back

1.5 The Ghost tells Hamlet a tale of horror. Saying that he is the spirit of Hamlet's father, he demands that Hamlet avenge King Hamlet's murder at the hands of Claudius. Hamlet, horrified, vows to "remember" and swears his friends to secrecy about what they have seen.

_____

3. **Mark me:** pay attention to me

HAMLET
 It waves me still.—Go on, I'll follow thee.
MARCELLUS
 You shall not go, my lord. ⌜*They hold back Hamlet.*⌝
HAMLET   Hold off your hands.
HORATIO
 Be ruled. You shall not go.   90
HAMLET   My fate cries out
 And makes each petty arture in this body
 As hardy as the Nemean lion's nerve.
 Still am I called. Unhand me, gentlemen.
 By heaven, I'll make a ghost of him that lets me! 95
 I say, away!—Go on. I'll follow thee.
         Ghost and Hamlet exit.
HORATIO
 He waxes desperate with imagination.
MARCELLUS
 Let's follow. 'Tis not fit thus to obey him.
HORATIO
 Have after. To what issue will this come?
MARCELLUS
 Something is rotten in the state of Denmark.   100
HORATIO
 Heaven will direct it.
MARCELLUS   Nay, let's follow him.
             They exit.

⌜Scene 5⌝
Enter Ghost and Hamlet.

HAMLET
 Whither wilt thou lead me? Speak. I'll go no
  further.
GHOST
 Mark me.

9. **lend thy serious hearing:** listen intently

11. **bound:** ready (The word also means "in duty bound" and "obligated," which is the sense to which the Ghost responds in the following line.)

16. **for:** during

21. **harrow up:** tear up (agricultural image)

22–23. **stars . . . spheres:** In Ptolemaic astronomy, each planet (star) was carried around the earth in a crystalline sphere.

25. **an end:** on end

26. **fearful porpentine:** uneasy (threatened) porcupine

27. **eternal blazon:** description of that which is eternal

HAMLET   I will.

GHOST   My hour is almost come   5
  When I to sulf'rous and tormenting flames
  Must render up myself.

HAMLET   Alas, poor ghost!

GHOST
  Pity me not, but lend thy serious hearing
  To what I shall unfold.   10

HAMLET   Speak. I am bound to hear.

GHOST
  So art thou to revenge, when thou shalt hear.

HAMLET   What?

GHOST   I am thy father's spirit,
  Doomed for a certain term to walk the night   15
  And for the day confined to fast in fires
  Till the foul crimes done in my days of nature
  Are burnt and purged away. But that I am forbid
  To tell the secrets of my prison house,
  I could a tale unfold whose lightest word   20
  Would harrow up thy soul, freeze thy young blood,
  Make thy two eyes, like stars, start from their
    spheres,
  Thy knotted and combinèd locks to part,
  And each particular hair to stand an end,   25
  Like quills upon the fearful porpentine.
  But this eternal blazon must not be
  To ears of flesh and blood. List, list, O list!
  If thou didst ever thy dear father love—

HAMLET   O God!   30

GHOST
  Revenge his foul and most unnatural murder.

HAMLET   Murder?

GHOST
  Murder most foul, as in the best it is,
  But this most foul, strange, and unnatural.

HAMLET
  Haste me to know 't, that I, with wings as swift   35

39. **duller . . . be:** you would be duller; **fat:** thick

40. **Lethe wharf:** bank of the river Lethe (the river of forgetfulness)

41. **Wouldst thou not:** if you did not

42. **orchard:** palace garden

44. **forgèd process:** false story

45. **Rankly abused:** completely misled

57–58. **decline / Upon:** to turn to (with the sense of "declining" as falling, bending downward)

65. **soft:** "enough," or "wait a minute"

69. **hebona:** a poison (The word may be linked to "henbane," a poisonous weed, or to "ebony," the sap of which was thought to be poisonous. Marlowe, in *The Jew of Malta*, mentions "the juice of hebon" as deadly.)

Orchard. (1.5.42)
From Octavio Boldoni, *Theatrum temporaneum* (1636).

As meditation or the thoughts of love,
May sweep to my revenge.

GHOST   I find thee apt;
And duller shouldst thou be than the fat weed
That roots itself in ease on Lethe wharf,   40
Wouldst thou not stir in this. Now, Hamlet, hear.
'Tis given out that, sleeping in my orchard,
A serpent stung me. So the whole ear of Denmark
Is by a forgèd process of my death
Rankly abused. But know, thou noble youth,   45
The serpent that did sting thy father's life
Now wears his crown.

HAMLET   O, my prophetic soul! My uncle!

GHOST
Ay, that incestuous, that adulterate beast,
With witchcraft of his ⌜wit,⌝ with traitorous gifts—   50
O wicked wit and gifts, that have the power
So to seduce!—won to his shameful lust
The will of my most seeming-virtuous queen.
O Hamlet, what (a) falling off was there!
From me, whose love was of that dignity   55
That it went hand in hand even with the vow
I made to her in marriage, and to decline
Upon a wretch whose natural gifts were poor
To those of mine.
But virtue, as it never will be moved,   60
Though lewdness court it in a shape of heaven,
So, (lust,) though to a radiant angel linked,
Will (sate) itself in a celestial bed
And prey on garbage.
But soft, methinks I scent the morning air.   65
Brief let me be. Sleeping within my orchard,
My custom always of the afternoon,
Upon my secure hour thy uncle stole,
With juice of cursèd hebona in a vial,
And in the porches of my ears did pour   70

71. **leprous distilment:** distillation causing a condition like leprosy

75. **posset:** clot

76. **eager:** acid

78–80. **a most instant tetter . . . body:** i.e., sores and scabs, as on a leper, covered my body with a vile crust like the bark of a tree **tetter:** a skin disease marked by sores and scabs **lazar-like:** like a leper

82. **dispatched:** dispossessed

84. **Unhousled . . . unaneled:** without having received final rites

90. **luxury:** lust

96. **matin:** morning

104. **globe:** Hamlet perhaps gestures to his head.

105. **table:** table-book or slate, used here metaphorically (Hamlet wants to wipe his memory clean, as one would erase a slate or table-book. Later [lines 114–16], he takes out actual "tables.")

The leprous distilment, whose effect
Holds such an enmity with blood of man
That swift as quicksilver it courses through
The natural gates and alleys of the body,
And with a sudden vigor it doth ⟨posset⟩   75
And curd, like eager droppings into milk,
The thin and wholesome blood. So did it mine,
And a most instant tetter barked about,
Most lazar-like, with vile and loathsome crust
All my smooth body.   80
Thus was I, sleeping, by a brother's hand
Of life, of crown, of queen at once dispatched,
Cut off, even in the blossoms of my sin,
Unhouseled, disappointed, unaneled,
No reck'ning made, but sent to my account   85
With all my imperfections on my head.
O horrible, O horrible, most horrible!
If thou hast nature in thee, bear it not.
Let not the royal bed of Denmark be
A couch for luxury and damnèd incest.   90
But, howsomever thou pursues this act,
Taint not thy mind, nor let thy soul contrive
Against thy mother aught. Leave her to heaven
And to those thorns that in her bosom lodge
To prick and sting her. Fare thee well at once.   95
The glowworm shows the matin to be near
And 'gins to pale his uneffectual fire.
Adieu, adieu, adieu. Remember me.   *(He exits.)*

HAMLET
O all you host of heaven! O earth! What else?
And shall I couple hell? O fie! Hold, hold, my heart,   100
And you, my sinews, grow not instant old,
But bear me ⟨stiffly⟩ up. Remember thee?
Ay, thou poor ghost, whiles memory holds a seat
In this distracted globe. Remember thee?
Yea, from the table of my memory   105

106. fond records: foolish jottings (**records** accented on the second syllable)

108. youth and observation: youthful observation

114. meet it is: it is appropriate that

125. Hillo, ho . . . bird, come: Hamlet mocks Marcellus's call, as if it were the call of a falconer.

The beggar Lazarus: "lazar-like." (1.5.79)
From Guillaume Guérault, *Figures de la Bible* (1565–70).

I'll wipe away all trivial, fond records,
All saws of books, all forms, all pressures past,
That youth and observation copied there,
And thy commandment all alone shall live
Within the book and volume of my brain,   110
Unmixed with baser matter. Yes, by heaven!
O most pernicious woman!
O villain, villain, smiling, damnèd villain!
My tables—meet it is I set it down
That one may smile and smile and be a villain.   115
At least I am sure it may be so in Denmark.
                                   ⌐*He writes.*⌐

So, uncle, there you are. Now to my word.
It is "adieu, adieu, remember me."
I have sworn 't.

                Enter Horatio and Marcellus.

HORATIO   My lord, my lord!   120
MARCELLUS   Lord Hamlet.
HORATIO   Heavens secure him!
HAMLET   So be it.
MARCELLUS   Illo, ho, ho, my lord!
HAMLET   Hillo, ho, ho, boy! Come, (bird,) come!   125
MARCELLUS
  How is 't, my noble lord?
HORATIO   What news, my lord?
HAMLET   O, wonderful!
HORATIO
  Good my lord, tell it.
HAMLET   No, you will reveal it.   130
HORATIO
  Not I, my lord, by heaven.
MARCELLUS   Nor I, my lord.
HAMLET
  How say you, then? Would heart of man once think
    it?
  But you'll be secret?   135

138. **arrant:** complete
142. **circumstance:** ceremony
154. **honest:** genuine
165. **Upon my sword:** an appropriate object on which to swear an oath, in that the hilts form a cross

A sword. (1.5.165)
From Jacobus a. Bruck,
Emblemata moralia & bellica (1615).

HORATIO/MARCELLUS Ay, by heaven, ⟨my lord.⟩

HAMLET
There's never a villain dwelling in all Denmark
But he's an arrant knave.

HORATIO
There needs no ghost, my lord, come from the grave
To tell us this.   140

HAMLET   Why, right, you are in the right.
And so, without more circumstance at all,
I hold it fit that we shake hands and part,
You, as your business and desire shall point you
(For every man hath business and desire,   145
Such as it is), and for my own poor part,
I will go pray.

HORATIO
These are but wild and whirling words, my lord.

HAMLET
I am sorry they offend you, heartily;
Yes, faith, heartily.   150

HORATIO   There's no offense, my lord.

HAMLET
Yes, by Saint Patrick, but there is, Horatio,
And much offense, too. Touching this vision here,
It is an honest ghost—that let me tell you.
For your desire to know what is between us, 155
O'ermaster 't as you may. And now, good friends,
As you are friends, scholars, and soldiers,
Give me one poor request.

HORATIO What is 't, my lord? We will.

HAMLET
Never make known what you have seen tonight. 160

HORATIO/MARCELLUS My lord, we will not.

HAMLET Nay, but swear 't.

HORATIO In faith, my lord, not I.

MARCELLUS Nor I, my lord, in faith.

HAMLET
Upon my sword.   165

170. **truepenny:** honest fellow

177. **Hic et ubique:** here and everywhere

184. **pioner:** a foot soldier who marches in advance of the army to dig trenches and clear the way; a digger or miner; **remove:** move to another spot

186. **as a stranger give it welcome:** welcome it as one should welcome a stranger

188. **your philosophy:** i.e., philosophy in general

189–202. **never . . . help you:** i.e., swear never to note, even through gestures and hints, that you know anything about me, no matter how strangely I act

190. **How . . . some'er:** howsoever

191–92. **As I . . . on:** since I may in the future think it appropriate to act bizarrely

194. **With arms . . . headshake:** with your arms folded or shaking your head in a knowing way

195. **doubtful:** ambiguous

MARCELLUS   We have sworn, my lord, already.

HAMLET   Indeed, upon my sword, indeed.

GHOST *cries under the stage*   Swear.

HAMLET
Ha, ha, boy, sayst thou so? Art thou there,
     truepenny?   170
Come on, you hear this fellow in the cellarage.
Consent to swear.

HORATIO   Propose the oath, my lord.

HAMLET
Never to speak of this that you have seen,
Swear by my sword.   175

GHOST, ⌜*beneath*⌝   Swear.

HAMLET
Hic et ubique? Then we'll shift our ground.
Come hither, gentlemen,
And lay your hands again upon my sword.
Swear by my sword   180
Never to speak of this that you have heard.

GHOST, ⌜*beneath*⌝   Swear by his sword.

HAMLET
Well said, old mole. Canst work i' th' earth so fast?
A worthy pioner! Once more remove, good friends.

HORATIO
O day and night, but this is wondrous strange.   185

HAMLET
And therefore as a stranger give it welcome.
There are more things in heaven and earth, Horatio,
Than are dreamt of in your philosophy. But come.
Here, as before, never, so help you mercy,
How strange or odd some'er I bear myself   190
(As I perchance hereafter shall think meet
To put an antic disposition on)
That you, at such times seeing me, never shall,
With arms encumbered thus, or this headshake,
Or by pronouncing of some doubtful phrase,   195

196. **an if:** if
198. **list:** should choose
200. **giving-out:** expression; **note:** indicate
204. **Rest, rest, perturbèd spirit:** These words suggest that Horatio and Marcellus have sworn the oath demanded by Hamlet and the Ghost; Q2 and F give no stage direction to indicate when they do so.

As "Well, well, we know," or "We could an if we
  would,"
Or "If we list to speak," or "There be an if they
  might,"
Or such ambiguous giving-out, to note   200
That you know aught of me—this do swear,
So grace and mercy at your most need help you.
GHOST, ⌈*beneath*⌉ Swear.
HAMLET
Rest, rest, perturbèd spirit.—So, gentlemen,
With all my love I do commend me to you,   205
And what so poor a man as Hamlet is
May do t' express his love and friending to you,
God willing, shall not lack. Let us go in together,
And still your fingers on your lips, I pray.
The time is out of joint. O cursèd spite   210
That ever I was born to set it right!
Nay, come, let's go together.

                              They exit.

The Tragedy of

HAMLET,

Prince of Denmark

ACT 2

2.1 Polonius sends his servant Reynaldo to Paris to question Laertes's acquaintances. Ophelia enters, deeply disturbed about a visit she has just had from an apparently mad Hamlet. Polonius decides that Hamlet has become insane because Ophelia is refusing to see him. Polonius rushes off to tell the king.

———————

4–5. make inquire / Of: ask questions about

8. Inquire me: i.e., inquire on my behalf; **Danskers:** Danes

9. what means: what is their supply of money

10. keep: live

12. encompassment and drift of question: roundabout conversation (Polonius's language itself tends to be roundabout.)

13–14. come you . . . touch it: i.e., you will come closer (to getting answers) than you would by specific questions

15. Take you, as 'twere: assume, as it were

⟨*ACT 2*⟩

⌜Scene 1⌝
Enter old Polonius with his man ⟨Reynaldo.⟩

POLONIUS
Give him this money and these notes, Reynaldo.
REYNALDO   I will, my lord.
POLONIUS
You shall do marvelous wisely, good Reynaldo,
Before you visit him, to make inquire
Of his behavior.   5
REYNALDO   My lord, I did intend it.
POLONIUS
Marry, well said, very well said. Look you, sir,
Inquire me first what Danskers are in Paris;
And how, and who, what means, and where they
    keep,   10
What company, at what expense; and finding
By this encompassment and drift of question
That they do know my son, come you more nearer
Than your particular demands will touch it.
Take you, as 'twere, some distant knowledge of him, 15
As thus: "I know his father and his friends
And, in part, him." Do you mark this, Reynaldo?
REYNALDO   Ay, very well, my lord.
POLONIUS
"And, in part, him, but," you may say, "not well.

73

21. **put on him:** accuse him of
22. **forgeries:** invented faults; **rank:** great; offensive
24. **wanton:** rebellious
25–26. **are companions . . . liberty:** are known to accompany youthful activity
27. **gaming:** gambling
29. **drabbing:** dealing with prostitutes
31. **season . . . charge:** make the charge seem less serious by your way of stating it   **season:** temper
33. **open to incontinency:** is habitually inclined to sexual indulgence
35. **quaintly:** cunningly
36. **taints of liberty:** slight faults that accompany independence
38–39. **A savageness . . . assault:** i.e., a wildness in untamed blood, which all young people can be accused of
44. **fetch of wit:** clever trick
46. **soiled i' th' working:** i.e., as cloth may be soiled as it is being worked with
48. **sound:** sound out or question
49. **prenominate crimes:** before-named wrongdoings
51. **closes . . . consequence:** agrees with you as follows
53. **addition:** form of address

74

But if 't be he I mean, he's very wild, 20
Addicted so and so." And there put on him
What forgeries you please—marry, none so rank
As may dishonor him, take heed of that,
But, sir, such wanton, wild, and usual slips
As are companions noted and most known 25
To youth and liberty.

REYNALDO   As gaming, my lord.

POLONIUS   Ay, or drinking, fencing, swearing,
Quarreling, drabbing—you may go so far.

REYNALDO   My lord, that would dishonor him. 30

POLONIUS
Faith, ⟨no,⟩ as you may season it in the charge.
You must not put another scandal on him
That he is open to incontinency;
That's not my meaning. But breathe his faults so
    quaintly 35
That they may seem the taints of liberty,
The flash and outbreak of a fiery mind,
A savageness in unreclaimèd blood,
Of general assault.

REYNALDO   But, my good lord— 40

POLONIUS   Wherefore should you do this?

REYNALDO   Ay, my lord, I would know that.

POLONIUS   Marry, sir, here's my drift,
And I believe it is a fetch of wit.
You, laying these slight sullies on my son, 45
As 'twere a thing a little soiled ⟨i' th'⟩ working,
Mark you, your party in converse, him you would
    sound,
Having ever seen in the prenominate crimes
The youth you breathe of guilty, be assured 50
He closes with you in this consequence:
"Good sir," or so, or "friend," or "gentleman,"
According to the phrase or the addition
Of man and country—

66. **o'ertook in 's rouse:** overcome by drink

69. **Videlicet:** namely, that is to say

69–70. **See . . . truth:** i.e., you can see this deceptive bait capture a real fish

71. **reach:** mental ability

72. **windlasses . . . bias:** indirect approaches, a **windlass** being an indirect course in hunting, the **bias** being the curve that brings the ball to the desired point in the game of bowls

75. **Shall you my son:** you shall (find out) my son

79. **in yourself:** yourself (instead of in reports)

The game of bowls. (2.1.72)
From *Le centre de l'amour* (1650).

REYNALDO   Very good, my lord.   55
POLONIUS   And then, sir, does he this, he does—what
  was I about to say? By the Mass, I was about to say
  something. Where did I leave?
REYNALDO   At "closes in the consequence," (at "friend,
  or so, and gentleman.")   60
POLONIUS
  At "closes in the consequence"—ay, marry—
  He closes thus: "I know the gentleman.
  I saw him yesterday," or "th' other day"
  (Or then, or then, with such or such), "and as you
    say,   65
  There was he gaming, there ⟨o'ertook⟩ in 's rouse,
  There falling out at tennis"; or perchance
  "I saw him enter such a house of sale"—
  Videlicet, a brothel—or so forth. See you now
  Your bait of falsehood take this carp of truth;   70
  And thus do we of wisdom and of reach,
  With windlasses and with assays of bias,
  By indirections find directions out.
  So by my former lecture and advice
  Shall you my son. You have me, have you not?   75
REYNALDO
  My lord, I have.
POLONIUS   God be wi' you. Fare you well.
REYNALDO   Good my lord.
POLONIUS
  Observe his inclination in yourself.
REYNALDO   I shall, my lord.   80
POLONIUS   And let him ply his music.
REYNALDO   Well, my lord.
POLONIUS
  Farewell.   *Reynaldo exits.*

                    Enter Ophelia.

       How now, Ophelia, what's the matter?

87. **closet:** private room

88. **doublet:** close-fitting jacket; **unbraced:** unfastened

89. **fouled:** dirty

90. **down-gyvèd to his ankle:** fallen down around his ankles like gyves or chains

114. **ecstasy:** madness

115. **violent property:** characteristic violence; **fordoes:** destroys

Man in gyves. (2.1.90)
From Cesare Vecellio,
Degli habiti antichi et moderni (1590).

OPHELIA
O, my lord, my lord, I have been so affrighted!   85
POLONIUS With what, i' th' name of God?
OPHELIA
My lord, as I was sewing in my closet,
Lord Hamlet, with his doublet all unbraced,
No hat upon his head, his stockings fouled,
Ungartered, and down-gyvèd to his ankle,   90
Pale as his shirt, his knees knocking each other,
And with a look so piteous in purport
As if he had been loosèd out of hell
To speak of horrors—he comes before me.
POLONIUS
Mad for thy love?   95
OPHELIA   My lord, I do not know,
But truly I do fear it.
POLONIUS   What said he?
OPHELIA
He took me by the wrist and held me hard.
Then goes he to the length of all his arm,   100
And, with his other hand thus o'er his brow,
He falls to such perusal of my face
As he would draw it. Long stayed he so.
At last, a little shaking of mine arm,
And thrice his head thus waving up and down,   105
He raised a sigh so piteous and profound
As it did seem to shatter all his bulk
And end his being. That done, he lets me go,
And, with his head over his shoulder turned,
He seemed to find his way without his eyes,   110
For out o' doors he went without their helps
And to the last bended their light on me.
POLONIUS
Come, go with me. I will go seek the King.
This is the very ecstasy of love,
Whose violent property fordoes itself   115

125. **coted:** observed

126. **wrack:** destroy; **beshrew my jealousy:** curse my suspicious thoughts

127. **proper to our age:** characteristic of the old

128. **cast beyond ourselves:** go too far (The image may come from casting a net, or the word **cast** may have the meaning of "plan, devise.")

130. **discretion:** good judgment

131. **close:** hidden

131–33. **might . . . love:** this love might cause more grief if hidden than hatred if told about

2.2 Claudius and Gertrude set Rosencrantz and Guildenstern, two boyhood friends of Hamlet, to spy on him to discover the cause of his apparent madness. After the returned ambassadors announce their success in stopping Fortinbras's planned invasion of Denmark, Polonius reports his "discovery" that Hamlet is mad for love. Claudius is unpersuaded but agrees to join Polonius in spying on Hamlet.

When Hamlet himself enters, he is confronted first by Polonius and then by Rosencrantz and Guildenstern, whom he quickly identifies as Claudius's spies. As they talk, a company of touring actors enters. Hamlet persuades one of them to deliver a speech, and recognizes, to his shame, that he has shown less intensity in avenging his father's murder than the actor has done in performance. Hamlet hopes that, when the players stage *The Murder of Gonzago* for the court, he can determine whether Claudius is guilty of King Hamlet's death.

---

6. **Sith:** since; **nor . . . nor:** neither . . . nor

And leads the will to desperate undertakings
As oft as any passions under heaven
That does afflict our natures. I am sorry.
What, have you given him any hard words of late?

OPHELIA
No, my good lord, but as you did command   120
I did repel his letters and denied
His access to me.

POLONIUS   That hath made him mad.
I am sorry that with better heed and judgment
I had not coted him. I feared he did but trifle   125
And meant to wrack thee. But beshrew my jealousy!
By heaven, it is as proper to our age
To cast beyond ourselves in our opinions
As it is common for the younger sort
To lack discretion. Come, go we to the King.   130
This must be known, which, being kept close, might
    move
More grief to hide than hate to utter love.
Come.

                                   They exit.

(Scene 2)
*Flourish. Enter King and Queen, Rosencrantz and
Guildenstern ⌈and Attendants.⌉*

KING
Welcome, dear Rosencrantz and Guildenstern.
Moreover that we much did long to see you,
The need we have to use you did provoke
Our hasty sending. Something have you heard
Of Hamlet's transformation, so call it,   5
Sith nor th' exterior nor the inward man
Resembles that it was. What it should be,
More than his father's death, that thus hath put him

12. **havlor:** manners
13. **vouchsafe your rest:** agree to stay
18. **opened:** laid bare, revealed
22. **gentry:** generosity (or, perhaps, courtesy)
32. **in the full bent:** fully, totally (The term suggests a bow, in archery, bent to its limit.)
40. **practices:** actions (with perhaps a suggestion of intrigues, maneuvers, and plots)

A bow "in the full bent." (2.2.32)
From Jacobus a. Bruck, *Emblemata moralia & bellica* (1615).

So much from th' understanding of himself
I cannot dream of. I entreat you both　　　　　　　10
That, being of so young days brought up with him
And sith so neighbored to his youth and havior,
That you vouchsafe your rest here in our court
Some little time, so by your companies
To draw him on to pleasures, and to gather　　　　　15
So much as from occasion you may glean,
[Whether aught to us unknown afflicts him thus]
That, opened, lies within our remedy.

QUEEN
Good gentlemen, he hath much talked of you,
And sure I am two men there is not living　　　　　20
To whom he more adheres. If it will please you
To show us so much gentry and goodwill
As to expend your time with us awhile
For the supply and profit of our hope,
Your visitation shall receive such thanks　　　　　25
As fits a king's remembrance.

ROSENCRANTZ　　　　　　　Both your Majesties
Might, by the sovereign power you have of us,
Put your dread pleasures more into command
Than to entreaty.　　　　　　　　　　　　　30

GUILDENSTERN　　　　But we both obey,
And here give up ourselves in the full bent
To lay our service freely at your feet,
To be commanded.

KING
Thanks, Rosencrantz and gentle Guildenstern.　　35

QUEEN
Thanks, Guildenstern and gentle Rosencrantz.
And I beseech you instantly to visit
My too much changèd son. Go, some of you,
And bring these gentlemen where Hamlet is.

GUILDENSTERN
Heavens make our presence and our practices　　40
Pleasant and helpful to him!

50. **Hunts . . . sure:** i.e., does not follow so successfully the trail of political cunning
55. **fruit:** dessert
59. **the main:** the central point
61. **sift:** examine closely (as if through a sieve)

A dog hunting the trail. (2.2.50)
From George Turberville, *The noble arte of venerie* (1611).

QUEEN   Ay, amen!

Rosencrantz and Guildenstern exit
⌈*with some Attendants.*⌉

Enter Polonius.

POLONIUS
Th' ambassadors from Norway, my good lord,
Are joyfully returned.

KING
Thou still hast been the father of good news.   45

POLONIUS
Have I, my lord? I assure my good liege
I hold my duty as I hold my soul,
Both to my God and to my gracious king,
And I do think, or else this brain of mine
Hunts not the trail of policy so sure   50
As it hath used to do, that I have found
The very cause of Hamlet's lunacy.

KING
O, speak of that! That do I long to hear.

POLONIUS
Give first admittance to th' ambassadors.
My news shall be the fruit to that great feast.   55

KING
Thyself do grace to them and bring them in.
                         ⌈*Polonius exits.*⌉
He tells me, my dear Gertrude, he hath found
The head and source of all your son's distemper.

QUEEN
I doubt it is no other but the main—
His father's death and our ⟨o'erhasty⟩ marriage.   60

KING
Well, we shall sift him.

Enter Ambassadors ⟨Voltemand and Cornelius ⌈*with*⌉
Polonius.⟩

65. **Upon our first:** at our first approach

71. **borne in hand:** systematically deceived; **arrests:** orders to desist

75. **give ... against:** attack, assault

84. **On such ... allowance:** according to such terms of safety for Denmark and of permission for Fortinbras

86. **likes:** pleases

93. **expostulate:** make a speech about

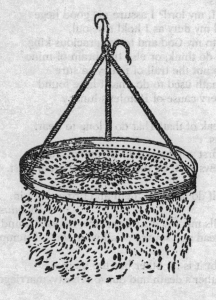

A sieve. (2.2.61)
From Geoffrey Whitney, *A choice of emblemes* (1586).

                              Welcome, my good friends.
  Say, Voltemand, what from our brother Norway?
VOLTEMAND
  Most fair return of greetings and desires.
  Upon our first, he sent out to suppress   65
  His nephew's levies, which to him appeared
  To be a preparation 'gainst the Polack,
  But, better looked into, he truly found
  It was against your Highness. Whereat, grieved
  That so his sickness, age, and impotence   70
  Was falsely borne in hand, sends out arrests
  On Fortinbras, which he, in brief, obeys,
  Receives rebuke from Norway, and, in fine,
  Makes vow before his uncle never more
  To give th' assay of arms against your Majesty.   75
  Whereon old Norway, overcome with joy,
  Gives him three-score thousand crowns in annual
     fee
  And his commission to employ those soldiers,
  So levied as before, against the Polack,   80
  With an entreaty, herein further shown,
                         ⌜*He gives a paper.*⌝
  That it might please you to give quiet pass
  Through your dominions for this enterprise,
  On such regards of safety and allowance
  As therein are set down.   85
KING   It likes us well,
  And, at our more considered time, we'll read,
  Answer, and think upon this business.
  Meantime, we thank you for your well-took labor.
  Go to your rest. At night we'll feast together.   90
  Most welcome home!
                    ⌜*Voltemand and Cornelius*⌝ *exit.*
POLONIUS   This business is well ended.
  My liege, and madam, to expostulate
  What majesty should be, what duty is,

97. brevity . . . wit: i.e., in a wise speech, a few words carry the central meaning

98. flourishes: ornaments

103. More . . . art: i.e., get to the point more quickly by cutting out the rhetorical ornamentations

104. I use no art: i.e., my language is natural

106. figure: figure of speech

113. Perpend: consider carefully

121. etc.: Polonius, in reading the letter, says "et cetera" in order to indicate that he is skipping over the letter's formal compliments.

123. stay: wait; **will be faithful:** will read accurately

124–27. Doubt . . . I love: Hamlet's poem plays on different meanings of **doubt:** (1) to be skeptical about (as about the ancient truths about the stars and the sun); (2) to suspect (that, e.g., truth might be a liar); (3) to disbelieve (e.g., Hamlet's love).

Why day is day, night night, and time is time   95
Were nothing but to waste night, day, and time.
Therefore, (since) brevity is the soul of wit,
And tediousness the limbs and outward flourishes,
I will be brief. Your noble son is mad.
"Mad" call I it, for, to define true madness,   100
What is 't but to be nothing else but mad?
But let that go.
QUEEN   More matter with less art.
POLONIUS
Madam, I swear I use no art at all.
That he's mad, 'tis true; 'tis true 'tis pity,   105
And pity 'tis 'tis true—a foolish figure,
But farewell it, for I will use no art.
Mad let us grant him then, and now remains
That we find out the cause of this effect,
Or, rather say, the cause of this defect,   110
For this effect defective comes by cause.
Thus it remains, and the remainder thus.
Perpend.
I have a daughter (have while she is mine)
Who, in her duty and obedience, mark,   115
Hath given me this. Now gather and surmise.
⌈*He reads.*⌉ *To the celestial, and my soul's idol, the*
most beautified Ophelia—
That's an ill phrase, a vile phrase; "beautified" is a
vile phrase. But you shall hear. Thus: ⌈*He reads.*⌉   120
In her excellent white bosom, these, etc.—
QUEEN   Came this from Hamlet to her?
POLONIUS
Good madam, stay awhile. I will be faithful.
⌈*He reads the*⌉ *letter.*
          Doubt thou the stars are fire,
               Doubt that the sun doth move,   125
          Doubt truth to be a liar,
               But never doubt I love.

128. ill . . . numbers: unskilled at writing verse

129. reckon my groans: count (and rhythmically count out) my lover's sighs

131–32. whilst . . . to him: i.e., while I still occupy this body

134. above: besides

145. played . . . table-book: remained silent, keeping this knowledge hidden as if I had put it in a desk or a diary

146. given . . . winking: made my heart close its eyes to what was going on

149. my young mistress: this young lady (i.e., Ophelia); **bespeak:** speak to

155–59. he . . . Fell into . . . madness: Polonius lists what were supposed to be the classic stages of the **declension** (decline) into love-madness: from **sadness,** to a **fast** (failure to eat), to a **watch** (insomnia), to **weakness,** to light-headedness, to insanity.

O dear Ophelia, I am ill at these numbers. I have not
art to reckon my groans, but that I love thee best, O
most best, believe it. Adieu.   130
                    Thine evermore, most dear lady, whilst
                        this machine is to him, Hamlet.
This, in obedience, hath my daughter shown me,
And more ⟨above,⟩ hath his solicitings,
As they fell out by time, by means, and place,   135
All given to mine ear.

KING   But how hath she received his love?

POLONIUS   What do you think of me?

KING
As of a man faithful and honorable.

POLONIUS
I would fain prove so. But what might you think,   140
When I had seen this hot love on the wing
(As I perceived it, I must tell you that,
Before my daughter told me), what might you,
Or my dear Majesty your queen here, think,
If I had played the desk or table-book   145
Or given my heart a ⟨winking,⟩ mute and dumb,
Or looked upon this love with idle sight?
What might you think? No, I went round to work,
And my young mistress thus I did bespeak:
"Lord Hamlet is a prince, out of thy star.   150
This must not be." And then I prescripts gave her,
That she should lock herself from ⟨his⟩ resort,
Admit no messengers, receive no tokens;
Which done, she took the fruits of my advice,
And he, repelled (a short tale to make),   155
Fell into a sadness, then into a fast,
Thence to a watch, thence into a weakness,
Thence to ⟨a⟩ lightness, and, by this declension,
Into the madness wherein now he raves
And all we mourn for.   160

KING, ⌜*to Queen*⌝   Do you think ⟨'tis⟩ this?

168. Take this from this: Polonius gestures to his head and his shoulder (or to his chain of office and his neck, or to his staff of office and his hand), indicating that he would yield up his life (or his office) if proved wrong.

171. center: the earth's center, which, in the Ptolemaic system, is also the center of the universe (See page 224.)

176. loose: turn her loose (The figure is that of releasing an animal from its chains, either for the hunt or for purposes of mating.)

177. arras: a hanging screen of rich tapestry fabric

186. board: i.e., speak to; **presently:** immediately

QUEEN It may be, very like.

POLONIUS
  Hath there been such a time (I would fain know
    that)
  That I have positively said " 'Tis so,"   165
  When it proved otherwise?

KING   Not that I know.

POLONIUS
  Take this from this, if this be otherwise.
  If circumstances lead me, I will find
  Where truth is hid, though it were hid, indeed,   170
  Within the center.

KING   How may we try it further?

POLONIUS
  You know sometimes he walks four hours together
  Here in the lobby.

QUEEN   So he does indeed.   175

POLONIUS
  At such a time I'll loose my daughter to him.
  ⌜*To the King.*⌝ Be you and I behind an arras then.
  Mark the encounter. If he love her not,
  And be not from his reason fall'n thereon,
  Let me be no assistant for a state,   180
  But keep a farm and carters.

KING   We will try it.

            Enter Hamlet (reading on a book.)

QUEEN
  But look where sadly the poor wretch comes
    reading.

POLONIUS
  Away, I do beseech you both, away.   185
  I'll board him presently. O, give me leave.
              King and Queen exit ⌜*with Attendants.*⌝
  How does my good Lord Hamlet?

HAMLET Well, God-a-mercy.

198. **a good kissing carrion:** This puzzling phrase is often changed to read "a god kissing carrion."

218. **wit:** understanding; **hams:** buttocks and thighs

220. **honesty:** good manners

POLONIUS Do you know me, my lord?

HAMLET Excellent well. You are a fishmonger. 190

POLONIUS Not I, my lord.

HAMLET Then I would you were so honest a man.

POLONIUS Honest, my lord?

HAMLET Ay, sir. To be honest, as this world goes, is to
be one man picked out of ten thousand. 195

POLONIUS That's very true, my lord.

HAMLET For if the sun breed maggots in a dead
dog, being a good kissing carrion—Have you a
daughter?

POLONIUS I have, my lord. 200

HAMLET Let her not walk i' th' sun. Conception is a
blessing, but, as your daughter may conceive,
friend, look to 't.

POLONIUS, ⌜*aside*⌝ How say you by that? Still harping on
my daughter. Yet he knew me not at first; he said I 205
was a fishmonger. He is far gone. And truly, in my
youth, I suffered much extremity for love, very near
this. I'll speak to him again.—What do you read, my
lord?

HAMLET Words, words, words. 210

POLONIUS What is the matter, my lord?

HAMLET Between who?

POLONIUS I mean the matter that you read, my lord.

HAMLET Slanders, sir; for the satirical rogue says here
that old men have gray beards, that their faces are 215
wrinkled, their eyes purging thick amber and
plum-tree gum, and that they have a plentiful lack of
wit, together with most weak hams; all which, sir,
though I most powerfully and potently believe, yet I
hold it not honesty to have it thus set down; for 220
yourself, sir, shall grow old as I am, if, like a crab,
you could go backward.

POLONIUS, ⌜*aside*⌝ Though this be madness, yet there is
method in 't.—Will you walk out of the air, my lord?

227. pregnant: full of meaning; **happiness:** aptness of phrasing

245. As . . . earth: like the general run of mortals

252. privates: intimates, with a pun on living within Fortune's "private parts" (This sexual punning begins with Hamlet's reference to Fortune's "favors" and continues in Hamlet's "in the secret parts of Fortune" and his calling Fortune "a strumpet.")

HAMLET Into my grave? 225

POLONIUS Indeed, that's out of the air. ⌈*Aside.*⌉ How
pregnant sometimes his replies are! A happiness
that often madness hits on, which reason and
⟨sanity⟩ could not so prosperously be delivered of. I
will leave him ⟨and suddenly contrive the means of 230
meeting between him⟩ and my daughter.—My lord,
I will take my leave of you.

HAMLET You cannot, ⟨sir,⟩ take from me anything that I
will more willingly part withal—except my life,
except my life, except my life. 235

POLONIUS Fare you well, my lord.

HAMLET, ⌈*aside*⌉ These tedious old fools.

Enter Guildenstern and Rosencrantz.

POLONIUS You go to seek the Lord Hamlet. There he is.

ROSENCRANTZ, ⌈*to Polonius*⌉ God save you, sir.
⌈*Polonius exits.*⌉

GUILDENSTERN My honored lord. 240

ROSENCRANTZ My most dear lord.

HAMLET My ⟨excellent⟩ good friends! How dost thou,
Guildenstern? Ah, Rosencrantz! Good lads, how do
you both?

ROSENCRANTZ
As the indifferent children of the earth. 245

GUILDENSTERN
Happy in that we are not ⟨overhappy.⟩
On Fortune's ⟨cap,⟩ we are not the very button.

HAMLET Nor the soles of her shoe?

ROSENCRANTZ Neither, my lord.

HAMLET Then you live about her waist, or in the 250
middle of her favors?

GUILDENSTERN Faith, her privates we.

HAMLET In the secret parts of Fortune? O, most true!
She is a strumpet. What news?

ROSENCRANTZ None, my lord, but ⟨that⟩ the world's 255
grown honest.

264. **goodly:** large

264–65. **confines:** places of confinement

282–84. **beggars bodies ... beggars' shadows:** i.e., if ambition is but a "shadow's shadow," then beggars (who are without ambition) are the only humans with substantial bodies and kings and heroes (ruled by ambition) are only the beggars' shadows

284. **fay:** faith

286. **wait upon:** accompany; serve

287. **sort you with:** put you in the same class with

HAMLET   Then is doomsday near. But your news is not
    true. (Let me question more in particular. What
    have you, my good friends, deserved at the hands of
    Fortune that she sends you to prison hither?   260
GUILDENSTERN   Prison, my lord?
HAMLET   Denmark's a prison.
ROSENCRANTZ   Then is the world one.
HAMLET   A goodly one, in which there are many con-
    fines, wards, and dungeons, Denmark being one o'   265
    th' worst.
ROSENCRANTZ   We think not so, my lord.
HAMLET   Why, then, 'tis none to you, for there is
    nothing either good or bad but thinking makes it
    so. To me, it is a prison.   270
ROSENCRANTZ   Why, then, your ambition makes it one.
    'Tis too narrow for your mind.
HAMLET   O God, I could be bounded in a nutshell and
    count myself a king of infinite space, were it not
    that I have bad dreams.   275
GUILDENSTERN   Which dreams, indeed, are ambition,
    for the very substance of the ambitious is merely
    the shadow of a dream.
HAMLET   A dream itself is but a shadow.
ROSENCRANTZ   Truly, and I hold ambition of so airy   280
    and light a quality that it is but a shadow's shadow.
HAMLET   Then are our beggars bodies, and our mon-
    archs and outstretched heroes the beggars' shad-
    ows. Shall we to th' court? For, by my fay, I cannot
    reason.   285
ROSENCRANTZ/GUILDENSTERN   We'll wait upon you.
HAMLET   No such matter. I will not sort you with the
    rest of my servants, for, to speak to you like an
    honest man, I am most dreadfully attended.) But,
    in the beaten way of friendship, what make you at   290
    Elsinore?
ROSENCRANTZ   To visit you, my lord, no other occasion.

295. too dear a halfpenny: not worth a halfpenny

307–8. the consonancy of our youth: the harmony we enjoyed when we were younger

309. by . . . dear: by whatever is more valuable

310. proposer: speaker; **charge you withal:** urge you with

313. of: on

316–17. my anticipation . . . discovery: my saying it first will keep you from having to reveal it

317–18. your secrecy . . . molt no feather: your promise of secrecy not be diminished

324. fretted: adorned

HAMLET Beggar that I am, I am ⟨even⟩ poor in thanks;
but I thank you, and sure, dear friends, my thanks
are too dear a halfpenny. Were you not sent for? 295
Is it your own inclining? Is it a free visitation?
Come, come, deal justly with me. Come, come; nay,
speak.

GUILDENSTERN What should we say, my lord?

HAMLET Anything but to th' purpose. You were sent 300
for, and there is a kind of confession in your looks
which your modesties have not craft enough to
color. I know the good king and queen have sent for
you.

ROSENCRANTZ To what end, my lord? 305

HAMLET That you must teach me. But let me conjure
you by the rights of our fellowship, by the consonancy of our youth, by the obligation of our ever-
preserved love, and by what more dear a better
proposer can charge you withal: be even and direct 310
with me whether you were sent for or no.

ROSENCRANTZ, ⌜to Guildenstern⌝ What say you?

HAMLET, ⌜aside⌝ Nay, then, I have an eye of you.—If
you love me, hold not off.

GUILDENSTERN My lord, we were sent for. 315

HAMLET I will tell you why; so shall my anticipation
prevent your discovery, and your secrecy to the
King and Queen molt no feather. I have of late, but
wherefore I know not, lost all my mirth, forgone all
custom of exercises, and, indeed, it goes so heavily 320
with my disposition that this goodly frame, the
earth, seems to me a sterile promontory; this most
excellent canopy, the air, look you, this brave o'er-
hanging firmament, this majestical roof, fretted
with golden fire—why, it appeareth nothing to me 325
but a foul and pestilent congregation of vapors.
What ⟨a⟩ piece of work is a man, how noble in
reason, how infinite in faculties, in form and mov-

329. **express:** well framed

330. **apprehension:** understanding

332. **quintessence:** the very essence (The word is usually used to describe that which transcends the four earthly essences, but here is used ironically to describe mankind as, in essence, "dust"—made from dust to return to dust. See Genesis 2.7, 3.19.)

340. **Lenten:** i.e., meager

341. **coted:** passed

345. **foil and target:** blunted smallsword and shield

346. **the humorous man:** the actor playing the eccentric character

347. **the clown:** the actor who plays the comic roles

348. **tickle o' th' sear:** i.e., easily made to laugh **sear:** the catch in a gunlock that keeps the hammer cocked (When the sear is tickle or loose, the gun goes off easily.); **the lady:** the actor playing the female role

350. **halt:** limp; go awkwardly or irregularly

353. **Their residence:** their remaining in the city

355–56. **their . . . innovation:** The **inhibition** that forces the tragedians from the city and the **innovation** that caused it may reflect London theatrical or political happenings.

361–62. **keeps . . . pace:** continues as usual

362–63. **an aerie of . . . little eyases:** a nest of young hawks (i.e., the child actors)

363. **cry out . . . question:** speak their lines in loud, shrill voices

ing how express and admirable; in action how like
an angel, in apprehension how like a god: the 330
beauty of the world, the paragon of animals—and
yet, to me, what is this quintessence of dust? Man
delights not me, ⟨no,⟩ nor women neither, though by
your smiling you seem to say so.

ROSENCRANTZ　My lord, there was no such stuff in my 335
thoughts.

HAMLET　Why did you laugh, then, when I said "man
delights not me"?

ROSENCRANTZ　To think, my lord, if you delight not in
man, what Lenten entertainment the players shall 340
receive from you. We coted them on the way, and
hither are they coming to offer you service.

HAMLET　He that plays the king shall be welcome—his
Majesty shall have tribute on me. The adventurous
knight shall use his foil and target, the lover shall 345
not sigh gratis, the humorous man shall end his
part in peace, ⟨the clown shall make those laugh
whose lungs are ⌈tickle⌉ o' th' sear,⟩ and the lady
shall say her mind freely, or the ⟨blank⟩ verse shall
halt for 't. What players are they? 350

ROSENCRANTZ　Even those you were wont to take such
delight in, the tragedians of the city.

HAMLET　How chances it they travel? Their residence,
both in reputation and profit, was better both ways.

ROSENCRANTZ　I think their inhibition comes by the 355
means of the late innovation.

HAMLET　Do they hold the same estimation they did
when I was in the city? Are they so followed?

ROSENCRANTZ　No, indeed are they not.

⟨HAMLET　How comes it? Do they grow rusty? 360

ROSENCRANTZ　Nay, their endeavor keeps in the wonted pace. But there is, sir, an aerie of children, little
eyases, that cry out on the top of question and are
most tyrannically clapped for 't. These are now the

365. berattle the common stages: noisily attack the public theaters

366-67. are afraid of goose quills: fear the satirical pens of the poets writing for boy actors

369. escoted: financially supported

369-70. pursue . . . sing: follow the acting profession only until their voices change in adolescence

376. tar: provoke, incite

377-79. There was . . . in the question: i.e, no plays were salable that did not take up the quarrel between the children's poets and the adult players

383. carry it away: carry off the victory

384-85. Hercules and his load too: i.e., the boy actors win over the whole world of playgoers (Hercules' load was the globe, which he bore on his shoulders for Atlas.)

387. mouths: contorted faces

389. picture in little: miniature portrait

390. 'Sblood: an oath (by Christ's or God's blood)

394. Th' appurtenance of: that which belongs to

395-96. comply . . . garb: use courteous action with you in this way

396. my extent: i.e., what I show

fashion and so ⌐berattle⌐ the common stages (so 365
they call them) that many wearing rapiers are afraid
of goose quills and dare scarce come thither.

HAMLET What, are they children? Who maintains 'em?
How are they escoted? Will they pursue the quality
no longer than they can sing? Will they not say 370
afterwards, if they should grow themselves to common players (as it is ⌐most like,⌐ if their means are
no better), their writers do them wrong to make
them exclaim against their own succession?

ROSENCRANTZ Faith, there has been much ⌐to-do⌐ on 375
both sides, and the nation holds it no sin to tar
them to controversy. There was for a while no
money bid for argument unless the poet and the
player went to cuffs in the question.

HAMLET Is 't possible?   380

GUILDENSTERN O, there has been much throwing
about of brains.

HAMLET Do the boys carry it away?

ROSENCRANTZ Ay, that they do, my lord—Hercules
and his load too.)   385

HAMLET It is not very strange; for my uncle is King of
Denmark, and those that would make mouths at
him while my father lived give twenty, forty, fifty, a
hundred ducats apiece for his picture in little.
'Sblood, there is something in this more than nat- 390
ural, if philosophy could find it out.

                        A flourish (for the Players.)

GUILDENSTERN There are the players.

HAMLET Gentlemen, you are welcome to Elsinore.
Your hands, come then. Th' appurtenance of welcome is fashion and ceremony. Let me comply 395
with you in this garb, (lest my) extent to the players,
which, I tell you, must show fairly outwards, should
more appear like entertainment than yours. You are
welcome. But my uncle-father and aunt-mother are
deceived.   400

402. mad north-north-west: only at certain times (when "the wind sits" in certain directions)

403. I know . . . a handsaw: a proverb that means "I can distinguish between things that do not resemble each other"

414. Roscius: an actor in the 1st century B.C.

417. Buzz, buzz: a rude response, suggesting that Polonius's news is old news

423–24. scene . . . unlimited: i.e., plays that observe the classical unities of time and place, as well as those that pay no attention to such limits

424. Seneca: a Roman philosopher and writer of tragedies

425. Plautus: a Roman writer of comedies; **For the law . . . liberty:** i.e., for plays that follow the rules of composition and those that do not

427. Jephthah: According to the biblical story (Judges 11.29–40), Jephthah unintentionally sacrificed his daughter through a rash vow. Hamlet goes on to sing lines from a popular ballad based on Jephthah's story.

432. passing: surpassingly, exceedingly

GUILDENSTERN In what, my dear lord?

HAMLET I am but mad north-north-west. When the wind is southerly, I know a hawk from a handsaw.

Enter Polonius.

POLONIUS Well be with you, gentlemen.

HAMLET Hark you, Guildenstern, and you too—at   405
each ear a hearer! That great baby you see there is not yet out of his swaddling clouts.

ROSENCRANTZ Haply he is the second time come to them, for they say an old man is twice a child.

HAMLET I will prophesy he comes to tell me of the   410
players; mark it.—You say right, sir, a Monday morning, 'twas then indeed.

POLONIUS My lord, I have news to tell you.

HAMLET My lord, I have news to tell you: when Roscius was an actor in Rome—   415

POLONIUS The actors are come hither, my lord.

HAMLET Buzz, buzz.

POLONIUS Upon my honor—

HAMLET Then came each actor on his ass.

POLONIUS The best actors in the world, either for   420
tragedy, comedy, history, pastoral, pastoral-comical, historical-pastoral, ⟨tragical-historical, tragical-comical-historical-pastoral,⟩ scene individable, or poem unlimited. Seneca cannot be too heavy, nor Plautus too light. For the law of writ and the liberty,   425
these are the only men.

HAMLET O Jephthah, judge of Israel, what a treasure hadst thou!

POLONIUS What a treasure had he, my lord?

HAMLET Why,   430
　　　　One fair daughter, and no more,
　　　　The which he lovèd passing well.

POLONIUS, ⌜*aside*⌝ Still on my daughter.

HAMLET Am I not i' th' right, old Jephthah?

440. lot: chance; **wot:** knows

443. row: stanza; **pious chanson:** scriptural ballad

444. abridgment: that which cuts short my recitation

447. valanced: fringed (i.e., with a beard)

449. my young lady and mistress: addressed to the boy actor who plays the women's parts

451. the altitude of a chopine: the height of the thick sole of a shoe called a "chopine"—i.e., the boy has grown several inches in height (See page 118.)

452–53. a piece . . . ring: Hamlet thus expresses his hope that the boy's voice is not **cracked** but is still suitable for female parts. (A coin is not lawful money if it has a crack that extends inward from the edge into the ring that surrounds the image of the sovereign's head.)

453. e'en to 't: go at it

454. fly at anything we see: i.e., undertake anything, no matter how difficult

455. straight: at once

456. quality: professional ability

461. caviary to the general: i.e., like caviar, too exotic for average tastes

463. cried . . . of: spoke with more authority than

464. digested: ordered, arranged

465. modesty: restraint

466. sallets: i.e., spicy (indelicate or vulgar) words

POLONIUS   If you call me "Jephthah," my lord: I have a   435
　　daughter that I love passing well.
HAMLET   Nay, that follows not.
POLONIUS   What follows then, my lord?
HAMLET   Why,
　　　　　　　　As by lot, God wot   440
and then, you know,
　　　　It came to pass, as most like it was—
the first row of the pious chanson will show you
more, for look where my abridgment comes.

　　　　　　　Enter the Players.

You are welcome, masters; welcome all.—I am glad   445
to see thee well.—Welcome, good friends.—O ⟨my⟩
old friend! Why, thy face is valanced since I saw thee
last. Com'st thou to beard me in Denmark?—What,
my young lady and mistress! ⟨By'r⟩ Lady, your lady-
ship is nearer to heaven than when I saw you last, by   450
the altitude of a chopine. Pray God your voice, like a
piece of uncurrent gold, be not cracked within the
ring. Masters, you are all welcome. We'll e'en to 't
like ⟨French⟩ falconers, fly at anything we see. We'll
have a speech straight. Come, give us a taste of your   455
quality. Come, a passionate speech.
⟨FIRST⟩ PLAYER   What speech, my good lord?
HAMLET   I heard thee speak me a speech once, but it
　　was never acted, or, if it was, not above once; for
　　the play, I remember, pleased not the million: 460
　　'twas caviary to the general. But it was (as I
　　received it, and others whose judgments in such
　　matters cried in the top of mine) an excellent play,
　　well digested in the scenes, set down with as much
　　modesty as cunning. I remember one said there   465
　　were no sallets in the lines to make the matter
　　savory, nor no matter in the phrase that might indict
　　the author of ⟨affectation,⟩ but called it an honest

470. **fine:** gaudy

471–73. **Aeneas' tale ... of Priam's slaughter:** Aeneas, hero of Virgil's *Aeneid*, tells Dido, queen of Carthage, stories of the Trojan War. Among them is that of Priam, king of Troy, who was killed by Pyrrhus seeking revenge for his father Achilles' death.

475. **Hyrcanian beast:** a tiger (Hyrcania, in Roman times, was the name of a region now in Iran at the southern end of the Caspian Sea. In the *Aeneid*, it is associated with tigers.)

479. **horse:** the wooden horse in which the Greeks hid themselves to gain entry into Troy (See page 114.)

482. **gules:** red (a heraldic term); **tricked:** decorated

487. **o'ersized:** covered as with "size," a glaze or filler

488. **carbuncles:** deep red glowing jewels

492. **discretion:** judgment, discernment

496. **Repugnant to:** opposing, resisting

498. **fell:** cruel

499. **senseless:** without human senses; **Ilium:** the fortress within Troy

method, [as wholesome as sweet and, by very much,
more handsome than fine.] One speech in 't I   470
chiefly loved. 'Twas Aeneas' (tale) to Dido, and
thereabout of it especially when he speaks of
Priam's slaughter. If it live in your memory, begin at
this line—let me see, let me see:

The rugged Pyrrhus, like th' Hyrcanian beast—   475
'tis not so; it begins with Pyrrhus:
The rugged Pyrrhus, he whose sable arms,
Black as his purpose, did the night resemble
When he lay couchèd in th' ominous horse,
Hath now this dread and black complexion smeared   480
With heraldry more dismal. Head to foot,
Now is he total gules, horridly tricked
With blood of fathers, mothers, daughters, sons,
Baked and impasted with the parching streets,
That lend a tyrannous and a damnèd light   485
To their lord's murder. Roasted in wrath and fire,
And thus o'ersizèd with coagulate gore,
With eyes like carbuncles, the hellish Pyrrhus
Old grandsire Priam seeks.
    So, proceed you.   490

POLONIUS 'Fore God, my lord, well spoken, with good
    accent and good discretion.

⟨FIRST⟩ PLAYER   *Anon he finds him*
Striking too short at Greeks. His antique sword,
Rebellious to his arm, lies where it falls,   495
Repugnant to command. Unequal matched,
Pyrrhus at Priam drives, in rage strikes wide;
But with the whiff and wind of his fell sword
Th' unnervèd father falls. ⟨Then senseless Ilium,⟩
Seeming to feel this blow, with flaming top   500
Stoops to his base, and with a hideous crash
Takes prisoner Pyrrhus' ear. For lo, his sword,
Which was declining on the milky head
Of reverend Priam, seemed i' th' air to stick.

509. **rack:** clouds high above, driven by the wind

514. **Cyclops:** Titans who forged thunderbolts for Jove, king of the Greco-Roman gods

515. **Mars:** the Roman god of war; **for proof eterne:** to stand the test of eternity

520. **fellies:** sections of the wheel's rim; **wheel:** Fortune was often pictured as controlling human life by turning a great wheel on which she stood or sat.

521. **nave:** hub of the wheel

525. **jig:** a lively, mocking song

526. **Hecuba:** the wife of Priam and queen of Troy

527. **mobled:** i.e., her head and face were muffled

531. **bisson rheum:** blinding tears; **clout:** piece of cloth

533. **lank and all o'erteemed:** shrunken and worn out with childbearing

536–37. **'Gainst . . . pronounced:** would have uttered treasonous statements against Fortune's rule

So as a painted tyrant Pyrrhus stood   505
(And,) like a neutral to his will and matter,
Did nothing.
But as we often see against some storm
A silence in the heavens, the rack stand still,
The bold winds speechless, and the orb below   510
As hush as death, anon the dreadful thunder
Doth rend the region; so, after Pyrrhus' pause,
Aroused vengeance sets him new a-work,
And never did the Cyclops' hammers fall
On Mars's armor, forged for proof eterne,   515
With less remorse than Pyrrhus' bleeding sword
Now falls on Priam.
Out, out, thou strumpet Fortune! All you gods
In general synod take away her power,
Break all the spokes and ⌜fellies⌝ from her wheel,   520
And bowl the round nave down the hill of heaven
As low as to the fiends!

POLONIUS This is too long.

HAMLET It shall to the barber's with your beard.—
  Prithee say on. He's for a jig or a tale of bawdry, or 525
  he sleeps. Say on; come to Hecuba.

(FIRST) PLAYER
But who, ah woe, had seen the mobled queen—

HAMLET "The mobled queen"?

POLONIUS That's good. ⟨⌜"Mobled⌝ queen" is good.⟩

(FIRST) PLAYER
Run barefoot up and down, threat'ning the flames   530
With (bisson rheum,) a clout upon that head
Where late the diadem stood, and for a robe,
About her lank and all o'erteemèd loins
A blanket, in the alarm of fear caught up—
Who this had seen, with tongue in venom steeped,   535
'Gainst Fortune's state would treason have
  pronounced.
But if the gods themselves did see her then

543. **milch:** wet with tears, milky
544. **passion:** deep emotion
545. **whe'er:** whether
549. **bestowed:** lodged, housed
550. **abstract:** summary
555. **God's bodykins:** a mild oath (by God's "little body")

The Trojan horse. (2.2.479)
From Diego de Saavedra Fajardo, *Le prince Chrestien* (1668).

When she saw Pyrrhus make malicious sport
In mincing with his sword her ⟨husband's⟩ limbs,   540
The instant burst of clamor that she made
(Unless things mortal move them not at all)
Would have made milch the burning eyes of heaven
And passion in the gods.

POLONIUS Look whe'er he has not turned his color and   545
has tears in 's eyes. Prithee, no more.

HAMLET 'Tis well. I'll have thee speak out the rest of
this soon.—Good my lord, will you see the players
well bestowed? Do you hear, let them be well used,
for they are the abstract and brief chronicles of the   550
time. After your death you were better have a bad
epitaph than their ill report while you live.

POLONIUS My lord, I will use them according to their
desert.

HAMLET God's ⟨bodykins,⟩ man, much better! Use ev-   555
ery man after his desert and who shall 'scape
whipping? Use them after your own honor and
dignity. The less they deserve, the more merit is in
your bounty. Take them in.

POLONIUS Come, sirs.   560

HAMLET Follow him, friends. We'll hear a play tomorrow. ⌜*As Polonius and Players exit, Hamlet speaks to*
the First Player.⌝ Dost thou hear me, old friend? Can
you play "The Murder of Gonzago"?

⌜FIRST⌝ PLAYER Ay, my lord.   565

HAMLET We'll ha 't tomorrow night. You could, for ⟨a⟩
need, study a speech of some dozen or sixteen
lines, which I would set down and insert in 't,
could you not?

⌜FIRST⌝ PLAYER Ay, my lord.   570

HAMLET Very well. Follow that lord—and look you
mock him not. ⌜*First Player exits.*⌝ My good friends,
I'll leave you till night. You are welcome to Elsinore.

ROSENCRANTZ Good my lord.

580–81. **Could . . . wanned:** i.e., could work his soul into such accord with his thought that, from his soul's working on his body, his face grew pale

583–84. **his whole function . . . conceit:** i.e., all the bodily powers that express emotion responding with outward appearances to match his thoughts

591. **Make mad . . . free:** i.e., madden guilty spectators and terrify those who are innocent

592. **amaze:** astound

594. **muddy-mettled:** dull-spirited; **peak:** mope

595. **John-a-dreams:** a proverbial name for an absent-minded dreamer; **unpregnant of:** unfilled by, and therefore never to give birth (to action)

598. **defeat:** overthrow

601–2. **gives me . . . lungs:** i.e., calls me an absolute liar

603. **'Swounds:** an oath, by Christ's wounds

606. **kites:** birds of prey

608. **kindless:** unnatural

HAMLET
Ay, so, good-bye to you.　　　　　　　　　　　　575
　　　　　⌜*Rosencrantz and Guildenstern*⌝ *exit.*
　　　　　　　Now I am alone.
O, what a rogue and peasant slave am I!
Is it not monstrous that this player here,
But in a fiction, in a dream of passion,
Could force his soul so to his own conceit　　　　580
That from her working all ⟨his⟩ visage wanned,
Tears in his eyes, distraction in his aspect,
A broken voice, and his whole function suiting
With forms to his conceit—and all for nothing!
For Hecuba!　　　　　　　　　　　　　　　585
What's Hecuba to him, or he to ⟨Hecuba,⟩
That he should weep for her? What would he do
Had he the motive and ⟨the cue⟩ for passion
That I have? He would drown the stage with tears
And cleave the general ear with horrid speech,　　590
Make mad the guilty and appall the free,
Confound the ignorant and amaze indeed
The very faculties of eyes and ears. Yet I,
A dull and muddy-mettled rascal, peak
Like John-a-dreams, unpregnant of my cause,　　595
And can say nothing—no, not for a king
Upon whose property and most dear life
A damned defeat was made. Am I a coward?
Who calls me "villain"? breaks my pate across?
Plucks off my beard and blows it in my face?　　600
Tweaks me by the nose? gives me the lie i' th' throat
As deep as to the lungs? Who does me this?
Ha! 'Swounds, I should take it! For it cannot be
But I am pigeon-livered and lack gall
To make oppression bitter, or ere this　　　　　605
I should ⟨have⟩ fatted all the region kites
With this slave's offal. Bloody, bawdy villain!
Remorseless, treacherous, lecherous, kindless
　　villain!

611. **brave:** admirable
615. **drab:** prostitute
616. **scullion:** kitchen servant
617. **About, . . . !:** i.e., turn around
619. **cunning:** art, skill; **scene:** performance
620. **presently:** instantly
626. **tent:** probe (as into a wound)
631. **spirits:** i.e., emotional states (such as **melan-choly**)
632. **Abuses:** deceives, deludes
633. **relative:** pertinent

A woman wearing chopines. (2.2.451)
From Pietro Bertelli,
Diuersarum nationum habitus (1594–96).

118

⟨O vengeance!⟩ 610
Why, what an ass am I! This is most brave,
That I, the son of a dear ⌜father⌝ murdered,
Prompted to my revenge by heaven and hell,
Must, like a whore, unpack my heart with words
And fall a-cursing like a very drab, 615
A ⟨scullion!⟩ Fie upon 't! Foh!
About, my brains!—Hum, I have heard
That guilty creatures sitting at a play
Have, by the very cunning of the scene,
Been struck so to the soul that presently 620
They have proclaimed their malefactions.
For murder, though it have no tongue, will speak
With most miraculous organ. I'll have these players
Play something like the murder of my father
Before mine uncle. I'll observe his looks; 625
I'll tent him to the quick. If he do blench,
I know my course. The spirit that I have seen
May be a ⟨devil,⟩ and the ⟨devil⟩ hath power
T' assume a pleasing shape; yea, and perhaps,
Out of my weakness and my melancholy, 630
As he is very potent with such spirits,
Abuses me to damn me. I'll have grounds
More relative than this. The play's the thing
Wherein I'll catch the conscience of the King.
                                        He exits.

To vengeance!
Why, what an ass am I! This is most brave,
That I, the son of a dear father murdered,
Prompted to my revenge by heaven and hell
Must, like a whore, unpack my heart with words
And fall a-cursing like a very drab,
A scullion! Fie upon't, foh!
About, my brains!—Hum, I have heard
That guilty creatures sitting at a play
Have by the very cunning of the scene
Been struck so to the soul that presently
They have proclaimed their malefactions;
For murder, though it have no tongue, will speak
With most miraculous organ. I'll have these players
Play something like the murder of my father
Before mine uncle. I'll observe his looks;
I'll tent him to the quick. If he do blench,
I know my course. The spirit that I have seen
May be a devil, and the devil hath power
T' assume a pleasing shape, yea, and perhaps
Out of my weakness and my melancholy,
As he is very potent with such spirits,
Abuses me to damn me. I'll have grounds
More relative than this. The play's the thing
Wherein I'll catch the conscience of the king.
                                          He exits.

The Tragedy of

HAMLET,

Prince of Denmark

ACT 3

3.1 After Rosencrantz and Guildenstern report their failure to find the cause of Hamlet's madness, Polonius places Ophelia where he and Claudius may secretly observe a meeting between her and Hamlet. Hamlet is at first courteous to Ophelia, but suddenly he turns on her: he denies having loved her, asks where her father is, attacks womankind, and tells her she should enter a nunnery. After Hamlet exits, Claudius decides that Hamlet's erratic behavior is not caused by love and announces a plan to send Hamlet on an embassy to England. Polonius persuades Claudius to take no action until Gertrude talks with Hamlet after the play, which is scheduled for that evening.

2. **puts . . . confusion:** acts in this distracted way

5. **distracted:** perturbed, unsettled

7. **forward . . . sounded:** i.e., eager to be questioned

14–15. **Niggard . . . reply:** not inclined to talk, but willing to answer fully our questions

16. **assay:** tempt

⌐Scene 1⌐
Enter King, Queen, Polonius, Ophelia, Rosencrantz,
Guildenstern, ⟨and⟩ Lords.

KING
  And can you by no drift of conference
  Get from him why he puts on this confusion,
  Grating so harshly all his days of quiet
  With turbulent and dangerous lunacy?

ROSENCRANTZ
  He does confess he feels himself distracted,   5
  But from what cause he will by no means speak.

GUILDENSTERN
  Nor do we find him forward to be sounded,
  But with a crafty madness keeps aloof
  When we would bring him on to some confession
  Of his true state.   10

QUEEN   Did he receive you well?

ROSENCRANTZ   Most like a gentleman.

GUILDENSTERN
  But with much forcing of his disposition.

ROSENCRANTZ
  Niggard of question, but of our demands
  Most free in his reply.   15

QUEEN   Did you assay him to any pastime?

ROSENCRANTZ
  Madam, it so fell out that certain players

18. **o'erraught:** overtook
28. **give . . . edge:** i.e., sharpen his desire
32. **closely:** privately
34. **Affront:** meet face to face
35. **espials:** spies
38. **as he is behaved:** according to how he acts

We o'erraught on the way. Of these we told him,
And there did seem in him a kind of joy
To hear of it. They are here about the court,   20
And, as I think, they have already order
This night to play before him.

POLONIUS   'Tis most true,
And he beseeched me to entreat your Majesties
To hear and see the matter.   25

KING
With all my heart, and it doth much content me
To hear him so inclined.
Good gentlemen, give him a further edge
And drive his purpose into these delights.

ROSENCRANTZ
We shall, my lord.   *Rosencrantz and Guildenstern*   30
                         ⌐*and Lords*⌐ *exit.*

KING   Sweet Gertrude, leave us ⟨too,⟩
For we have closely sent for Hamlet hither,
That he, as 'twere by accident, may here
Affront Ophelia.
Her father and myself ⟨⟨lawful espials⟩⟩   35
⟨Will⟩ so bestow ourselves that, seeing unseen,
We may of their encounter frankly judge
And gather by him, as he is behaved,
If 't be th' affliction of his love or no
That thus he suffers for.   40

QUEEN   I shall obey you.
And for your part, Ophelia, I do wish
That your good beauties be the happy cause
Of Hamlet's wildness. So shall I hope your virtues
Will bring him to his wonted way again,   45
To both your honors.

OPHELIA   Madam, I wish it may.
                         ⌐*Queen exits.*⌐

POLONIUS
Ophelia, walk you here.—Gracious, so please you,

51–52. show . . . loneliness: i.e., Ophelia's apparent reading of a Bible or prayer book would give a pretext for her being alone

52. to blame: i.e., guilty, blameworthy

59–61. The harlot's . . . word: i.e., the pock-marked cheek of the whore is not uglier, when compared to the illusion of beauty she creates with cosmetics, than is what I have done in comparison to my story of what happened

73. rub: obstacle (a technical term from the game of bowls, where a "rub" is any obstruction that hinders or deflects the course of the bowl)

75. shuffled off this mortal coil: i.e., untangled ourselves from the flesh; also, detached ourselves from the turmoil of human affairs.

77. makes calamity of so long life: i.e., makes us put up with unhappiness for such a long time

We will bestow ourselves. ⌜*To Ophelia.*⌝ Read on this
   book,   50
That show of such an exercise may color
Your ⟨loneliness.⟩—We are oft to blame in this
('Tis too much proved), that with devotion's visage
And pious action we do sugar o'er
The devil himself.   55

KING, ⌜*aside*⌝ O, 'tis too true!
How smart a lash that speech doth give my
   conscience.
The harlot's cheek beautied with plast'ring art
Is not more ugly to the thing that helps it   60
Than is my deed to my most painted word.
O heavy burden!

POLONIUS
I hear him coming. ⟨Let's⟩ withdraw, my lord.
                                ⌜*They withdraw.*⌝

Enter Hamlet.

HAMLET
To be or not to be—that is the question:
Whether 'tis nobler in the mind to suffer   65
The slings and arrows of outrageous fortune,
Or to take arms against a sea of troubles
And, by opposing, end them. To die, to sleep—
No more—and by a sleep to say we end
The heartache and the thousand natural shocks   70
That flesh is heir to—'tis a consummation
Devoutly to be wished. To die, to sleep—
To sleep, perchance to dream. Ay, there's the rub,
For in that sleep of death what dreams may come,
When we have shuffled off this mortal coil,   75
Must give us pause. There's the respect
That makes calamity of so long life.
For who would bear the whips and scorns of time,
Th' oppressor's wrong, the proud man's contumely,

80. **despised:** unrequited (accent on first syllable)

81. **office:** i.e., those in office

83. **his quietus make:** settle his own account (from *quietus est,* a legal term meaning "he is quit")

84. **bare bodkin:** a mere dagger (or, an unsheathed dagger); **fardels:** burdens, loads

87. **undiscovered:** unexplored; **bourn:** frontier

88. **puzzles:** i.e., paralyzes

91. **conscience:** i.e., knowledge, consciousness

92. **native hue:** natural color

93. **cast:** shade

94. **pitch:** height (the *pitch* is the highest point in a falcon's flight); **moment:** importance

95. **With this regard:** on this account; **their currents turn awry:** i.e., the great enterprises are like rivers that, turned aside from their main channels, lose momentum and become stagnant

96. **Soft you now:** an exclamation to interrupt speech ("wait a moment," "hold," "enough")

The pangs of despised love, the law's delay, 80
The insolence of office, and the spurns
That patient merit of th' unworthy takes,
When he himself might his quietus make
With a bare bodkin? Who would fardels bear,
To grunt and sweat under a weary life, 85
But that the dread of something after death,
The undiscovered country from whose bourn
No traveler returns, puzzles the will
And makes us rather bear those ills we have
Than fly to others that we know not of? 90
Thus conscience does make cowards (of us all,)
And thus the native hue of resolution
Is (sicklied) o'er with the pale cast of thought,
And enterprises of great pitch and moment
With this regard their currents turn awry 95
And lose the name of action.—Soft you now,
The fair Ophelia.—Nymph, in thy orisons
Be all my sins remembered.

OPHELIA   Good my lord,
How does your Honor for this many a day? 100

HAMLET   I humbly thank you, well.

OPHELIA
My lord, I have remembrances of yours
That I have longèd long to redeliver.
I pray you now receive them.

HAMLET
No, not I. I never gave you aught. 105

OPHELIA
My honored lord, you know right well you did,
And with them words of so sweet breath composed
As made (the) things more rich. Their perfume
   lost,
Take these again, for to the noble mind 110
Rich gifts wax poor when givers prove unkind.
There, my lord.

113. **honest:** chaste (with perhaps also the meaning of "truthful")

118. **discourse to:** conversation with

123. **his:** its

124. **sometime:** formerly; **paradox:** a statement contrary to what is generally thought

125. **the time:** the present age

127–29. **virtue . . . relish of it:** The metaphor here is of grafting a bud or branch to produce better fruit. Virtue, Hamlet says, may be grafted onto (may **inoculate**) sinful human nature (**our old stock**), but the sinfulness will still leave its taste (**relish**) in the fruit that is produced.

131. **nunnery:** convent (The word was sometimes used mockingly to refer to a brothel.)

132–33. **indifferent honest:** reasonably virtuous

Grafting ("inoculating") tree stock. (3.1.128)
From Marco Bussato, *Giardino di agricoltura* (1599).

HAMLET Ha, ha, are you honest?

OPHELIA My lord?

HAMLET Are you fair? 115

OPHELIA What means your lordship?

HAMLET That if you be honest and fair, (your honesty)
should admit no discourse to your beauty.

OPHELIA Could beauty, my lord, have better commerce than with honesty? 120

HAMLET Ay, truly, for the power of beauty will sooner
transform honesty from what it is to a bawd than
the force of honesty can translate beauty into his
likeness. This was sometime a paradox, but now
the time gives it proof. I did love you once. 125

OPHELIA Indeed, my lord, you made me believe so.

HAMLET You should not have believed me, for virtue
cannot so (inoculate) our old stock but we shall
relish of it. I loved you not.

OPHELIA I was the more deceived. 130

HAMLET Get thee (to) a nunnery. Why wouldst thou be
a breeder of sinners? I am myself indifferent honest, but yet I could accuse me of such things that it
were better my mother had not borne me: I am
very proud, revengeful, ambitious, with more of- 135
fenses at my beck than I have thoughts to put them
in, imagination to give them shape, or time to act
them in. What should such fellows as I do crawling
between earth and heaven? We are arrant knaves
(all;) believe none of us. Go thy ways to a nunnery. 140
Where's your father?

OPHELIA At home, my lord.

HAMLET Let the doors be shut upon him that he may
play the fool nowhere but in 's own house. Farewell.

OPHELIA O, help him, you sweet heavens! 145

HAMLET If thou dost marry, I'll give thee this plague
for thy dowry: be thou as chaste as ice, as pure as
snow, thou shalt not escape calumny. Get thee to a

151. **monsters:** cuckolds (In the standard joke, a cuckold had horns growing out of the forehead; see page 140.)

157. **nickname:** call by the wrong name

157–58. **make . . . ignorance:** call your immorality ignorance (The word **wantonness** may here have the less frequent meaning of "affectation.")

159. **on 't:** of it

164–65. **courtier's . . . sword:** i.e., the courtier's eye, the scholar's tongue, the soldier's sword

167. **glass of fashion:** mirror of proper behavior; **mold of form:** model of attractiveness

172. **out of time:** out of correct rhythm

173. **blown:** vigorous, fresh (The word, applied to flowers in bloom, picks up the earlier **rose of the . . . state.**)

174. **Blasted with ecstasy:** blighted by madness

176. **affections:** emotions, mental state

180. **doubt:** fear; **the hatch and the disclose:** Both **hatch** and **disclose** mean to break out of the egg— here, the "egg" on which Hamlet's melancholy **sits on brood** (line 179).

nunnery, farewell. Or if thou wilt needs marry,
marry a fool, for wise men know well enough what 150
monsters you make of them. To a nunnery, go, and
quickly too. Farewell.

OPHELIA　Heavenly powers, restore him!

HAMLET　I have heard of your paintings ⟨too,⟩ well
enough. God hath given you one face, and you 155
make yourselves another. You jig and amble, and
you ⟨lisp;⟩ you nickname God's creatures and make
your wantonness ⟨your⟩ ignorance. Go to, I'll no
more on 't. It hath made me mad. I say we will have
no more marriage. Those that are married already, 160
all but one, shall live. The rest shall keep as they are.
To a nunnery, go.　　　　　　　　　　*He exits.*

OPHELIA
O, what a noble mind is here o'erthrown!
The courtier's, soldier's, scholar's, eye, tongue,
　　sword, 165
⟨Th' expectancy⟩ and rose of the fair state,
The glass of fashion and the mold of form,
Th' observed of all observers, quite, quite down!
And I, of ladies most deject and wretched,
That sucked the honey of his musicked vows, 170
Now see ⟨that⟩ noble and most sovereign reason,
Like sweet bells jangled, out of time and harsh;
That unmatched form and stature of blown youth
Blasted with ecstasy. O, woe is me
T' have seen what I have seen, see what I see! 175

KING, ⌜*advancing with*⌝ Polonius
Love? His affections do not that way tend;
Nor what he spake, though it lacked form a little,
Was not like madness. There's something in his soul
O'er which his melancholy sits on brood,
And I do doubt the hatch and the disclose 180
Will be some danger; which for to prevent,
I have in quick determination

187. **something-settled:** somehow fixed
197. **round:** plainspoken
199. **find him not:** i.e., does not discover his secret

3.2 Hamlet gives direction to the actors and asks Horatio to help him observe Claudius's reaction to the play. When the court arrive, Hamlet makes bawdy and bitter comments to Ophelia. The traveling actors perform, in dumb show and then with dialogue, a story that includes many elements of Claudius's alleged seduction of Gertrude and murder of King Hamlet. At the moment that the Player King is murdered in his garden by his nephew, Claudius stops the play and rushes out. Hamlet is exuberant that the Ghost's word has been proved true. Rosencrantz and Guildenstern return to tell Hamlet that Claudius is furious and that Gertrude wishes to see Hamlet at once in her sitting room. Hamlet promises himself that he will not harm her, though he will "speak daggers."

---

3. **I had as lief:** I'd just as soon

Thus set it down: he shall with speed to England
For the demand of our neglected tribute.
Haply the seas, and countries different,   185
With variable objects, shall expel
This something-settled matter in his heart,
Whereon his brains still beating puts him thus
From fashion of himself. What think you on 't?

POLONIUS
It shall do well. But yet do I believe   190
The origin and commencement of his grief
Sprung from neglected love.—How now, Ophelia?
You need not tell us what Lord Hamlet said;
We heard it all.—My lord, do as you please,
But, if you hold it fit, after the play   195
Let his queen-mother all alone entreat him
To show his grief. Let her be round with him;
And I'll be placed, so please you, in the ear
Of all their conference. If she find him not,
To England send him, or confine him where   200
Your wisdom best shall think.

KING   It shall be so.
Madness in great ones must not ⟨unwatched⟩ go.
                                        They exit.

⌜Scene 2⌝
Enter Hamlet and three of the Players.

HAMLET Speak the speech, I pray you, as I pronounced
it to you, trippingly on the tongue; but if you mouth
it, as many of our players do, I had as lief the
town-crier spoke my lines. Nor do not saw the air
too much with your hand, thus, but use all gently;   5
for in the very torrent, tempest, and, as I may say,
whirlwind of your passion, you must acquire and
beget a temperance that may give it smoothness. O,

9. **robustious:** noisy, boisterous

11. **groundlings:** spectators who stood rather than sat, and thus paid less to go to the theater

12. **capable of:** able to appreciate

14. **Termagant:** imaginary Muslim god, shown in early drama as noisy and unrestrained

15. **Herod:** Herod of Judea, who appears in medieval drama as a raging tyrant

20. **modesty:** moderation, absence of excess

21. **from:** opposite to

22. **playing:** acting

25. **the . . . time:** i.e., the present exactly as it is

26. **his:** its; **pressure:** shape

26-27. **come tardy off:** done inadequately

27. **unskillful:** those lacking judgment

28-29. **the censure . . . one:** the judgment of even one of which

29. **allowance:** estimation

32. **not to speak it profanely:** not intending to be profane in what I'm about to say

33. **Christians:** an informal usage, meaning humans as opposed to animals

36. **journeymen:** hirelings who work for daily wages

38. **indifferently:** pretty well

42. **of them:** i.e., some of them

43. **barren:** dull, not intelligent

it offends me to the soul to hear a robustious, periwig-pated fellow tear a passion to tatters, to very 10 rags, to split the ears of the groundlings, who for the most part are capable of nothing but inexplicable dumb shows and noise. I would have such a fellow whipped for o'erdoing Termagant. It out-Herods Herod. Pray you, avoid it. 15

PLAYER   I warrant your Honor.

HAMLET   Be not too tame neither, but let your own discretion be your tutor. Suit the action to the word, the word to the action, with this special observance, that you o'erstep not the modesty of 20 nature. For anything so o'erdone is from the purpose of playing, whose end, both at the first and now, was and is to hold, as 'twere, the mirror up to nature, to show virtue her ⟨own⟩ feature, scorn her own image, and the very age and body of the time 25 his form and pressure. Now this overdone or come tardy off, though it makes the unskillful laugh, cannot but make the judicious grieve, the censure of ⟨the⟩ which one must in your allowance o'erweigh a whole theater of others. O, there be players that I 30 have seen play and heard others ⟨praise⟩ (and that highly), not to speak it profanely, that, neither having th' accent of Christians nor the gait of Christian, pagan, nor man, have so strutted and bellowed that I have thought some of nature's 35 journeymen had made men, and not made them well, they imitated humanity so abominably.

PLAYER   I hope we have reformed that indifferently with us, ⟨sir.⟩

HAMLET   O, reform it altogether. And let those that play 40 your clowns speak no more than is set down for them, for there be of them that will themselves laugh, to set on some quantity of barren spectators to laugh too, though in the meantime some neces-

57. **my conversation coped withal:** my experience has brought me into contact with

61. **revenue:** accent on second syllable

65. **pregnant:** ready (to bend)

66. **thrift:** profit

67. **dear:** highly prized

68. **election:** choice

74. **commeddled:** mixed together

"Groundlings." (3.2.11)
From Gabriel Rollenhagen,
Nucleus emblematum selectissimorum (1611).

138

sary question of the play be then to be considered.   45
That's villainous and shows a most pitiful ambition
in the fool that uses it. Go make you ready.
                                    (Players exit.)

Enter Polonius, Guildenstern, and Rosencrantz.

How now, my lord, will the King hear this piece of
work?
POLONIUS   And the Queen too, and that presently.   50
HAMLET   Bid the players make haste. *(Polonius exits.)*
  Will you two help to hasten them?
ROSENCRANTZ   Ay, my lord.   *They exit.*
HAMLET   What ho, Horatio!

                Enter Horatio.

HORATIO   Here, sweet lord, at your service.   55
HAMLET
  Horatio, thou art e'en as just a man
  As e'er my conversation coped withal.
HORATIO
  O, my dear lord—
(HAMLET)   Nay, do not think I flatter,
  For what advancement may I hope from thee   60
  That no revenue hast but thy good spirits
  To feed and clothe thee? Why should the poor be
    flattered?
  No, let the candied tongue lick absurd pomp
  And crook the pregnant hinges of the knee   65
  Where thrift may follow fawning. Dost thou hear?
  Since my dear soul was mistress of her choice
  And could of men distinguish, her election
  Hath sealed thee for herself. For thou hast been
  As one in suffering all that suffers nothing,   70
  A man that Fortune's buffets and rewards
  Hast ta'en with equal thanks; and blessed are those
  Whose blood and judgment are so well
    commeddled

75. **pipe:** small wind instrument, like a flute

84. **comment:** observation

85. **occulted:** deliberately hidden

86. **unkennel:** reveal, as when a fox is driven from its lair

89. **Vulcan's stithy:** forge of the Roman god of fire and metalworking

99. **chameleon's dish:** Chameleons were thought to live off air.

A cuckold. (3.1.151)
From *Bagford Ballads* (printed in 1878).

That they are not a pipe for Fortune's finger   75
To sound what stop she please. Give me that man
That is not passion's slave, and I will wear him
In my heart's core, ay, in my heart of heart,
As I do thee.—Something too much of this.—
There is a play tonight before the King.   80
One scene of it comes near the circumstance
Which I have told thee of my father's death.
I prithee, when thou seest that act afoot,
Even with the very comment of thy soul
Observe my uncle. If his occulted guilt   85
Do not itself unkennel in one speech,
It is a damnèd ghost that we have seen,
And my imaginations are as foul
As Vulcan's stithy. Give him heedful note,
For I mine eyes will rivet to his face,   90
And, after, we will both our judgments join
In censure of his seeming.
HORATIO   Well, my lord.
If he steal aught the whilst this play is playing
And 'scape ⟨detecting⟩, I will pay the theft.   95
                              ⟨*Sound a flourish.*⟩
HAMLET They are coming to the play. I must be idle.
   Get you a place.

Enter Trumpets and Kettle Drums. ⟨Enter⟩ King, Queen,
Polonius, Ophelia, ⟨Rosencrantz, Guildenstern, and other
   Lords attendant with ⌜*the King's*⌝ *guard carrying*
                          torches.⟩

KING How fares our cousin Hamlet?
HAMLET Excellent, i' faith, of the chameleon's dish. I
   eat the air, promise-crammed. You cannot feed   100
   capons so.
KING I have nothing with this answer, Hamlet. These
   words are not mine.
HAMLET No, nor mine now. ⌜*To Polonius.*⌝ My lord, you
   played once i' th' university, you say?   105

132. **your only jig-maker:** the best comic of them all

138. **a suit of sables:** clothing trimmed with sable furs

POLONIUS That did I, my lord, and was accounted a
    good actor.

HAMLET What did you enact?

POLONIUS I did enact Julius Caesar. I was killed i' th'
    Capitol. Brutus killed me.   110

HAMLET It was a brute part of him to kill so capital a
    calf there.—Be the players ready?

ROSENCRANTZ Ay, my lord. They stay upon your pa-
    tience.

QUEEN Come hither, my dear Hamlet, sit by me.   115

HAMLET No, good mother. Here's metal more
    attractive.   ⌜*Hamlet takes a place near Ophelia.*⌝

POLONIUS, ⌜*to the King*⌝ Oh, ho! Do you mark that?

HAMLET Lady, shall I lie in your lap?

OPHELIA No, my lord.   120

⟨HAMLET I mean, my head upon your lap?

OPHELIA Ay, my lord.⟩

HAMLET Do you think I meant country matters?

OPHELIA I think nothing, my lord.

HAMLET That's a fair thought to lie between maids'   125
    legs.

OPHELIA What is, my lord?

HAMLET Nothing.

OPHELIA You are merry, my lord.

HAMLET Who, I?   130

OPHELIA Ay, my lord.

HAMLET O God, your only jig-maker. What should a
    man do but be merry? For look you how cheerfully
    my mother looks, and my father died within 's two
    hours.   135

OPHELIA Nay, 'tis twice two months, my lord.

HAMLET So long? Nay, then, let the devil wear black,
    for I'll have a suit of sables. O heavens, die two
    months ago, and not forgotten yet? Then there's
    hope a great man's memory may outlive his life half 140
    a year. But, by'r Lady, he must build churches, then,

142. **suffer not thinking on:** endure oblivion

142–43. **the hobby-horse:** a character in morris dances (The song that Hamlet quotes expresses sorrow that such figures are gone and forgotten.)

144 SD. **Dumb show:** a scene without words

158. **miching mallecho:** skulking misdeed (**Miching** is dialect for "sneaking," **mallecho** is the Spanish *malhecho*, "misdeed.")

160. **Belike:** perhaps; **argument:** plot

168. **naught:** naughty, indecent

A hobby-horse. (3.2.143)
From *Morris dancers . . .* (Anon., n.d.).

or else shall he suffer not thinking on, with the
hobby-horse, whose epitaph is "For oh, for oh, the
hobby-horse is forgot."

The trumpets sounds. Dumb show follows.

Enter a King and a Queen, ⟨very lovingly,⟩ the Queen   145
embracing him and he her. ⟨She kneels and makes show of
protestation unto him.⟩ He takes her up and declines his
head upon her neck. He lies him down upon a bank of
flowers. She, seeing him asleep, leaves him. Anon
⟨comes⟩ in another man, takes off his crown, kisses it, pours   150
poison in the sleeper's ears, and leaves him. The Queen
returns, finds the King dead, makes passionate action. The
poisoner with some three or four come in again, seem to
condole with her. The dead body is carried away. The
poisoner woos the Queen with gifts. She seems harsh   155
awhile but in the end accepts ⟨his⟩ love.

⌐*Players exit.*⌐

OPHELIA   What means this, my lord?
HAMLET   Marry, this ⟨is miching⟩ mallecho. It means
   mischief.
OPHELIA   Belike this show imports the argument of the   160
   play.

Enter Prologue.

HAMLET   We shall know by this fellow. The players
   cannot keep ⟨counsel;⟩ they'll tell all.
OPHELIA   Will he tell us what this show meant?
HAMLET   Ay, or any show that you will show him. Be   165
   not you ashamed to show, he'll not shame to tell you
   what it means.
OPHELIA   You are naught, you are naught. I'll mark the
   play.
PROLOGUE

> For us and for our tragedy,   170
> Here stooping to your clemency,
> We beg your hearing patiently.   ⌐*He exits.*⌐

173. **posy of a ring:** a poem inscribed in a ring

176. **Phoebus' cart:** the chariot of the sun god, which appears to make its cycle around the earth annually. (The language of this play-within-the-play is set apart from that surrounding it by complicated word order and noticeably poetic language.)

177. **Neptune's salt wash:** the ocean **Neptune:** Roman god of the sea; **Tellus:** Roman goddess of the earth

180. **Hymen:** god of marriage

186. **distrust you:** fear for you

188. **For women . . . love:** This line is part of an incomplete couplet; perhaps the completing line was dropped in the printing house, or perhaps the couplet was incompletely crossed out by Shakespeare.

189-90. **women's . . . extremity:** i.e., women's love and fear are parallel: where they love, they also fear

196. **My operant powers . . . leave to do:** my vital powers cease to function

HAMLET Is this a prologue or the posy of a ring?
OPHELIA 'Tis brief, my lord.
HAMLET As woman's love. 175

Enter ⌈the Player⌉ King and Queen.

PLAYER KING
Full thirty times hath Phoebus' cart gone round
Neptune's salt wash and Tellus' ⟨orbèd⟩ ground,
And thirty dozen moons with borrowed sheen
About the world have times twelve thirties been
Since love our hearts and Hymen did our hands 180
Unite commutual in most sacred bands.

PLAYER QUEEN
So many journeys may the sun and moon
Make us again count o'er ere love be done!
But woe is me! You are so sick of late,
So far from cheer and from ⟨your⟩ former state, 185
That I distrust you. Yet, though I distrust,
Discomfort you, my lord, it nothing must.
[For women fear too much, even as they love,]
And women's fear and love hold quantity,
In neither aught, or in extremity. 190
Now what my ⟨love⟩ is, proof hath made you know,
And, as my love is sized, my fear is so:
[Where love is great, the littlest doubts are fear;
Where little fears grow great, great love grows there.]

PLAYER KING
Faith, I must leave thee, love, and shortly too. 195
My operant powers their functions leave to do.
And thou shalt live in this fair world behind,
Honored, beloved; and haply one as kind
For husband shalt thou—

PLAYER QUEEN   *O, confound the rest!* 200
Such love must needs be treason in my breast.
In second husband let me be accurst.
None wed the second but who killed the first.

204. **wormwood:** i.e., bitter, harsh
205. **instances:** causes
206. **thrift:** worldly profit
211. **Purpose is but the slave to memory:** i.e., a purpose must be remembered if it is to be carried out
212. **validity:** vigor
215–16. **Most . . . debt:** i.e., we conveniently forget the promises we make to ourselves
220. **enactures:** enactments
223. **aye:** ever
231. **try:** test (his friendship)
235. **devices still:** plans always

HAMLET That's wormwood!

PLAYER QUEEN

  The instances that second marriage move   205
  Are base respects of thrift, but none of love.
  A second time I kill my husband dead
  When second husband kisses me in bed.

PLAYER KING

  I do believe you think what now you speak,
  But what we do determine oft we break.   210
  Purpose is but the slave to memory,
  Of violent birth, but poor validity,
  Which now, the fruit unripe, sticks on the tree
  But fall unshaken when they mellow be.
  Most necessary 'tis that we forget   215
  To pay ourselves what to ourselves is debt.
  What to ourselves in passion we propose,
  The passion ending, doth the purpose lose.
  The violence of either grief or joy
  Their own enactures with themselves destroy.   220
  Where joy most revels, grief doth most lament;
  Grief ⟨joys,⟩ joy grieves, on slender accident.
  This world is not for aye, nor 'tis not strange
  That even our loves should with our fortunes change;
  For 'tis a question left us yet to prove   225
  Whether love lead fortune or else fortune love.
  The great man down, you mark his favorite flies;
  The poor, advanced, makes friends of enemies.
  And hitherto doth love on fortune tend,
  For who not needs shall never lack a friend,   230
  And who in want a hollow friend doth try
  Directly seasons him his enemy.
  But, orderly to end where I begun:
  Our wills and fates do so contrary run
  That our devices still are overthrown;   235
  Our thoughts are ours, their ends none of our own.
  So think thou wilt no second husband wed,
  But die thy thoughts when thy first lord is dead.

242. **An anchor's cheer:** an anchorite's (hermit's) food and drink

243. **opposite . . . joy:** obstacle that makes joy's face turn pale (or, perhaps, that deprives joy's face of all expression)

251. **rock:** soothe

256. **argument:** plot

261. **Tropically:** i.e., as a trope, a figure of speech

265. **free:** innocent

266–67. **Let . . . unwrung:** a proverb that says, in effect: let guilty persons flinch; we have clear consciences **galled jade:** a horse with raw skin **withers:** ridge between the horse's shoulders **unwrung:** not chafed

269. **a chorus:** a character who (as in Shakespeare's *Henry V*) tells the audience what they are about to see

PLAYER QUEEN
  Nor earth to me give food, nor heaven light,
  Sport and repose lock from me day and night,   **240**
  [*To desperation turn my trust and hope,*
  ⌜*An*⌝ *anchor's cheer in prison be my scope.*]
  Each opposite that blanks the face of joy
  Meet what I would have well and it destroy.
  Both here and hence pursue me lasting strife,   **245**
  If, once a widow, ever I be wife.

HAMLET If she should break it now!

PLAYER KING
  'Tis deeply sworn. Sweet, leave me here awhile.
  My spirits grow dull, and fain I would beguile
  The tedious day with sleep.   ⟨*Sleeps.*⟩ **250**

PLAYER QUEEN   *Sleep rock thy brain,*
  And never come mischance between us twain.
                    ⌜*Player Queen exits.*⌝

HAMLET Madam, how like you this play?

QUEEN The lady doth protest too much, methinks.

HAMLET O, but she'll keep her word.   **255**

KING Have you heard the argument? Is there no offense in 't?

HAMLET No, no, they do but jest, poison in jest. No offense i' th' world.

KING What do you call the play?   **260**

HAMLET "The Mousetrap." Marry, how? Tropically. This play is the image of a murder done in Vienna. Gonzago is the duke's name, his wife Baptista. You shall see anon. 'Tis a knavish piece of work, but what of that? Your Majesty and we that have free **265** souls, it touches us not. Let the galled jade wince; our withers are unwrung.

Enter Lucianus.

This is one Lucianus, nephew to the king.

OPHELIA You are as good as a chorus, my lord.

270–71. **I could . . . dallying:** i.e., I could play the role of narrator at a puppet show in which you and your lover are shown making love

273–74. **take off mine edge:** make me less sharp; satisfy my desire (Hamlet gives a sexual meaning to Ophelia's "You are keen" [i.e., sharp, penetrating] and responds with this double entendre.)

275. **better and worse:** more witty and more offensive

276. **so you mis-take:** i.e., in the same way, you take falsely (Wives promise to "take" their husbands "for better, for worse.")

278–79. **the croaking . . . revenge:** Hamlet here amusingly condenses two lines from the anonymous *The True Tragedy of Richard III* (c. 1591): "The screeking raven sits croaking for revenge. / Whole herds of beasts comes bellowing for revenge."

282. **Confederate season:** i.e., time being my ally; **else:** otherwise

284. **With Hecate's ban:** by the curse of Hecate, the goddess of sorcery and witchcraft

292. **false fire:** discharge of a gun loaded only with powder

HAMLET I could interpret between you and your love, 270
    if I could see the puppets dallying.

OPHELIA You are keen, my lord, you are keen.

HAMLET It would cost you a groaning to take off mine
    edge.

OPHELIA Still better and worse. 275

HAMLET So you mis-take your husbands.—Begin,
    murderer. ⟨Pox,⟩ leave thy damnable faces and
    begin. Come, the croaking raven doth bellow for
    revenge.

LUCIANUS
  Thoughts black, hands apt, drugs fit, and time 280
    agreeing,
  ⟨Confederate⟩ season, else no creature seeing,
  Thou mixture rank, of midnight weeds collected,
  With Hecate's ban thrice blasted, thrice ⟨infected,⟩
  Thy natural magic and dire property 285
  On wholesome life ⟨usurp⟩ immediately.
                ⟨*Pours the poison in his ears.*⟩

HAMLET He poisons him i' th' garden for his estate. His
    name's Gonzago. The story is extant and written in
    very choice Italian. You shall see anon how the
    murderer gets the love of Gonzago's wife. 290
                  ⌜*Claudius rises.*⌝

OPHELIA The King rises.

⟨HAMLET What, frighted with false fire?⟩

QUEEN How fares my lord?

POLONIUS Give o'er the play.

KING Give me some light. Away! 295

POLONIUS Lights, lights, lights!
               All but Hamlet and Horatio exit.

HAMLET
  Why, let the strucken deer go weep,
    The hart ungallèd play.
  For some must watch, while some must sleep:
    Thus runs the world away. 300

301. **feathers:** worn on actors' hats

302. **turn Turk with me:** turn against me

303. **Provincial:** possibly, of Provence (in France); **razed:** slashed decoratively

303-4. **a fellowship in a cry of players:** a partnership in a theater company

307. **Damon:** renowned, in Roman mythology, for the depth of his friendship for his friend Pythias

308. **dismantled:** stripped

310. **pajock:** possibly "peacock" (In the natural history of Shakespeare's day, the peacock had a reputation for lust and cruelty.)

311. **rhymed:** The obvious rhyme word is *ass.*

317-18. **recorders:** wooden flutes with mouth pieces

320. **perdy:** from the French *par dieu,* "by God"

327-28. **distempered:** upset (with a second meaning of "ill," which is how Hamlet chooses to interpret it)

330. **choler:** biliousness (The word has a second meaning of "anger," which Hamlet plays on at line 334.)

333. **purgation:** medical cleansing; spiritual purification

Would not this, sir, and a forest of feathers (if the
rest of my fortunes turn Turk with me) with ⟨two⟩
Provincial roses on my razed shoes, get me a
fellowship in a cry of players?

HORATIO Half a share.   305

HAMLET A whole one, I.
For thou dost know, O Damon dear,
    This realm dismantled was
Of Jove himself, and now reigns here
    A very very—pajock.   310

HORATIO You might have rhymed.

HAMLET O good Horatio, I'll take the ghost's word for
a thousand pound. Didst perceive?

HORATIO Very well, my lord.

HAMLET Upon the talk of the poisoning?   315

HORATIO I did very well note him.

HAMLET Ah ha! Come, some music! Come, the record-
ers!
For if the King like not the comedy,
    Why, then, belike he likes it not, perdy.   320
Come, some music!

Enter Rosencrantz and Guildenstern.

GUILDENSTERN Good my lord, vouchsafe me a word
with you.

HAMLET Sir, a whole history.

GUILDENSTERN The King, sir—   325

HAMLET Ay, sir, what of him?

GUILDENSTERN Is in his retirement marvelous distempered.

HAMLET With drink, sir?

GUILDENSTERN No, my lord, with choler.   330

HAMLET Your wisdom should show itself more richer
to signify this to the doctor, for for me to put him to
his purgation would perhaps plunge him into more
choler.

336. **start:** shy away (like a nervous or wild horse)
344. **wholesome:** sane
345. **pardon:** permission to depart
355. **admiration:** wonder
360. **closet:** private chamber
364. **by these ... stealers:** i.e., by these hands (The phrase borrows from the catechism, where one is told "to keep [one's] hands from picking and stealing.")

GUILDENSTERN   Good my lord, put your discourse into   335
  some frame and ⟨start⟩ not so wildly from my
  affair.

HAMLET   I am tame, sir. Pronounce.

GUILDENSTERN   The Queen your mother, in most great
  affliction of spirit, hath sent me to you.   340

HAMLET   You are welcome.

GUILDENSTERN   Nay, good my lord, this courtesy is not
  of the right breed. If it shall please you to make me
  a wholesome answer, I will do your mother's
  commandment. If not, your pardon and my return   345
  shall be the end of ⟨my⟩ business.

HAMLET   Sir, I cannot.

ROSENCRANTZ   What, my lord?

HAMLET   Make you a wholesome answer. My wit's
  diseased. But, sir, such answer as I can make, you   350
  shall command—or, rather, as you say, my mother.
  Therefore no more but to the matter. My mother,
  you say—

ROSENCRANTZ   Then thus she says: your behavior hath
  struck her into amazement and admiration.   355

HAMLET   O wonderful son that can so 'stonish a mother! But is there no sequel at the heels of this
  mother's admiration? Impart.

ROSENCRANTZ   She desires to speak with you in her
  closet ere you go to bed.   360

HAMLET   We shall obey, were she ten times our mother. Have you any further trade with us?

ROSENCRANTZ   My lord, you once did love me.

HAMLET   And do still, by these pickers and stealers.

ROSENCRANTZ   Good my lord, what is your cause of   365
  distemper? You do surely bar the door upon your
  own liberty if you deny your griefs to your friend.

HAMLET   Sir, I lack advancement.

ROSENCRANTZ   How can that be, when you have the
  voice of the King himself for your succession in   370
  Denmark?

372. **"While the grass grows"**: The rest of the proverb reads "the horse starves."

373. **something musty**: somewhat stale, i.e., so familiar it need not be quoted in full (The proverb, in Latin, was in use 350 years before *Hamlet* was written.)

376–77. **go . . . toil**: try to get to the windward side of me, as if to force me into a trap (Hamlet speaks as if they were hunters and he their quarry.)

381. **this pipe**: the recorder

387. **ventages**: finger holes, or **stops** (line 390), of the recorder

396. **sound me**: (1) play me like a musical instrument; (2) measure my depths, as with a fathom line; (3) test me for my secrets (a triple pun)

397. **compass**: (1) full range of an instrument's sound; (2) limits, scope

399. **organ**: musical instrument; **'Sblood**: an oath (by God's, or Christ's, blood)

402. **fret**: (1) annoy; (2) provide an instrument with frets (On stringed instruments, frets are the raised parts that guide the fingers.)

HAMLET Ay, sir, but "While the grass grows"—the proverb is something musty.

Enter the Players with recorders.

O, the recorders! Let me see one. ⌐*He takes a recorder and turns to Guildenstern.*¬ To withdraw 375 with you: why do you go about to recover the wind of me, as if you would drive me into a toil?

GUILDENSTERN O, my lord, if my duty be too bold, my love is too unmannerly.

HAMLET I do not well understand that. Will you play 380 upon this pipe?

GUILDENSTERN My lord, I cannot.

HAMLET I pray you.

GUILDENSTERN Believe me, I cannot.

HAMLET I do beseech you. 385

GUILDENSTERN I know no touch of it, my lord.

HAMLET It is as easy as lying. Govern these ventages with your fingers and ⟨thumb,⟩ give it breath with your mouth, and it will discourse most eloquent music. Look you, these are the stops. 390

GUILDENSTERN But these cannot I command to any utt'rance of harmony. I have not the skill.

HAMLET Why, look you now, how unworthy a thing you make of me! You would play upon me, you would seem to know my stops, you would pluck 395 out the heart of my mystery, you would sound me from my lowest note to ⟨the top of⟩ my compass; and there is much music, excellent voice, in this little organ, yet cannot you make it speak. 'Sblood, do you think I am easier to be played on than a pipe? 400 Call me what instrument you will, though you ⟨can⟩ fret me, you cannot play upon me.

Enter Polonius.

God bless you, sir.

413. by and by: soon, before long; or, perhaps, right away

427. Nero: murderer of his mother Agrippina

431. How . . . somever: however; **shent:** punished

432. give them seals: i.e., validate my words (by putting them into action)

ROSENCRANTZ: ... ...
will you do you go about to recover the wind
of me, as if you would drive me into a toil?

GUILDENSTERN: O, my lord, if my duty be too bold, my
love is too unmannerly.

HAMLET: I do not well understand that. Will you play
upon this pipe?

GUILDENSTERN: My lord, I cannot.

HAMLET: I pray you.

GUILDENSTERN: Believe me, I cannot.

HAMLET: I do beseech you.

GUILDENSTERN: I know no touch of it, my lord.

HAMLET: It is as easy as lying. Govern these ventages
with your fingers and thumb, give it breath with
your mouth, and it will discourse most eloquent
music. Look you, these are the stops.

GUILDENSTERN: But these cannot I command to any
utterance of harmony. I have not the skill.

HAMLET: Why, look you now, how unworthy a thing
you make of me! You would play upon me, you
would seem to know my stops, you would pluck
out the heart of my mystery, you would sound me
from my lowest note to the top of my compass;
and there is much music, excellent voice, in this
little organ, yet cannot you make it speak. 'Sblood,
do you think I am easier to be played on than a pipe?
Call me what instrument you will, though you can
fret me, you cannot play upon me.

Enter Polonius.

POLONIUS My lord, the Queen would speak with you,
and presently.   405

HAMLET Do you see yonder cloud that's almost in
shape of a camel?

POLONIUS By th' Mass, and 'tis like a camel indeed.

HAMLET Methinks it is like a weasel.

POLONIUS It is backed like a weasel.   410

HAMLET Or like a whale.

POLONIUS Very like a whale.

(HAMLET) Then I will come to my mother by and by.
⌜*Aside.*⌝ They fool me to the top of my bent.—I will
come by and by.   415

(POLONIUS) I will say so.

(HAMLET) "By and by" is easily said. Leave me,
friends.

⌜*All but Hamlet exit.*⌝

'Tis now the very witching time of night,
When churchyards yawn and hell itself (breathes)   420
out
Contagion to this world. Now could I drink hot
blood
And do such (bitter) business as the day
Would quake to look on. Soft, now to my mother.   425
O heart, lose not thy nature; let not ever
The soul of Nero enter this firm bosom.
Let me be cruel, not unnatural.
I will speak (daggers) to her, but use none.
My tongue and soul in this be hypocrites: 430
How in my words somever she be shent,
To give them seals never, my soul, consent.

He exits.

3.3 Claudius orders Rosencrantz and Guildenstern to take Hamlet to England immediately. Polonius arrives to tell Claudius of his plans to spy on Hamlet's conversation with Gertrude. Left alone, Claudius reveals to the audience his remorse for killing his brother, and he tries to pray. Hamlet comes upon him kneeling and draws his sword, but then stops to think that if he kills Claudius at prayer, Claudius will go to heaven. Hamlet decides to kill Claudius when the king is committing a sin so that Claudius will instead go to hell. After Hamlet leaves, Claudius rises, saying that he has been unable to pray.

----

1. **I . . . not:** i.e., I do not like the way he is acting
3. **dispatch:** prepare at once
5. **The terms of our estate:** my position as a king
12. **single and peculiar:** individual and private
14. **noyance:** injury
16. **cess:** cessation, decease
17. **gulf:** whirlpool
21. **mortised:** securely fastened
25. **Arm you . . . to:** i.e., prepare yourself for

⌜Scene 3⌝
Enter King, Rosencrantz, and Guildenstern.

KING
  I like him not, nor stands it safe with us
  To let his madness range. Therefore prepare you.
  I your commission will forthwith dispatch,
  And he to England shall along with you.
  The terms of our estate may not endure   5
  Hazard so near 's as doth hourly grow
  Out of his brows.
GUILDENSTERN   We will ourselves provide.
  Most holy and religious fear it is
  To keep those many many bodies safe   10
  That live and feed upon your Majesty.
ROSENCRANTZ
  The single and peculiar life is bound
  With all the strength and armor of the mind
  To keep itself from noyance, but much more
  That spirit upon whose weal depends and rests   15
  The lives of many. The cess of majesty
  Dies not alone, but like a gulf doth draw
  What's near it with it; or it is a massy wheel
  Fixed on the summit of the highest mount,
  To whose ⟨huge⟩ spokes ten thousand lesser things   20
  Are mortised and adjoined, which, when it falls,
  Each small annexment, petty consequence,
  Attends the boist'rous ⟨ruin.⟩ Never alone
  Did the king sigh, but ⟨with⟩ a general groan.
KING
  Arm you, I pray you, to this speedy voyage,   25
  For we will fetters put about this fear,
  Which now goes too free-footed.
ROSENCRANTZ   We will haste us.
          ⌜*Rosencrantz and Guildenstern*⌝ *exit.*

        Enter Polonius.

31–32. tax him home: reprimand him strongly

36. of vantage: from the vantage point of concealment

41. primal eldest curse: The first curse, which condemned Cain to a life of "a fugitive and a vagabond," was laid on him for his murder of his brother, Abel (Genesis 4.10–12).

50–51. Whereto ... offense?: i.e., what purpose does mercy serve except to confront the face of condemnation? (The promise of the New Testament is that mercy, in the person of Christ, will, at the Last Judgment, oppose itself to the face of the offended Deity, and thus secure forgiveness of our sins.)

53–54. forestallèd ... down: i.e., the twofold force of prayer is that we not be "led into temptation" and that we be "forgiven our trespasses"

60. th' offense: that which has been gained through the crime

61. currents: course of events

62. Offense's gilded hand: the golden hand of the offender, "gilded" through money illegally obtained; **shove by:** thrust aside

POLONIUS
  My lord, he's going to his mother's closet.
  Behind the arras I'll convey myself   30
  To hear the process. I'll warrant she'll tax him
    home;
  And, as you said (and wisely was it said),
  'Tis meet that some more audience than a mother,
  Since nature makes them partial, should o'erhear   35
  The speech of vantage. Fare you well, my liege.
  I'll call upon you ere you go to bed
  And tell you what I know.

KING   Thanks, dear my lord.
                              ⌜*Polonius*⌝ *exits.*
  O, my offense is rank, it smells to heaven;   40
  It hath the primal eldest curse upon 't,
  A brother's murder. Pray can I not,
  Though inclination be as sharp as will.
  My stronger guilt defeats my strong intent,
  And, like a man to double business bound,   45
  I stand in pause where I shall first begin
  And both neglect. What if this cursèd hand
  Were thicker than itself with brother's blood?
  Is there not rain enough in the sweet heavens
  To wash it white as snow? Whereto serves mercy   50
  But to confront the visage of offense?
  And what's in prayer but this twofold force,
  To be forestallèd ere we come to fall,
  Or (pardoned) being down? Then I'll look up.
  My fault is past. But, O, what form of prayer   55
  Can serve my turn? "Forgive me my foul murder"?
  That cannot be, since I am still possessed
  Of those effects for which I did the murder:
  My crown, mine own ambition, and my queen.
  May one be pardoned and retain th' offense?   60
  In the corrupted currents of this world,
  Offense's gilded hand may ⟨shove⟩ by justice,

64. **'tis not so above:** this is not the case in heaven

65. **There is no shuffling:** in heaven, one cannot escape through evasion

65–68. **the action . . . in evidence:** i.e., in God's court, the legal action must be brought in accord with the facts; we are forced even to testify against ourselves

68. **rests:** remains

72. **limèd:** trapped, like a bird caught in birdlime

73. **engaged:** entangled; **Make assay:** put forth all your efforts

80. **would be scanned:** i.e., needs to be examined

84. **hire and salary:** i.e., something Claudius should pay me for

85. **grossly, full of bread:** in the full enjoyment of the world (See Ezekiel 16.49: "Pride, fullness of bread, and abundance of idleness.")

87. **audit:** final account

89. **heavy with him:** i.e., his spirit is in a serious condition

90. **him:** i.e., Claudius

93. **know thou a more horrid hent:** i.e., wait for a more horrible occasion

And oft 'tis seen the wicked prize itself
Buys out the law. But 'tis not so above:
There is no shuffling; there the action lies   65
In his true nature, and we ourselves compelled,
Even to the teeth and forehead of our faults,
To give in evidence. What then? What rests?
Try what repentance can. What can it not?
Yet what can it, when one cannot repent?   70
O wretched state! O bosom black as death!
O limèd soul, that, struggling to be free,
Art more engaged! Help, angels! Make assay.
Bow, stubborn knees, and heart with strings of steel
Be soft as sinews of the newborn babe.   75
All may be well.   ⌜*He kneels.*⌝

                    Enter Hamlet.

HAMLET
Now might I do it ⟨pat,⟩ now he is a-praying,
And now I'll do 't.   ⌜*He draws his sword.*⌝
                    And so he goes to heaven,
And so am I ⟨revenged.⟩ That would be scanned: 80
A villain kills my father, and for that,
I, his sole son, do this same villain send
To heaven.
Why, this is ⟨hire⟩ and ⟨salary,⟩ not revenge.
He took my father grossly, full of bread,   85
With all his crimes broad blown, as flush as May;
And how his audit stands who knows save heaven.
But in our circumstance and course of thought
'Tis heavy with him. And am I then revenged
To take him in the purging of his soul,   90
When he is fit and seasoned for his passage?
No.
Up sword, and know thou a more horrid hent.
                    ⌜*He sheathes his sword.*⌝
When he is drunk asleep, or in his rage,

100. **stays:** waits
101. **This physic:** this medicine (i.e., this postponement of the killing; or, Claudius's purging of himself through prayer)

3.4 In Gertrude's room, Polonius hides behind a tapestry. Hamlet's entrance so alarms Gertrude that she cries out for help. Polonius echoes her cry, and Hamlet, thinking Polonius to be Claudius, stabs him to death. Hamlet then verbally attacks his mother for marrying Claudius. In the middle of Hamlet's attack, the Ghost returns to remind Hamlet that his real purpose is to avenge his father's death. Gertrude cannot see the Ghost and pities Hamlet's apparent madness. After the Ghost exits, Hamlet urges Gertrude to abandon Claudius's bed. He then tells her about Claudius's plan to send him to England and reveals his suspicions that the journey is a plot against him, which he resolves to counter violently. He exits dragging out Polonius's body.

1. **straight:** immediately; **lay home to him:** reprove him thoroughly
7. **round:** blunt
9. **fear me not:** don't doubt me

Or in th' incestuous pleasure of his bed, 95
At game a-swearing, or about some act
That has no relish of salvation in 't—
Then trip him, that his heels may kick at heaven,
And that his soul may be as damned and black
As hell, whereto it goes. My mother stays. 100
This physic but prolongs thy sickly days.
⌈*Hamlet*⌉ *exits.*

KING, ⌈*rising*⌉
My words fly up, my thoughts remain below;
Words without thoughts never to heaven go.
He exits.

⌈Scene 4⌉
Enter ⟨Queen⟩ and Polonius.

POLONIUS
He will come straight. Look you lay home to him.
Tell him his pranks have been too broad to bear
with
And that your Grace hath screened and stood
between 5
Much heat and him. I'll silence me even here.
Pray you, be round ⟨with him.

HAMLET, *within* Mother, mother, mother!⟩
QUEEN I'll ⟨warrant⟩ you. Fear me not. Withdraw,
I hear him coming. 10
⌈*Polonius hides behind the arras.*⌉

Enter Hamlet.

HAMLET Now, mother, what's the matter?
QUEEN
Hamlet, thou hast thy father much offended.
HAMLET
Mother, you have my father much offended.

14. **idle:** foolish
18. **forgot me:** forgotten who I am
24. **glass:** mirror
29. **Dead for a ducat:** i.e., dead, I'll wager a ducat

"Heaven's face does glow." (3.4.57)
From Richard Day,
A booke of Christian prayers (1590).

QUEEN
  Come, come, you answer with an idle tongue.
HAMLET
  Go, go, you question with a wicked tongue.   15
QUEEN
  Why, how now, Hamlet?
HAMLET   What's the matter now?
QUEEN
  Have you forgot me?
HAMLET   No, by the rood, not so.
  You are the Queen, your husband's brother's wife,   20
  And (would it were not so) you are my mother.
QUEEN
  Nay, then I'll set those to you that can speak.
HAMLET
  Come, come, and sit you down; you shall not budge.
  You go not till I set you up a glass
  Where you may see the ⟨inmost⟩ part of you.   25
QUEEN
  What wilt thou do? Thou wilt not murder me?
  Help, ho!
POLONIUS, ⌈*behind the arras*⌉   What ho! Help!
HAMLET
  How now, a rat? Dead for a ducat, dead.
                    ⌈*He ⟨kills Polonius⟩ by thrusting a rapier
                              through the arras.*⌉
POLONIUS, ⌈*behind the arras*⌉
  O, I am slain!   30
QUEEN   O me, what hast thou done?
HAMLET   Nay, I know not. Is it the King?
QUEEN
  O, what a rash and bloody deed is this!
HAMLET
  A bloody deed—almost as bad, good mother,
  As kill a king and marry with his brother.   35
QUEEN
  As kill a king?

45. **damnèd custom:** habitual wickedness

46. **proof:** invulnerable (like armor); **sense:** feeling

55. **contraction:** i.e., the marriage contract

57. **rhapsody:** jumble

58. **this . . . mass:** i.e., the earth

59. **against the doom:** when Judgment Day comes

60. **Is thought-sick:** i.e., Heaven is thought-sick

62. **That roars . . . index:** i.e., that receives such a violent introduction (The index was the "table of contents" introducing a book.)

64. **counterfeit presentment:** representation in portraits (These are perhaps miniatures—Claudius's on a chain around Gertrude's neck, King Hamlet's around Prince Hamlet's neck—or are perhaps paintings hung upon the wall.)

66. **Hyperion:** the sun god, the most beautiful of the pagan deities; **front:** brow

68. **A station . . . Mercury:** a way of standing that is like that of the winged messenger of the gods

HAMLET   Ay, lady, it was my word.
⌈*He pulls Polonius' body from behind the arras.*⌉
Thou wretched, rash, intruding fool, farewell.
I took thee for thy better. Take thy fortune.
Thou find'st to be too busy is some danger.   40
⌈*To Queen.*⌉ Leave wringing of your hands. Peace, sit
  you down,
And let me wring your heart; for so I shall
If it be made of penetrable stuff,
If damnèd custom have not brazed it so   45
That it be proof and bulwark against sense.

QUEEN
What have I done, that thou dar'st wag thy tongue
In noise so rude against me?

HAMLET   Such an act
That blurs the grace and blush of modesty,   50
Calls virtue hypocrite, takes off the rose
From the fair forehead of an innocent love
And sets a blister there, makes marriage vows
As false as dicers' oaths——O, such a deed
As from the body of contraction plucks   55
The very soul, and sweet religion makes
A rhapsody of words! Heaven's face does glow
O'er this solidity and compound mass
With heated visage, as against the doom,
Is thought-sick at the act.   60

QUEEN   Ay me, what act
That roars so loud and thunders in the index?

HAMLET
Look here upon this picture and on this,
The counterfeit presentment of two brothers.
See what a grace was seated on this brow,   55
Hyperion's curls, the front of Jove himself,
An eye like Mars' to threaten and command,
A station like the herald Mercury
New-lighted on a ⟨heaven⟩-kissing hill,

74. **ear:** i.e., of a cereal plant like wheat
75. **Blasting:** blighting; **his:** its
76. **leave to feed:** stop feeding
77. **batten:** glut yourself; **moor:** barren land
79. **heyday:** state of excitement; **blood:** passion
81. **Sense:** perception through the senses
83. **apoplexed:** suffering from apoplexy, hence without sensation or consciousness
84. **sense ... thralled:** i.e., the five senses are never so subjected by lunacy (Hamlet's argument is that, even in madness, Gertrude's senses would have **reserved some quantity of choice** [line 85]—i.e., retained a trace of the power to choose.)
87. **cozened:** tricked; **hoodman-blind:** the game of blindman's buff
89. **sans all:** without the other senses
91. **so mope:** be so stupefied
93. **mutine:** incite rebellion
94–95. **be ... fire:** i.e., melt like the wax in a burning candle
95–98. **Proclaim ... will:** i.e., do not call it shameful when youthful passion acts impetuously, since the frost of age is itself aflame and reason is acting as a pander for desire instead of controlling it
101. **grainèd:** indelible ("Grain" was a "fast" or permanent dye.)
102. **leave their tinct:** give up their color
104. **enseamèd:** greasy

A combination and a form indeed	70
Where every god did seem to set his seal
To give the world assurance of a man.
This was your husband. Look you now what follows.
Here is your husband, like a mildewed ear
Blasting his wholesome brother. Have you eyes?	75
Could you on this fair mountain leave to feed
And batten on this moor? Ha! Have you eyes?
You cannot call it love, for at your age
The heyday in the blood is tame, it's humble
And waits upon the judgment; and what judgment	80
Would step from this to this? [Sense sure you have,
Else could you not have motion; but sure that sense
Is apoplexed; for madness would not err,
Nor sense to ecstasy was ne'er so thralled,
But it reserved some quantity of choice	85
To serve in such a difference.] What devil was 't
That thus hath cozened you at hoodman-blind?
[Eyes without feeling, feeling without sight,
Ears without hands or eyes, smelling sans all,
Or but a sickly part of one true sense	90
Could not so mope.] O shame, where is thy blush?
Rebellious hell,
If thou canst mutine in a matron's bones,
To flaming youth let virtue be as wax
And melt in her own fire. Proclaim no shame	95
When the compulsive ardor gives the charge,
Since frost itself as actively doth burn,
And reason (panders) will.
QUEEN   O Hamlet, speak no more!
Thou turn'st my eyes into my (very) soul,	100
And there I see such black and (grainèd) spots
As will (not) leave their tinct.
HAMLET   Nay, but to live
In the rank sweat of an enseamèd bed,
Stewed in corruption, honeying and making love	105
Over the nasty sty!

112. **a vice of kings:** a buffoon of a king (a reference to the comic Vice of the morality plays)

113. **cutpurse:** thief

123. **lapsed in time and passion:** i.e., having let time slip by and passion cool

124. **important:** importunate, urgent

128. **amazement on thy mother sits:** i.e., your mother is in a state of extreme shock

130. **Conceit:** imagination

135. **incorporal:** immaterial

137. **in th' alarm:** waked by the call to arms

138. **hair, like life in excrements:** as if hair, a lifeless outgrowth ("excrement"), had come to life

139. **an end:** on end

QUEEN   O, speak to me no more!
   These words like daggers enter in my ears.
   No more, sweet Hamlet!
HAMLET   A murderer and a villain,   110
   A slave that is not twentieth part the (tithe)
   Of your precedent lord; a vice of kings,
   A cutpurse of the empire and the rule,
   That from a shelf the precious diadem stole
   And put it in his pocket—   115
QUEEN   No more!
HAMLET   A king of shreds and patches—

                   Enter Ghost.

   Save me and hover o'er me with your wings,
   You heavenly guards!—What would your gracious
      figure?   120
QUEEN   Alas, he's mad.
HAMLET
   Do you not come your tardy son to chide,
   That, lapsed in time and passion, lets go by
   Th' important acting of your dread command?
   O, say!   125
GHOST   Do not forget. This visitation
   Is but to whet thy almost blunted purpose.
   But look, amazement on thy mother sits.
   O, step between her and her fighting soul.
   Conceit in weakest bodies strongest works.   130
   Speak to her, Hamlet.
HAMLET   How is it with you, lady?
QUEEN   Alas, how is 't with you,
   That you do bend your eye on vacancy
   And with th' incorporal air do hold discourse?   135
   Forth at your eyes your spirits wildly peep,
   And, as the sleeping soldiers in th' alarm,
   Your bedded hair, like life in excrements,
   Start up and stand an end. O gentle son,

144. **capable:** responsive
147. **effects:** purposes
148. **want:** lack
155. **in . . . lived:** dressed as he did when he lived
158. **ecstasy:** madness
165. **gambol from:** skip away from
166. **flattering unction:** soothing salve

Mercury. (3.4.68)
From Giovanni Battista Cavalleriis,
Antiquarum statuarum (1585–94).

Upon the heat and flame of thy distemper   140
Sprinkle cool patience! Whereon do you look?

HAMLET
On him, on him! Look you how pale he glares.
His form and cause conjoined, preaching to stones,
Would make them capable. ⌐*To the Ghost.*⌐ Do not
    look upon me,   145
Lest with this piteous action you convert
My stern effects. Then what I have to do
Will want true color—tears perchance for blood.

QUEEN   To whom do you speak this?

HAMLET   Do you see nothing there?   150

QUEEN
Nothing at all; yet all that is I see.

HAMLET   Nor did you nothing hear?

QUEEN   No, nothing but ourselves.

HAMLET
Why, look you there, look how it steals away!
My father, in his habit as he lived!   155
Look where he goes even now out at the portal!
                                            Ghost exits.

QUEEN
This is the very coinage of your brain.
This bodiless creation ecstasy
Is very cunning in.

HAMLET   ⟨Ecstasy?⟩   160
My pulse as yours doth temperately keep time
And makes as healthful music. It is not madness
That I have uttered. Bring me to the test,
And ⟨I⟩ the matter will reword, which madness
Would gambol from. Mother, for love of grace,   165
Lay not that flattering unction to your soul
That not your trespass but my madness speaks.
It will but skin and film the ulcerous place,
Whiles rank corruption, mining all within,
Infects unseen. Confess yourself to heaven,   170

174. **fatness:** grossness; **pursy:** fat, flabby

176. **curb:** bow

182–83. **That monster . . . devil:** This passage may contain mistakes in the printing (editors often change "devil" to "evil"). The general meaning may be: "Custom, a monster that consumes all sense, is therefore like a devil in suggesting evil habits."

184. **use:** habit

186. **aptly:** easily

190. **either ⌈. . .⌉ the devil:** A word seems to have been lost; Q2 reads "either the devil"; many editors (to complete the line and the thought) insert the verb "master," found in the quarto of *Hamlet* printed in 1611.

196. **their scourge and minister:** heaven's scourge (of punishment—and therefore subject to punishment himself) and heaven's minister (agent of divine retribution) **their:** heaven's

200. **remains behind:** is yet to come

Repent what's past, avoid what is to come,
And do not spread the compost on the weeds
To make them ranker. Forgive me this my virtue,
For, in the fatness of these pursy times,
Virtue itself of vice must pardon beg,   175
Yea, curb and woo for leave to do him good.

QUEEN
O Hamlet, thou hast cleft my heart in twain!

HAMLET
O, throw away the worser part of it,
And ⟨live⟩ the purer with the other half!
Good night. But go not to my uncle's bed.   180
Assume a virtue if you have it not.
[That monster, custom, who all sense doth eat,
Of habits devil, is angel yet in this,
That to the use of actions fair and good
He likewise gives a frock or livery   185
That aptly is put on.] Refrain ⟨tonight,⟩
And that shall lend a kind of easiness
To the next abstinence, [the next more easy;
For use almost can change the stamp of nature
And either ⌜. . .⌝ the devil or throw him out   190
With wondrous potency.] Once more, good night,
And, when you are desirous to be blest,
I'll blessing beg of you. For this same lord
                              ⌜*Pointing to Polonius.*⌝
I do repent; but heaven hath pleased it so
To punish me with this and this with me,   195
That I must be their scourge and minister.
I will bestow him and will answer well
The death I gave him. So, again, good night.
I must be cruel only to be kind.
This bad begins, and worse remains behind.   200
[One word more, good lady.]

QUEEN   What shall I do?

203. **Not . . . means . . . :** After this general statement of negation, Hamlet lists the things he would have Gertrude *not* do (e.g., go to bed with Claudius).

206. **reechy:** filthy

210. **'Twere good you let him know:** said very sarcastically, as are lines 211–18

212. **paddock:** toad; **gib:** tomcat

213. **Such dear concernings:** such important matters

215–18. **Unpeg the basket . . . and break your own neck down:** The story that Hamlet alludes to here is lost. **Unpeg:** unfasten **To try conclusions:** to experiment

229–30. **to have the enginer . . . petard:** to have the maker of military devices blown up by his own explosives (See page 184.)

230–31. **and 't . . . I will:** i.e., with any luck, I will

234. **packing:** leaving the country; carrying off a burden

HAMLET
Not this by no means that I bid you do:
Let the bloat king tempt you again to bed,
Pinch wanton on your cheek, call you his mouse, 205
And let him, for a pair of reechy kisses
Or paddling in your neck with his damned fingers,
Make you to ravel all this matter out
That I essentially am not in madness,
But mad in craft. 'Twere good you let him know, 210
For who that's but a queen, fair, sober, wise,
Would from a paddock, from a bat, a gib,
Such dear concernings hide? Who would do so?
No, in despite of sense and secrecy,
Unpeg the basket on the house's top, 215
Let the birds fly, and like the famous ape,
To try conclusions, in the basket creep
And break your own neck down.

QUEEN
Be thou assured, if words be made of breath
And breath of life, I have no life to breathe 220
What thou hast said to me.

HAMLET
I must to England, you know that.

QUEEN   Alack,
I had forgot! 'Tis so concluded on.

HAMLET
[There's letters sealed; and my two schoolfellows, 225
Whom I will trust as I will adders fanged,
They bear the mandate; they must sweep my way
And marshal me to knavery. Let it work,
For 'tis the sport to have the enginer
Hoist with his own petard; and 't shall go hard 230
But I will delve one yard below their mines
And blow them at the moon. O, 'tis most sweet
When in one line two crafts directly meet.]
This man shall set me packing.

239. to draw toward an end with you: to come to the end of my business with you (with a pun on **draw**, as Hamlet drags him away)

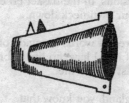

A petard. (3.4.230)
From Louis de Gaya,
A treatise of the arms . . . (1678).

I'll lug the guts into the neighbor room.   235
Mother, good night indeed. This counselor
Is now most still, most secret, and most grave,
Who was in life a foolish prating knave.—
Come, sir, to draw toward an end with you.
Good night, mother.   240
⌜*They*⌝ *exit,* ⟨*Hamlet tugging in Polonius.*⟩

The Tragedy of

HAMLET,
Prince of Denmark

ACT 4

4.1 Gertrude reports Polonius's death to Claudius, who sends Rosencrantz and Guildenstern to find Hamlet and recover the body.

———————

  1. **matter:** significance
 11. **brainish apprehension:** brain-sick belief
 12. **unseen:** hidden
 13. **heavy:** dreadful
 18. **laid to us, whose providence:** charged against me, whose foresight

⌜ACT 4⌝

⌜Scene 1⌝

Enter King and Queen, with Rosencrantz and
Guildenstern.

KING

There's matter in these sighs; these profound heaves
You must translate; 'tis fit we understand them.
Where is your son?

QUEEN

[Bestow this place on us a little while.]

⌜*Rosencrantz and Guildenstern exit.*⌝

Ah, mine own lord, what have I seen tonight!   5

KING   What, Gertrude? How does Hamlet?

QUEEN

Mad as the sea and wind when both contend
Which is the mightier. In his lawless fit,
Behind the arras hearing something stir,
Whips out his rapier, cries "A rat, a rat,"   10
And in this brainish apprehension kills
The unseen good old man.

KING   O heavy deed!

It had been so with us, had we been there.
His liberty is full of threats to all—   15
To you yourself, to us, to everyone.
Alas, how shall this bloody deed be answered?
It will be laid to us, whose providence

189

19. **short:** i.e., on a short leash; **out of haunt:** away from others

23. **divulging:** coming to light

26–27. **like . . . base:** perhaps, like a vein of gold in a mine of base metals; or, perhaps, like gold that separates out as liquid from base metals when the metal is heated

32–33. **with all our majesty . . . excuse:** i.e., with all my royal authority I must countenance, and with all my skill I must excuse

34. **join you . . . aid:** find others to help you

41. **and what's untimely done:** Both Q2 and F print this short line; the four lines following in Q2 require that some words be inserted to provide a reference for "Whose whisper" in line 42. Many editions accept the 18th-century editorial insertion of "So haply slander" to complete line 41.

43. **As level . . . blank:** with as sure an aim as the cannon hitting its mark

Should have kept short, restrained, and out of haunt
This mad young man. But so much was our love,   20
We would not understand what was most fit,
But, like the owner of a foul disease,
To keep it from divulging, let it feed
Even on the pith of life. Where is he gone?

QUEEN
To draw apart the body he hath killed,   25
O'er whom his very madness, like some ore
Among a mineral of metals base,
Shows itself pure: he weeps for what is done.

KING O Gertrude, come away!
The sun no sooner shall the mountains touch   30
But we will ship him hence; and this vile deed
We must with all our majesty and skill
Both countenance and excuse.—Ho, Guildenstern!

Enter Rosencrantz and Guildenstern.

Friends both, go join you with some further aid.
Hamlet in madness hath Polonius slain,   35
And from his mother's closet hath he dragged him.
Go seek him out, speak fair, and bring the body
Into the chapel. I pray you, haste in this.
                    ⟨*Rosencrantz and Guildenstern exit.*⟩
Come, Gertrude, we'll call up our wisest friends
And let them know both what we mean to do   40
And what's untimely done. ⌜. . .⌝
[Whose whisper o'er the world's diameter,
As level as the cannon to his blank
Transports his poisoned shot, may miss our name
And hit the woundless air.] O, come away!   45
My soul is full of discord and dismay.

                              They exit.

4.2 Hamlet refuses to tell Rosencrantz and Guild-enstern where he has put Polonius's body.

---

6. **dust . . . kin:** "for dust thou art, and unto dust shalt thou return" (Genesis 3.19)

12–13. **to be demanded . . . what replication:** being questioned by . . . what reply

15. **countenance:** favorable looks

17–18. **like an ape an apple:** as an ape keeps an apple

23. **sleeps in:** is not understood by

⌜Scene 2⌝
⟨*Enter Hamlet.*⟩

HAMLET   Safely stowed.

⟨GENTLEMEN, *within*   Hamlet! Lord Hamlet!⟩

HAMLET   But soft, what noise? Who calls on Hamlet?
  O, here they come.

    Enter Rosencrantz, ⟨Guildenstern,⟩ and others.

ROSENCRANTZ
  What have you done, my lord, with the dead body?   5
HAMLET
  ⟨Compounded⟩ it with dust, whereto 'tis kin.
ROSENCRANTZ
  Tell us where 'tis, that we may take it thence
  And bear it to the chapel.
HAMLET   Do not believe it.
ROSENCRANTZ   Believe what?   10
HAMLET   That I can keep your counsel and not mine
  own. Besides, to be demanded of a sponge, what
  replication should be made by the son of a king?
ROSENCRANTZ   Take you me for a sponge, my lord?
HAMLET   Ay, sir, that soaks up the King's countenance,   15
  his rewards, his authorities. But such officers do the
  King best service in the end. He keeps them like ⟨an
  ape⟩ an apple in the corner of his jaw, first mouthed,
  to be last swallowed. When he needs what you have
  gleaned, it is but squeezing you, and, sponge, you   20
  shall be dry again.
ROSENCRANTZ   I understand you not, my lord.
HAMLET   I am glad of it. A knavish speech sleeps in a
  foolish ear.
ROSENCRANTZ   My lord, you must tell us where the   25
  body is and go with us to the King.
HAMLET   The body is with the King, but the King is not
  with the body. The King is a thing—

30–31. Hide fox . . . : perhaps a line from a child's game like hide-and-seek

4.3 Hamlet is brought to Claudius, who tells him that he is to leave immediately for England. Alone, at the end of this scene, Claudius discloses to the audience that he is sending Hamlet to his death.

———————

4. loved of: loved by; **distracted:** unsettled
6–7. where 'tis so . . . offense: i.e., where the people love with their eyes instead of their reason, they judge the punishment (the **scourge**) rather than the crime (the **offense**)
7. To bear . . . even: to manage everything smoothly and evenly
9. Deliberate pause: the result of careful thought
9–10. Diseases . . . relieved: Proverbial: desperate diseases require desperate remedies.

GUILDENSTERN A "thing," my lord?

HAMLET Of nothing. Bring me to him. (Hide fox, and   30
all after!)

They exit.

⌜Scene 3⌉
Enter King and two or three.

KING
I have sent to seek him and to find the body.
How dangerous is it that this man goes loose!
Yet must not we put the strong law on him.
He's loved of the distracted multitude,
Who like not in their judgment, but their eyes;   5
And, where 'tis so, th' offender's scourge is weighed,
But never the offense. To bear all smooth and even,
This sudden sending him away must seem
Deliberate pause. Diseases desperate grown
By desperate appliance are relieved   10
Or not at all.

Enter Rosencrantz.

                How now, what hath befallen?

ROSENCRANTZ
Where the dead body is bestowed, my lord,
We cannot get from him.

KING   But where is he?   15

ROSENCRANTZ
Without, my lord; guarded, to know your pleasure.

KING
Bring him before us.

ROSENCRANTZ   Ho! Bring in the lord.

They enter ⌜with Hamlet.⌉

KING Now, Hamlet, where's Polonius?

HAMLET At supper.   20

23. **convocation of politic worms:** perhaps an allusion to the Diet of Worms, a **convocation** (council) summoned at the city of Worms by the Holy Roman emperor in 1521

35. **progress:** royal journey

45. **Which . . . grieve:** which we tender as dearly (value as highly) as we dearly (deeply) grieve

49. **at help:** favorable

50. **tend:** attend you, wait for you; **bent:** ready

KING At supper where?

HAMLET Not where he eats, but where he is eaten. A
  certain convocation of politic worms are e'en at
  him. Your worm is your only emperor for diet. We
  fat all creatures else to fat us, and we fat ourselves   25
  for maggots. Your fat king and your lean beggar is
  but variable service—two dishes but to one table.
  That's the end.

[KING Alas, alas!

HAMLET A man may fish with the worm that hath eat   30
  of a king and eat of the fish that hath fed of that
  worm.]

KING What dost thou mean by this?

HAMLET Nothing but to show you how a king may go a
  progress through the guts of a beggar.   35

KING Where is Polonius?

HAMLET In heaven. Send thither to see. If your messenger find him not there, seek him i' th' other
  place yourself. But if, indeed, you find him not
  within this month, you shall nose him as you go up   40
  the stairs into the lobby.

KING, ⌜to Attendants.⌝ Go, seek him there.

HAMLET He will stay till you come. ⌜Attendants exit.⌝

KING
  Hamlet, this deed, for thine especial safety
  (Which we do tender, as we dearly grieve   45
  For that which thou hast done) must send thee
    hence
  (With fiery quickness.) Therefore prepare thyself.
  The bark is ready, and the wind at help,
  Th' associates tend, and everything is bent   50
  For England.

HAMLET For England?

KING Ay, Hamlet.

HAMLET Good.

KING
  So is it, if thou knew'st our purposes.   55

56. **I see a cherub . . . :** Heaven's angels (cherubim), Hamlet suggests, can see Claudius's purposes.

63. **at foot:** at his heels, close behind

67. **England:** the king of England

68. **As . . . sense:** as my power may give you a sense thereof (i.e., of the value of retaining my love)

69. **cicatrice:** scar

70-71. **thy free awe . . . us:** i.e., awe of Denmark's power makes England pay **homage** (acknowledge allegiance, or perhaps, pay tribute) to Denmark

71-72. **thou . . . process:** i.e., England may not lightly regard my royal command

74. **present:** immediate

75. **the hectic:** continual fever

77. **Howe'er my haps:** whatever my fortunes

4.4 Fortinbras and his army march across Hamlet's path on their way to Poland. Hamlet finds in Fortinbras's vigorous activity a model for himself in avenging his father's murder; Hamlet resolves upon bloody action.

2-4. **by his license . . . Over his kingdom:** in formal language, Fortinbras, having been given **license** from Claudius to **march** across Denmark, now asks for an escort (see 2.2.81-85) **conveyance of:** escort during

HAMLET
I see a cherub that sees them. But come, for
  England.
Farewell, dear mother.

KING   Thy loving father, Hamlet.

HAMLET
My mother. Father and mother is man and wife,   60
Man and wife is one flesh, ⟨and⟩ so, my mother.—
Come, for England.   *He exits.*

KING
Follow him at foot; tempt him with speed aboard.
Delay it not. I'll have him hence tonight.
Away, for everything is sealed and done   65
That else leans on th' affair. Pray you, make haste.
                    ⌜*All but the King exit.*⌝
And England, if my love thou hold'st at aught
(As my great power thereof may give thee sense,
Since yet thy cicatrice looks raw and red
After the Danish sword, and thy free awe   70
Pays homage to us), thou mayst not coldly set
Our sovereign process, which imports at full,
By letters congruing to that effect,
The present death of Hamlet. Do it, England,
For like the hectic in my blood he rages,   75
And thou must cure me. Till I know 'tis done,
Howe'er my haps, my joys ⟨were ne'er begun.⟩
                    He exits.

                    ⌜Scene 4⌝
        Enter Fortinbras with his army over the stage.

FORTINBRAS
Go, Captain, from me greet the Danish king.
Tell him that by his license Fortinbras
Craves the conveyance of a promised march
Over his kingdom. You know the rendezvous.

5. **would aught with us:** wishes anything of me
(Note his use of the royal "we.")

6. **in his eye:** in his presence

9. **softly:** slowly

16. **the main:** the main part

18. **with no addition:** without added details

20. **the name:** the mere name of conquest

21. **To pay . . . farm it:** I would not pay five ducats
to rent it

23. **ranker:** higher; **in fee:** outright

27. **Will not debate . . . this straw:** are not enough
to pay for settling this trifling quarrel

28. **impostume:** abscess

29. **without:** on the outside

If that his Majesty would aught with us,   5
We shall express our duty in his eye;
And let him know so.
CAPTAIN   I will do 't, my lord.
FORTINBRAS   Go softly on.   ⌜*All but the Captain exit.*⌝

[*Enter Hamlet, Rosencrantz,* ⌜*Guildenstern,*⌝ *and others.*

HAMLET   Good sir, whose powers are these?   10
CAPTAIN   They are of Norway, sir.
HAMLET   How purposed, sir, I pray you?
CAPTAIN   Against some part of Poland.
HAMLET   Who commands them, sir?
CAPTAIN
The nephew to old Norway, Fortinbras.   15
HAMLET
Goes it against the main of Poland, sir,
Or for some frontier?
CAPTAIN
Truly to speak, and with no addition,
We go to gain a little patch of ground
That hath in it no profit but the name.   20
To pay five ducats, five, I would not farm it;
Nor will it yield to Norway or the Pole
A ranker rate, should it be sold in fee.
HAMLET
Why, then, the Polack never will defend it.
CAPTAIN
Yes, it is already garrisoned.   25
HAMLET
Two thousand souls and twenty thousand ducats
Will not debate the question of this straw.
This is th' impostume of much wealth and peace,
That inward breaks and shows no cause without
Why the man dies.—I humbly thank you, sir.   30
CAPTAIN   God be wi' you, sir.   ⌜*He exits.*⌝
ROSENCRANTZ   Will 't please you go, my lord?

34. **inform against:** denounce

38–39. **discourse, . . . before and after:** power of thought that looks into the past and the future

41. **fust:** become moldy

42. **Bestial oblivion:** mindlessness like the beasts'

42–43. **craven scruple / Of thinking:** cowardly hesitation that results from thinking

49. **gross as earth:** as evident as the earth itself

53. **Makes mouths at:** makes faces at (i.e., holds in contempt)

56–59. **Rightly . . . at the stake:** i.e., to be truly great, one should not fight except when the argument is itself great, unless honor is at risk   **at the stake:** at risk (as in gambling)

64. **trick of fame:** illusion of honor

66. **Whereon . . . cause:** on which the numbers of fighting men do not have room to fight the battle

HAMLET
  I'll be with you straight. Go a little before.
                      ⌈*All but Hamlet exit.*⌉
  How all occasions do inform against me
  And spur my dull revenge. What is a man   35
  If his chief good and market of his time
  Be but to sleep and feed? A beast, no more.
  Sure He that made us with such large discourse,
  Looking before and after, gave us not
  That capability and godlike reason   40
  To fust in us unused. Now whether it be
  Bestial oblivion or some craven scruple
  Of thinking too precisely on th' event
  (A thought which, quartered, hath but one part
    wisdom   45
  And ever three parts coward), I do not know
  Why yet I live to say "This thing's to do,"
  Sith I have cause, and will, and strength, and means
  To do 't. Examples gross as earth exhort me:
  Witness this army of such mass and charge,   50
  Led by a delicate and tender prince,
  Whose spirit with divine ambition puffed
  Makes mouths at the invisible event,
  Exposing what is mortal and unsure
  To all that fortune, death, and danger dare,   55
  Even for an eggshell. Rightly to be great
  Is not to stir without great argument,
  But greatly to find quarrel in a straw
  When honor's at the stake. How stand I, then,
  That have a father killed, a mother stained,   60
  Excitements of my reason and my blood,
  And let all sleep, while to my shame I see
  The imminent death of twenty thousand men
  That for a fantasy and trick of fame
  Go to their graves like beds, fight for a plot   65
  Whereon the numbers cannot try the cause,

67–68. Which is not . . . hide the slain: which is not large enough to be a tomb or receptacle for those who will be killed   **continent:** container

---

4.5 Reports reach Gertrude that Ophelia is mad. Ophelia enters singing about death and betrayal. After Ophelia has gone, Claudius agonizes over her madness and over the stir created by the return of an angry Laertes. When Laertes breaks in on Claudius and Gertrude, Claudius asserts his innocence with regard to Polonius's death. The reappearance of the mad Ophelia is devastating to Laertes.

---

3. **distract:** distraught; **will needs be:** must be
6. **tricks:** plots, deception
8. **Spurns enviously at straws:** takes offense angrily at trifles; **in doubt:** obscurely (?)
9–11. **Her speech . . . to collection:** her speech makes no sense, but its very formlessness makes her hearers draw conclusions
12. **botch . . . up:** patch together
13–15. **Which . . . make one think:** the words, together with her gestures, would make one think
22. **as sin's true nature is:** i.e., sin, in its true nature, is a sickness of the soul
23. **toy:** trifle; **amiss:** disaster
24. **artless:** awkward, stupid; **jealousy:** unreasonable suspicions
25. **spills:** destroys; **spilt:** divulged

Which is not tomb enough and continent
To hide the slain? O, from this time forth
My thoughts be bloody or be nothing worth!

⌜*He exits.*⌝

⌜Scene 5⌝
Enter Horatio, ⟨Queen,⟩ and a Gentleman.

QUEEN   I will not speak with her.
GENTLEMAN   She is importunate,
  Indeed distract; her mood will needs be pitied.
QUEEN   What would she have?
GENTLEMAN
  She speaks much of her father, says she hears   5
  There's tricks i' th' world, and hems, and beats her
    heart,
  Spurns enviously at straws, speaks things in doubt
  That carry but half sense. Her speech is nothing,
  Yet the unshapèd use of it doth move   10
  The hearers to collection. They ⟨aim⟩ at it
  And botch the words up fit to their own thoughts;
  Which, as her winks and nods and gestures yield
    them,
  Indeed would make one think there might be   15
    thought,
  Though nothing sure, yet much unhappily.
HORATIO
  'Twere good she were spoken with, for she may
    strew
  Dangerous conjectures in ill-breeding minds.   20
QUEEN   Let her come in.   ⌜*Gentleman exits.*⌝
  ⌜*Aside.*⌝ To my sick soul (as sin's true nature is),
  Each toy seems prologue to some great amiss.
  So full of artless jealousy is guilt,
  It spills itself in fearing to be spilt.   25

28–31. **How should I . . . shoon:** Ophelia sings a version of a ballad preserved in many editions of music of the time. The song continues in lines 34–37 and 41, 43–45.

30. **cockle hat:** A hat with a cockle shell denoted a pilgrim returning from the shrine of St. James of Compostela.

31. **shoon:** shoes

44. **did not go:** The word "not" has been inserted into the ballad, perhaps as Ophelia's addition, or perhaps by mistake by the printer.

47. **God dild you:** God yield (reward) you

47–48. **the owl . . . daughter:** According to an old story, an ungenerous baker's daughter was transformed into an owl as punishment for her stinginess.

50. **Conceit upon:** i.e., (she is) thinking about

Pilgrim with cockle hat and staff. (4.5.30)
From Henry Peacham, *Minerua Britanna* (1612).

(Enter Ophelia distracted.)

OPHELIA
Where is the beauteous Majesty of Denmark?

QUEEN How now, Ophelia?

OPHELIA ⌜*sings*⌝
How should I your true love know
From another one?
By his cockle hat and staff   30
And his sandal shoon.

QUEEN
Alas, sweet lady, what imports this song?

OPHELIA Say you? Nay, pray you, mark.
⌜*Sings.*⌝ *He is dead and gone, lady,*
He is dead and gone;   35
At his head a grass-green turf,
At his heels a stone.

Oh, ho!

QUEEN Nay, but Ophelia—

OPHELIA Pray you, mark.   40
⌜*Sings.*⌝ *White his shroud as the mountain snow—*

Enter King.

QUEEN Alas, look here, my lord.

OPHELIA ⌜*sings*⌝
Larded all with sweet flowers;
Which bewept to the ground did not go
With true-love showers.   45

KING How do you, pretty lady?

OPHELIA Well, God dild you. They say the owl was a
baker's daughter. Lord, we know what we are but
know not what we may be. God be at your table.

KING Conceit upon her father.   50

OPHELIA Pray let's have no words of this, but when
they ask you what it means, say you this:

53–60. Tomorrow . . . more: The song alludes to the ancient custom that the first girl a man sees on Valentine's day is to be his truelove. The song continues in lines 63–68, 70–71. **betime:** early **dupped:** opened

63. Gis: Jesus

66. Cock: a substitution for "God" in oaths

74. cannot . . . weep: cannot help weeping

83. spies: individual soldiers sent by the army to scout out the territory

85–86. most violent . . . remove: the cause, through his violence, of his justly earned removal **author:** cause

86. muddied: stirred up, confused

⌜*Sings.*⌝ Tomorrow is Saint Valentine's day,
    All in the morning betime,
    And I a maid at your window,   55
    To be your Valentine.
    Then up he rose and donned his clothes
    And dupped the chamber door,
    Let in the maid, that out a maid
    Never departed more.   60

KING Pretty Ophelia—

OPHELIA
  Indeed, without an oath, I'll make an end on 't:
⌜*Sings.*⌝ By Gis and by Saint Charity,
    Alack and fie for shame,
    Young men will do 't, if they come to 't;   65
    By Cock, they are to blame.
    Quoth she "Before you tumbled me,
    You promised me to wed."
He answers:
    "So would I 'a done, by yonder sun,   70
    An thou hadst not come to my bed."

KING How long hath she been thus?

OPHELIA I hope all will be well. We must be patient,
  but I cannot choose but weep to think they would
  lay him i' th' cold ground. My brother shall know of   75
  it. And so I thank you for your good counsel. Come,
  my coach! Good night, ladies, good night, sweet
  ladies, good night, good night.   ⟨*She exits.*⟩

KING
  Follow her close; give her good watch, I pray you.
              ⌜*Horatio exits.*⌝
  O, this is the poison of deep grief. It springs   80
  All from her father's death, and now behold!
  O Gertrude, Gertrude,
  When sorrows come, they come not single spies,
  But in battalions: first, her father slain;
  Next, your son gone, and he most violent author   85
  Of his own just remove; the people muddied,

89–90. **we have . . . greenly:** I have acted foolishly

91. **In hugger-mugger:** without proper ceremony

96. **in clouds:** i.e., in a cloud of suspicion

97. **wants not buzzers:** does not lack gossipers

99. **of matter beggared:** lacking facts

100. **Will nothing stick . . . arraign:** not hesitate to accuse me of the crime

101–3. **this . . . superfluous death:** this (battalion of troubles) kills me over and over, as if I were shot at by a **murd'ring piece,** a cannon that scatters its shots

105. **Attend:** listen

106. **Switzers:** Swiss bodyguards

109–12. **The ocean . . . your officers:** i.e., Laertes and his followers are overbearing the king's officers as quickly and pitilessly as an ocean flooding its flatlands **overpeering of his list:** overflowing its shore **head:** armed force

113–16. **as the world . . . They cry:** as if the world were to begin right now, with tradition and custom completely forgotten **ratifiers and props of every word:** probably refers to **Antiquity** and **custom,** the supports of words and promises

117. **Caps:** Their caps, that is, are thrown into the air.

Thick, and unwholesome in ⟨their⟩ thoughts and
　　whispers
For good Polonius' death, and we have done but
　　greenly　　　　　　　　　　　　　　　　　　　90
In hugger-mugger to inter him; poor Ophelia
Divided from herself and her fair judgment,
Without the which we are pictures or mere beasts;
Last, and as much containing as all these,
Her brother is in secret come from France,　　　95
Feeds on ⟨his⟩ wonder, keeps himself in clouds,
And wants not buzzers to infect his ear
With pestilent speeches of his father's death,
Wherein necessity, of matter beggared,
Will nothing stick our person to arraign　　　　100
In ear and ear. O, my dear Gertrude, this,
Like to a murd'ring piece, in many places
Gives me superfluous death.

　　　　　　　　　　　　　　　　A noise within.

⟨QUEEN　Alack, what noise is this?⟩
KING　Attend!　　　　　　　　　　　　　　　　105
　　Where is my Switzers? Let them guard the door.

　　　　　　　　　Enter a Messenger.

　　What is the matter?
MESSENGER　　　　　　Save yourself, my lord.
　　The ocean, overpeering of his list,
　　Eats not the flats with more impiteous haste　　110
　　Than young Laertes, in a riotous head,
　　O'erbears your officers. The rabble call him "lord,"
　　And, as the world were now but to begin,
　　Antiquity forgot, custom not known,
　　The ratifiers and props of every word,　　　　115
　　⟨They⟩ cry "Choose we, Laertes shall be king!"
　　Caps, hands, and tongues applaud it to the clouds,
　　"Laertes shall be king! Laertes king!"

　　　　　　　　　　　　　　　　A noise within.

120. **counter:** In hunting, a dog goes "counter" when it follows the trail in the wrong direction.
122. **without:** outside
132. **cuckold:** betrayed husband
134. **true:** faithful, chaste
137. **fear our:** fear for my
139. **would:** i.e., what it would like to do
140. **his:** its

QUEEN
  How cheerfully on the false trail they cry.
  O, this is counter, you false Danish dogs!   120
KING The doors are broke.

                Enter Laertes with others.

LAERTES
  Where is this king?—Sirs, stand you all without.
ALL No, let's come in!
LAERTES I pray you, give me leave.
ALL We will, we will.   125
LAERTES
  I thank you. Keep the door. ⌜*Followers exit.*⌝ O, thou
    vile king,
  Give me my father!
QUEEN   Calmly, good Laertes.
LAERTES
  That drop of blood that's calm proclaims me   130
    bastard,
  Cries "cuckold" to my father, brands the harlot
  Even here between the chaste unsmirchèd brow
  Of my true mother.
KING   What is the cause, Laertes,   135
  That thy rebellion looks so giant-like?—
  Let him go, Gertrude. Do not fear our person.
  There's such divinity doth hedge a king
  That treason can but peep to what it would,
  Acts little of his will.—Tell me, Laertes,   140
  Why thou art thus incensed.—Let him go,
    Gertrude.—
  Speak, man.
LAERTES Where is my father?
KING Dead.   145
QUEEN
  But not by him.
KING   Let him demand his fill.

148. **juggled with:** manipulated and thus deceived

152. **both . . . negligence:** I don't care what happens to me in this world or the next

154. **throughly:** thoroughly

162. **swoopstake:** a term from gambling, as is **draw**; literally, take all the stakes on the gambling table (Here the meaning is "are you determined to take revenge on friends and enemies both?")

168. **life-rend'ring pelican:** The mother pelican was thought to feed her young with her own blood.

173. **sensibly:** intensely

174. **level:** intelligible, plain

179. **virtue:** power

LAERTES
  How came he dead? I'll not be juggled with.
  To hell, allegiance! Vows, to the blackest devil!
  Conscience and grace, to the profoundest pit!   150
  I dare damnation. To this point I stand,
  That both the worlds I give to negligence,
  Let come what comes, only I'll be revenged
  Most throughly for my father.
KING Who shall stay you?   155
LAERTES My will, not all the ⟨world.⟩
  And for my means, I'll husband them so well
  They shall go far with little.
KING   Good Laertes,
  If you desire to know the certainty   160
  Of your dear father, is 't writ in your revenge
  That, swoopstake, you will draw both friend and
     foe,
  Winner and loser?
LAERTES None but his enemies.   165
KING Will you know them, then?
LAERTES
  To his good friends thus wide I'll ope my arms
  And, like the kind life-rend'ring pelican,
  Repast them with my blood.
KING   Why, now you speak   170
  Like a good child and a true gentleman.
  That I am guiltless of your father's death
  And am most sensibly in grief for it,
  It shall as level to your judgment 'pear
  As day does to your eye.   175
            A noise within: ⟨Let her come in.
LAERTES⟩ How now, what noise is that?

        Enter Ophelia.

  O heat, dry up my brains! Tears seven times salt
  Burn out the sense and virtue of mine eye!

180–81. **paid . . . beam:** avenged (The image is of putting an excess of weight in one scale until it overbalances the other scale, or **turns the beam.**)

185. **fine in:** refined by

186. **instance of itself:** sample or proof of its refined nature (In this case, the sample is Ophelia's wits, which, Laertes says, have been sent after the dead Polonius.)

193. **could not move thus:** could not be this moving

194–95. **You must sing ". . . a-down-a":** Ophelia perhaps instructs others on the stage to sing refrains to her song.

195. **the wheel:** perhaps, the refrain of the song; or, perhaps the turning of the spinning wheel, to which motion ballads were sung

196. **false steward:** perhaps a reference to a story or ballad no longer known

198. **This nothing's . . . matter:** this nonsense speaks more eloquently than does serious speech

199. **There's rosemary:** Ophelia begins here to distribute real or imaginary flowers.

202. **document:** lesson, instruction

202–3. **thoughts . . . fitted:** i.e., Ophelia has wisely linked **thoughts** and **remembrance**

204. **fennel:** In flower symbolism, fennel symbolized flattery and deceit.

205. **rue:** symbol of sorrow or repentance

207. **with a difference:** a heraldic term for a variation in a coat of arms, but here meaning, perhaps, "for a different reason"; **daisy:** symbol of dissembling

208. **violets:** symbol of faithfulness

211. **Thought:** melancholy; **passion:** suffering

By heaven, thy madness shall be paid with weight 180
Till our scale turn the beam! O rose of May,
Dear maid, kind sister, sweet Ophelia!
O heavens, is 't possible a young maid's wits
Should be as mortal as ⟨an old⟩ man's life?
⟨Nature is fine in love, and, where 'tis fine, 185
It sends some precious instance of itself
After the thing it loves.⟩

OPHELIA ⌜*sings*⌝
  They bore him barefaced on the bier,
  ⟨*Hey non nonny, nonny, hey nonny,*⟩
  And in his grave rained many a tear. 190
Fare you well, my dove.

LAERTES
Hadst thou thy wits and didst persuade revenge,
It could not move thus.

OPHELIA You must sing "A-down a-down"—and you
"Call him a-down-a."—O, how the wheel becomes 195
it! It is the false steward that stole his master's
daughter.

LAERTES This nothing's more than matter.

OPHELIA There's rosemary, that's for remembrance.
Pray you, love, remember. And there is pansies, 200
that's for thoughts.

LAERTES A document in madness: thoughts and remembrance fitted.

OPHELIA There's fennel for you, and columbines.
There's rue for you, and here's some for me; we 205
may call it herb of grace o' Sundays. You ⟨must⟩ wear
your rue with a difference. There's a daisy. I would
give you some violets, but they withered all when
my father died. They say he made a good end.
⌜*Sings.*⌝ *For bonny sweet Robin is all my joy.* 210

LAERTES
Thought and afflictions, passion, hell itself
She turns to favor and to prettiness.

219. **poll:** head
230. **collateral:** i.e., as an accessory
231. **find us touched:** find me implicated
239. **hatchment:** tablet displaying his coat of arms
240. **ostentation:** ceremony
242. **That:** so that

Rosemary. (4.5.199)
From *The grete herball . . .* (1529).

OPHELIA ⌈*sings*⌉

>*And will he not come again?*
>*And will he not come again?*
>>*No, no, he is dead.*
>>*Go to thy deathbed.*
>*He never will come again.*

>*His beard was as white as snow,*
>⟨*All*⟩ *flaxen was his poll.*
>>*He is gone, he is gone,*
>>*And we cast away moan.*
>*God 'a mercy on his soul.*

And of all Christians' souls, ⟨I pray God.⟩ God be wi'
you.   ⟨*She exits.*⟩

LAERTES Do you ⟨see⟩ this, O God?   225

KING
  Laertes, I must commune with your grief,
  Or you deny me right. Go but apart,
  Make choice of whom your wisest friends you will,
  And they shall hear and judge 'twixt you and me.
  If by direct or by collateral hand   230
  They find us touched, we will our kingdom give,
  Our crown, our life, and all that we call ours,
  To you in satisfaction; but if not,
  Be you content to lend your patience to us,
  And we shall jointly labor with your soul   235
  To give it due content.

LAERTES   Let this be so.
  His means of death, his obscure funeral
  (No trophy, sword, nor hatchment o'er his bones,
  No noble rite nor formal ostentation)   240
  Cry to be heard, as 'twere from heaven to earth,
  That I must call 't in question.

KING   So you shall,
  And where th' offense is, let the great ax fall.
  I pray you, go with me.   245

                                    They exit.

4.6 Horatio is given a letter from Hamlet telling of the prince's boarding of a pirate ship and his subsequent return to Denmark.

---

10. **th' ambassador:** i.e., Hamlet

14. **overlooked:** read; **means:** means of access

16. **pirate . . . appointment:** pirate ship well equipped for battle

17–18. **put on a compelled valor:** became, under compulsion, courageous

21. **thieves of mercy:** merciful thieves

23. **repair thou:** come

25–26. **too light for the bore of the matter:** too light for the caliber of the gun; i.e., inadequate

⌜Scene 6⌝
Enter Horatio and others.

HORATIO What are they that would speak with me?

GENTLEMAN Seafaring men, sir. They say they have
letters for you.

HORATIO Let them come in. ⌜*Gentleman exits.*⌝ I do not
know from what part of the world I should be   5
greeted, if not from Lord Hamlet.

Enter Sailors.

SAILOR God bless you, sir.

HORATIO Let Him bless thee too.

SAILOR He shall, sir, ⟨an 't⟩ please Him. There's a letter
for you, sir. It came from th' ambassador that was   10
bound for England—if your name be Horatio, as I
am let to know it is.   ⌜*He hands Horatio a letter.*⌝

HORATIO ⟨*reads the letter*⟩ *Horatio, when thou shalt have
overlooked this, give these fellows some means to the
King. They have letters for him. Ere we were two days*   15
*old at sea, a pirate of very warlike appointment gave
us chase. Finding ourselves too slow of sail, we put on
a compelled valor, and in the grapple I boarded them.
On the instant, they got clear of our ship; so I alone
became their prisoner. They have dealt with me like*   20
*thieves of mercy, but they knew what they did: I am to
do a ⟨good⟩ turn for them. Let the King have the letters
I have sent, and repair thou to me with as much speed
as thou wouldst fly death. I have words to speak in
thine ear will make thee dumb; yet are they much too*   25
*light for the ⟨bore⟩ of the matter. These good fellows
will bring thee where I am. Rosencrantz and Guildenstern hold their course for England; of them I have
much to tell thee. Farewell.*

⟨*He*⟩ *that thou knowest thine,*   30
Hamlet.

32. **way:** means of access

4.7 Claudius, in conversation with Laertes, also gets a letter from Hamlet announcing the prince's return. Claudius enlists Laertes's willing help in devising another plot against Hamlet's life. Laertes agrees to kill Hamlet with a poisoned rapier in a fencing match. If he fails, Claudius will give Hamlet a poisoned cup of wine. Gertrude interrupts their plotting to announce that Ophelia has drowned.

---

1. **my acquittance seal:** ratify my acquittal, i.e., acknowledge my innocence
8. **capital:** deadly
10. **mainly:** greatly
12. **unsinewed:** weak
16. **conjunctive:** closely joined
17. **star . . . sphere:** In Ptolemaic astronomy each planet (**star**) was carried around earth in a crystalline sphere from which it was inseparable.
19. **count:** accounting, judgment
20. **the general gender:** the common people
22. **Work . . . stone:** function like springs of water that petrify wood
23. **Convert his gyves:** transform his shackles

Come, I will ⟨give⟩ you way for these your letters
And do 't the speedier that you may direct me
To him from whom you brought them.

They exit.

⌜Scene 7⌝
Enter King and Laertes.

KING
Now must your conscience my acquittance seal,
And you must put me in your heart for friend,
Sith you have heard, and with a knowing ear,
That he which hath your noble father slain
Pursued my life.   5
LAERTES   It well appears. But tell me
Why you ⟨proceeded⟩ not against these feats,
So criminal and so capital in nature,
As by your safety, greatness, wisdom, all things else,
You mainly were stirred up.   10
KING   O, for two special reasons,
Which may to you perhaps seem much unsinewed,
But yet to me they're strong. The Queen his mother
Lives almost by his looks, and for myself
(My virtue or my plague, be it either which),   15
She is so ⟨conjunctive⟩ to my life and soul
That, as the star moves not but in his sphere,
I could not but by her. The other motive
Why to a public count I might not go
Is the great love the general gender bear him,   20
Who, dipping all his faults in their affection,
Work like the spring that turneth wood to stone,
Convert his gyves to graces, so that my arrows,
Too slightly timbered for so ⟨loud a wind,⟩
Would have reverted to my bow again,   25
But not where I have aimed them.
LAERTES
And so have I a noble father lost,

28. **terms:** condition

29. **if praises . . . again:** if I may praise what she used to be

30–31. **Stood challenger . . . perfections:** her worth challenged all the age to equal her excellence

50. **naked:** defenseless

52. **pardon:** permission

57. **character:** handwriting

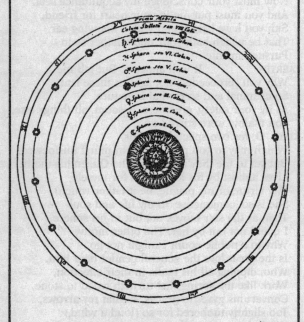

Ptolemaic universe. (4.7.17)
From Marcus Manilius, *The sphere of . . .* (1675).

A sister driven into desp'rate terms,
Whose worth, if praises may go back again.
Stood challenger on mount of all the age   30
For her perfections. But my revenge will come.

KING
Break not your sleeps for that. You must not think
That we are made of stuff so flat and dull
That we can let our beard be shook with danger
And think it pastime. You shortly shall hear more. 35
I loved your father, and we love ourself,
And that, I hope, will teach you to imagine—

Enter a Messenger with letters.

⟨How now? What news?⟩
MESSENGER   Letters, my lord, from
  Hamlet.⟩   40
  These to your Majesty, this to the Queen.
KING   From Hamlet? Who brought them?
MESSENGER
  Sailors, my lord, they say. I saw them not.
  They were given me by Claudio. He received them
  [Of him that brought them.]   45
KING   Laertes, you shall hear
  them.—
  Leave us.   ⟨*Messenger exits.*⟩
  ⌐Reads.⌐ *High and mighty, you shall know I am set*
  naked on your kingdom. Tomorrow shall I beg leave to 50
  see your kingly eyes, when I shall (first asking ⟨your⟩
  pardon) thereunto recount the occasion of my sudden
  ⟨and more strange⟩ return. ⟨Hamlet.⟩
  What should this mean? Are all the rest come back?
  Or is it some abuse and no such thing?   55
LAERTES   Know you the hand?
KING   'Tis Hamlet's character. "Naked"—
  And in a postscript here, he says "alone."
  Can you ⟨advise⟩ me?

68. **So:** provided that

70. **checking at:** refusing to continue (The image is of a falcon in flight turning away from the prey she is supposed to be pursuing.); **that:** if that (i.e., if)

72. **device:** devising, planning

75. **uncharge the practice:** not blame his death on our plot **uncharge:** lift a burden from **practice:** stratagem, treachery

79. **organ:** agent, instrument

83. **Your . . . parts:** all of your qualities combined

86. **unworthiest siege:** least important rank

88. **A very . . . youth:** a mere decoration in youth's cap

89–92. **youth no less becomes . . . graveness:** i.e., clothes worn by youth are as becoming to the young as the garments of age are to their comfortably prosperous wearers **sables:** rich robes with sable trim **weeds:** garments **Importing:** signifying

LAERTES
I am lost in it, my lord. But let him come.   60
It warms the very sickness in my heart
That I ⟨shall⟩ live and tell him to his teeth
"Thus didst thou."

KING   If it be so, Laertes
(As how should it be so? how otherwise?),   65
Will you be ruled by me?

LAERTES   Ay, my lord,
So you will not o'errule me to a peace.

KING
To thine own peace. If he be now returned,
As ⟨checking⟩ at his voyage, and that he means   70
No more to undertake it, I will work him
To an exploit, now ripe in my device,
Under the which he shall not choose but fall;
And for his death no wind of blame shall breathe,
But even his mother shall uncharge the practice   75
And call it accident.

[**LAERTES**   My lord, I will be ruled,
The rather if you could devise it so
That I might be the organ.

KING   It falls right.   80
You have been talked of since your travel much,
And that in Hamlet's hearing, for a quality
Wherein they say you shine. Your sum of parts
Did not together pluck such envy from him
As did that one, and that, in my regard,   85
Of the unworthiest siege.

LAERTES   What part is that, my lord?

KING
A very ribbon in the cap of youth—
Yet needful too, for youth no less becomes
The light and careless livery that it wears   90
Than settled age his sables and his weeds,
Importing health and graveness.] Two months since

95. **can well:** are skillful

98. **As had he been:** as if he had been; **encorpsed and demi-natured:** made into a single body (with the horse) to form a double-natured creature like the centaur (half man, half horse)

99. **brave:** noble; **topped:** surpassed

100–1. **in forgery . . . he did:** in imagining his feats, I fall short of his actual performance

108. **made confession of you:** acknowledged you

110. **art and exercise . . . defense:** theory and practice of fencing

113. **'scrimers:** fencers (French *escrimeurs*)

119. **play:** fence

A centaur. (4.7.98)
From Gabriel Rollenhagen,
Nucleus emblematum selectissimorum (1611).

Here was a gentleman of Normandy.
I have seen myself, and served against, the French,
And they can well on horseback, but this gallant   95
Had witchcraft in 't. He grew unto his seat,
And to such wondrous doing brought his horse
As had he been encorpsed and demi-natured
With the brave beast. So far he topped ⟨my⟩ thought
That I in forgery of shapes and tricks   100
Come short of what he did.

LAERTES   A Norman was 't?

KING   A Norman.

LAERTES
Upon my life, Lamord.

KING   The very same.   105

LAERTES
I know him well. He is the brooch indeed
And gem of all the nation.

KING   He made confession of you
And gave you such a masterly report
For art and exercise in your defense,   110
And for your rapier most especial,
That he cried out 'twould be a sight indeed
If one could match you. [The 'scrimers of their
   nation
He swore had neither motion, guard, nor eye,   115
If you opposed them.] Sir, this report of his
Did Hamlet so envenom with his envy
That he could nothing do but wish and beg
Your sudden coming-o'er, to play with you.
Now out of this—   120

LAERTES   What out of this, my lord?

KING
Laertes, was your father dear to you?
Or are you like the painting of a sorrow,
A face without a heart?

LAERTES   Why ask you this?   125

128. **passages of proof:** proven instances

129. **qualifies:** diminishes, lessens

131. **snuff:** the burned part of the wick of a candle

132. **is at a like goodness still:** remains always at the same level of perfection

133. **pleurisy:** excess (not to be confused with the disease of the same name)

134. **his own too-much:** its own excess

139-40. **spendthrift . . . by easing:** According to old notions of medicine, a sigh eases distress but draws blood away from the heart.

140. **to . . . th' ulcer:** i.e., to the main point

142. **indeed:** in fact; also, in action

145. **should murder sanctuarize:** i.e., should protect a murderer (like Hamlet) from punishment

149. **put on those shall:** incite those who shall

151. **in fine:** in conclusion

153. **remiss:** carelessly indifferent

154. **generous:** noble-minded

157. **unbated:** not blunted (as rapiers for such matches should be); **a pass of practice:** a treacherous thrust

KING

  Not that I think you did not love your father,
  But that I know love is begun by time
  And that I see, in passages of proof,
  Time qualifies the spark and fire of it.
  [There lives within the very flame of love   130
  A kind of wick or snuff that will abate it,
  And nothing is at a like goodness still;
  For goodness, growing to a pleurisy,
  Dies in his own too-much. That we would do
  We should do when we would; for this "would"   135
    changes
  And hath abatements and delays as many
  As there are tongues, are hands, are accidents;
  And then this "should" is like a ⌜spendthrift⌝ sigh,
  That hurts by easing. But to the quick of th' ulcer:] 140
  Hamlet comes back; what would you undertake
  To show yourself indeed your father's son
  More than in words?

LAERTES   To cut his throat i' th' church.

KING

  No place indeed should murder sanctuarize;   145
  Revenge should have no bounds. But, good Laertes,
  Will you do this? Keep close within your chamber.
  Hamlet, returned, shall know you are come home.
  We'll put on those shall praise your excellence
  And set a double varnish on the fame   150
  The Frenchman gave you; bring you, in fine,
    together
  And wager ⟨on⟩ your heads. He, being remiss,
  Most generous, and free from all contriving,
  Will not peruse the foils, so that with ease,   155
  Or with a little shuffling, you may choose
  A sword unbated, and in a ⟨pass⟩ of practice
  Requite him for your father.

161. **of a mountebank:** from a quack doctor
162. **mortal:** deadly
163. **cataplasm:** poultice
164. **Collected from:** composed of; **simples:** medicinal plants; **virtue:** medicinal power
167. **contagion:** poison that infects the blood
167–68. **if . . . death:** if I scratch him he will die
171. **May fit us to our shape:** may suit our plan
172–73. **drift . . . performance:** intention reveal itself through our bungling
175. **back or second:** backup position
176. **blast in proof:** blow up in the testing
177. **your cunnings:** yours and Hamlet's skills
184. **stuck:** thrust (a fencing term)
190. **askant:** aslant

LAERTES   I will do 't,
  And for ⟨that⟩ purpose I'll anoint my sword.   160
  I bought an unction of a mountebank
  So mortal that, but dip a knife in it,
  Where it draws blood no cataplasm so rare,
  Collected from all simples that have virtue
  Under the moon, can save the thing from death   165
  That is but scratched withal. I'll touch my point
  With this contagion, that, if I gall him slightly,
  It may be death.
KING   Let's further think of this,
  Weigh what convenience both of time and means   170
  May fit us to our shape. If this should fail,
  And that our drift look through our bad
      performance,
  'Twere better not assayed. Therefore this project
  Should have a back or second that might hold   175
  If this did blast in proof. Soft, let me see.
  We'll make a solemn wager on your cunnings—
  I ha 't!
  When in your motion you are hot and dry
  (As make your bouts more violent to that end)   180
  And that he calls for drink, I'll have prepared
      him
  A chalice for the nonce, whereon but sipping,
  If he by chance escape your venomed stuck,
  Our purpose may hold there.—But stay, what   185
      noise?

                    Enter Queen.

QUEEN
  One woe doth tread upon another's heel,
  So fast they follow. Your sister's drowned, Laertes.
LAERTES Drowned? O, where?
QUEEN
  There is a willow grows askant the brook   190

191. **hoar:** gray
192. **Therewith:** i.e., with willow garlands
193. **long purples:** orchids
194. **liberal:** plainspoken
195. **cold:** chaste
198. **envious sliver:** malicious branch
202. **lauds:** hymns
203. **incapable of:** without ability to understand
204. **endued:** naturally adapted
213. **It . . . trick:** i.e., weeping is natural
214–15. **When these . . . out:** when these tears are shed, my female-like weakness will be spent

That shows his ⟨hoar⟩ leaves in the glassy stream.
Therewith fantastic garlands did she make
Of crowflowers, nettles, daisies, and long purples,
That liberal shepherds give a grosser name,
But our cold maids do "dead men's fingers" call   195
  them.
There on the pendant boughs her coronet weeds
Clamb'ring to hang, an envious sliver broke,
When down her weedy trophies and herself
Fell in the weeping brook. Her clothes spread wide, 200
And mermaid-like awhile they bore her up,
Which time she chanted snatches of old lauds,
As one incapable of her own distress
Or like a creature native and endued
Unto that element. But long it could not be   205
Till that her garments, heavy with their drink,
Pulled the poor wretch from her melodious lay
To muddy death.

LAERTES   Alas, then she is drowned.

QUEEN Drowned, drowned.   210

LAERTES
Too much of water hast thou, poor Ophelia,
And therefore I forbid my tears. But yet
It is our trick; nature her custom holds,
Let shame say what it will. When these are gone,
The woman will be out.—Adieu, my lord.   215
I have a speech o' fire that fain would blaze,
But that this folly drowns it.   *He exits.*

KING   Let's follow, Gertrude.
How much I had to do to calm his rage!
Now fear I this will give it start again.   220
Therefore, let's follow.

                    They exit.

The Tragedy of

HAMLET,
Prince of Denmark

ACT 5

5.1 Hamlet, returned from his journey, enters a graveyard with Horatio where a gravedigger is singing as he digs. Hamlet tries to find out who the grave is for and meditates on the skulls that are being dug up. A funeral procession approaches. Hamlet soon realizes that the corpse is Ophelia's. When Laertes in his grief leaps into her grave and curses Hamlet as the cause of Ophelia's death, Hamlet comes forward. He and Laertes struggle, with Hamlet protesting his own love and grief for Ophelia.

---

0 SD. **Enter Gravedigger and Another:** In Q2 and Folio *Hamlet*, this stage direction reads "Enter two clowns," thus indicating that the Gravedigger and his companion were played by actors who did comic roles.

4. **straight:** straightway, immediately; **crowner:** coroner; **sat on her:** conducted a formal inquest into her death; **finds it:** decided that her death warrants

9. **se offendendo:** in self-offense (the gravedigger's mistake for the common legal phrase *se defendendo*, "in self-defense")

11. **wittingly:** deliberately

12. **Argal:** a mistake for Latin *ergo*, "therefore"

15. **Give me leave:** let me go on

17. **will he, nill he:** willy-nilly, whether wished or not

23. **'quest:** inquest

⌜ACT 5⌝

⌜Scene 1⌝
Enter ⌜Gravedigger and Another.⌝

⌜GRAVEDIGGER⌝ Is she to be buried in Christian burial,
  when she willfully seeks her own salvation?

OTHER I tell thee she is. Therefore make her grave
  straight. The crowner hath sat on her and finds it
  Christian burial.   5

⌜GRAVEDIGGER⌝ How can that be, unless she drowned
  herself in her own defense?

OTHER Why, 'tis found so.

⌜GRAVEDIGGER⌝ It must be ⟨se offendendo;⟩ it cannot be
  else. For here lies the point: if I drown myself   10
  wittingly, it argues an act, and an act hath three
  branches—it is to act, to do, to perform. ⟨Argal,⟩ she
  drowned herself wittingly.

OTHER Nay, but hear you, goodman delver—

⌜GRAVEDIGGER⌝ Give me leave. Here lies the water;   15
  good. Here stands the man; good. If the man go to
  this water and drown himself, it is (will he, nill he)
  he goes; mark you that. But if the water come to him
  and drown him, he drowns not himself. Argal, he
  that is not guilty of his own death shortens not his   20
  own life.

OTHER But is this law?

⌜GRAVEDIGGER⌝ Ay, marry, is 't—crowner's 'quest law.

239

27. **there thou sayst:** you said it correctly
28. **count'nance:** legal approval
30. **even-Christian:** their fellow Christians
32. **hold up:** maintain
34. **bore arms:** was given heraldic insignia (with a pun on "arms" as part of the body)
41. **Go to:** an exclamation of impatience
53. **unyoke:** i.e., quit, as a farmer does when he unyokes his team of oxen
56. **Mass:** by the Mass

OTHER   Will you ha' the truth on 't? If this had not been
a gentlewoman, she should have been buried out o'   25
Christian burial.

⌈GRAVEDIGGER⌉   Why, there thou sayst. And the more
pity that great folk should have count'nance in this
world to drown or hang themselves more than
their even-Christian. Come, my spade. There is no   30
ancient gentlemen but gard'ners, ditchers, and
grave-makers. They hold up Adam's profession.

OTHER   Was he a gentleman?

⌈GRAVEDIGGER⌉   He was the first that ever bore arms.

⟨OTHER   Why, he had none.   35

⌈GRAVEDIGGER⌉   What, art a heathen? How dost thou
understand the scripture? The scripture says Adam
digged. Could he dig without arms?⟩ I'll put another question to thee. If thou answerest me not to the
purpose, confess thyself—   40

OTHER   Go to!

⌈GRAVEDIGGER⌉   What is he that builds stronger than
either the mason, the shipwright, or the carpenter?

OTHER   The gallows-maker; for that ⟨frame⟩ outlives a
thousand tenants.   45

⌈GRAVEDIGGER⌉   I like thy wit well, in good faith. The
gallows does well. But how does it well? It does
well to those that do ill. Now, thou dost ill to say the
gallows is built stronger than the church. Argal, the
gallows may do well to thee. To 't again, come.   50

OTHER   "Who builds stronger than a mason, a shipwright, or a carpenter?"

⌈GRAVEDIGGER⌉   Ay, tell me that, and unyoke.

OTHER   Marry, now I can tell.

⌈GRAVEDIGGER⌉   To 't.   55

OTHER   Mass, I cannot tell.

⟨*Enter Hamlet and Horatio afar off.*⟩

⌈GRAVEDIGGER⌉   Cudgel thy brains no more about it,

58–59. your . . . beating: i.e., a stupid donkey does not move more quickly because it is beaten

63–66, 73–76, 96–99, 122–23. In youth . . . : The words of the Gravedigger's song are found, with variations, printed in Richard Tottel's *Miscellany* (1557), entitled "The aged lover renounceth love." The "O" and "a's" (lines 65–66) may mark the breathing or grunts of the Gravedigger, or may be part of his song, much of which makes little sense.

69–70. Custom . . . easiness: i.e., habit makes it easy for him

71. of little employment: not frequently used

72. hath the daintier sense: is more sensitive

78. jowls: dashes

81. o'erreaches: gets the better of

for your dull ass will not mend his pace with
beating. And, when you are asked this question
next, say "a grave-maker." The houses he makes   60
lasts till doomsday. Go, get thee in, and fetch me a
stoup of liquor.

⌈*The Other Man exits
and the Gravedigger digs and sings.*⌉

In youth when I did love, did love,
    Methought it was very sweet
To contract—O—the time for—a—my behove,   65
    O, methought there—a—was nothing—a—meet.

HAMLET   Has this fellow no feeling of his business? He
sings in grave-making.

HORATIO   Custom hath made it in him a property of
easiness.   70

HAMLET   'Tis e'en so. The hand of little employment
hath the daintier sense.

⌈**GRAVEDIGGER**⌉ (*sings*)
    But age with his stealing steps
    Hath clawed me in his clutch,
    And hath shipped me into the land,   75
    As if I had never been such.

⌈*He digs up a skull.*⌉

HAMLET   That skull had a tongue in it and could sing
once. How the knave jowls it to the ground as if
'twere Cain's jawbone, that did the first murder!
This might be the pate of a politician which this ass   80
now o'erreaches, one that would circumvent God,
might it not?

HORATIO   It might, my lord.

HAMLET   Or of a courtier, which could say "Good
morrow, sweet lord! How dost thou, sweet lord?"   85
This might be my Lord Such-a-one that praised my
Lord Such-a-one's horse when he went to beg it,
might it not?

HORATIO   Ay, my lord.

91. chapless: without a lower jaw; **mazard:** head (a slang term)

94. loggets: a game played by throwing pieces of wood at a stake

101. quiddities: hair-splitting definitions

102. quillities: subtle distinctions, quibbles; **tenures:** holdings

104. sconce: head (a slang term)

106–7. his statutes, his recognizances . . . : Hamlet begins here a list of legal terms referring to buying and holding property.

112. indentures: contracts

113. conveyances: deeds; **this box:** i.e., this skull

114. inheritor: owner

A chapless skull. (5.1.91)
From Henry Peacham, *Minerua Britanna* (1612).

HAMLET Why, e'en so. And now my Lady Worm's,   90
chapless and knocked about the ⟨mazard⟩ with a
sexton's spade. Here's fine revolution, an we had
the trick to see 't. Did these bones cost no more the
breeding but to play at loggets with them? Mine
ache to think on 't.   95

⌜GRAVEDIGGER⌝ ⟨sings⟩
          A pickax and a spade, a spade,
          For and a shrouding sheet,
          O, a pit of clay for to be made
          For such a guest is meet.

                              ⌜*He digs up more skulls.*⌝

HAMLET There's another. Why may not that be the   100
skull of a lawyer? Where be his quiddities now, his
quillities, his cases, his tenures, and his tricks? Why
does he suffer this mad knave now to knock him
about the sconce with a dirty shovel and will not tell
him of his action of battery? Hum, this fellow might   105
be in 's time a great buyer of land, with his statutes,
his recognizances, his fines, his double vouchers,
his recoveries. ⟨Is this the fine of his fines and the
recovery of his recoveries,⟩ to have his fine pate full
of fine dirt? Will ⟨his⟩ vouchers vouch him no more   110
of his purchases, and ⟨double ones too,⟩ than the
length and breadth of a pair of indentures? The very
conveyances of his lands will scarcely lie in this box,
and must th' inheritor himself have no more, ha?

HORATIO Not a jot more, my lord.   115

HAMLET Is not parchment made of sheepskins?

HORATIO Ay, my lord, and of calves' skins too.

HAMLET They are sheep and calves which seek out
assurance in that. I will speak to this fellow.—
Whose grave's this, sirrah?   120

⌜GRAVEDIGGER⌝ Mine, sir.

  ⌜*Sings.*⌝   ⟨O,⟩ *a pit of clay for to be made*
                ⟨*For such a guest is meet.*⟩

125. **out on 't:** outside of it
129. **quick:** living
131. **quick:** quickly moving
140. **absolute:** precise
140–41. **by the card:** i.e., with precision
143–45. **the age ... kibe:** i.e., the present age has become so affected that peasants walk on the very heels of courtiers **picked:** affected **his kibe:** the courtier's sore heel

HAMLET I think it be thine indeed, for thou liest in 't.
⌜GRAVEDIGGER⌝ You lie out on 't, sir, and therefore 'tis 125
    not yours. For my part, I do not lie in 't, yet it is
    mine.
HAMLET Thou dost lie in 't, to be in 't and say it is thine.
    'Tis for the dead, not for the quick; therefore thou
    liest. 130
⌜GRAVEDIGGER⌝ 'Tis a quick lie, sir; 'twill away again
    from me to you.
HAMLET What man dost thou dig it for?
⌜GRAVEDIGGER⌝ For no man, sir.
HAMLET What woman then? 135
⌜GRAVEDIGGER⌝ For none, neither.
HAMLET Who is to be buried in 't?
⌜GRAVEDIGGER⌝ One that was a woman, sir, but, rest
    her soul, she's dead.
HAMLET How absolute the knave is! We must speak by 140
    the card, or equivocation will undo us. By the
    Lord, Horatio, this three years I have took note of
    it: the age is grown so picked that the toe of the
    peasant comes so near the heel of the courtier, he
    galls his kibe.—How long hast thou been grave- 145
    maker?
⌜GRAVEDIGGER⌝ Of ⟨all⟩ the days i' th' year, I came to 't
    that day that our last King Hamlet overcame
    Fortinbras.
HAMLET How long is that since? 150
⌜GRAVEDIGGER⌝ Cannot you tell that? Every fool can
    tell that. It was that very day that young Hamlet
    was born—he that is mad, and sent into England.
HAMLET Ay, marry, why was he sent into England?
⌜GRAVEDIGGER⌝ Why, because he was mad. He shall 155
    recover his wits there. Or if he do not, 'tis no great
    matter there.
HAMLET Why?
⌜GRAVEDIGGER⌝ 'Twill not be seen in him there. There
    the men are as mad as he. 160

170. **pocky:** rotten, as if infected with syphilis

171. **scarce hold the laying in:** barely hold together long enough to be buried

177. **your water:** i.e., water

177–78. **your . . . body:** i.e., bodies **whoreson:** vile

178. **lien you:** lain

HAMLET How came he mad?

⌈GRAVEDIGGER⌉ Very strangely, they say.

HAMLET How "strangely"?

⌈GRAVEDIGGER⌉ Faith, e'en with losing his wits.

HAMLET Upon what ground?   165

⌈GRAVEDIGGER⌉ Why, here in Denmark. I have been
    sexton here, man and boy, thirty years.

HAMLET How long will a man lie i' th' earth ere he rot?

⌈GRAVEDIGGER⌉ Faith, if he be not rotten before he die
    (as we have many pocky corses (nowadays) that will 170
    scarce hold the laying in), he will last you some
    eight year or nine year. A tanner will last you nine
    year.

HAMLET Why he more than another?

⌈GRAVEDIGGER⌉ Why, sir, his hide is so tanned with his 175
    trade that he will keep out water a great while; and
    your water is a sore decayer of your whoreson dead
    body. Here's a skull now hath lien you i' th' earth
    three-and-twenty years.

HAMLET Whose was it?   180

⌈GRAVEDIGGER⌉ A whoreson mad fellow's it was.
    Whose do you think it was?

HAMLET Nay, I know not.

⌈GRAVEDIGGER⌉ A pestilence on him for a mad rogue!
    He poured a flagon of Rhenish on my head once. 185
    This same skull, sir, was, sir, Yorick's skull, the
    King's jester.

HAMLET This?

⌈GRAVEDIGGER⌉ E'en that.

HAMLET, ⌈*taking the skull*⌉ (Let me see.) Alas, poor 190
    Yorick! I knew him, Horatio—a fellow of infinite
    jest, of most excellent fancy. He hath bore me on his
    back a thousand times, and now how abhorred in
    my imagination it is! My gorge rises at it. Here hung
    those lips that I have kissed I know not how oft. 195
    Where be your gibes now? your gambols? your

199. **chapfallen:** without the lower jaw; also, perhaps, dejected

199–200. **my lady's chamber:** i.e., the room of the gentlewoman you would entertain

201. **favor:** appearance

204. **Alexander:** Alexander the Great, who died in 323 B.C. as ruler of the known world

212. **curiously:** elaborately

215. **modesty:** moderation, reserve

220. **Imperious:** imperial; majestic

223. **flaw:** gust of wind

226. **maimèd:** impaired, diminished

228. **Fordo:** destroy; **some estate:** high rank

229. **Couch we:** let us hide

songs? your flashes of merriment that were wont to
set the table on a roar? Not one now to mock your
own grinning? Quite chapfallen? Now get you to my
lady's ⟨chamber,⟩ and tell her, let her paint an inch   200
thick, to this favor she must come. Make her laugh
at that.—Prithee, Horatio, tell me one thing.

HORATIO   What's that, my lord?

HAMLET   Dost thou think Alexander looked o' this
fashion i' th' earth?   205

HORATIO   E'en so.

HAMLET   And smelt so? Pah! ⌜*He puts the skull down.*⌝

HORATIO   E'en so, my lord.

HAMLET   To what base uses we may return, Horatio!
Why may not imagination trace the noble dust of   210
Alexander till he find it stopping a bunghole?

HORATIO   'Twere to consider too curiously to consider
so.

HAMLET   No, faith, not a jot; but to follow him thither,
with modesty enough and likelihood to lead it, ⟨as   215
thus:⟩ Alexander died, Alexander was buried, Alexander returneth to dust; the dust is earth; of earth
we make loam; and why of that loam whereto he
was converted might they not stop a beer barrel?
Imperious Caesar, dead and turned to clay,   220
Might stop a hole to keep the wind away.
O, that that earth which kept the world in awe
Should patch a wall t' expel the ⟨winter's⟩ flaw!

*Enter King, Queen, Laertes, ⟨Lords attendant,⟩ and the
corpse ⌜of Ophelia, with a Doctor of Divinity.⌝*

But soft, but soft awhile! Here comes the King,
The Queen, the courtiers. Who is this they follow?   225
And with such maimèd rites? This doth betoken
The corse they follow did with desp'rate hand
Fordo its own life. 'Twas of some estate.
Couch we awhile and mark.   ⌜*They step aside.*⌝

234. **doubtful:** suspicious

235. **but that . . . order:** except for the fact that the king's command overrides the rule of the church

236–37. **in ground . . . trumpet:** in unhallowed ground been buried until the Judgment Day (See 1 Corinthians 15.51–52: ". . . for the trumpet shall sound, and the dead shall be raised incorruptible. . . .")

237. **For:** instead of

238. **Shards:** bits of pottery

240. **crants:** garlands

241. **strewments:** flowers strewn on a grave

241–42. **bringing . . . burial:** being brought to the grave, her last home, to the sound of the bell

246. **such rest:** i.e., to pray for such rest

247. **peace-parted:** i.e., that depart in peace

252. **howling:** i.e., in hell

254. **Sweets to the sweet:** sweet flowers to the sweet maiden

260–61. **thy most . . . Deprived thee of:** i.e., deprived you of your mind

LAERTES	What ceremony else?	230
HAMLET	That is Laertes, a very noble youth. Mark.	
LAERTES	What ceremony else?	

DOCTOR
  Her obsequies have been as far enlarged
  As we have warranty. Her death was doubtful,
  And, but that great command o'ersways the order,   235
  She should in ground unsanctified been lodged
  Till the last trumpet. For charitable prayers
  ⟨Shards,⟩ flints, and pebbles should be thrown on
    her.
  Yet here she is allowed her virgin crants,   240
  Her maiden strewments, and the bringing home
  Of bell and burial.

LAERTES
  Must there no more be done?

DOCTOR   No more be done.
  We should profane the service of the dead   245
  To sing a requiem and such rest to her
  As to peace-parted souls.

LAERTES   Lay her i' th' earth,
  And from her fair and unpolluted flesh
  May violets spring! I tell thee, churlish priest,   250
  A minist'ring angel shall my sister be
  When thou liest howling.

HAMLET, ⌈*to Horatio*⌉   What, the fair Ophelia?

QUEEN   Sweets to the sweet, farewell!
                      ⌈*She scatters flowers.*⌉
  I hoped thou shouldst have been my Hamlet's wife;   255
  I thought thy bride-bed to have decked, sweet maid,
  And not have strewed thy grave.

LAERTES   O, treble woe
  Fall ten times ⟨treble⟩ on that cursèd head
  Whose wicked deed thy most ingenious sense   260
  Deprived thee of!—Hold off the earth awhile,
  Till I have caught her once more in mine arms.
                    (Leaps in the grave.)

265. **Pelion:** a high mountain on which, in Greek mythology, the giants placed Mount Ossa in their attempt to scale Mount Olympus

269. **wand'ring stars:** planets

275. **splenitive:** quick-tempered

289. **forbear him:** be patient with him

290. **thou't:** thou wilt

291. **Woo't:** wilt thou

293. **eisel:** vinegar

Now pile your dust upon the quick and dead,
Till of this flat a mountain you have made
T' o'ertop old Pelion or the skyish head   265
Of blue Olympus.
HAMLET, ⌈*advancing*⌉
                    What is he whose grief
Bears such an emphasis, whose phrase of sorrow
Conjures the wand'ring stars and makes them stand
Like wonder-wounded hearers? This is I,   270
Hamlet the Dane.
LAERTES, ⌈*coming out of the grave*⌉
                    The devil take thy soul!
HAMLET   Thou pray'st not well.   ⌈*They grapple.*⌉
I prithee take thy fingers from my throat,
For though I am not splenitive ⟨and⟩ rash,   275
Yet have I in me something dangerous,
Which let thy wisdom fear. Hold off thy hand.
KING   Pluck them asunder.
QUEEN   Hamlet! Hamlet!
ALL   Gentlemen!   280
HORATIO   Good my lord, be quiet.
                    ⌈*Hamlet and Laertes are separated.*⌉
HAMLET
Why, I will fight with him upon this theme
Until my eyelids will no longer wag!
QUEEN   O my son, what theme?
HAMLET
I loved Ophelia. Forty thousand brothers   285
Could not with all their quantity of love
Make up my sum. What wilt thou do for her?
KING   O, he is mad, Laertes!
QUEEN   For love of God, forbear him.
HAMLET   'Swounds, show me what thou't do.   290
Woo't weep, woo't fight, woo't fast, woo't tear
    thyself,
Woo't drink up eisel, eat a crocodile?

296. **quick:** alive

299. **the burning zone:** that zone in the celestial sphere, paralleling the earth's equator, in which the sun seems to circle the earth

300. **Ossa:** See note to line 265.

304. **Anon:** soon

305. **golden couplets:** twin birds covered with yellow down; **disclosed:** hatched

312. **wait upon him:** accompany him

313. **in:** by thinking of

315. **to the present push:** into immediate action

I'll do 't. Dost (thou) come here to whine?
To outface me with leaping in her grave? 295
Be buried quick with her, and so will I.
And if thou prate of mountains, let them throw
Millions of acres on us, till our ground,
Singeing his pate against the burning zone,
Make Ossa like a wart. Nay, an thou'lt mouth, 300
I'll rant as well as thou.

QUEEN   This is mere madness;
And (thus) awhile the fit will work on him.
Anon, as patient as the female dove
When that her golden couplets are disclosed, 305
His silence will sit drooping.

HAMLET   Hear you, sir,
What is the reason that you use me thus?
I loved you ever. But it is no matter.
Let Hercules himself do what he may, 310
The cat will mew, and dog will have his day.
                                        Hamlet exits.

KING
I pray thee, good Horatio, wait upon him.
                                        Horatio exits.
⌜*To Laertes.*⌝ Strengthen your patience in our last
    night's speech.
We'll put the matter to the present push.— 315
Good Gertrude, set some watch over your son.—
This grave shall have a living monument.
An hour of quiet (shortly) shall we see;
Till then in patience our proceeding be.
                                        They exit.

5.2 In the hall of the castle, Hamlet tells Horatio how he discovered the king's plot against him and how he turned the tables on Rosencrantz and Guildenstern. Osric enters to ask, on Claudius's behalf, that Hamlet fence with Laertes. Hamlet agrees to the contest, despite his misgivings.

Hamlet is winning the match when Gertrude drinks from the poisoned cup that Claudius has prepared for Hamlet. Laertes then wounds Hamlet with the poisoned rapier. In the scuffle that follows, Hamlet forces an exchange of rapiers, and Hamlet wounds Laertes. As Gertrude dies, Laertes, himself dying, discloses his and Claudius's plot against Hamlet. Hamlet kills Claudius. Before Hamlet dies, he asks Horatio to tell the full story that has led to these deaths and names Fortinbras heir to the Danish throne. After Hamlet's death, Fortinbras arrives, claims the crown, and orders a military funeral for Hamlet.

----

6. **mutines:** mutineers; **bilboes:** shackles

8. **indiscretion:** acting impulsively

9. **pall:** lose strength; **learn:** teach

11. **our ends:** outcome of our actions

12. **Rough-hew them how we will:** no matter how roughly we ourselves shape them

23. **Larded:** ornamented

25. **bugs and goblins in my life:** causes of alarm if I were allowed to live **bugs:** bugbears

26. **on . . . bated:** As soon as the document has been read, Hamlet is to be executed, the immediacy of the execution not being reduced (**bated**) by any delay (**leisure**).

⌈Scene 2⌉

Enter Hamlet and Horatio.

HAMLET
So much for this, sir. Now shall you see the other.
You do remember all the circumstance?

HORATIO   Remember it, my lord!

HAMLET
Sir, in my heart there was a kind of fighting
That would not let me sleep. ⟨Methought⟩ I lay   5
Worse than the mutines in the ⟨bilboes.⟩ Rashly—
And praised be rashness for it: let us know,
Our indiscretion sometime serves us well
When our deep plots do pall; and that should learn
    us   10
There's a divinity that shapes our ends,
Rough-hew them how we will—

HORATIO   That is most
    certain.

HAMLET   Up from my cabin,   15
My sea-gown scarfed about me, in the dark
Groped I to find out them; had my desire,
Fingered their packet, and in fine withdrew
To mine own room again, making so bold
⟨My fears forgetting manners⟩ to unfold   20
Their grand commission; where I found, Horatio,
A royal knavery—an exact command,
Larded with many several sorts of reasons
Importing Denmark's health and England's too,
With—ho!—such bugs and goblins in my life,   25
That on the supervise, no leisure bated,
No, not to stay the grinding of the ax,
My head should be struck off.

HORATIO   Is 't possible?

HAMLET
Here's the commission. Read it at more leisure.   30
                        ⌈*Handing him a paper.*⌉

34. **Or:** before

36. **fair:** in the clear hand of a clerk

37–38. **hold it . . . A baseness:** consider it, as our statesmen do, a lower-class skill

40. **yeoman's:** substantial, loyal

41. **effect:** substance

44–52. **As England . . . allowed:** In this passage, Hamlet parodies the formal language he used in writing the **new commission. tributary:** a nation that pays tribute (a form of tax) to its conqueror

47. **stand . . . amities:** serve to link their friendships

48. **suchlike ases of great charge:** similar "whereas" legal phrases of great significance

52. **shriving time:** time for confession

54. **ordinant:** working to control events

55. **signet:** small seal

56. **model:** replica

58. **Subscribed it, gave 't th' impression:** signed it, sealed it with the signet on wax

60. **changeling:** exchange (As the fairies substituted elves or imps for human babies, so Hamlet has replaced the king's document with his own forged one.)

61. **what to this was sequent:** what followed this

But wilt thou hear now how I did proceed?
HORATIO   I beseech you.
HAMLET
  Being thus benetted round with ⌜villainies,⌝
  Or I could make a prologue to my brains,
  They had begun the play. I sat me down,   35
  Devised a new commission, wrote it fair—
  I once did hold it, as our statists do,
  A baseness to write fair, and labored much
  How to forget that learning; but, sir, now
  It did me yeoman's service. Wilt thou know   40
  Th' effect of what I wrote?
HORATIO   Ay, good my lord.
HAMLET
  An earnest conjuration from the King,
  As England was his faithful tributary,
  As love between them like the palm might flourish, 45
  As peace should still her wheaten garland wear
  And stand a comma 'tween their amities,
  And many suchlike ⌜ases⌝ of great charge,
  That, on the view and knowing of these contents,
  Without debatement further, more or less,   50
  He should those bearers put to sudden death,
  Not shriving time allowed.
HORATIO   How was this sealed?
HAMLET
  Why, even in that was heaven ordinant.
  I had my father's signet in my purse,   55
  Which was the model of that Danish seal;
  Folded the writ up in the form of th' other,
  ⟨Subscribed⟩ it, gave 't th' impression, placed it
    safely,
  The changeling never known. Now, the next day 60
  Was our sea-fight; and what to this was sequent
  Thou knowest already.
HORATIO
  So Guildenstern and Rosencrantz go to 't.

65. **defeat:** destruction
66. **insinuation:** winding themselves into the affair
67. **baser:** inferior
68. **pass:** thrust; **fell:** fierce
71. **Does . . . upon—:** is it not now my duty—
73. **election:** The play suggests, here and elsewhere, that the Danish king is somehow elected.
74. **angle:** fishhook; **proper:** very
77. **quit:** requite, pay back
80. **In:** into
87–88. **by . . . his:** I see the portrait of Laertes's situation in that of my own
89. **bravery:** boastful showiness

"Put your bonnet to his right use:
'tis for the head." (5.2.105–6)
From *Bagford Ballads* (printed in 1878).

HAMLET
⟨Why, man, they did make love to this employment.⟩
They are not near my conscience. Their defeat   65
Does by their own insinuation grow.
'Tis dangerous when the baser nature comes
Between the pass and fell incensèd points ·
Of mighty opposites.

HORATIO   Why, what a king is this!   70

HAMLET
Does it not, think thee, stand me now upon—
He that hath killed my king and whored my mother,
Popped in between th' election and my hopes,
Thrown out his angle for my proper life,
And with such cozenage—is 't not perfect   75
   conscience
⟨To quit him with this arm? And is 't not to be
   damned
To let this canker of our nature come
In further evil?   80

HORATIO
It must be shortly known to him from England
What is the issue of the business there.

HAMLET
It will be short. The interim's mine,
And a man's life's no more than to say "one."
But I am very sorry, good Horatio,   85
That to Laertes I forgot myself,
For by the image of my cause I see
The portraiture of his. I'll ⌜court⌝ his favors.
But, sure, the bravery of his grief did put me
Into a tow'ring passion.   90

HORATIO   Peace, who comes here?⟩

Enter ⟨Osric,⟩ a courtier.

OSRIC Your lordship is right welcome back to Denmark.

95. **waterfly**: an iridescent insect

99–100. **Let a beast . . . king's mess**: if a man, no matter how bestial, has enough money he will be welcome at the king's table **crib**: stall of an ox **mess**: place where groups (usually military) were fed

105. **Put your bonnet . . . use**: i.e., put on your hat. (Hats were commonly worn by men, even indoors, but removed in the presence of superiors. Osric continues to hold his hat in his hand despite Hamlet's insistence; see 5.2.117.)

110. **indifferent**: somewhat

112. **complexion**: temperament

118–95. Throughout these passages, Osric's language is florid, affected, and imprecise; Hamlet answers him in a style even more exaggerated. Often we can only guess at what they may be saying.

122–23. **the card or calendar of gentry**: the model of courtly manners (?)

124. **continent**: that which contains

125. **definement**: definition; **perdition**: loss

126–28. **to divide him . . . quick sail**: to inventory his qualities would stagger one's memory, but the inventory would fall short of his excellence (?)

HAMLET I ⟨humbly⟩ thank you, sir. ⌜*Aside to Horatio.*⌝
Dost know this waterfly? 95

HORATIO, ⌜*aside to Hamlet*⌝ No, my good lord.

HAMLET, ⌜*aside to Horatio*⌝ Thy state is the more gracious, for 'tis a vice to know him. He hath much
land, and fertile. Let a beast be lord of beasts and his
crib shall stand at the king's mess. 'Tis a chough, 100
but, as I say, spacious in the possession of dirt.

OSRIC Sweet lord, if your lordship were at leisure, I
should impart a thing to you from his Majesty.

HAMLET I will receive it, sir, with all diligence of
spirit. ⟨Put⟩ your bonnet to his right use: 'tis for the 105
head.

OSRIC I thank your lordship; it is very hot.

HAMLET No, believe me, 'tis very cold; the wind is
northerly.

OSRIC It is indifferent cold, my lord, indeed. 110

HAMLET But yet methinks it is very ⟨sultry⟩ and hot ⟨for⟩
my complexion.

OSRIC Exceedingly, my lord; it is very sultry, as
'twere—I cannot tell how. My lord, his Majesty
bade me signify to you that he has laid a great wager 115
on your head. Sir, this is the matter—

HAMLET I beseech you, remember. ⌜*He motions to
Osric to put on his hat.*⌝

OSRIC Nay, good my lord, for my ease, in good faith.
[Sir, here is newly come to court Laertes—believe
me, an absolute ⌜gentleman,⌝ full of most excellent 120
differences, of very soft society and great showing.
Indeed, to speak ⌜feelingly⌝ of him, he is the card or
calendar of gentry, for you shall find in him the
continent of what part a gentleman would see.

HAMLET Sir, his definement suffers no perdition in 125
you, though I know to divide him inventorially
would dozy th' arithmetic of memory, and yet but
yaw neither, in respect of his quick sail. But, in the

129–33. a soul . . . nothing more: Hamlet's mockingly affected language says, in essence, that Laertes is a fine man, so special that he can be matched only by his image in a mirror; everyone else in comparison to him is only his shadow.

135–36. wrap . . . breath? i.e., why are we talking about him?

138. possible: i.e., possible for Osric

140. nomination: naming

143. all 's: all his

148. approve: commend

154–55. imputation: reputation

155. meed: merit

155–56. unfellowed: unmatched

158. Rapier and dagger: In rapier fencing, the rapier, carried in the right hand, led the attack; the dagger, in the left hand, parried the opponent's attack.

162–63. poniards: daggers; **assigns: accessories; girdle, hangers, and so:** sword belt, attaching straps, and so forth

164. carriages: literally, wheeled supports on which cannons are mounted; **dear to fancy:** fancifully designed

verity of extolment, I take him to be a soul of great
article, and his infusion of such dearth and rareness 130
as, to make true diction of him, his semblable is his
mirror, and who else would trace him, his umbrage,
nothing more.

OSRIC   Your lordship speaks most infallibly of him.

HAMLET   The concernancy, sir? Why do we wrap the 135
gentleman in our more rawer breath?

OSRIC   Sir?

HORATIO, ⌈*aside to Hamlet*⌉ Is 't not possible to understand in another tongue? You will to 't, sir, really.

HAMLET, ⌈*to Osric*⌉ What imports the nomination of 140
this gentleman?

OSRIC   Of Laertes?

HORATIO, ⌈*aside*⌉ His purse is empty already; all 's
golden words are spent.

HAMLET   Of him, sir.   145

OSRIC   I know you are not ignorant—

HAMLET   I would you did, sir. Yet, in faith, if you did, it
would not much approve me. Well, sir?]

OSRIC   You are not ignorant of what excellence Laertes
is—   150

[HAMLET   I dare not confess that, lest I should compare
with him in excellence. But to know a man well
were to know himself.

OSRIC   I mean, sir, for ⌈his⌉ weapon. But in the imputation laid on him by them, in his meed he's unfel- 155
lowed.]

HAMLET   What's his weapon?

OSRIC   Rapier and dagger.

HAMLET   That's two of his weapons. But, well—

OSRIC   The King, sir, hath wagered with him six Barba- 160
ry horses, against the which he has impawned, as I
take it, six French rapiers and poniards, with their
assigns, as girdle, ⟨hangers,⟩ and so. Three of the
carriages, in faith, are very dear to fancy, very

165. **responsive:** well matched

166. **liberal conceit:** imaginative design (?)

167. **What call you the "carriages"?:** i.e., what are you calling "carriages"?

168–69. **edified by the margent:** aided through a note in the margin

178. **laid:** bet

178–79. **a dozen passes between yourself and him:** a dozen exchanges between Hamlet and Laertes

180–81. **twelve for nine:** No one has satisfactorily explained this phrase so that it fits in with the terms of the wager.

182. **vouchsafe the answer:** consent to meet Laertes in this match (Hamlet chooses to understand the statement differently.)

187. **breathing time of day:** the time I take my exercise

188. **foils:** weapons blunted for fencing

195. **commend:** offer my services (The word also means "praise," as Hamlet takes it at lines 196–97.)

197–98. **for 's turn:** for his purpose (i.e., to praise him)

responsive to the hilts, most delicate carriages, and 165
of very liberal conceit.

HAMLET What call you the "carriages"?

[HORATIO, ⌈*aside to Hamlet*⌉ I knew you must be edified
by the margent ere you had done.]

OSRIC The ⟨carriages,⟩ sir, are the hangers. 170

HAMLET The phrase would be more germane to the
matter if we could carry a cannon by our sides. I
would it ⟨might⟩ be "hangers" till then. But on. Six
Barbary horses against six French swords, their
assigns, and three liberal-conceited carriages— 175
that's the French bet against the Danish. Why is this
all ⌈"impawned,"⌉ ⟨as⟩ you call it?

OSRIC The King, sir, hath laid, sir, that in a dozen
passes between yourself and him, he shall not
exceed you three hits. He hath laid on twelve for 180
nine, and it would come to immediate trial if your
lordship would vouchsafe the answer.

HAMLET How if I answer no?

OSRIC I mean, my lord, the opposition of your person
in trial. 185

HAMLET Sir, I will walk here in the hall. If it please his
Majesty, it is the breathing time of day with me. Let
the foils be brought, the gentleman willing, and the
King hold his purpose, I will win for him, an I can.
If not, I will gain nothing but my shame and the odd 190
hits.

OSRIC Shall I deliver you ⟨e'en⟩ so?

HAMLET To this effect, sir, after what flourish your
nature will.

OSRIC I commend my duty to your lordship. 195

HAMLET Yours. ⌈*Osric exits.*⌉ ⟨He⟩ does well to commend it himself. There are no tongues else for 's
turn.

HORATIO This lapwing runs away with the shell on his
head. 200

201. **comply . . . with his dug:** say polite things to the breast he was about to nurse from

203. **drossy:** worthless

204. **tune:** manner of speaking

204–7. **out . . . opinions:** perhaps, out of repeated social encounters, they have got a collection of frothy language that wins acceptance from refined persons

207–8. **blow . . . out:** In this image, Osric and his kind are themselves composed of froth; when one blows on them to see if there is anything to them, they collapse like bubbles.

215–16. **If . . . ready:** if the king is ready, so am I

219. **In happy time:** opportunely (a courteous phrase)

220–21. **use some gentle entertainment:** receive him in a friendly way

225–226. **at the odds:** with the odds (advantage) allowed me

230. **gaingiving:** misgiving

232. **repair:** coming

233–34. **a special providence . . . a sparrow:** See Matthew 10.29–31: "Are not two sparrows sold for a farthing, and one of them shall not fall on the ground without your Father? . . . Fear ye not, therefore, ye are of more value than many sparrows."

HAMLET   He did ⟨comply,⟩ sir, with his dug before he
   sucked it. Thus has he (and many more of the same
   breed that I know the drossy age dotes on) only got
   the tune of the time, and, out of an habit of
   encounter, a kind of ⟨yeasty⟩ collection, which car-   205
   ries them through and through the most ⌜fanned⌝
   and ⟨winnowed⟩ opinions; and do but blow them to
   their trial, the bubbles are out.

[*Enter a Lord.*

LORD   My lord, his Majesty commended him to you by
   young Osric, who brings back to him that you   210
   attend him in the hall. He sends to know if your
   pleasure hold to play with Laertes, or that you will
   take longer time.
HAMLET   I am constant to my purposes. They follow
   the King's pleasure. If his fitness speaks, mine is   215
   ready now or whensoever, provided I be so able as
   now.
LORD   The King and Queen and all are coming down.
HAMLET   In happy time.
LORD   The Queen desires you to use some gentle   220
   entertainment to Laertes before you fall to play.
HAMLET   She well instructs me.   ⌜*Lord exits.*⌝]
HORATIO   You will lose, my lord.
HAMLET   I do not think so. Since he went into France, I
   have been in continual practice. I shall win at the   225
   odds; ⟨but⟩ thou wouldst not think how ill all's here
   about my heart. But it is no matter.
HORATIO   Nay, good my lord—
HAMLET   It is but foolery, but it is such a kind of
   ⟨gaingiving⟩ as would perhaps trouble a woman.   230
HORATIO   If your mind dislike anything, obey it. I will
   forestall their repair hither and say you are not fit.
HAMLET   Not a whit. We defy augury. There is ⟨a⟩
   special providence in the fall of a sparrow. If it be
   ⟨now,⟩ 'tis not to come; if it be not to come, it will be   235

237-38. **of aught he leaves knows:** knows anything about what he leaves behind

238. **betimes:** early

241. **This presence:** this royal audience

243. **needs:** necessarily

244. **sore:** severe, grave

246. **Roughly awake:** harshly awaken

255. **disclaiming from:** proclaiming my innocence (disavowing all part in); **purposed:** intended

257. **That I have:** as if I had

259. **in nature:** in terms of my natural affection for my father and for my sister

261. **terms of honor:** offense to my honor

262-65. **will no reconcilement . . . ungored:** will accept of reconciliation until experts in those questions give a decision that may serve as a precedent for making peace, thus freeing my reputation from a charge of dishonor **voice:** authority **name ungored:** reputation unwounded

now; if it be not now, yet it ⟨will⟩ come. The
readiness is all. Since no man of aught he leaves
knows, what is 't to leave betimes? Let be.

A table prepared. ⟨Enter⟩ Trumpets, Drums, and Officers
with cushions, King, Queen, ⌜*Osric,*⌝ *and all the state,*
foils, daggers, ⟨flagons of wine,⟩ and Laertes.

KING
  Come, Hamlet, come and take this hand from me.
                    ⌜*He puts Laertes' hand into Hamlet's.*⌝
HAMLET, ⌜*to Laertes*⌝
  Give me your pardon, sir. I have done you wrong;   240
  But pardon 't as you are a gentleman. This presence
    knows,
  And you must needs have heard, how I am punished
  With a sore distraction. What I have done
  That might your nature, honor, and exception   245
  Roughly awake, I here proclaim was madness.
  Was 't Hamlet wronged Laertes? Never Hamlet.
  If Hamlet from himself be ta'en away,
  And when he's not himself does wrong Laertes,
  Then Hamlet does it not; Hamlet denies it.   250
  Who does it, then? His madness. If 't be so,
  Hamlet is of the faction that is wronged;
  His madness is poor Hamlet's enemy.
  ⟨Sir, in this audience⟩
  Let my disclaiming from a purposed evil   255
  Free me so far in your most generous thoughts
  That I have shot my arrow o'er the house
  And hurt my brother.
LAERTES   I am satisfied in nature,
  Whose motive in this case should stir me most   260
  To my revenge; but in my terms of honor
  I stand aloof and will no reconcilement
  Till by some elder masters of known honor
  I have a voice and precedent of peace
  To ⟨keep⟩ my name ungored. But ⟨till⟩ that time   265

269. frankly: freely, willingly

272. your foil: the background against which you will shine (a courteous pun on the word **foils**, used at line 270 to request the blunted weapons)

274. Stick fiery off: stand out in brilliant contrast

280. laid the odds . . . side: i.e., the king's stake, much greater than Laertes's, is bet on Hamlet, who here again claims to be weaker than Laertes

282. we have therefore odds: we have been given "odds" (in that Laertes must make three more hits than Hamlet in order to win)

283. Let me see another: Here Laertes selects the sharpened, poisoned rapier.

284. This likes me: I like this; **have all a length:** are all the same length

285 SD. play: fence

288. quit in answer of the third exchange: requite (Laertes) for earlier hits by scoring the third hit

291. union: large pearl

I do receive your offered love like love
And will not wrong it.

HAMLET   I embrace it freely
And will this brothers' wager frankly play.—
Give us the foils. (Come on.)   270

LAERTES   Come, one for me.

HAMLET
I'll be your foil, Laertes; in mine ignorance
Your skill shall, like a star i' th' darkest night,
Stick fiery off indeed.

LAERTES   You mock me, sir.   275

HAMLET   No, by this hand.

KING
Give them the foils, young Osric. Cousin Hamlet,
You know the wager?

HAMLET   Very well, my lord.
Your Grace has laid the odds o' th' weaker side.   280

KING
I do not fear it; I have seen you both.
But, since he is better, we have therefore odds.

LAERTES
This is too heavy. Let me see another.

HAMLET
This likes me well. These foils have all a length?

OSRIC   Ay, my good lord.   285

                              (*Prepare to play.*)

KING
Set me the stoups of wine upon that table.—
If Hamlet give the first or second hit
Or quit in answer of the third exchange,
Let all the battlements their ordnance fire.
The King shall drink to Hamlet's better breath,   290
And in the cup an (union) shall he throw,
Richer than that which four successive kings
In Denmark's crown have worn. Give me the cups,

294. **kettle:** kettledrum
314. **napkin:** handkerchief
315. **carouses:** drinks a toast

And let the kettle to the trumpet speak,
The trumpet to the cannoneer without, 295
The cannons to the heavens, the heaven to earth,
"Now the King drinks to Hamlet." Come, begin.
And you, the judges, bear a wary eye.

> *Trumpets the while.*

HAMLET Come on, sir.
LAERTES Come, my lord. (*They play.*) 300
HAMLET One.
LAERTES No.
HAMLET Judgment!
OSRIC A hit, a very palpable hit.
LAERTES Well, again. 305
KING
Stay, give me drink.—Hamlet, this pearl is thine.
Here's to thy health.

> ⌜*He drinks and then drops the pearl in the cup.*⌝
> *Drum, trumpets, and shot.*
> Give him the cup.

HAMLET
I'll play this bout first. Set it by awhile.
Come. ⌜*They play.*⌝ Another hit. What say you? 310
LAERTES
(A touch, a touch.) I do confess 't.
KING
Our son shall win.
QUEEN   He's fat and scant of breath.
Here, Hamlet, take my napkin; rub thy brows.
The Queen carouses to thy fortune, Hamlet. 315

> ⌜*She lifts the cup.*⌝

HAMLET Good madam.
KING Gertrude, do not drink.
QUEEN
I will, my lord; I pray you pardon me. ⌜*She drinks.*⌝
KING, ⌜*aside*⌝
It is the poisoned cup. It is too late.

326. **pass:** thrust

327. **make a wanton of me:** play with me as if I were a child

330 SD. **in scuffling they change rapiers:** This stage direction, in Q1, reads "they catch one anothers' rapiers," which suggests that Hamlet forces the exchange through a contemporary method of disarm called the "left-hand seizure" (see woodcut).

336. **woodcock:** a proverbially stupid bird; **mine own springe:** caught in my own trap

The left-hand seizure. (5.2.330 SD)
From Sainct Didier, *Traicte contenant . . .* (1573).

HAMLET
  I dare not drink yet, madam—by and by.   320

QUEEN Come, let me wipe thy face.

LAERTES, ⌜*to Claudius*⌝
  My lord, I'll hit him now.

KING   I do not think 't.

LAERTES, ⌜*aside*⌝
  And yet it is almost against my conscience.

HAMLET
  Come, for the third, Laertes. You do but dally.   325
  I pray you pass with your best violence.
  I am ⟨afeard⟩ you make a wanton of me.

LAERTES Say you so? Come on.   ⟨*Play.*⟩

OSRIC Nothing neither way.

LAERTES Have at you now!   330

⌜*Laertes wounds Hamlet. Then ⟨in scuffling they change*
          rapiers,⟩ and Hamlet wounds Laertes.⌝

KING Part them. They are incensed.

HAMLET Nay, come again.

                      ⌜*The Queen falls.*⌝

OSRIC Look to the Queen there, ho!

HORATIO
  They bleed on both sides.—How is it, my lord?

OSRIC How is 't, Laertes?   335

LAERTES
  Why as a woodcock to mine own springe, Osric.
                      ⌜*He falls.*⌝
  I am justly killed with mine own treachery.

HAMLET
  How does the Queen?

KING   She swoons to see them bleed.

QUEEN
  No, no, the drink, the drink! O, my dear Hamlet!   340
  The drink, the drink! I am poisoned.   ⌜*She dies.*⌝

HAMLET
  O villainy! Ho! Let the door be locked.   ⌜*Osric exits.*⌝
  Treachery! Seek it out.

348. **Unbated and envenomed:** sharp and poisoned

357. **union:** probable pun on "union" as "pearl" and "union" in marriage and death

360. **tempered:** mixed, compounded

366. **this chance:** these events

367. **mutes:** actors without speaking parts

368. **fell sergeant:** cruel sergeant at arms (arresting officer)

LAERTES

It is here, Hamlet. ⟨Hamlet,⟩ thou art slain.
No med'cine in the world can do thee good.   345
In thee there is not half an hour's life.
The treacherous instrument is in ⟨thy⟩ hand,
Unbated and envenomed. The foul practice
Hath turned itself on me. Lo, here I lie,
Never to rise again. Thy mother's poisoned.   350
I can no more. The King, the King's to blame.

HAMLET

The point envenomed too! Then, venom, to thy
    work.   ⟨*Hurts the King.*⟩

ALL Treason, treason!

KING

O, yet defend me, friends! I am but hurt.   355

HAMLET

Here, thou incestuous, ⟨murd'rous,⟩ damnèd Dane,
Drink off this potion. Is ⟨thy union⟩ here?
        ⌜*Forcing him to drink the poison.*⌝
Follow my mother.   ⟨*King dies.*⟩

LAERTES   He is justly served.

It is a poison tempered by himself.   360
Exchange forgiveness with me, noble Hamlet.
Mine and my father's death come not upon thee,
Nor thine on me.   ⟨*Dies.*⟩

HAMLET

Heaven make thee free of it. I follow thee.—
I am dead, Horatio.—Wretched queen, adieu.—   365
You that look pale and tremble at this chance,
That are but mutes or audience to this act,
Had I but time (as this fell sergeant, Death,
Is strict in his arrest), O, I could tell you—
But let it be.—Horatio, I am dead.   370
Thou livest; report me and my cause aright
To the unsatisfied.

HORATIO   Never believe it.

382. Absent thee from felicity awhile: i.e., keep yourself from the happiness of death

386–88. Young Fortinbras . . . volley: i.e., Fortinbras, returning victoriously from Poland, has shot off a volley of gunfire to salute the ambassadors approaching from England

390. o'ercrows: triumphs over

393. voice: vote

394–95. occurrents . . . solicited: occurrences that have brought on

396. O, O, O, O!: This series of *O*s, usually omitted by editors, may simply be an indication for the actor to make the sounds appropriate to Hamlet's dying.

I am more an antique Roman than a Dane.
Here's yet some liquor left. ⌜*He picks up the cup.*⌝ 375
HAMLET   As thou'rt a man,
Give me the cup. Let go! By heaven, I'll ha 't.
O God, Horatio, what a wounded name,
Things standing thus unknown, shall I leave behind
    me!   380
If thou didst ever hold me in thy heart,
Absent thee from felicity awhile
And in this harsh world draw thy breath in pain
To tell my story.
                    A march afar off ⟨and ⌜*shot*⌝ *within.⟩*
                    What warlike noise is this?   385

                    Enter Osric.

OSRIC
Young Fortinbras, with conquest come from Poland,
To th' ambassadors of England gives
This warlike volley.
HAMLET   O, I die, Horatio!
The potent poison quite o'ercrows my spirit.   390
I cannot live to hear the news from England.
But I do prophesy th' election lights
On Fortinbras; he has my dying voice.
So tell him, with th' occurrents, more and less,
Which have solicited—the rest is silence.   395
⟨O, O, O, O!⟩   ⟨*Dies.*⟩
HORATIO
Now cracks a noble heart. Good night, sweet prince,
And flights of angels sing thee to thy rest.
                                        ⌜*March within.*⌝
Why does the drum come hither?

Enter Fortinbras with the ⌜*English*⌝ *Ambassadors ⟨with
         Drum, Colors, and Attendants.⟩*

FORTINBRAS   Where is this sight?   400

403. **This quarry ... havoc:** this heap of dead bodies proclaims that havoc has been at work

404. **toward:** in preparation

409. **senseless:** incapable of sensing

410. **him:** i.e., Claudius

417. **jump upon this bloody question:** so immediately after this bloody quarrel

420. **stage:** platform

424. **casual:** occurring by chance

425. **put on:** instigated

428. **deliver:** tell

432. **rights of memory:** rights remembered

433. **Which ... me:** which my presence here at this advantageous time invites me to claim

HORATIO   What is it you would see?
  If aught of woe or wonder, cease your search.
FORTINBRAS
  This quarry cries on havoc. O proud Death,
  What feast is toward in thine eternal cell
  That thou so many princes at a shot   405
  So bloodily hast struck?
AMBASSADOR   The sight is dismal,
  And our affairs from England come too late.
  The ears are senseless that should give us hearing
  To tell him his commandment is fulfilled,   410
  That Rosencrantz and Guildenstern are dead.
  Where should we have our thanks?
HORATIO   Not from his
    mouth,
  Had it th' ability of life to thank you.   415
  He never gave commandment for their death.
  But since, so jump upon this bloody question,
  You from the Polack wars, and you from England,
  Are here arrived, give order that these bodies
  High on a stage be placed to the view,   420
  And let me speak to ⟨th'⟩ yet unknowing world
  How these things came about. So shall you hear
  Of carnal, bloody, and unnatural acts,
  Of accidental judgments, casual slaughters,
  Of deaths put on by cunning and ⟨forced⟩ cause,   425
  And, in this upshot, purposes mistook
  Fall'n on th' inventors' heads. All this can I
  Truly deliver.
FORTINBRAS   Let us haste to hear it
  And call the noblest to the audience.   430
  For me, with sorrow I embrace my fortune.
  I have some rights of memory in this kingdom,
  Which now to claim my vantage doth invite me.
HORATIO
  Of that I shall have also cause to speak,

435-36. And from his mouth . . . on more: i.e., with words from Hamlet's mouth, whose "voice" will be seconded by others.

437. presently: immediately

440. On . . . happen: i.e., happen as a result of plots and errors

443. put on: put to the test

444. passage: passing, death

448. field: field of battle

And from his mouth whose voice will draw ⟨on⟩　　435
  more.
But let this same be presently performed
Even while men's minds are wild, lest more
  mischance
On plots and errors happen.　　　　　　　　440
FORTINBRAS　　　　　　　　　Let four captains
Bear Hamlet like a soldier to the stage,
For he was likely, had he been put on,
To have proved most royal; and for his passage,
The soldier's music and the rite of war　　445
Speak loudly for him.
Take up the bodies. Such a sight as this
Becomes the field but here shows much amiss.
Go, bid the soldiers shoot.
　　　　　　They exit, ⟨marching, after the which a peal of
　　　　　　　　　　　　ordnance are shot off.⟩

And from his mouth whose voice will draw you

near.

But for this same, he present, personal?

Even while men's minds are wild, lest more

mischance

On plots and errors happen.

FORTINBRAS   Let four captains

Bear Hamlet like a soldier to the stage;

For he was likely, had he been put on,

To have proved most royal; and for his passage

The soldier's music, and the rite of war

Speak loudly for him.

Take up the bodies. Such a sight as this

Becomes the field but here shows much amiss.

Go, bid the soldiers shoot.

They go out, marching; after the which a peal of
ordnance are shot off.

Textual Notes

The reading of the present text appears to the left of the square bracket. The earliest sources of readings not in Q2, the Second Quarto text (upon which this edition is based), are indicated as follows: **Q1** is the First Quarto of 1603; **Q3** is the Third Quarto of 1611; **Q4** is the Fourth Quarto of ?1622; **Q5** is the Fifth Quarto of 1637; **F** is the First Folio of 1623; **F2** is the Second Folio of 1632; **F3** is the Third Folio of 1663–64; **F4** is the Fourth Folio of 1685; **Ed.** is an earlier editor of Shakespeare, beginning with Rowe in 1709. No sources are given for emendations of punctuation or for corrections of obvious typographical errors, like turned letters that produce no known word. **SD** means stage direction; **SP** means speech prefix; **uncorr.** means first or uncorrected state; **corr.** means second or corrected state; ~ stands in place of a word already quoted before the square bracket; ⌃ indicates the omission of a punctuation mark.

1.1. 15. ho!] Q2; *omit* F 19. soldier] F; souldiers Q2 39. we have two nights seen] Q2; we two Nights haue seene F 46. SD *a half-line later in* F 47. off] Q2, F (of) 50. he] Q2; it F 51. harrows] F; horrowes Q2 53. Speak to] Q2; Question F 72. he] Q2; *omit* F 74. Polacks] Ed.; pollax Q2; Pollax F 76. jump] Q2; iust F 84. why . . . cast] F; with . . . cost Q2 100. those] F; these Q2 101. of] Q2; on F 103. returned] F; returne Q2 105. comart] Q2; Cou'nant F 106. designed] F2; desseigne Q2; designe F 110. lawless] Q2; Landlesse F 115. compulsatory] Q2; Compulsatiue F 120–37. Q2 *only* 133. feared] Ed.; feare Q2 137. SD *Ghost*] Q2; *Ghost againe.* F 139. SD *omit* F 150. you] F; your Q2 151. SD *omit* F 153. strike it] Q2; strike at it F 156. SD *omit* Q2; *1 line later in* F 165. morn] Q2; day F 173. say] Q2; sayes F 175. This] Q2; The F 176. dare stir] Q2; can walke F 178. takes] Q2; talkes F 179. that] Q2; the F 182. eastward] Q2; Easterne F 190. convenient] Q2; conueniently F

1.2. 0. SD *the Council . . . Cornelius]* Hamlet, Polonius, Laer-
tes, and his Sister Ophelia, Lords Attendant F   1. SP KING] F;
Claud. Q2   9. to] Q2; of F   11. an . . . a] Q2; one . . . one
F   21. this] Q2; the F   35. bearers] Q2; bearing F   40. SP
CORNELIUS/VOLTEMAND] Q2; *Volt.* F   41. SD F; *omit* Q2   52.
My dread lord] Q2; Dread my Lord F   60. Hath] Q2; He hath
F   60–62. wrung . . . consent] Q2 *only*   69. so, my] F; so
much my Q2   70. nighted] Q2; nightly F   80. good] F; coold
Q2   85. shapes] Q3; chapes Q2; shewes F   86. denote] F;
deuote Q2   100. a] F; or Q2   116. you.] F; ~ ˌ Q2   123. pray
thee] Q2; prythee F   131. heaven] Q2; Heauens F   132. SD
Flourish . . . exit.] Q2; *Exeunt | Manet Hamlet.* F   133. sullied]
Q2 (sallied); solid F   136. self-slaughter] F; seale slaughter
Q2   136. God, God] Q2; God, O God F   137. weary] F; wary
Q2   138. Seem] Q2; Seemes F   139. on 't, ah fie! 'Tis] Q2; on't?
Oh fie, fie, 'tis F   141. merely.] F; ~ ˌ Q2   141. to this] F; thus
Q2   145. beteem] Q2; beteene F   147. would] F; should Q2
153. even she ˌ] Ed.; euen she. F; *omit* Q2   154. God] Q2;
Heauen F   160. in] Q2; of F   164. SD *Barnardo*] Q2; *Barnard*
F   177. hear] Q2; haue F   182. you to drink deep ere] F; you
for to drinke ere Q2   185. see] F; *omit* Q2   190. Or ever I had
seen] Q2; Ere I had euer seene F   192. Where] Q2; Oh where
F   205. God's] Q2; Heauens F   210. at point exactly] Q2; at all
points exactly F   212. stately ˌ . . . them.] Q2 (them;); ~: . . .
~ ˌ F   214. distilled] Q2; bestil'd F   219. Where, as] Q1
(Where as); Whereas Q2, F   224. watch] Q2; watcht F   237.
Indeed, sirs] Q2; Indeed, indeed Sirs F   239, 241, 243. SP ALL]
Q2; *Both.* F   254. Very like. Stayed] Q2; Very like, very like:
staid F   257. SP BARNARDO/MARCELLUS] Ed.; *Both.* Q2; *All.*
F   259. grizzled] Q2; grisly F   262. tonight] Q4; to nigh Q2; to
Night F   263. walk] Q2; wake F   264. warrant it] Q2; warrant
you it F   269. tenable] Q2; treble F   270. whatsomever] Q2;
whatsoeuer F   276. loves] Q2; loue F   276. SD *All . . . exit.*]
Ed.; *Exeunt.* Q2, F *printing it 1 line earlier*   279. Foul] F; fonde
Q2

1.3. 0. SD *his sister*] Q2; *omit* F   3. convey] Q2; Conuoy
F   3. is] F; in Q2   6. favor] Q2; fauours F   9. Forward] Q2;
Froward F   10. perfume and] Q2; *omit* F   15. bulk] F; bulkes

Q2   19. will] Q2; feare F   21. *omit* Q2   24. safety] Q2; sanctity
F   24. the health] Ed.; health Q2, F   24. this whole] Q2; the
weole F   30. particular act and place] Q2; peculiar Sect and
force F   38. you in] Q2; within F   44. their] Q2; the F   50.
watchman] Q2; watchmen F   53. like] F; *omit* Q2   56. SD *1
line earlier in* Q2   62. for. There,] Q2 (~, ~ ͜); ~ ͜ ~: F   63.
thee] Q2; you F   65. Look] Q2; See F   68. Those] Q2; The
F   69. unto] Q2; to F   71. new-hatched] Q2; vnhatch't F   71.
courage] Q2; Comrade F   80. Are] F; Or Q2   81. be] F; boy
Q2   82. loan] F; loue Q2   83. dulls the] F; dulleth Q2   89.
you.]~ ͜ Q2   89. invests] Q2; inuites F   96. Lord] Q2; L.
F   107. you?] ~ ͜ Q2   115. these] Q2; his F   118. Running]
Ed.; Wrong Q2; Roaming F   123. With almost all the holy
vows] Q2; with all the vowes F   124. springes] F; springs
Q2   126. Lends] Q2; Giues F   129. From] Q2; For F   129.
time] Q2; time Daughter F   130. something] Q2; somewhat
F   132. parle] Q2; parley F   134. tether] F; tider Q2   137. that
dye] Q2; the eye F   138. imploratory] F; imploratotors Q2
139. bawds] Ed.; bonds Q2, F   140. beguile] F; beguide Q2

   1.4.   0. SD *and*] Q2; *omit* F   1. it is] Q2; is it F   2. a] F; *omit*
Q2   6. It then] Q2; then it F   7. SD Q2; *omit* F   10. wassail]
Q2; wassels F   16. But] Q2; And F   19–41. Q2 *only*   19. revel]
Q5; reueale Q2   30. the] Ed.; their Q2   39. evil] Ed.; eale
Q2   47. intents] Q2; euents F   50. O, answer] Q2; Oh, oh,
answer F   54. interred] Q2; enurn'd F   61. the reaches] Q2;
thee; reaches F   62. SD *Ghost beckons.*] Ed.; *Beckins.* Q2; *Ghost
beckens Hamlet.* F   67. waves] Q2; wafts F   70. I will] Q2; will I
F   78. summit] Ed.; somnet Q2; Sonnet F   80. assume] Q2;
assumes F   82. madness?] ~ , Q2; ~ ͜ F   83–86. Q2 *only*   87.
waves] Q2; wafts F   89. hands] Q2; hand F   92. arture] Q2;
Artire F   97. imagination] F; imagion Q2

   1.5.   1. Whither] Q2; Where F   24. knotted] Q2; knotty
F   26. fearful] Q2; fretfull F   28. List, list, O] Q2; list *Hamlet*,
oh F   30. God] Q2; Heauen F   35. Haste me] Q2; Hast, hast me
F   35. that I, with] Q2; That with F   40. roots] Q2; rots F   50.
wit] Ed; wits Q2, F   50. with] Q2; hath F   52. to his] Q2; to to
this F   54. a] F; *omit* Q2   62. lust] F; but Q2   63. sate] F; sort
Q2   65. morning] Q2; Mornings F   67. of] Q2; in F   69.

hebona] Q2; Hebenon F   71. leprous] Q2; leaperous F   75. posset] F; possesse Q2   76. eager] Q2; Aygre F   78. barked] Q2; bak'd F   82. of queen] Q2; and Queene F   84. unaneled] F; vnanueld Q2   86. With all] F; Withall Q2   91. howsomever] Q2; howsoeuer F   91. pursues] Q2; pursuest F   98. adieu, adieu. Remember] Q2; adue, *Hamlet*: remember F   98. SD F; *omit* Q2   100. Hold, hold, my] Q2; hold my F   102. stiffly] F; swiftly Q2   111. Yes, by] Q2; yes, yes, by F   114. My tables— meet] Q2; My Tables, my Tables; meet F   119. SD *1 line later in* F, *which prefixes line 120* "Hor & Mar. within."   122. Heavens] Q2; Heauen F   123. SP HAMLET] Q2; *Mar.* F   124. SP MARCEL-LUS] Q2; *Hor.* F   125. bird] F; and Q2   136. SP HORATIO/MAR-CELLUS] Ed.; *Booth.* Q2; *Both.* F   136. my lord] F; *omit* Q2   144. desire] Q2; desires F   147. I will] Q2; Look you, Ile F   148. whirling] Q2; hurling F   152. Horatio] Q2; my Lord F   161. SP HORATIO/MARCELLUS] Ed.; *Booth.* Q2; *Both.* F   168. SP *Ghost.* Q2, F   177. our] Q2; for F   180–81. *lines transposed in* F   182. by his sword] Q2; *omit* F   183. earth] Q2; ground F   188. your] Q2; our F   190. some'er] Q2; so ere F   193. times] Q2; time F   194. this] Q2; thus F   196. Well, well, we] Q2; well, we F   198. they] Q2; there F   201. this do swear] Q2; this not to doe F   202. you] Q2; you: | Swear F   205. With all] F; Withall Q2

2.1.   0. SD *old . . . Reynaldo*] Ed.; *old Polonius, with his man or two* Q2; *Polonius, and Reynoldo* F   1. this] Q2; his F   3. marvelous] Q2; maruels F   4. to make inquire] Q2; you make inquiry F   16. As] Q2; And F   31. no] F; *omit* Q2   38. unre-claimèd] Q2; vnreclaim'd F   44. wit] Q2; warrant F   46. i' th'] F; with Q2   49. seen ⌐.] Q2; ~. F   53. or] Q2; and F   59–60. at "friend . . . gentleman."] F; *omit* Q2   62. closes thus] Q2; closes with you thus F   64. such or such] Q2; such and such F   66. o'ertook] F; or tooke Q2   70. take . . . carp] Q2; takes . . . Cape F   83. SD *Reynaldo exits.*] Q2; *Exit.* F. *Both* Q2 *and* F *set* SD *1 line earlier.*   85. O, my lord] Q2; Alas F   86. i' th' . . . God] Q2; in the . . . Heauen F   87. closet] Q2; Chamber F   107. As] Q2; That F   109. shoulder] Q2; shoulders F   111. helps] Q2; helpe F   113. Come] Q2; *omit* F   117. passions] Q2;

passion F 124. heed] Q2; speed F 125. feared] Q2; feare
F 127. By heaven] Q2; It seemes F 134. Come] Q2; *omit* F
2.2. 0. SD *Flourish.*] Q2; *omit* F 0. SD *and Attendants*] *omit*
Q2; *Cum aliis* F 5. so call] Q2; so I call F 6. Sith nor] Q2;
Since not F 10. dream] Q2; deeme F 12. sith . . . havior] Q2;
since . . . humour F 16. occasion] Q2; Occasions F 17. Q2;
omit F 20. is] Q2; are F 31. But] Q2; *omit* F 33. service] Q2;
Seruices F 39. these] Q2; the F 42. Ay] Q2; *omit* F 42. SD
Q2; *Exit.* F, *set 1 line earlier* 46. I assure my] Q2; Assure you,
my F 48. and] Q2; one F 51. it hath] Q2; I haue F 53. do I]
Q2; I do F 55. fruit] Q2; Newes F 57. dear Gertrude] Q2;
sweet Queene F 60. o'erhasty] F; hastie Q2 61. SD *Enter . . .
Polonius.*] *Enter Polonius, Voltumand, and Cornelius.* F, *set 1 line
earlier in both* Q2 *and* F 62. my] Q2; *omit* F 77. three-score]
Q2; three F 81. shown] Q2 (shone); F 83. this] Q2; his F 91.
SD *Voltemand and Cornelius exit.*] Ed.; *Exeunt Embassadors.*
Q2; *Exit Ambass.* F 92. is well] Q2; is very well F 97. since] F;
omit Q2 106. 'tis 'tis] Q2; it is F 116. SD *He reads.*] Ed.; *The
Letter.* F; *omit* Q2 120. Thus] Q2; these F 121. *etc.*] Q2; *omit*
F 123. SD *He reads the letter.*] *Letter.* Q2; *omit* F 133. shown]
Q2; shew'd F 134. above] F; about Q2 134. solicitings] Q2;
soliciting F 146. winking] F; working Q2 149. bespeak:] Q2
(~,); ~ ˌ F 151. prescripts] Q2; Precepts F 152. his] F; her
Q2 155. repelled] Q2; repulsed F 157. watch] F; wath Q2
158. a] F; *omit* Q2 159. wherein] Q2; whereon F 160.
mourn] Q2; waile F 161. 'tis] F; *omit* Q2 162. like] Q2; likely
F 175. does] Q2; ha's F 181. But] Q2; And F 182. SD Q2 *1
line earlier;* F *one-half line earlier* 190. Excellent well] Q2;
Excellent, excellent well F 195. ten] Q2; two F 202. but, as]
Q2; but not as F 206. far gone] Q2; farre gone, farre gone
F 213. that you read] Q2; you meane F 214. rogue] Q2; slaue
F 216. and] Q2; or F 217. lack] Q2; locke F 218. most] Q2;
omit F 220–21. for yourself] Q2; for you your selfe F 221.
shall grow] Q2; should be F 229. sanity] F; sanctity Q2 230–
31. and . . . him] F; *omit* Q2 231. My lord] Q2; My Honourable
Lord F 232. will take] Q2; I will most humbly | Take F 233.
sir] F; *omit* Q2 234. will more] F; will not more Q2 234–35.

except my life, except my life, except my life] Q2; except my life,
my life F   237. SD *2 lines earlier in* Q2; *1 line later in* F   238.
the] Q2; my F   242. excellent] F; extent Q2   246. overhappy.]
F; euer happy ‸ Q2   247. cap] F; lap Q2   254. What news] Q2;
What's the newes F   255. that] F; *omit* Q2   258–89. Let . . .
attended] F; *omit* Q2   286. SP ROSENCRANTZ/GUILDENSTERN]
Ed.; *Both* F   293. even] F; euer Q2   300. Anything] Q2; Why
any thing F   301. of] Q2; *omit* F   310. can] Q2; could F   317.
discovery, and your] Q2; discovery of your F   318. Queen‸]
Q2; ~: F   320. exercises] Q2; exercise F   320. heavily] Q2;
heauenly F   324. firmament] Q2; *omit* F   325. appeareth noth-
ing] Q2; appeares no other thing F   326. but] Q2; then F   327.
a] F; *omit* Q2   328. faculties] Q2; faculty F   328–30. moving
‸ . . . admirable; . . . action ‸ . . . angel, . . . apprehension ‸] F
(~ ‸ . . . ~? . . . ~, . . . ~? . . . ~,);   ~, . . . ~ ‸ . . . ~, . . . ~ ‸
. . . ~, Q2   333. no] F; *omit* Q2   333. women] Q2; Woman
F   337. then] Q2; *omit* F   344. on] Q2; of F   347–48. the
clown . . . sear] F; *omit* Q2   348. tickle] Ed.; tickled F   349.
blank] F; black Q2   351. such] Q2; *omit* F   359. are they] Q2;
they are F   360–85. F; *omit* Q2   365. berattle] F2; be-ratled
F   372. most like] Ed.; like most F   375. to-do] ~ ‸ ~ F   386.
very] Q2; *omit* F   387. mouths] Q2; mowes F   388. fifty] Q2;
omit F   390. 'Sblood] Q2; *omit* F   394. then] Q2; *omit* F   396.
this] Q2; the F   396. lest my] F; let me Q2   407. swaddling] Q2;
swathing F   408. Haply] Q2, F (Happily)   410. prophesy ‸] Q2;
~. F   411. sir, a] Q2; Sir: for a F   412. then] Q2; so F   415.
was] Q2; *omit* F   419. came] Q2; can F   421–22. pastoral-
comical, historical-pastoral] Q2; ~-~-~-~ F   422–23. tragical-
. . . -pastoral] F; *omit* Q2   443. pious] Q2; *Pons* F   444. abridgment comes] Q2; Abridgments come F   444. SD *Enter the
Players.*] Q2; *Enter foure or fiue Players.* F   446. my] F; *omit*
Q2   447. Why] Q2; *omit* F   447. valanced] Q2; valiant F   449.
By'r] F; by Q2   450. to] Q2; *omit* F   454. French falconers] F;
friendly Fankners Q2   457, 493, 527, 530. SP FIRST] F; *omit*
Q2   457. good] Q2; *omit* F   462. judgments] Q2; iudgement
F   466. were] Q2; was F   468. affectation] F; affection Q2
469–70. as wholesome . . . fine] Q2; *omit* F   470. One speech]
Q2; One cheefe Speech F   471. tale] F; talke Q2   472. when]

Q2; where F   481. *dismal.*] F (~:); ~ ‸ Q2   482. *total*] Q2; to
take F   485. *a damnèd*] Q2; damnèd F   486. *lord's murder*] Q2;
vilde Murthers F   490. Q2; *omit* F   496. *matched*] Q2; match
F   499. *Then . . . Ilium*] F; *omit* Q2   500. *this*] Q2; his F   506.
And] F; *omit* Q2   520. *fellies*] Ed.; follies Q2; Fallies F   527. *ah
woe . . . moblèd*] Q2; O who . . . inobled F   528. *moblèd*] Q2;
inobled F   529. "Moblèd queen" is good] Ed.; *omit* Q2; Inobled
Queene is good F   530. *flames*] Q2; flame F   531. *bisson
rheum*] F; *Bison* rehume Q2   531. *upon*] Q2; about F   540.
husband's] F; husband Q2   546. Prithee] Q2; Pray you F   547–
48. of this] Q2; *omit* F   550. abstract] Q2; Abstracts F   552.
live] Q2; liued F   555. bodykins] F; bodkin Q2   555. much]
Q2; *omit* F   556. shall] Q2; should F   562. SD *As . . . Player.*]
this ed.; *Exeunt Pol. and Players.* Q2 *after line 573; Exit Polon.* F
after line 560   566. ha 't] Q2 (hate), F   567. a] F; *omit* Q2   567.
dozen or] F; dosen lines, or Q2   573. till] Q2 (tell); til F   575.
good-bye to you] Q2 (God buy to you); God buy'ye F   575. SD
Rosencrantz . . . exit.] *Exeunt.* Q2; *Exeunt. Manet Hamlet.* F, *both
after line 574*   580. own] Q2; whole F   581. his] F; the Q2
581. wanned] Q2; warm'd F   583. and] Q2 (an); and F   586. to
Hecuba] F; to her Q2   588. the cue] F; that Q2   593. faculties]
Q2; faculty F   603. 'Swounds] Q2; Why F   606. have] F; a
Q2   607. offal. Bloody, bawdy] Q2 (~, ~, ~); Offall, bloudy: a
Bawdy F   610. F; *omit* Q2   611. Why] Q2; Who F   611. I! This]
Q2; I? I sure, this F   612. a] Q2; the F   612. father] Q3; *omit*
Q2, F   616. scullion] F; stallyon Q2   617. brains!—Hum, I]
Q2; Braine. | I F   626. do] Q2; but F   628. a] Q2; the F   628.
devil . . . devil] F; deale . . . deale Q2

3.1.   0. SD *and*] F; *omit* Q2   1. And] Q2 (An); And F   1.
conference] Q2; circumstance F   18. o'erraught] Q2; ore-
wrought F   20. here] Q2; *omit* F   29. into] Q2; on | To F   30.
SD Q2; *Exeunt.* F   31. too] F; two Q2   33. here] Q2; there
F   35. lawful espials] F; *omit* Q2   36. Will] F; Wee'le Q2   39.
no ‸] Q2; ~. F   52. loneliness] F; lowlines Q2   54. sugar] Q2;
surge F   56. too] Q2; *omit* F   63. Let's] F; *omit* Q2   63. SD
Enter Hamlet.] Q2 *1 line earlier;* F *Exeunt. Enter Hamlet*   68.
die,] F; ~ ‸ Q2   68. sleep—] ~ ‸ Q2, F   72. wished.] F; ~ ‸
Q2   72. die,] ~ ‸ Q2, F   79. proud] Q2; poore F   80. despised]

Q2; dispriz'd F   84. would fardels] Q2; would these Fardles
F   91. of us all] F; *omit* Q2   93. sicklied] F; sickled Q2   94.
pitch] Q2; pith F   95. awry] Q2; away F   101. well] Q2; well,
well, well F   105. not I] Q2; no F   106. you know] Q2; I know
F   108. the] F; these Q2   108–9. Their . . . lost] Q2; then . . .
left F   117. your honesty] F; you Q2   120. with] Q2; your
F   128. inoculate] F; euocutat Q2   131. to] F; *omit* Q2   137.
in, imagination˄] Q2; ~˄~, F   139. earth and heaven] Q2;
Heauen and Earth F   140. all] F; *omit* Q2   144. nowhere] Q2;
no way F   149. nunnery, farewell] Q2; Nunnery. Go, Farewell
F   153. Heavenly] Q2; O heauenly F   154. paintings] Q2;
pratlings F   154. too] F; *omit* Q2   155–56. hath . . . face . . .
yourselves] Q2; has . . . pace . . . your selfe F   156. jig and] Q2;
gidge, you F   157. lisp] F; list Q2   157. you nickname] Q2; and
nickname F   158. wantonness your] F; wantonness Q2   160.
marriage] Q2; Marriages F   166. expectancy] F; expectation
Q2   169. And] Q2; Haue F   170. musicked] Q2; Musicke
F   171. that] F; what Q2   172. time] Q2; tune F   173. stature]
Q2; Feature F   175. Q2 *uncorr. prints* "Exit."   176. SP KING,
advancing with Polonius] Ed.; *Enter King and Polonius.* Q2,
F   178. soul˄] Q2; ~? F   181. for] Q2; *omit* F   191. his] Q2;
this F   197. grief] Q2; Greefes F   203. unwatched] F; vn-
matcht Q2

3.2.   0. *three*] Q2; *two or thrée* F   1. pronounced] F; pro-
noun'd Q2   3. our] Q2; your F   4. town-crier spoke] Q2;
town-crier had spoke F   5. with] Q2; *omit* F   6–7. say, whirlwind of your passion] Q2; say) the Whirle-winde of (Passion
F   9. hear] Q2; see F   13. would] Q2; could F   20. o'erstep]
Q2; ore-stop F   24. own] F; *omit* Q2   27. makes] Q2; make
F   29. the] F; *omit* Q2   31. praise] F; praysd Q2   34. nor man]
Q2; or Norman F   39. sir] F; *omit* Q2   47. SD *Players exit.*] F;
omit Q2   47. SD *Enter . . . Rosencrantz.*] *placed as in* F; *2 lines
later in* Q2   51. SD *Polonius exits.*] F; *omit* Q2   53. ROSENCRANTZ
Ay] Q2; BOTH. We will F   53. SD *They exit.*] F; *Exeunt they two.*
Q2   54. SD *1 line earlier in* F   59. SP HAMLET] F; *omit* Q2   64.
lick] Q2; like F   66. fawning] Q2; faining F   67. her] Q2; my
F   68. distinguish, her election] F; ~˄ ~~, Q2   69. Hath] F;
S'hath Q2   72. Hast] Q2; Hath F   74. commeddled] Q2; co-

mingled F   84. thy] Q2; my F   89. heedful] Q2; needful F   92.
In] Q2; To F   95. detecting] F; detected Q2   95. SD *omit* Q2;
following 97 SD *in* F   97. SD *2 lines earlier in* Q2, F   97. SD *the
King's*] Ed.; *his* F *torches*] *Torches. Danish March* F   104. mine
now. My] ~~ ⌃ ~ Q2; ~. ~~ F   106. did I] Q2; I did F   108.
What] Q2; And what F   115. SP QUEEN] F; *Ger.* Q2   115. dear]
Q2; good F   121–22. F; *omit* Q2   144. SD *The . . . follows.*] Q2;
Hoboyes play. The dumbe shew enters. F   145. *a Queen*] Q2;
Queene F   145. *very lovingly*] F; *omit* Q2   146. *and he her*] Q2;
omit F   146–47. *She . . . him*] F; *omit* Q2   148. *He lies*] Q2;
Layes F   150. *comes*] F; *come* Q2   150. *another man*] Q2; *a
Fellow* F   150. *it, pours*] Q2; *it, and powres* F   151. *sleeper's*]
Q2; *Kings* F   151. *leaves him*] Q2; *Exits* F   152. *dead, makes*]
Q2; *dead, and makes* F   153. *three or four*] Q2; *two or three
Mutes* F   153–54. *come . . . seem to condole*] Q2; *comes . . .
seeming to lament* F   155. *harsh*] Q2; *loath and vnwilling*
F   156. *his*] F; *omit* Q2   156. SD *Players exit.*] Ed.; *Exeunt* F;
omit Q2   158. is miching] F; munching Q2   158. It] Q2; that
F   161. SD *one-half line later in* Q2; *after line 169 in* F   162. this
fellow] Q2; these Fellowes F   163. counsel] F; *omit* Q2   164.
he] Q2; they F   175. SD *and Queen*] Q2; *and his Queene* F   176
and hereafter to line 248. SP PLAYER KING] Ed.; *King* Q2,
F   177. *orbèd*] F; orb'd the Q2   182 and hereafter until line
251. SP PLAYER QUEEN] *Quee.* Q2; *Bap.* F   185. *your*] F; our
Q2   185. *former*] Q2; *forme* F   188. Q2; *omit* F   189. And] Q2;
For F   189. hold] Q2; holds F   190. In] F; Eyther none, in
Q2   191. love] F; Lord Q2   193–94. Q2; *omit* F   196. their] Q2;
my F   204. That's] Q2; Wormwood F   205. SP *omit* Q2; *Bapt.*
F   209. you ⌃] Q2; ~. F   213. the] Q2; like F   219. either] Q2;
other F   220. enactures] Q2; ennactors F   222. joys] F; ioy
Q2   227. favorite] Q2; fauourites F   239. me give] Q2; giue me
F   241–42. Q2; *omit* F   242. An] Ed.; And Q2   246. once
a . . . be wife] F; once I be a . . . be a wife Q2   247. printed after
line 245 in Q2   252. SD Ed.; *Exeunt.* Q2; *Exit* F   254. doth
protest] Q2; protests F   261. how?] F; ~ ⌃ Q2   267. SD *1 line
later in* Q2   269. as good as a] Q2; a good F   276. your] Q2;
omit F   277. Pox] F; *omit* Q2   282. Confederate] F; Considerat
Q2   284. infected] F; inuected Q2   286. usurp] F; vsurps

Q2   286. SD F; *omit* Q2   288. written] Q2; writ F   289. very]
Q2; *omit* F   292. F; *omit* Q2   296. SP POLONIUS] Q2; *All.*
F   300. *Thus*] Q2; So F   302. two] F; *omit* Q2   304. players]
Q2; players, sir F   321. SD *placed as in* Q2; *after line 316 in*
F   330. lord, with] Q2; Lord, rather with F   332. the] Q2; his
F   333. into more] Q2; into farre more F   336. start] F; stare
Q2   346. my] F; *omit* Q2   348. SP ROSENCRANTZ] Q2; *Guild.*
F   350. answer] Q2; answers F   351. as] Q2; *omit* F   358.
Impart] Q2; *omit* F   364. And do] Q2; And I do F   366.
surely . . . upon] Q2; freely . . . of F   372. sir] Q2; *omit* F   373.
SD *after line 371 in* Q2; *Enter one with a Recorder.* F   374.
recorders] Q2; recorder F   374. one] Q2; *omit* F   387. It
is . . . ventages] Q2; 'Tis . . . Ventiges F   388. fingers] Q2; fin-
ger F   388. thumb] F; the vmber Q2   389. eloquent] Q2;
excellent F   397. the top of] F; *omit* Q2   399. speak. 'Sblood]
Q2; Why F   400. think I] Q2; thinke, that I F   401–2. you can
fret] F; you fret Q2   402. me, you] F; me not, you Q2   402. SD
1 line later in Q2, F   406–7. yonder . . . of] Q2; that . . . like
F   408. Mass, and 'tis] Q2; Misse, and it's F   413. SP HAMLET]
F; *omit* Q2   413. I will] Q2; will I F   416. SP POLONIUS] F; *omit*
Q2   417. SP HAMLET] F; *omit* Q2   417–18. Leave me, friends]
placed here in F; *after line 415 in* Q2   418. SD *omit* Q2; *Exit.* F
after line 416   420. breathes] F; breakes Q2   424. bitter business as the day] F; busines as the bitter day Q2   429. daggers] F;
dagger Q2   432. SD Q2; *omit* F

   3.3.   6. near 's] Q2; dangerous F   7. brows] Q2; Lunacies
F   15. weal] Q2; spirit F   16. cess] Q2; cease F   18. or] Q2;
omit F   19. summit] Ed.; somnet Q2, F   20. huge] F; hough
Q2   23. ruin] F; raine Q2   24. with] F; *omit* Q2   26. about]
Q2; vpon F   28. SP ROSENCRANTZ] Q2; *Both.* F   28. SD
Rosencrantz . . . exit.] Ed.; *Exeunt Gent.* Q2, F   39. SD *Polonius
exits.*] Ed.; *Exit.* Q2 *after line 38*; *omit* F   54. pardoned] F;
pardon Q2   62. shove] F; showe Q2   77. pat] F; *omit* Q2   77.
a-praying] Q2; praying F   80. revenged] F; reuendge Q2   82.
sole] Q2; foule F   84. Why] Q2; Oh F   84. hire and salary] F;
base and silly Q2   86. With all] F; Withal Q2   86. flush] Q2;
fresh F   96. game, a-swearing] Q2; gaming, swearing F

   3.4.   0. SD Queen] F; *Gertrard* Q2   7. with him] F; *omit*

Q2   8. F; *omit* Q2   9. SP *and hereafter in 3.4 and 4.1* QUEEN] F; *Ger.* Q2, *except line 61: "Quee."*   9. warrant] F; wait Q2   10. SD *Enter Hamlet.*] *placed as in* F; Q2 *after line 7*   15. a wicked] Q2; an idle F   21. And (would it . . . so)] And‸ would it . . . so, Q2; But‸ would you . . . so. F   25. inmost] F; most Q2   27. Help] Q2; Helpe, helpe F   28. Help] Q2; helpe, helpe, helpe F   29. SD *kills Polonius.*] F *1 line later; omit* Q2   39. better] Q2; Betters F   46. be] Q2; is F   51. off] Q2 (of); off F   53. sets] Q2; makes F   57–58. glow‸ I O'er] Q2; glow, I Yea F   59. heated] Q2; tristfull F   62. That] F; *Ham.* That Q2   63. SP HAMLET] F; *omit* Q2   65. this] Q2; his F   67. and] Q2; or F   69. heaven] F; heaue, a Q2   75. brother] Q2; breath F   81–86. Sense . . . difference] Q2; *omit* F   88–91. Eyes . . . mope] Q2; *omit* F   98. And] Q2; As F   98. panders] F; pardons Q2   100. eyes into my very soul] F; very eyes into my soule Q2   101. grainèd] F; greeued Q2   102. not leave their] F; leaue there their Q2   111. tithe] F; kyth Q2   117. SD *1 line earlier in* Q2, F   119. your] Q2; you F   134. do] Q2; *omit* F   135. th' incorporal] Q2; their corporall F   149. whom] Q2; who F   156. SD *Ghost exits.*] Q2; *Exit.* F   160. F; *omit* Q2   164. I] F; *omit* Q2   166. that] Q2; a F   172. on] Q2; or F   173. ranker] Q2; ranke F   174. these] Q2; this F   179. live] F; leaue Q2   181. Assume] F; Assune Q2   182–86. That . . . on] Q2; *omit* F   186. on.] ~‸ Q2   186. Refrain tonight] F; to refraine night Q2   188–91. the . . . potency] Q2; *omit* F   200. This] Q2; Thus F   201. Q2; *omit* F   204. bloat] Q2; blunt F   208. ravel] F; rouell Q2   210. mad] Q2; made F   225–33. Q2; *omit* F   236. night‸ indeed] Q2; ~. ~F   238. a foolish] F; a most foolish Q2   240. SD *They . . . Polonius.*] Ed.; *Exit.* Q2; *Exit Hamlet . . . Polonius.* F

4.1.   0. SD *Enter . . . Guildenstern.*] Q2; *Enter King.* F   1. matter] Q2; matters F   4. Q2; *omit* F   5. mine own] Q2; my good F   7. sea] Q2; Seas F   10. Whips out his rapier, cries] Q2; He whips his Rapier out, and cries F   11. this] Q2; his F   23. let] Q2; let's F   33. SD *Enter . . . Guildenstern.*] Q2 *1 line earlier;* F *one-half line earlier*   36. mother's closet] Q2; Mother Clossets F   36. dragged] F; dreg'd Q2   38. SD *Rosencrantz . . . exit.*] F (*Exit Gent.*); *omit* Q2   42–45. Whose . . . air] Q2; *omit* F

4.2.   0. SD *Enter Hamlet.*] F; *Enter Hamlet, Rosencraus, and*

others. Q2 2. F; *omit* Q2 3. SP HAMLET] F; *omit* Q2 3. But
soft] Q2; *omit* F 4. SD *Enter . . . others.*] F (*Enter Ros. and
Guildensterne.*) 6. Compounded] F; Compound Q2 17–18.
an ape] F; *omit* Q2 18. an apple] Q2; *omit* F 30–31. Hide . . .
after] F; *omit* Q2

4.3. 0. SD *Enter . . . three.*] Q2; *Enter King.* F 7. never] Q2;
neerer F 11. SD *Enter Rosencrantz.*] F; *Enter Rosencraus and
all the rest.* Q2 18. Ho . . . lord] Q2; Hoa, *Guildensterne?* Bring
in my Lord. F 18. SD *They . . . Hamlet.*] Ed.; *They enter.* Q2;
Enter Hamlet and Guildensterne. F 23. politic] Q2; *omit* F 25.
ourselves] Q2; our selfe F 27. service—two] Q2 (~, ~);
seruice to F 29–32. Q2; *omit* F 33. SP KING] F; *King. King.*
Q2 38. there] F; thrre Q2 39. if, indeed] Q2; indeed, if F 40.
within] Q2; *omit* F 44. deed, for] Q2; deed of thine, for F 48.
With fiery quickness] F; *omit* Q2 50. is] Q2; at F 56. them]
Q2; him F 61. and so] F; so Q2 73. congruing] Q2; coniuring
F 77. were ne'er begun] F; will nere begin Q2

4.4. 0. SD *Enter . . . stage.*] Q2; *Enter Fortinbras with an
Armie.* F 3. Craves] Q2; Claimes F 9. softly] Q2; safely F 9.
SD *All . . . others.*] Ed.; *Enter Hamlet, Rosencraus, &c.* Q2; *Exit.*
F 10–69. Q2; *omit* F 20. name.] ~ . Q2

4.5. 0. SD *Queen*] F; *Gertrard* Q2; *Enter Queene and Horatio.*
F 2, 5. SP GENTLEMAN] Q2; *Hor.* F 11. aim] F; yawne Q2 15.
might] Q2; would F 18. SP HORATIO] Q2; *Qu.* F 21. SP
QUEEN] Ed.; *omit* Q2, F 22. SP To] F; *Quee.* Q2 25. SD
Enter . . . distracted.] F; *Enter Ophelia.* Q2 *after line 21* 28. SD
sings] Ed.; *shee sings.* Q2 *after line 27; omit* F 34. SD *Sings*] Ed.;
Song. Q2 *after line 35; omit* F 38. Q2; *omit* F 41. SD *Enter
King.*] Q2; *after line 37 in* F 43. SD *sings*] Ed.; *Song.* Q2 *after
line 44; omit* F 43. all] Q2; *omit* F 44. ground] Q2; graue
F 47. God] F; good Q2 51. Pray let's] Q2; Pray you let's
F 53. SD *Sings*] Ed.; *Song.* Q2 *after line 53; omit* F 62. Indeed,
without] Q2; Indeed la? without F 69. Q2; *omit* F 70. 'a] Q2;
ha F 72. thus] Q2; this F 74. would] Q2; should F 77–78.
Good . . . good . . . good . . . good] F; God . . . god . . . god
. . . god Q2 78. SD F; *omit* Q2 81. and now behold] Q2; *omit*
F 83. sorrows come] Q2; sorrowes comes F 84. battalions]
Q2; Battaliaes F 87. their] F; *omit* Q2 96. Feeds] Q2; Keepes

F 96. his] F; this Q2 100. person] Q2; persons F 104. F; *omit* Q2 105. Q2; *omit* F 106. is] Q2; are F 106. SD *after line 103* Q2, F 116. They] F; The Q2 118. SD *A noise within.*] Q2 *1 line later; Noise within.* F *2 lines later* 121. SD *Enter . . . others.*] Q2 *1 line earlier; Enter Laertes.* F *1 line earlier* 122. this king?— Sirs] Q2 (~ ~? ~); the King, sirs? F 130. that's calm] Q2; that calme F 156. world] F; worlds Q2 161. father, is 't] Q2; Fathers death, if F 162. swoopstake] Ed.; soopstake Q2, F 168. pelican] Q2; Politician F 173. sensibly] Q2; sensible F 174. 'pear] Q2; pierce F 176. F; *Laer.* Let her come in. Q2, *printed after "Enter Ophelia."* 177. SP LAERTES] F; *omit* Q2 177. SD *Enter Ophelia.* F *1 line earlier;* Q2 *after line 175* 180. with] Q2; by F 181. turn] Q2; turnes F 184. an old] F; a poore Q2 185–87. F; *omit* Q2 188. SD *sings*] Ed.; *Song.* Q2 *after line 188; omit* F 189. F; *omit* Q2 190. in . . . rained] Q2; on . . . raines F 194. A-down a-down] Q2; downe a-downe F 200. you] Q2; *omit* F 200. pansies] Q2; Paconcies F 204. columbines] F; colembines Q2 206. herb of grace] Q2; Herbe-Grace F 206. You] Q2; Oh you F 206. must] F; may Q2 211. afflictions] Q2; Affliction F 213. SD *sings*] Ed.; *Song.* Q2 *after line 213; omit* F 218. was] Q2; *omit* F 219. All] F; *omit* Q2 222. God 'a mercy] Q2; Gramercy F 223. Christians'] Q2; Christian F 223. I pray God] F; *omit* Q2 224. SD *She exits.*] *omit* Q2; *Exeunt Ophelia* F 225. see] F; *omit* Q2 225. O God] Q2; you Gods F 226. commune] Q2; common F 238. funeral] Q2; buriall F 242. call 't] Q2; call F

4.6. 0. SD *Enter . . . others.*] Q2; *Enter Horatio, with an Attendant.* F 2. SP GENTLEMAN] Q2; *Ser.* F 2. Seafaring men] Q2; Saylors F 6. greeted,] ~. Q2 6. SD *Enter Sailors.*] Q2; *Enter Saylor.* F 9. an 't] F; and Q2 10. came from th' ambassador] Q2; comes from th'Ambassadours F 13. SP HORATIO] Q2; *omit* F 16. warlike] Q2; Warlicke F 18. and] Q2; *omit* F 22. good] F; *omit* Q2 23. speed] Q2; hast F 25. thine] Q2; your F 26. bore] F; bord Q2 30. He] F; So Q2 32. SP Come] F; *Hor.* Come Q2 32. give] F; *omit* Q2 34. SD *They exit.*] Ed.; *Exeunt.* Q2; *Exit.* F

4.7. 7. proceeded] F; proceede Q2 8. criminal] Q2; crimefull F 9. greatness] Q2; *omit* F 13. But] Q2; And F 16.

conjunctive] F; concliue Q2   22. Work] Q2; Would F   24. loud
a wind] F; loued Arm'd Q2   26. But . . . have aimed] Q2;
And . . . had arm'd F   29. Whose worth] Q2; Who was F   37.
SD *with letters*] Q2; *omit* F   38–40. F; *omit* Q2   41. SP These]
Ed.; *Messen.* These Q2; This F   45. Q2; *omit* F   51. *your*] F; you
Q2   52. *the occasion*] Q2; th'Occasions F   53. *and more
strange*] F; *omit* Q2   53. *Hamlet*] F; *omit* Q2   54. SP What] F;
King. What Q2   55. and] Q2; Or F   59. advise] F; deuise
Q2   62. shall] F; *omit* Q2   67–68. Ay . . . will] Q2; If so you'l
F   70. checking] F; the King Q2   77–92. LAERTES . . .
graveness] Q2; *omit* F   92. Two months since] Q2; Some two
Monthes hence F   95. can] Q2; ran F   96. unto] Q2; into
F   99. topped] Q2; past F   99. my] F; me Q2   104. Lamord]
Q2; *Lamound* F   107. the] Q2; our F   111. especial] Q2;
especially F   113–16. The . . . them] Q2; *omit* F   119. you] Q2;
him F   121. What] Q2; Why F   130–40. Q2; *omit* F   139.
spendthrift] Q5; spend thirfts Q2   142. yourself indeed your
. . . son] Q2; your selfe your . . . sonne indeed F   153. on] F;
ore Q2   157. pass] F; pace Q2   160. that] F; *omit* Q2   162.
that, but dip] Q2; I but dipt F   171. shape.] Ed.; ~ ˌ Q2; ~ ,
F   176. did] Q2; should F   177. cunnings] Q2; commings
F   180. that] Q2; the F   181. prepared] F; prefard Q2   185–
86. But . . . noise] Q2; how sweet Queene F   188. they] Q2;
they'l F   190. askant the] Q2; aslant a F   191. hoar] F; horry
Q2   192. make] Q2; come F   195. our cold] F; our cull-cold
Q2   199. her] Q2; the F   202. lauds] Q2; tunes F   206. their]
Q2; her F   207. lay] Q2; buy F   209. she is] Q2; is she F   217.
drowns] Q2; doubts F

5.1.   0. SD *Enter . . . Another*.] Ed.; *Enter two Clownes.* Q2,
F   1 and throughout scene SP GRAVEDIGGER] Ed.; *Clowne* Q2,
F   2. when she] Q2; that F   3. is. Therefore] Q2; is, and
therefore F   9. *se offendendo*] F; so offended Q2   12. to act]
Q2; an Act F   12. do, to] Q2; doe, and to F   12. Argal] F; or all
Q2   35–38. OTHER . . . arms] F; *omit* Q2   44. frame] F; *omit*
Q2   56. SD F; *omit* Q2   60. houses he] Q2; Houses that he
F   61. in, and] Q2; to *Yaughan* F   62. stoup] F; soope Q2   62.
SD this ed.; *Sings.* F; *Song.* Q2 *after line 63*   66. *a . . . a*] Q2;
omit F   67. SP HAMLET] F; *Enter Hamlet and Horatio. Ham.*

Q2 67. business? He] Q2 (busines? a); businesse, that he
F 68. in] Q2; at F 72. daintier] F; dintier Q2 73. SD *sings*] F;
Song. Q2 *after line 73* 74. *clawed*] Q2; *caught* F 75. *into*] Q2;
intill F 80. This] Q2; It F 81. now] Q2; *omit* F 81. o'erreach-
es] Q2; o're Offices F 81. would] Q2; could F 85. thou, sweet]
Q2; thou, good F 87. went] Q2; meant F 91. mazard] F;
massene Q2 92. an] Q2 (and); if F 96. SD *sings*] F; *Song*.
Q2 100. may] Q2; might F 101. of . . . quiddities] Q2; of
of . . . Quiddits F 102. quillities] Q2 (quillites); Quillets F
103. mad] Q2; rude F 108–9. Is . . . recoveries] F; *omit* Q2
110. his] F; *omit* Q2 111. double ones too] F; doubles Q2
113. scarcely] Q2; hardly F 117. calves'] Q2; Calue F 118.
which] Q2; that F 120. sirrah] Q2; Sir F 122. *O*] F; or
Q2 123. F; *omit* Q2 126. in 't, yet] Q2; in't; and yet F 142.
this . . . took] Q2; these . . . taken F 144. heel of the]
heeles of our F 145–46. been grave-maker] Q2; been a Graue-
maker F 147. all] F; *omit* Q2 152. that very] Q2; the very
F 153. is] Q2; was F 159. him there] Q2; him F 167. sexton]
Q2; sixteene F 169. Faith] Q2; Ifaith F 170. nowadays] F;
omit Q2 178. now hath lien you] Q2; now: this Scul, has laine
F 186. sir, was, sir, Yorick's] Q2; Sir, this same Scull sir, was
Yoricks F 190. Let me see] F; *omit* Q2 192. bore] Q2; borne
F 193–94. and now how abhorred in my imagination it is] Q2;
And how abhorred my Imagination is F 198. Not] Q2; No
F 199. grinning] Q2; Ieering F 200. chamber] F; table Q2
215–16. as thus] F; *omit* Q2 217. to] Q2; into F 220. Imperi-
ous] Q2; Imperiall F 223. winter's] F; waters Q2 223. SD
Enter . . . attendant.] Ed.; *Enter K. Q. Laertes and the corse.* Q2
*after line 224; Enter King, Queene, Laertes, and a Coffin, with
Lords attendant.* F *after line 224* 224. awhile] Q2; aside F 225.
this] Q2; that F 227. desp'rate] Q2; disperate F 228. of] Q2;
omit F 233, 244. SP DOCTOR] Q2; *Priest*. F 234. warranty] Q2;
warrantis F 236. been] Q2; haue F 237. prayers] Q2; praier
F 238. Shards] F; *omit* Q2 240. crants] Q2; Rites F 246. a]
Q2; sage F 257. have] Q2; t'haue F 258. treble woe] Q2;
terrible woer F 259. treble] F; double Q2 262. SD F; *omit*
Q2 267. grief] Q2; griefes F 269. Conjures] Q2; Coniure
F 275. For] Q2; Sir F 275. and] F; *omit* Q2 276. in me

something] Q2; something in me F   277. wisdom . . . Hold off]
Q2; wisenesse . . . Away F   280. Q2; *omit* F   281. SP HORATIO]
Q2; *Gen.* F   290. 'Swounds] Q2; Come F   291. woo't fast] Q2;
omit F   294. thou] F; *omit* Q2   302. SP QUEEN] Q2; *King.*
F   303. thus] F; this Q2   305. couplets] Q2; Cuplet F   311. SD
Hamlet exits.] Q2; *Exit.* F   312. thee] Q2; you F   312. SD
Horatio exits.] Q2 *here completes the SD begun in its margin 1 line*
above as "Exit Hamlet" with "and Horatio."; omit F   313. your]
Q2; you F   318. shortly] F; thirtie Q2

    5.2.   1. shall you] Q2; let me F   5. Methought] F; my thought
Q2   6. bilboes] F; bilbo Q2   7. praised] Q2; praise F   9.
deep . . . learn] Q2; deare . . . teach F   9. pall] Q2 *uncorr.;* fall
Q2 *corr.;* paule F   20. unfold] Q2; vnseale F   22. A] Q2; Oh
F   23. reasons] Q2; reason F   31. now] Q2; me F   33. villain-
ies] Ed.; villaines Q2, F   34. Or] Q2; Ere F   41. Th' effect] Q2;
The effects F   45. like . . . might] Q2; as . . . should F   48.
ases] Ed.; as sir Q2; Assis F   49. knowing] Q2; know F   51.
those] Q2; the F   54. ordinant] Q2; ordinate F   57. the form]
Q2; forme F   58. Subscribed] F; Subscribe Q2   61. sequent]
Q2; sement F   64. F; *omit* Q2   65. defeat] Q2; debate
F   71. think] Q2; thinkst F   77–91. F; *omit* Q2   88. court] Ed.;
count F   91. SD *Enter . . . courtier.*] *Enter a Courtier.* Q2; *Enter*
young Osricke. F   92 and thereafter SP OSRIC] F; *Cour.* Q2   94.
humbly] F; humble Q2   101. say] Q2; saw F   102. lordship]
Q2; friendship F   104. sir] Q2; *omit* F   105. Put] F; *omit*
Q2   111. But yet] Q2; *omit* F   111. sultry . . . for] F; sully . . .
or Q2   114. how. My] Q2; how; but my F   118. good my lord]
Q2; in good faith F   119–48. Q2; *omit* F   120. gentleman] Q3;
gentlemen Q2   122. feelingly] Q3; sellingly Q2 *uncorr.;* felling-
ly Q2 *corr.*   127. dozy] Q2 *uncorr.;* dazzie Q2 *corr.*   128. yaw]
Q2 *uncorr.;* raw Q2 *corr.*   139. to 't] Q2 *uncorr.;* doo't Q2
corr.   150. is] Q2; is at his weapon F   151–56. Q2; *omit*
F   154. his] Q5; this Q2   160. King, sir, hath wagered] Q2; sir
King ha's wag'd F   161. has impawned] Q2; impon'd F   163.
hangers] F; hanger Q2   163. and] Q2; or F   168–69. Q2; *omit*
F   170. carriages] F; carriage Q2   172. a] Q2; *omit* F   173.
might be] F; be Q2 *uncorr.;* be might Q2 *corr.*   173. on. Six] Q2
(on, six); on sixe F   176. bet] Q2; but F   176–77. this all

"impawned," as you] Ed.; this all you Q2; this impon'd as
F 178. laid, sir, that] Q2; laid that F 179. yourself] Q2; you
F 180–81. hath laid on . . . nine . . . it] Q2; hath one . . . mine
. . . that F 189. an] Q2 (and); if F 192. deliver] Q2; redeliuer
F 192. e'en] F; *omit* Q2 196. Yours . . . He does] Ed.; Yours
doo's Q2; Yours, yours; hee does F 198. turn] Q2; tongue
F 201. did comply, sir] did sir Q2 *uncorr.*; did so sir Q2 *corr.*;
did Complie F 202–3. has . . . many . . . breed] Q2; had . . .
mine . . . Beauy F 204. out of an] Q2; outward F 205. yeasty]
F; histy Q2 206–7. fanned and winnowed] Ed.; prophane and
trennowed Q2; fond and winnowed F 208. trial] Q2; tryalls
F 208 SD–222. Q2; *omit* F 223. lose, my] Q2; lose this wager,
my F 226. but] F; *omit* Q2 226. how ill all's here] Q2; how all
heere F 230. gaingiving] F; gamgiuing Q2 231. it] Q2; *omit*
F 233. a] F; *omit* Q2 235. now] F; *omit* Q2 236. will] F; well
Q2 237–38. of aught he leaves knows, what] Q2; ha's ought of
what he leaues. What F 238. SD Q2; *Enter King, Queene,
Laertes and Lords, with other Attendants with Foyles, and Gaunt-
lets, a Table and Flagons of Wine on it.* F 244. a] Q2; *omit*
F 254. F; *omit* Q2 258. brother] Q2; Mother F 265. keep] F;
omit Q2 265. ungored] Q2; ungorg'd F 265. till] F; all
Q2 268. I embrace] Q2; I do embrace F 270. Come on] F;
omit Q2 274. off] Q2 (of) 282. better] Q2; better'd F 285.
SD F *1 line earlier; omit* Q2 291. union] F; Vnice Q2 294.
trumpet] Q2; Trumpets F 298. SD Q2; *omit* F 300. my lord]
Q2; on sir F 300. SD F; *omit* Q2 307. SD Q2 (*after line 304
and adding "Florish, a peece goes off."; Trumpets sound, and shot
goes off.* F *after line 308* 309. it] Q2; *omit* F 311. A touch, a
touch] F; *omit* Q2 311. confess 't] Q2; confesse F 314.
Here . . . napkin] Q2; Heere's a Napkin F 325. do] Q2; *omit*
F 327. afeard] F; sure Q2 328. SD F; *omit* Q2 330. SD F;
omit Q2 336. own] Q2; *omit* F 344. Hamlet. Hamlet] F;
Hamlet Q2 346. an hour's] Q2; houre of F 347. thy] F; my
Q2 353. SD F; *omit* Q2 356. murd'rous] F; *omit* Q2 357. off]
Q2 (of) 357. thy union] F; the Onixe Q2 358. SD F; *omit*
Q2 363. SD F; *omit* Q2 371. cause aright] Q2; causes right
F 378. God] Q2; good F 379. I leave] Q2; liue F 384. SD *A
march a farre off.* Q2; *March afarre off, and shout within.* F 396.

F; *omit* Q2 396. SD F; *omit* Q2 397. cracks] Q2; cracke F 399. SD Q2; *Enter Fortinbras and English Ambassador, with Drumme, Colours, and Attendants.* F 403. This] Q2; His F 403. proud] F; prou'd Q2 405. shot] Q2; shoote F 421. th'] F; *omit* Q2 425. forced] F; for no Q2 433. now] Q2; are F 434. also] Q2; always F 435. on] F; no Q2 444. royal] Q2; royally F 445. rite] Q2; rites F 447. bodies] Q2; body F 449. SD *Exeunt.* Q2; *Exeunt . . . off.* F

Hamlet:
A Modern Perspective

Michael Neill

The great Russian director Vsevolod Meyerhold used to maintain that "if all the plays ever written suddenly disappeared and only *Hamlet* miraculously survived, all the theaters in the world would be saved. They could all put on *Hamlet* and be successful."[1] Perhaps Meyerhold exaggerated because of his frustration—he was prevented from ever staging the tragedy by Soviet dictator Joseph Stalin, who apparently thought it too dangerous to be performed—but Meyerhold's sense of *Hamlet*'s extraordinary breadth of appeal is amply confirmed by its stage history. Praised by Shakespeare's contemporaries for its power to "please all" as well as "to please the wiser sort,"[2] it provided his company with an immediate and continuing success. It was equally admired by popular audiences at the Globe on the Bankside, by academic playgoers "in the two Universities of Cambridge and Oxford," and at court—where it was still in request in 1637, nearly forty years after its first performance. And in 1609, the sea captain William Keeling considered the play ideal for amateur performance by his crew, "to keepe [them] from idleness and unlawful games, or sleepe" during a lengthy West African cruise.

In the four centuries since it was first staged, *Hamlet* has never lost its theatrical appeal, remaining today the most frequently performed of Shakespeare's tragedies. At the same time, it has developed a reputation as the most intellectually puzzling of his plays, and it has already attracted more commentary than any other work in English except the Bible. Even today, when criticism stresses the importance of the reader's role in "constructing" the texts of the past, there is something astonishing about *Hamlet*'s capacity to accommodate the most bafflingly different readings.[3]

In the early nineteenth century, for instance, Romantic critics read it as the psychological study of a prince too delicate and sensitive for his public mission; to later nineteenth-century European intellectuals, the hero's anguish and self-reproach spoke so eloquently of the disillusionment of revolutionary failure that in czarist Russia "Hamletism" became the acknowledged term for political vacillation and disengagement. Our own century, not surprisingly, has discovered a more violent and disturbing play: to the French poet Paul Valéry, the tragedy seemed to embody the European death wish revealed in the carnage and devastation of the First World War; in the mid-1960s the English director Peter Hall staged it as a work expressing the political despair of the nuclear age; for the Polish critic Jan Kott, as for the Russian filmmaker Gregori Kozintsev, the play became "a drama of a political crime" in a state not unlike Stalin's Soviet empire;[4] while the contemporary Irish poet Seamus Heaney finds in it a metaphor for the murderous politics of revenge presently devouring his native Ulster:

> I am Hamlet the Dane,
> skull handler, parablist,
> smeller of rot
>
> in the state, infused
> with its poisons,
> pinioned by ghosts
> and affections
>
> murders and pieties[5]

Even the major "facts" of the play—the status of the Ghost, or the real nature of Hamlet's "madness"—are seen very differently at different times. Samuel Johnson, for example, writing in the 1760s, had no doubt that the hero's "madness," a source of "much mirth" to eighteenth-century audiences, was merely "pretended," but twentieth-century Hamlets onstage, even if they are not the full-fledged neurotics invented by Freud and his disciple Ernest Jones, are likely to show some signs of actual madness. Modern readings, too, while still fascinated by the hero's intellectual and emotional complexities, are likely to emphasize those characteristics that are least compatible with the idealized "sweet prince" of the Victorians—the diseased suspicion of women, revealed in his obsession with his mother's sexuality and his needless cruelty to Ophelia, his capacity for murderous violence (he dies with the blood of five people on his hands), and his callous indifference to the killing of such relative innocents as Polonius, Rosencrantz, and Guildenstern.

Hamlet's ability to adapt itself to the preconceptions of almost any audience, allowing the viewers, in the play's own sardonic phrase, to "botch the words up fit to their own thoughts" (4.5.12), results partly from the boldness of its design. Over the sensationalism and rough energy of a conventional revenge plot is placed a sophisticated psychological drama whose most intense action belongs to the interior world of soliloquy: Hamlet agrees to revenge his father's death at the urging of the Ghost, and thus steps into an old-fashioned revenge tragedy; but it is Hamlet's inner world, revealed to us in his soliloquies (speeches addressed not to other characters but to the audience, as if the character were thinking aloud), that equally excites our attention. It is as if two plays are occurring simultaneously.

Although *Hamlet* is often thought of as the most
personal of Shakespeare's tragedies, Shakespeare did
not invent the story of revenge that the play tells. The
story was an ancient one, belonging originally to Norse
saga. The barbaric narrative of murder and revenge—of
a king killed by his brother, who then marries the dead
king's widow, of the young prince who must pretend to
be mad in order to save his own life, who eludes a series
of traps laid for him by his wicked uncle, and who finally
revenges his father's death by killing the uncle—had
been elaborated in the twelfth-century *Historiae Danicae*
of Saxo Grammaticus, and then polished up for sixteenth-century French readers in François de Belle-
forest's *Histoires Tragiques*. It was first adapted for the
English theater in the late 1580s in the form of the
so-called Ur-*Hamlet*, a play attributed to Thomas Kyd
(unfortunately now lost) that continued to hold the stage
until at least 1596; and it may well be that, when
Shakespeare began work on *Hamlet* about 1599, he had
no more lofty intention than to polish up this slightly
tarnished popular favorite. But Shakespeare's wholesale
rewriting produced a *Hamlet* so utterly unlike Kyd's
work that its originality was unmistakable even to playgoers familiar with Kyd's play.

The new tragedy preserved the outline of the old
story, and took over Kyd's most celebrated contribu-
tions—a ghost crying for revenge, and a play-within-
the-play that sinisterly mirrors the main plot; but by
focusing upon the perplexed interior life of the hero,
Shakespeare gave a striking twist to what had been a
brutally straightforward narrative. On the levels of both
revenge play and psychological drama, the play develops
a preoccupation with the hidden, the secret, and the
mysterious that does much to account for its air of
mystery. In Maynard Mack's words, it is "a play in the

interrogative mood" whose action deepens and complicates, rather than answers, the apparently casual question with which it begins, "Who's there?"[6]

"The Cheer and Comfort of Our Eye": *Hamlet* and Surveillance

The great subject of revenge drama, before *Hamlet*, was the moral problem raised by private, personal revenge: i.e., should the individual take revenge into his own hands or leave it to God? Kyd's *The Spanish Tragedy* (and, one assumes, his lost play about Hamlet as well) captured on the stage the violent contradictions of the Elizabethan attitudes toward this form of "wild justice." The surprising thing about Shakespeare's *Hamlet* is that it barely glances at the ethical argument raised by a hero's taking justice into his own hands—an argument central to *The Spanish Tragedy*. Of course, the controversy about the morality of private revenge must have provided an important context for the original performances of the play, giving an ominous force to Hamlet's fear that the spirit he has seen "may be a devil" luring him to damnation (2.2.628). But Shakespeare simply takes this context for granted, and goes on to discover a quite different kind of political interest in his plot— one that may help to explain the paranoiac anxieties it was apparently capable of arousing in a dictator like Stalin.

Turning away from the framework of ethical debate, Shakespeare used Saxo's story of Hamlet's pretended madness and delayed revenge to explore the brutal facts about survival in an authoritarian state. Here too the play could speak to Elizabethan experience, for we should not forget that the glorified monarchy of Queen

Elizabeth I was sustained by a vigorous network of spies and informers. Indeed, one portrait of Elizabeth shows her dressed in a costume allegorically embroidered with eyes and ears, partly to advertise that her watchers and listeners were everywhere. Shakespeare's Elsinore, too—the castle governed by Claudius and home to Hamlet—is full of eyes and ears; and behind the public charade of warmth, magnanimity, and open government that King Claudius so carefully constructs, the lives of the King's subjects are exposed to merciless inquisition.

It is symbolically appropriate that the play should begin with a group of anxious watchers on the battlemented walls of the castle, for nothing and no one in Claudius's Denmark is allowed to go "unwatched": every appearance must be "sifted" or "sounded," and every secret "opened." The King himself does not hesitate to eavesdrop on the heir apparent; and his chief minister, Polonius, will meet his death lurking behind a curtain in the same squalid occupation. But they are not alone in this: the wholesale corruption of social relationships, even the most intimate, is an essential part of Shakespeare's chilling exposure of authoritarian politics. Denmark, Hamlet informs Rosencrantz and Guildenstern accurately enough, is "a prison" (2.2.262); and the treachery of these former school friends of Hamlet illustrates how much, behind the mask of uncle Claudius's concern, his court is ruled by the prison-house customs of the stool pigeon and the informer. How readily first Ophelia and then Gertrude allow themselves to become passive instruments of Polonius's and Claudius's spying upon the Prince; how easily Rosencrantz and Guildenstern are persuaded to put their friendship with Hamlet at the disposal of the state. Even Laertes's affectionate relationship with his sister is tainted by a desire to install himself as a kind of censor, a "watchman" to the fortress of her heart (1.3.50). In this he is all too like his father, Polonius, who makes himself an interiorized Big Brother, engraving his cautious precepts on Laertes's memory (1.3.65 ff.) and telling Ophelia precisely what she is permitted to think and feel:

OPHELIA
  I do not know, my lord, what I should think.
POLONIUS
  Marry, I will teach you. Think yourself a baby. . . .
                   (1.3.113–14)

Polonius is the perfect inhabitant of this court: busily policing his children's sexuality, he has no scruple about prostituting his daughter in the interests of state security, for beneath his air of senile wordiness and fatherly anxiousness lies an ingrained cynicism that allows him both to spy on his son's imagined "drabbing" in Paris and to "loose" his daughter as a sexual decoy to entrap the Prince.

  Hamlet's role as hero at once sets him apart from this prison-house world and yet leads him to become increasingly entangled in its web of surveillance. To the admiring Ophelia, Hamlet remains "Th' observed of all observers" (3.1.168), but his obvious alienation has resulted in his being "observed" in a much more sinister sense. He is introduced in Act 1, scene 2, as a mysteriously taciturn watcher and listener whose glowering silence calls into question the pomp and bustle of the King's wordy show, just as his mourning blacks cast suspicion on the showy costumes of the court. Yet he himself, we are quickly made to realize, is the object of a dangerously inquisitive stare—what the King smoothly calls "the cheer and comfort of our eye" (1.2.120). The

full meaning of that silky phrase will be disclosed on
Claudius's next appearance, when, after Hamlet has met
the Ghost and has begun to appear mad, Claudius
engages Rosencrantz and Guildenstern to probe his
nephew's threatening transformation (2.2.1–18). "Madness in great ones," the King insists, "must not unwatched go" (3.1.203):

> There's something in his soul
> O'er which his melancholy sits on brood,
> And I do doubt the hatch and the disclose
> Will be some danger.   (3.1.178–81)

But of course Hamlet's madness is as much disguise
as it is revelation; and while the Prince is the most
ruthlessly observed character in the play, he is also its
most unremitting observer. Forced to master his opponent's craft of smiling villainy, he becomes not merely
an actor but also a dramatist, ingeniously using a troupe
of traveling players, with their "murder in jest," to
unmask the King's own hypocritical "show."

The scene in which the Players present *The Murder of
Gonzago*, the play that Hamlet calls "The Mousetrap,"
brings the drama of surveillance to its climax. We in the
audience become participants in the drama's claustro-
phobic economy of watching and listening, as our
attention moves to and fro between the various groups
on the stage, gauging the significance of every word,
action, and reaction, sharing the obsessional gaze that
Hamlet describes to Horatio:

> Observe my uncle . . . Give him heedful note,
> For I mine eyes will rivet to his face,
> And, after, we will both our judgments join
> In censure of his seeming.   (3.2.85–92)

"The Mousetrap" twice reenacts Claudius's murder of his brother—first in the dumb show and then in the play proper—drawing out the effect so exquisitely that the King's enraged interruption produces an extraordinary discharge of tension. An audience caught up in Hamlet's wild excitement is easily blinded to the fact that this seeming climax is, in terms of the revenge plot, at least, a violent anticlimax. Kyd's *Spanish Tragedy* had developed the play-within-the-play as a perfect vehicle for the ironies of revenge, allowing the hero to take his actual revenge in the very act of staging the villain's original crime. Hamlet's play, however, does not even make public Claudius's forbidden story. Indeed, while it serves to confirm the truth of what the Ghost has said, the only practical effect of the Prince's theatrical triumph is to hand the initiative decisively to Claudius. In the scenes that follow, Hamlet shows himself capable of both instinctive violence and of cold-blooded calculation, but his behavior is purely reactive. Otherwise he seems oddly paralyzed by his success—a condition displayed in the prayer scene (3.3.77–101) where he stands behind the kneeling Claudius with drawn sword, "neutral to his will and matter," uncannily resembling the frozen revenger described in the First Player's speech about Pyrrhus standing over old Priam (2.2.493 ff.). All Hamlet can do is attempt to duplicate the triumph of "The Mousetrap" in his confrontation with Gertrude by holding up to her yet another verbal mirror, in which she is forced to gaze in horror on her "inmost part" (3.4.25).

Hamlet's sudden loss of direction after the "Mousetrap" scene lasts through the fourth act of the play until he returns from his sea voyage in that mysteriously altered mood on which most commentators remark—a kind of fatalism that makes him the largely passive servant of a plot that he now does little to advance or impede. It is as if the springing of the "Mousetrap" leaves Hamlet with nowhere to go—primarily because it leaves him with nothing to say. But from the very beginning, his struggle with Claudius has been conceived as a struggle for the control of language—a battle to determine what can and cannot be uttered.

Speaking the Unspeakable: *Hamlet* and Memory

If surveillance is one prop of the authoritarian state, the other is its militant regulation of speech. As Claudius flatters the court into mute complicity with his theft of both the throne and his dead brother's wife, he genially insists "You cannot speak of reason to the Dane / And lose your voice" (1.2.44–45); but an iron wall of silence encloses the inhabitants of his courtly prison. While the flow of royal eloquence muffles inconvenient truths, ears here are "fortified" against dangerous stories (1.1.38) and lips sealed against careless confession: "Give thy thoughts no tongue," Polonius advises Laertes, ". . . Give every man thine ear, but few thy voice . . . reserve thy judgment" (1.3.65–75). Hamlet's insistent warnings to his fellow watchers on the battlements "Never to speak of this that you have seen" (1.5.174) urge the same caution: "Let it be tenable in your silence still. . . . Give it an understanding but no tongue" (1.2.269–71). What for them is merely common prudence, however, is for the hero an absolute prohibition and an intolerable burden: ". . . break, my heart, for I must hold my tongue" (1.2.164).

Hamlet has only two ways of rupturing this enforced silence. The "pregnant" wordplay of his "mad" satire, as

Polonius uneasily recognizes (2.2.226–27), is one way, but it amounts to no more than inconclusive verbal fencing. Soliloquy is a more powerful resource because, since it is heard by no one (except the audience), its impenetrable privacy defines Hamlet's independence from the corrupt public world. From his first big speech in the play, he has made such hiddenness the badge of his resistance to the King and Queen: "I have that within which passes show" (1.2.88), he announces. What is at issue here is not simply a contrast between hypocrisy and true grief over the loss of his king and father: rather, Hamlet grounds his very claim to integrity upon a notion that true feeling can never be expressed: it is only "that . . . which *passes show*" that can escape the taint of hypocrisy, of "acting." It is as if, in this world of remorseless observation, the self can survive only as a ferociously defended secret, something treasured for the very fact of its hiddenness and impenetrability. Unlike Gertrude, unlike Ophelia, unlike those absorbent "sponges" Rosencrantz and Guildenstern, Hamlet must insist he is not made of "penetrable stuff."

If Hamlet's "antic disposition" is the guardian of his rebellious inwardness, soliloquy is where this inwardness lives, a domain which (if we except Claudius's occasional flickers of conscience) no other character is allowed to inhabit. Hamlet's soliloquies bulk so large in our response to the play because they not only guarantee the existence of the hero's secret inner life; they also, by their relentless self-questioning, imply the presence of still more profoundly secret truths "hid within the center": "I *do not know* / Why yet I live to say 'This thing's to do,' / Sith I have cause, and will, and strength, and means / To do 't" (4.4.46–49). The soliloquies are the focus of the play's preoccupation with speaking and silence. Hamlet is set apart from those around him by his access to this region of private utterance: in it he can, as it were, "be bounded in a nutshell and count [himself] a king of infinite space" (2.2.273–74).

Yet there is a paradox here: the isolation of soliloquy is at once his special strength and the source of peculiar anguish. It saves him from the fate of Ophelia, who becomes "Divided from herself and her fair judgment" (4.5.92) by her grief at Polonius's death and hasty burial; accustomed to speak only in the voice that others allow her, dutifully resolved to "think nothing, my lord" (3.2.124), she is left with no language other than the disconnected fragments of her madness to express outrage at a murder which authority seems determined to conceal. Hamlet, by contrast, finds in soliloquy an arena where the unspeakable can be uttered. But the very fact that these are words that others do not hear also makes soliloquy a realm of noncommunication, of frustrating silence—a prison as well as a fortress in which the speaker beats his head unavailingly against the walls of his own cell. Thus the soliloquy that ends Act 2 reproaches itself for a kind of speechlessness—the mute ineffectuality of a "John-a-dreams," who, unlike the Player, "can *say* nothing"—and at the same time mocks itself as a torrent of empty language, a mere unpacking of the heart with words (2.2.593–616). For all their eloquence, the soliloquies serve in the end only to increase the tension generated by the pressure of forbidden utterance.

It is from this pressure that the first three acts of the play derive most of their extraordinary energy; and the energy is given a concrete dramatic presence in the form of the Ghost. The appearance of a ghost demanding vengeance was a stock device borrowed from the Roman playwright Seneca; and the Ur-*Hamlet* had been notorious for its ghost, shrieking like an oysterwife,

"Hamlet, revenge!" But the strikingly unconventional thing about Shakespeare's Ghost is its melancholy preoccupation with the silenced past and its plangent cry of "Remember me" (1.5.98) which makes remembrance seem more important than revenge. "The struggle of humanity against power," the Czech novelist Milan Kundera has written, "is the struggle of memory against forgetfulness"; and this Ghost, which stands for all that has been erased by the bland narratives of King Claudius, is consumed by the longing to speak that which power has rendered unspeakable. The effect of the Ghost's narrative upon Hamlet is to infuse him with the same desire; indeed, once he has formally inscribed its watchword—"Remember me"—on the tables of his memory, he is as if possessed by the Ghost, seeming to mime its speechless torment when he appears to Ophelia, looking "As if he had been loosèd out of hell / To speak of horrors" (2.1.93–94).

For all its pathos of silenced longing, the Ghost remains profoundly ambivalent, and not just because Elizabethans held such contradictory beliefs about ghosts.[7] The ambivalence is dramatized in a particularly disturbing detail: as the Ghost pours his story into Hamlet's ear (the gesture highlighted by the Ghost's incantatory repetition of "hear" and "ear"), we become aware of an uncanny parallel between the Ghost's act of narration and the murder the Ghost tells about:

> 'Tis given out that, sleeping in my orchard,
> A serpent stung me. So the whole ear of Denmark
> Is by a forgèd process of my death
> Rankly abused. . . .
> Upon my secure hour thy uncle stole,
> With juice of cursèd hebona in a vial,
> And in the porches of my ears did pour
> The leprous distilment . . .   (1.5.42–71)

If Claudius's propaganda has abused "the whole ear of Denmark" like a second poisoning, the Ghost's own story enters Hamlet's "ears of flesh and blood" like yet another corrosive. The fact that it is a story that demands telling, and that its narrator is "an honest ghost," cannot alter the fact that it will work away in Hamlet's being like secret venom until he in turn can vent it in revenge.

The "Mousetrap" play is at once a fulfillment and an escape from that compulsion. It gives, in a sense, a public voice to the Ghost's silenced story. But it is only a metaphoric revenge. Speaking daggers and poison but using none, Hamlet turns out only to have written his own inability to bring matters to an end. It is no coincidence, then, that he should foresee the conclusion of his own tragedy as being the product of someone else's script: "There's a divinity that shapes our ends, / Rough-hew them how we will" (5.2.11–12).

"To Tell My Story": Unfinished *Hamlet*

In the last scene of the play, the sense that Hamlet's story has been shaped by Providence—or by a playwright other than Hamlet—is very strong: the swordplay with Laertes is a theatrical imitation of dueling that becomes the real thing, sweetly knitting up the paralyzing disjunction between action and acting; at the same time, revenge is symmetrically perfected in the spectacle of Claudius choking on "a poison tempered by himself," Laertes "justly killed with his own treachery," and the Queen destroyed in the vicious pun that has her poisoned by Claudius's "union." Yet Hamlet's consoling fatalism does not survive the final slaughter. Instead, he faces his end tormented by a sense of incompleteness, of a story still remaining to be told:

> You that look pale and tremble at this chance,
> That are but mutes or audience to this act,
> Had I but time (as this fell sergeant, Death,
> Is strict in his arrest), O, I could tell you—
> But let it be.   (5.2.366–70)

Within a few lines Hamlet's distinctive voice, which has dominated his own tragedy like that of no other Shakespearean hero, will be cut off in midsentence by the arrest of death—and "the rest is silence" (5.2.395).

The play is full of such unfinished, untold, or perhaps even untellable tales, from Barnardo's interrupted story of the Ghost's first appearance to the Player's unfinished rendition of "Aeneas' tale to Dido" and the violently curtailed performance of *The Murder of Gonzago*. In the opening scene the Ghost itself is cut off, before it can speak, by the crowing of a cock; and when it returns and speaks to Hamlet, it speaks first about a story it cannot tell:

> But that I am forbid
> To tell the secrets of my prison house,
> I could a tale unfold whose lightest word
> Would harrow up thy soul, freeze thy
>   young blood . . .   (1.5.18–21)

Even the tale it *is* permitted to unfold is, ironically, one of murderous interruption and terrible incompleteness:

> *Cut off*, even in the blossoms of my sin,
> Unhouseled, disappointed, unaneled,
> No reck'ning made, but sent to my account
> With all my *imperfections* on my head.
>   (1.5.83–86)

Act 5 at last produces the formal reckoning of this imperfect account, yet it leaves Hamlet once again echoing the Ghost's agony of frustrated utterance.

But what, we might ask, can there be left to tell, beyond what we have already seen and heard? It seems to be part of the point, a last reminder of Hamlet's elusive "mystery," that we shall never know. The Prince has, of course, insisted that Horatio remain behind "to tell my story"; but the inadequacy of Horatio's response only intensifies the sense of incompleteness. All that his stolid imagination can offer is that bald plot summary of "accidental judgments [and] casual slaughters," which, as Anne Barton protests, leaves out "everything that seems important" about the play and its protagonist.[8] Nor is Fortinbras's attempt to make "The soldier's music and the rite of war / Speak loudly for him" (5.2.445–46) any more satisfactory: for the military strongman's cannon are no better tuned to speak for Hamlet than the player's pipe.

It would be a mistake, of course, to underestimate the dramatic significance of Horatio's story or of the "music and the rite of war"—these last gestures of ritual consolation—especially in a play where, beginning with the obscene confusion of Claudius's "mirth in funeral" and including Polonius's "hugger-mugger" interment and Ophelia's "maimed rites," we have seen the dead repeatedly degraded by the slighting of their funeral pomps. In this context it matters profoundly that Hamlet alone is accorded the full dignity of obsequies suited to his rank, for it signals his triumph over the oblivion to which Claudius is fittingly consigned, and, in its gesture back toward Hamlet's story as Shakespeare has told it (so much better than Horatio does), it brings Hamlet's story to a heroic end.

"The Undiscovered Country":
Hamlet and the Secrets of Death

How we respond to the ending of *Hamlet*—both as revenge drama and as psychological study—depends in part on how we respond to yet a third level of the play—that is, to *Hamlet* as a prolonged meditation on death. The play is virtually framed by two encounters with the dead: at one end is the Ghost, at the other a pile of freshly excavated skulls. The skulls (all but one) are nameless and silent; the Ghost has an identity (though a "questionable" one) and a voice; yet they are more alike than might at first seem. For this ghost, though invulnerable "as the air," is described as a "dead corse," a "ghost . . . come from the grave," its appearance suggesting a grotesque disinterment of the buried king (1.4.52–57; 1.5.139). The skulls for their part may be silent, but Hamlet plays upon each to draw out its own "excellent voice" ("That skull had a tongue in it and could sing once": 5.1.77–78), just as he engineered that "miraculous organ" of the Ghost's utterance, the "Mousetrap."

There is a difference, however: Hamlet's dressing up the skulls with shreds of narrative ("as if 'twere Cain's jawbone . . . This might be the pate of a politician . . . or of a courtier . . . Why may not that be the skull of a lawyer": 5.1.78–101) only serves to emphasize their mocking anonymity, until the Gravedigger offers to endow one with a precise historical identity: "This same skull . . . was . . . Yorick's skull, the King's jester" (5.1.186–87). Hamlet is delighted: now memory can begin its work of loving resurrection. But how does the Gravedigger *know?* The answer is that of course he cannot; and try as Hamlet may to cover this bare bone with the flesh of nostalgic recollection, he cannot escape the wickedly punning reminder of "this *same*

skull" that all skulls indeed look frightfully the same.
Ironically, even Yorick's distinctive trademark, his grin,
has become indistinguishable from the mocking leer of
that grand jester of the *Danse Macabre*, Death the Antic:
"Where be your gibes now? . . . Not one now to mock
your own grinning?"; so that even as he holds it, the
skull's identity appears to drain away into the anonymous *memento mori* sent to adorn "my lady's" dressing
table. It might as well be Alexander the Great's; or
Caesar's; or anyone's. It might as well be what it will one
day become—a handful of clay, fit to stop a beer barrel.
    It is significant that (with the trivial exception of 4.4)
the graveyard scene is the only one to take place outside
the confines of Claudius's castle-prison. As the "common" place to which all stories lead, the graveyard both
invites narrative and *silences* it. Each blank skull at once
poses and confounds the question with which the tragedy itself began, "Who's there?," subsuming all human
differences in awful likeness: "As you are now," goes the
tombstone verse, "so once was I / As I am now, so shall
you be." In the graveyard all stories collapse into one
reductive history ("Alexander died, Alexander was buried, Alexander returneth to dust": 5.1.216–17). In this
sense the Gravedigger is the mocking counterpart of the
Player: and the houses of oblivion that gravediggers
make challenge the players' memorial art by lasting "till
doomsday" (5.1.61). Hamlet shares with the Gravedigger the same easy good-fellowship he extends to the
play's other great outsider, the First Player; but the
Gravedigger asserts a more sinister kind of intimacy
with his claim to have begun his work "that very day that
young Hamlet was born" (5.1.152–53). In this moment
he identifies himself as the Prince's mortal double, the
Sexton Death from the *Danse Macabre* who has been
preparing him a grave from the moment of birth.
    If there is a final secret to be revealed, then, about that

"undiscovered country" on which Hamlet's imagination broods, it is perhaps only the Gravedigger's spade that can uncover it. For his digging lays bare the one thing we can say for certain lies hidden "within" the mortal show of the flesh—the emblems of Death himself, that *Doppelgänger* who shadows each of us as the mysterious Lamord (*La Mort*) shadows Laertes. If there is a better story, one that would confer on the rough matter of life the consolations of form and significance, it is, the play tells us, one that cannot finally be told; for it exists on the other side of language, to be tantalizingly glimpsed only at the point when Hamlet is about to enter the domain of the inexpressible. The great and frustrating achievement of this play, its most ingenious and tormenting trick, the source of its endlessly belabored mystery, is to persuade us that such a story might exist, while demonstrating its irreducible hiddenness. The only story Hamlet is given is that of a hoary old revenge tragedy, which he persuades himself (and us) can never denote him truly; but it is a narrative frame that nothing (not even inaction) will allow him to escape. The story of our lives, the play wryly acknowledges, is always the wrong story; but the rest, after all, is silence.

———————

1. Dmitri Shostakovich, *Testimony: The Memoirs of Dmitri Shostakovich*, as related to and edited by Solomon Volkow, trans. Antonina W. Bouis (London: Faber, 1981), p. 84.

2. See F. E. Halliday, *A Shakespeare Companion, 1564–1964* (Harmondsworth: Penguin, 1964), pp. 435, 209; see also pp. 262 and 403.

3. The most lucid guide to this critical labyrinth, though he deals with no work later than 1960, is probably still Morris Weitz, *Hamlet and the Philosophy of Literary Criticism* (London: Faber, 1964).

4. Jan Kott, *Shakespeare Our Contemporary* (London: Methuen, 1964).

5. Excerpt from "Viking Dublin: Trial Pieces" from *Poems, 1965–1975* by Seamus Heaney. Copyright © 1975, 1980 by Seamus Heaney. Reprinted by permission of Farrar, Straus and Giroux, Inc. Permission for use of these lines from *North* by Seamus Heaney, published by Faber and Faber Limited, is also acknowledged.

6. See Mack's classic essay, "The World of *Hamlet*," *Yale Review* 41 (1952): 502–23; Mack's approach is significantly extended in Harry Levin's *The Question of Hamlet* (New York: Oxford University Press, 1959).

7. The most balanced treatment of this and other contentious historical issues in the play is in Roland M. Frye, *The Renaissance Hamlet* (Princeton: Princeton University Press, 1984).

8. Introduction to T.J.B. Spencer, ed., *Hamlet* (Harmondsworth: Penguin, 1980), p. 52. See also James L. Calderwood's *To Be and Not To Be: Negation and Metadrama in "Hamlet"* (New York: Columbia University Press, 1983).

Further Reading

Hamlet

Calderwood, James L. *To Be and Not To Be: Negation and Metadrama in "Hamlet."* New York: Columbia University Press, 1983.

Calderwood addresses *Hamlet* as a staged performance, as both a verbal and a visual sign. He finds the play dominated by "Shakespeare's negative mode," in which multiple meanings coexist in seeming contradiction. As his title suggests, however, Calderwood finds that rather than resolve contradictions the play ultimately accepts and contains them.

Frye, Roland M. *The Renaissance Hamlet: Issues and Responses in 1600.* Princeton: Princeton University Press, 1984.

Frye investigates Renaissance attitudes toward rebellion, conscience, regicide, incest, retribution, and mourning in an attempt to reconstruct the responses of the audience for which *Hamlet* was originally written. In light of his findings, Frye proposes that an Elizabethan audience would have recognized the perplexing issues Hamlet faced and ultimately found him morally heroic.

Hawkes, Terence. *"Telmah."* In Patricia Parker and Geoffrey Hartman, eds., *Shakespeare and the Question of Theory.* London: Methuen, 1985.

Hawkes argues that *Hamlet*'s vitality resides in its contradictions and therefore proposes that the play be treated as a site in which multiple and conflicting interpretations may coexist without one claiming "primacy" or "authority." He offers the title *Telmah* (*Hamlet* backward) to suggest "a sense of an ever-present potential challenge and contradiction *within* and *implied by* the text that we name *Hamlet*."

Kott, Jan. "*Hamlet* in the Mid-Century." In *Shakespeare Our Contemporary*. London: Methuen, 1964.

Envisioning an ideal performance of *Hamlet* as one true to Shakespeare and modern at the same time, Kott discusses productions—both real and imagined—that satisfy this formula. As an example of a *Hamlet* modern in both psychological and dramatic qualities, he describes a Polish production of 1956 produced on the heels of the Soviet Communist party's 20th Congress. Under this shadow, the play became a "political drama par excellence."

Kyd, Thomas. *The Spanish Tragedy*. London, 1594.

Shakespeare may have drawn on *The Spanish Tragedy* (c. 1589) when he wrote *Hamlet*, for Kyd's drama includes many elements also found in Shakespeare's play: the ghost, the difficulty in verifying the truth of the ghost's words, the resulting need for delay, a feigning of madness, the play-within-a-play, and the moral perplexities facing a sensitive man called to revenge. In both incident and situation, *The Spanish Tragedy* provides a remarkable counterpoint to *Hamlet*.

Levin, Harry. *The Question of Hamlet*. New York: Oxford University Press, 1959.

Levin focuses on the general atmosphere of questioning within the play, identifying three dominant figures of speech—which are each "simultaneously a figure of thought": direct inquiry, doubt, and irony. According to Levin, the play's—and Hamlet's—pervasive irony serves as a synthesizing figure that allows us to confront, though not solve, the contradictions posed by the play's interrogative mood.

Mack, Maynard. "The World of *Hamlet*." *Yale Review* 41 (1952): 502–23.

Mack describes the "imaginative environment" of *Hamlet* as one dominated by disabling incomprehensibility and a pervasive sense of mortality. Hamlet, in the play's final act, ultimately comes to comprehend this world and what it means to live in it.

Mowat, Barbara A. "The Form of *Hamlet*'s Fortunes." *Renaissance Drama* 19 (1988): 97–126.

Mowat surveys editions of *Hamlet* from Nicholas Rowe's in 1709 to the present day, tracing the conflation of the Second Quarto (Q2) and First Folio (F) texts to demonstrate that "the text of Q2/F *Hamlet* . . . has been radically unstable, multiform." In fact, she finds that "the situation of the text in the 1980s . . . is more typical than unusual, as editors create their own *Hamlet*s, breaking away from the editorial consensus."

Neely, Carol Thomas. " 'Documents in Madness': Reading Madness and Gender in Shakespeare's Tragedies and Early Modern Culture." *Shakespeare Quarterly* 42 (1991): 315–38.

Chronicling the English fascination with madness in the period from 1580 to 1640, Neely undertakes to examine "how representations of madness in Shakespeare's tragedies function within wider cultural contexts." While the gender distinctions initiated by Shakespeare's representations of madness often prove oppressive to women, Neely contends that these representations also serve as vehicles for social critique through "unsettling productions or indecorous interventions by performers."

Schleiner, Louise. "Latinized Greek Drama in Shakespeare's Writing of *Hamlet*." *Shakespeare Quarterly* 41 (1990): 29–48.

Schleiner proposes that Aeschylus' *Oresteia* and Euripides' *Orestes* possibly influenced Shakespeare's *Hamlet*. Though scholars have generally thought that Shakespeare read relatively little Greek, Schleiner claims that he may have had access to the two Greek plays through Latin translations and a pair of English plays of 1599 entitled *Agamemnon* and *Orestes' Furies*.

Showalter, Elaine. "Representing Ophelia: Women, Madness, and the Responsibilities of Feminist Criticism." In Patricia Parker and Geoffrey Hartman, eds., *Shakespeare and the Question of Theory*. London: Methuen, 1985.

Tracing the representations of Ophelia in painting, theatrical productions, literary criticism, and psychoanalytic criticism, Showalter demonstrates how the various depictions of Ophelia's insanity and sexuality reflect cultural norms. The representation of Ophelia "depends on attitudes toward women and madness" in the culture at large. Thus the pious Ophelia of the Augustan age and the schizophrenic heroine of modern productions derive from the same figure but reflect radically different eras.

Weitz, Morris. *Hamlet and the Philosophy of Literary Criticism*. London: Faber, 1964.

Through an exploration of the history of *Hamlet* criticism, Weitz investigates "the traditional question, What is Criticism?" The first part of his book consists of a systematic exposition of some of the major critics of *Hamlet*. In the second part Weitz outlines what he sees as the main issues in *Hamlet* criticism, including "Is Hamlet mad?," "Does Hamlet vacillate?," "Is Ophelia honest, weak, in love with Hamlet?," "Is Gertrude an adulteress?," "Why is Hamlet tragic?," and many more.

Werstine, Paul. "The Textual Mystery of *Hamlet*." *Shakespeare Quarterly* 39 (1988): 1–26.

Werstine contends that attempts to discover the origins of the many variations between the early printed texts of *Hamlet* are likely to fail for lack of information. He suggests that we simply read "what we have," i.e., the early printed texts themselves. Examining the Folio and Second Quarto texts of *Hamlet* that are yoked together in most modern editions, he demonstrates that the combination results in a play more mysterious than either of the two versions taken singly.

Shakespeare's Language

Abbott, E. A. *A Shakespearian Grammar*. New York: Haskell House, 1972.

This compact reference book, first published in 1870, helps with many difficulties in Shakespeare's language. It systematically accounts for a host of differences between Shakespeare's usage and sentence structure and our own.

Blake, Norman. *Shakespeare's Language: An Introduction*. New York: St. Martin's Press, 1983.

This general introduction to Elizabethan English discusses various aspects of the language of Shakespeare and his contemporaries, offering possible meanings for hundreds of ambiguous constructions.

Dobson, E. J. *English Pronunciation, 1500–1700*. 2 vols. Oxford: Clarendon Press, 1968.

This long and technical work includes chapters on spelling (and its reformation), phonetics, stressed vowels, and consonants in early modern English.

Houston, John. *Shakespearean Sentences: A Study in Style and Syntax*. Baton Rouge: Louisiana State University Press, 1988.

Houston studies Shakespeare's stylistic choices, considering matters such as sentence length and the relative positions of subject, verb, and direct object. Examining plays throughout the canon in a roughly chronological, developmental order, he analyzes how sentence structure is used in setting tone, in characterization, and for other dramatic purposes.

Onions, C. T. *A Shakespeare Glossary*. Oxford: Clarendon Press, 1986.

This revised edition updates Onions's standard, selective glossary of words and phrases in Shakespeare's plays that are now obsolete, archaic, or obscure.

Partridge, Eric. *Shakespeare's Bawdy*. London: Routledge & Kegan Paul, 1955.

After an introductory essay, "The Sexual, the Homosexual, and Non-Sexual Bawdy in Shakespeare," Partridge provides a comprehensive glossary of "bawdy" phrases and words from the plays.

Robinson, Randal. *Unlocking Shakespeare's Language: Help for the Teacher and Student*. Urbana, Ill.: National Council of Teachers of English and the ERIC Clearinghouse on Reading and Communication Skills, 1989.

Specifically designed for the high-school and undergraduate college teacher and student, Robinson's book addresses the problems that most often hinder present-day readers of Shakespeare. Through work with his own students, Robinson found that many readers today are particularly puzzled by such stylistic characteristics as subject-verb inversion, interrupted structures, and compression. He shows how our own colloquial language contains comparable structures, and thus helps students recognize such structures when they find them in Shakespeare's plays. This book supplies worksheets—with examples from major plays—to illuminate and remedy such problems as unusual sequences of words and the separation of related parts of sentences.

Shakespeare's Life

Baldwin, T. W. *William Shakspere's Petty School.* Urbana: University of Illinois Press, 1943.

Baldwin here investigates the theory and practice of the petty school, the first level of education in Elizabethan England. He focuses on that educational system primarily as it is reflected in Shakespeare's art.

Baldwin, T. W. *William Shakspere's Small Latine and Lesse Greeke.* 2 vols. Urbana: University of Illinois Press, 1944.

Baldwin attacks the view that Shakespeare was an uneducated genius—a view that had been dominant among Shakespeareans since the eighteenth century. Instead, Baldwin shows, the educational system of Shakespeare's time would have given the playwright a strong background in the classics, and there is much in the plays that shows how Shakespeare benefited from such an education.

Beier, A. L., and Roger Finlay, eds. *London 1500–1800: The Making of the Metropolis.* New York: Longman, 1986.

Focusing on the economic and social history of early modern London, these collected essays probe aspects of metropolitan life, including "Population and Disease," "Commerce and Manufacture," and "Society and Change."

Bentley, G. E. *Shakespeare's Life: A Biographical Handbook*. New Haven: Yale University Press, 1961.
This "just-the-facts" account presents the surviving documents of Shakespeare's life against an Elizabethan background.

Chambers, E. K. *William Shakespeare: A Study of Facts and Problems*. 2 vols. Oxford: Clarendon Press, 1930.
Analyzing in great detail the scant historical data, Chambers's complex, scholarly study considers the nature of the texts in which Shakespeare's work is preserved.

Cressy, David. *Education in Tudor and Stuart England*. London: Edward Arnold, 1975.
This volume collects sixteenth-, seventeenth-, and early-eighteenth-century documents detailing aspects of formal education in England, such as the curriculum, the control and organization of education, and the education of women.

Dutton, Richard. *William Shakespeare: A Literary Life*. New York: St. Martin's Press, 1989.
Not a biography in the traditional sense, Dutton's very readable work nevertheless "follows the contours of Shakespeare's life" as he examines Shakespeare's career as playwright and poet, with consideration of his patrons, theatrical associations, and audience.

Fraser, Russell. *Young Shakespeare*. New York: Columbia University Press, 1988.
Fraser focuses on Shakespeare's first thirty years, paying attention simultaneously to his life and art.

De Grazia, Margreta. *Shakespeare Verbatim: The Reproduction of Authenticity and the Apparatus of 1790*. Oxford: Clarendon Press, 1991.

De Grazia traces and discusses the development of such editorial criteria as authenticity, historical periodization, factual biography, chronological developments, and close reading, locating as the point of origin Edmond Malone's 1790 edition of Shakespeare's works. There are interesting chapters on the First Folio and on the "legendary" versus the "documented" Shakespeare.

Schoenbaum, S. *William Shakespeare: A Compact Documentary Life*. New York: Oxford University Press, 1977.
This standard biography economically presents the essential documents from Shakespeare's time in an accessible narrative account of the playwright's life.

Shakespeare's Theater

Bentley, G. E. *The Profession of Player in Shakespeare's Time, 1590–1642*. Princeton: Princeton University Press, 1984.
Bentley readably sets forth a wealth of evidence about performance in Shakespeare's time, with special attention to the relations between player and company, and the business of casting, managing, and touring.

Berry, Herbert. *Shakespeare's Playhouses*. New York: AMS Press, 1987.
Berry's six essays collected here discuss (with illustrations) varying aspects of the four playhouses in which Shakespeare had a financial stake: the Theatre in Shoreditch, the Blackfriars, and the first and second Globe.

Cook, Ann Jennalie. *The Privileged Playgoers of Shakespeare's London*. Princeton: Princeton University Press, 1981.
Cook's work argues, on the basis of sociological,

economic, and documentary evidence, that Shakespeare's audience—and the audience for English Renaissance drama generally—consisted mainly of the "privileged."

Greg, W. W. *Dramatic Documents from the Elizabethan Playhouses.* 2 vols. Oxford: Clarendon Press, 1931.

Greg itemizes and briefly describes almost all the play manuscripts that survive from the period 1590 to around 1660, including, among other things, players' parts. His second volume offers facsimiles of selected manuscripts.

Gurr, Andrew. *Playgoing in Shakespeare's London.* Cambridge: Cambridge University Press, 1987.

Gurr charts how the theatrical enterprise developed from its modest beginnings in the late 1560s to become a thriving institution in the 1600s. He argues that there were important changes over the period 1567–1644 in the playhouses, the audience, and the plays.

Harbage, Alfred. *Shakespeare's Audience.* New York: Columbia University Press, 1941.

Harbage investigates the fragmentary surviving evidence to interpret the size, composition, and behavior of Shakespeare's audience.

Hattaway, Michael. *Elizabethan Popular Theatre: Plays in Performance.* London: Routledge & Kegan Paul, 1982.

Beginning with a study of the popular drama of the late Elizabethan age—a description of the stages, performance conditions, and acting of the period—this volume concludes with an analysis of five well-known plays of the 1590s, one of them (*Titus Andronicus*) by Shakespeare.

Shapiro, Michael. *Children of the Revels: The Boy Companies of Shakespeare's Time and Their Plays.* New York: Columbia University Press, 1977.

Shapiro chronicles the history of the amateur and quasi-professional child companies that flourished in London at the end of Elizabeth's reign and the beginning of James's.

The Publication of Shakespeare's Plays

Blayney, Peter. *The First Folio of Shakespeare.* Hanover, Md.: Folger, 1991.

Blayney's accessible account of the printing and later life of the First Folio—an amply illustrated catalogue to a 1991 Folger Shakespeare Library exhibition—analyzes the mechanical production of the First Folio, describing how the Folio was made, by whom and for whom, how much it cost, and its ups and downs (or, rather, downs and ups) since its printing in 1623.

Hinman, Charlton. *The Printing and Proof-Reading of the First Folio of Shakespeare.* 2 vols. Oxford: Clarendon Press, 1963.

In the most arduous study of a single book ever undertaken, Hinman attempts to reconstruct how the Shakespeare First Folio of 1623 was set into type and run off the press, sheet by sheet. He also provides almost all the known variations in readings from copy to copy.

Hinman, Charlton. *The Norton Facsimile: The First Folio of Shakespeare.* New York: W. W. Norton, 1968.

This facsimile presents a photographic reproduction of an "ideal" copy of the First Folio of Shakespeare; Hinman attempts to represent each page in its most fully corrected state.

Key to
Famous Lines and Phrases

For this relief much thanks.   [Francisco—1.1.8]

. . . prologue to the omen coming on
                          [Horatio—1.1.135]

. . . the morn in russet mantle clad
                          [Horatio—1.1.181]

A little more than kin and less than kind.
                          [Hamlet—1.2.67]

O, that this too, too sullied flesh would melt
                          [Hamlet—1.2.133]

. . . frailty, thy name is woman!   [Hamlet—1.2.150]

In my mind's eye   [Hamlet—1.2.193]

A countenance more in sorrow than in anger.
                          [Horatio—1.2.247]

. . . the primrose path of dalliance   [Ophelia—1.3.54]

This above all: to thine own self be true
                          [Polonius—1.3.84]

Something is rotten in the state of Denmark.
                          [Marcellus—1.4.100]

Murder most foul, as in the best it is   [Ghost—1.5.33]

Leave her to heaven [Ghost—1.5.93]

. . . one may smile and smile and be a villain.
[Hamlet—1.5.115]

There are more things in heaven and earth, Horatio,
Than are dreamt of in your philosophy.
[Hamlet—1.5.187–88]

The time is out of joint. [Hamlet—1.5.210]

. . . brevity is the soul of wit [Polonius—2.2.97]

More matter with less art. [Queen—2.2.103]

Though this be madness, yet there is method in 't.
[Polonius—2.2.223–24]

. . . there is nothing either good or bad but thinking
makes it so. [Hamlet—2.2.268–70]

What a piece of work is a man . . . [Hamlet—2.2.327]

I am but mad north-north-west. . . . I know a hawk
from a handsaw. [Hamlet—2.2.402–3]

. . . caviary to the general. [Hamlet—2.2.461]

Use every man after his desert and who shall 'scape
whipping? [Hamlet—2.2.555–57]

O, what a rogue and peasant slave am I!
[Hamlet—2.2.577]

What's Hecuba to him, or he to Hecuba
[Hamlet—2.2.586]

. . . the devil hath power
T' assume a pleasing shape   [Hamlet—2.2.628–29]

The play's the thing   [Hamlet—2.2.633]

To be or not to be—that is the question
                              [Hamlet—3.1.64]

The glass of fashion and the mold of form,
Th' observed of all observers   [Ophelia—3.1.167–68]

It out-Herods Herod.   [Hamlet—3.2.14–15]

Suit the action to the word, the word to the action
                              [Hamlet—3.2.18–19]

The lady doth protest too much, methinks.
                              [Queen—3.2.254]

A king of shreds and patches   [Hamlet—3.4.117]

. . . 'tis the sport to have the enginer
Hoist with his own petard   [Hamlet—3.4.229–30]

How all occasions do inform against me
                              [Hamlet—4.4.34]

There's such divinity doth hedge a king
                              [King—4.5.138]

Alas, poor Yorick! I knew him, Horatio
                              [Hamlet—5.1.190–91]

Imperious Cæsar, dead and turned to clay
                              [Hamlet—5.1.220]

Sweets to the sweet   [Gertrude—5.1.254]

There's a divinity that shapes our ends
                        [Hamlet—5.2.11]

There is a special providence in the fall of a
  sparrow.   [Hamlet—5.2.233–34]

Washington Square Press Relaunches the Enriched Classics Series with Each New Edition Featuring Expanded and Updated Reader's Supplements

ADVENTURES OF HUCKLEBERRY FINN
Mark Twain................88805-X/$4.99

THE GOOD EARTH
Pearl S. Buck................51012-6/$6.99

LAME DEER, SEEKER OF VISIONS
John (Fire) Lame Deer & Erdoes. . . .88802-1/$5.50

MY ANTONIA
Willa Cather................89086-7/$5.50

OEDIPUS THE KING
Sophocles....................88048/$5.50

THE SCARLET LETTER
Nathaniel Hawthorne...........51011-8/$4.99

DR. JEKYLL AND MR. HYDE
Robert Louis Stevenson.........53210-3/$3.99

FRANKENSTEIN
Mary Shelley................53150-6/$4.99

THE RED BADGE OF COURAGE
Stephen Crane................00275-9/$5.99

A TALE OF TWO CITIES
Charles Dickens..............00274-0/$5.99

A CHRISTMAS CAROL
Charles Dickens..............52078-4/$3.99

JANE EYRE
Charlotte Brontë..............01479-x/$5.99

WUTHERING HEIGHTS
Emily Brontë................01480-3/$5.99

WSP

S*THE NEW FOLGER LIBRARY*
HAKESPEARE
SET FREE

Teaching Series edited by Peggy O'Brien,
Director, Teaching Shakespeare Institute

Romeo and Juliet
Macbeth
and
A Midsummer Night's Dream
☐ 76046-7/$18.00

Hamlet
and
Henry IV, Part 1
☐ 76048-3/$18.00

Twelfth Night
and
Othello
☐ 76047-5/$18.00

WSP

Simon & Schuster Mail Order
200 Old Tappan Rd., Old Tappan, N.J. 07675
Please send me the audio I have checked above. I am enclosing $_____ (please add $3.95 to cover postage and handling plus your applicable local sales tax). Send check or money order — no cash or C.O.D.'s please. Allow up to six weeks for delivery. You may use VISA/MASTERCARD: card number, expiration date and customer signature must be included.

Name _____

Address _____

City _____ State/Zip _____

VISA/MASTERCARD Card # _____ Exp.Date _____

Signature _____
                                                              1089-01